STORM GOD

The Legend

Michael McMahon

Kildanore

STORM GOD *The Legend*
Kildanore Press, Blanchardstown, Dublin 1992

© Michael McMahon 1992
Cover design: Fran Dempsey © 1992
Painted by: Markus Rischar, The Little Animated Film
　　　　　　Factory, Dublin.

With special thanks to Gabriel Byrne and Lee Dunne, two of the best, Paul Kenny and Henry Solomon.

All rights reserved. No part of this publication may be reproduced, stored in a retrieval system, or transmitted in any form or by any means, electronic, mechanical, photocopying, recording, or otherwise, without the prior permission in writing of the publisher.

Typesetting: Kildanore Press, Dublin
Film Separations: Irish Photo Limited, Dublin
Printed by The Guernsey Press Company

For Maria

Drawing on ancient Irish, Celtic, and Norse legends, **STORM GOD** is a work of fiction, — an adventure. The writer has woven *The Legend,* primarily as an entertainment. Poetic licence has been used, and if the use of a term such as 'manuscripts' is not historically accurate within the timescale (the pre-Christian Millennium), such use is valid within the context of this story, and the world it inhabits.

Similarly, the use of the term 'high king', which has a later historical base, is used merely to denote a superior king. The world of **STORM GOD** is one where anything is possible. Doubt is suspended, allowing the imagination to experience a world that might, and perhaps should have, existed.

List of names and pronunciations:

Ceolmhar	Keyolvar
Deirbhne	Dervne
Brian	Breen
Aobhne	Eveneh
Dubhghall	Duvgal
Díele	Deela
dún	Doon
Samhain	Souwin

PROLOGUE

The island lay out to sea, four hours sailing time from the mainland in good weather. Visible, even through the winter mists, its dark rocky coastline and high cliffs were beginning to feel the first of the many winter storms which were common in that part of the world.

On the cliff top two dark brooding men stood watching the waves pound relentlessly against the rocks below. They held their cloaks tightly against the driving wind and spray, their heads protected by their helmets, ignoring the fierce gale which blew over them and disturbed the sea with such force.

The older of the two men, the leader, looked hard at the mist-shrouded peaks on the mainland beyond, his eyes never wavering, his gaze fixed, strong and determined. As he watched, noisy gulls circled and screeched overhead, their cries carrying far in the wind. The leader turned to his companion.

"We will begin soon," he said, his cold grey eyes returning to the object of his interest.

The younger man, who had the same dark features as his leader, nodded.

"You have done your work well," the leader continued. "You have earned the reward I shall give you when I have taken the high king's place..."

He spoke without emotion so that his words, though sincerely meant, had the effect of seeming otherwise. The younger man thanked his leader in the same manner, but the leader was so much absorbed in the horizon that he did not notice the hate in his companion's voice.

After some time the leader turned and began to walk back towards the village, some distance away, followed by the younger man. The rain and mist slowly enveloped the distant mountains, and the sea roared with anger as the storm broke.

CHAPTER ONE

It was snowing again. For two days there had been a respite, but now it came down once more, isolating the dún. There was no sign that it would ever stop, no break in the cold grey clouds hiding the winter sun.

The dún was quiet, no one daring to stir out of doors, and the snow lay undisturbed on the ground where it fell. A dog howled somewhere, and then was quiet.

Creidne the storyteller, gazing out the window, was once again filled with depression and gloom. He cursed the time of year, and the dreary days yet to come. He cursed the fact that he could not travel. He hated being confined to the dún, having to remain within the walls of the king's house, unable to hunt, unable to visit the other dúns, to gather stories or to tell his own.

It was the same every winter. A terrible gloom would come over him, and he became, in spite of all his efforts, a moody and disagreeable man and, by the time spring arrived, probably the most unpopular man in the dún.

He watched the smoke rise from the houses of the merchants and freemen, all now sitting snugly by their fires, the straw roofs of their houses groaning under the weight of snow. He heard the dog bark again, the sound carrying far in the silence, and he thought to himself how this really was the worst time of year. Many of the bards and the other storytellers counted the winter as a good time for the telling of their tales and the singing of their songs, the darkened rooms and winter fires adding character to the fantasy, but Creidne would have none of it. He was fiercely loyal to the summer, and even from the time when the first leaves began to fall in autumn, he was already looking ahead to the following summer.

He liked the winter for one reason only. There were no raids from the Formorian pirates — a hard and cruel people who came over the sea in ships and who raided up and down the coast, terrorising the villages and settlements.

The rough seas and bad weather kept them away, as well as the other rival kings and chiefs who were constantly at war with each other. All of them were now forced, like Creidne, to remain by their winter fires, bringing, if only for a few short months, peace to the countryside.

Creidne hated the glory that was made of war. It filled him with despair and anger that those whose specialty was killing were the highest honoured among his people. He and other men of learning were looked upon with disdain, amounting almost to contempt, by the warriors who regarded themselves as the sole class to whom respect was due.

Creidne did not generally have much contact with the warriors, except for one or two with whom he was friendly.

In spite of his dislike for the time of year, it gave him time to study, to be alone with his manuscripts. Where he lived, in the high king's house, there were many manuscripts for him to read, collected over the years and jealously guarded by the bards and druids into whose care they had been given. Creidne's skill lay not in his being merely able to read and write but, because like the other bards and storytellers he had given so many years to the study of the laws and customs of his people, that he was able to recite the law and other important facts about the lives of the heroes and kings long since dead.

It was only after many years of learning and study, and when he could be said to be able to recite everything by heart, that a man was accepted into the ranks of the bards.

The years had been kind to Creidne. He was still young, his hair retaining most of its colour with only a few flecks of grey here and there, his beard too, which he kept uncommonly trim. He had risen fast in the high king's household, and he was now the king's chief bard and lawmaker.

In spite of this, and the esteem in which he was held, he was a man alone, without any real friends, a man who had given his life to the service of his king and his people. He asked for nothing in return except the right to peace, and the time to study his manuscripts, time also to travel, without which he felt sure he would have gone insane.

Down below in the courtyard, a man crossed from the building beyond and entered the house where Creidne had his quarters. Creidne watched him idly as he passed beneath his window, at the footprints left behind in the virgin snow.

The high king's house was a large stone building, the only one in the dún, built square and enclosing the courtyard across which the man had just walked. The house was spacious, two stories high, housing not alone the high king and his family, but also many of his warriors, as well as his bards and musicians and the other people who made up the household of a rich and powerful king. Although the house was of stone, the roof, like the roofs of the other houses, was thatch, beneath which great beams of wood criss-crossed the ceiling, supporting the great weight, now made ever heavier by the snow.

The high king lived in that part of the building from which the man had just emerged, and when he disappeared into the building Creidne occupied, the storyteller had expected to hear the sound of footsteps outside his door, but there was only silence.

He thought about the high king. The Samhain feast was close, a most important festival to celebrate the coming of winter, for which he had prepared a new story to tell which would mark the occasion, and to which all the chiefs and kings subject to the high king's authority would come. Creidne disliked Samhain. It was a sinister time, a time of death, a time for spirits to roam the winter countryside. It made him uneasy, and although he was not afraid of death, he suddenly felt cold and frightened.

He turned away from the window and returned to his manuscripts. The room was sparsely furnished, with only a small pallet for sleeping, two chairs and along the wall on one side, a bookcase filled with manuscripts and writing materials.

It was the room of a scholar. He sat by the table and poured some wine into his cup from the jug which he kept there, sipping the wine as he read the page spread out before him. For a long time he remained oblivious of anything except his own thoughts as the afternoon turned into evening, and darkness fell.

Creidne rose and lit the lamps with a taper from the fire which burned bright at one wall, and was about to sit down again when there was a knock on his door.

"Come in," he called, and the door opened.

"May I speak with you?" the man said, peering round the door before entering.

"Come in Blamad, come in," Creidne said warmly, glad to be able to converse with someone for a while, glad too that it was this man.

Blamad entered. He was a big man, with a slight beard. On his face there were several scars, yet in spite of these he was still handsome. His hair was long and dark and banded at the forehead. There was a long scar running down his forearm onto his hand, a reminder of an encounter he'd had with a Formorian raiding party.

Taking off the fur cloak he had been wearing, he was dressed now in a brown tunic and breeches which were tucked into his boots, still wet from the snow.

"I hope you're well today Creidne," he said smiling broadly.

"I'm as well as I can be on such a day," came the reply. Blamad was one of the few warriors whom Creidne liked. He pointed to the jug.

"Take some wine. It'll take the chill from your bones. Then pull over a chair and we'll sit by the fire and talk."

Blamad looked at him, smiling once more.

"There's no fooling you, is there?" he said lightly. Creidne smiled back.

"I know that the high king's champion does not come to see the high king's bard on a grey winter's day — and in the evening too — without some good cause." He looked at Blamad.

"How did you fare last night?" he asked, changing the subject for the moment. Blamad shook his head.

"That Nemedian took my money again. He's gifted with the dice, or else the gods are on his side," he said good humouredly.

Creidne laughed. Blamad's passion for gambling was well known, as was the fact that Carriog the Nemedian always beat him. Always. Blamad had never been able to match him, but still he kept on trying.

"Some day you will learn," Creidne said, pouring more wine.

"Now, tell me why you have come," he continued, becoming more serious. Blamad drank slowly from his cup, then began.

"The high king himself asked me to come and speak to you. There is grave news which concerns us all. Early today a messenger came from the king's brother Brian. He'd been travelling for days through the snow and was exhausted and in a bad way by the time he reached our dún. I am not certain that he will survive. Anyway, Brian sent a message to tell the king that a large force of Formorians have landed close to Brians' dún, and have begun to build a settlement as if they intend to stay. He sent raiding parties against them, but already they are too strong and they beat his men off with great loss. Brian is afraid now that when spring comes they will be too strong for him to resist, and so he has asked for our help. He says that the Formorians have a new leader. A man called Vitrig..."

"Vitrig. I know that name," Creidne said, frowning. Blamad looked at him, puzzled, Creidne explained.

"Years ago I went to the land of the Picts, to a place where some of our people had settled. The Picts had made a treaty with us and we left each other alone, but the Formorians were constantly raiding the coast, Pictish villages as well as ours, and we lived in terror most of the time. There was, even then, one man whose name was feared above all the others, and that man's name was Vitrig. He was spoken of then as a rising young chief, cruel even by their standards, a hard, cold, ruthless warrior with no humanity, no spark of decency in him at all. The mere mention of his name filled men with great fear and many of our people abandoned their villages and moved further inland to escape him, and his cruelty.

"Brian also says this," Blamad said. "He's gone further inland than any Formorian has dared to."

"Do you think he intends to come this far?" Creidne asked, unable to believe that even a man like Vitrig would take such a risk and move so far inland, away from his ships, where he might be vulnerable.

"The high king thinks that he might. They've been building up to this for a long time. It's nearly three years since they raided seriously, so I think perhaps the king might be right."

Blamad spoke about the Formorians with detachment. He was for too long a warrior, and he had seen too many battles, to be unduly concerned. It was inevitable that when spring came, war would follow. It was the way of things, it had always been that way and he could not see it ever being any other way.

For as long as he had lived there had been Formorian raids, for as long as his father's lifetime before him, they had come when winter ended, when the sea was calm again after the storms. His father had died fighting Formorians, but he could not say that he hated them for it. They were his natural enemies and he expected them to try to kill his people, just as he and his people tried to kill them. That too, was the way of things, that too would never change. He was sure of it.

"What did Brian say about his own people?" Creidne asked.

"He does not think that they are in danger yet," Blamad replied. "He has a strong army of his own, the match for any Formorian, but he is concerned about some of his chiefs who will not join him against their enemy, chiefs who grow a little stronger and think they do not need the protection of their king. Still, he believes that he will be able to pacify and unify his chiefs before spring comes, but I do not envy him his task."

"It never changes," Creidne said quietly. He was gazing into the fire. The glow lit his face, catching the moisture in his eyes.

"What never changes?"

"Since our people took the island," Creidne said, all the time looking into the flames, his eyes distant, "and the Danaan people were no more, no even before that, when Nemed and his people ruled the island, the Formorians have come year after year raiding our coasts, killing, burning and taking slaves. I find it strange that none of our kings or chiefs have ever thought of going over to that island of theirs and destroying them all, for that is what we will have to do or they will continue to plague our people, even long after we are dead. If we do not kill them all, they will come back time and time again to hurt us..."

Creidne, normally the most peaceful of men, surprised Blamad by this speech, so out of character. However, he continued in like manner.

"I pray that the gods curse them for bringing death and misery to our people. I pray that the gods will destroy them utterly for their cruelty."

Blamad did not reply. He did not know what to say. He sat watching Creidne's face as the bard gazed into the fire, and he knew that Creidne was not a coward because he was a scholar, as many other warriors believed. Instead, he saw that he had a grim and determined nature, a fire and a lust for vengeance as far as the Formorians were concerned, and it surprised him to see it in one so normally calm and passive and without malice.

In the darkness they sat by the fire, the oil lamps flickering when the breeze caught them. The crackling logs on the fire were the only disturbance of the silence, the two men enjoying each other's company, and the solitude of their own thoughts for a long time. Finally, Creidne spoke again.

"You still have not told me why you have come to see me," he said quietly, afraid to break the spell of peace which had grown in the room.

"The high king wishes to see you tonight," Blamad replied gravely. "He has something to ask of you. Something which I know you will do for him."

"What is this something you speak of?" Creidne asked, curiously.

"I cannot tell you. It is for the king to tell you. It must come from him. Have patience, storyteller, and you will soon know his wish." Blamad rose from the chair and put his cup down.

"I must go now," he said. "I have many things to attend to before I go to the king again. You serve a good wine, my friend.

"I will see you later," he said, and was gone, leaving Creidne wondering what it was the high king wished to see him about at such a late hour.

He remained by the fire, staring into the flames, feeling the heat burn his face. He was suddenly apprehensive and wondered if the king's request had anything to do with the messenger who had come from Brian that day. He decided to do as Blamad had asked and wait until later, but he was intensely curious.

Blamad was with the king when Creidne entered the private chamber. They were seated at a table set in the centre of the room, while two slaves stood nearby with food and wine, ready to serve as soon as the king gave the command.

Carriog the Nemedian was also with them, a tall dark-featured man, unsmiling, who remained by Blamad's side.

"Come in, Creidne, and welcome," the high king said, beckoning him to a chair.

"Sit down here, beside me." Creidne sat.

"You may serve the food now." The slaves laid the food on the table, returning with jugs of wine and goblets which they set before each of the men. Having done this, the king waved them away.

"You may leave us now. We will attend to ourselves."

The slaves withdrew and, when the door had closed behind them, the king relaxed and smiled a little.

"You'll like this wine," he said to Creidne, knowing the bard's pride in his own wine. He poured some into a cup. It tasted good, and Creidne nodded his approval.

The king smiled. He was a young man, not yet three years king, but already his dark hair was slightly flecked with grey, a sign of the troubled times in which he had come to the throne. He was beardless and this emphasised his youth, while his hair, which was shoulder length, was banded with a gold band. He wore a long flowing robe belted at the waist, the whole picture being that of a gentle weak man, belying the fact that he was a strong and wise king, respected by his own people, if not understood by those who opposed him.

"You are wondering why I have asked you to come here and in private, away from the assembly hall, but I have good reasons," he said directly to Creidne, putting down his goblet.

"Blamad has told you about the Formorians landing, and Brian's fear that they will overrun his lands, but what Blamad did not know, what he still does not know, is that the Grey

Druid has now taken arms against us, and is threatening to come here and fight us."

The king spoke quietly and calmly as he always did, no matter how serious or deep the crisis, his unshakable demeanour having calmed many quarrels among his volatile warriors.

Blamad nearly choked on the wine he had just begun to drink.

"I'm sorry, my Lord," he said, wiping his tunic.

"So you should get a shock, Blamad," the king replied.

"This news makes the Formorian threat doubly serious, and I cannot help but believe that the Formorians and the Druid, however unlikely it sounds, have made an agreement and are working together. Even while he was talking peace with us, the Druid must have been planning such a move. If the Druid and his Picts are allies with the Formorians, then you all know that we shall be in serious trouble when spring comes. It is well that Samhain is close, it is well that winter sets in, or we should be in trouble without having time to prepare for it. The chiefs and other kings will be gathering here in a few days, so I will speak to them, warn them of the threat which faces us all, try to persuade them of the danger. I'm afraid, Creidne, that you will not tell your tales at this year's feast, because I have a far more important task for you, something which may well decide our future."

He looked at Creidne for a moment. The storyteller's face showed the disappointment he felt. Nevertheless, he waited for the king to finish. "As you know, Morna my queen, is with her foster father Ceolmhar in the north. She will winter there. I want you to go to Ceolmhar's dún and tell him what I have told you. Tell him to gather his people together at the first coming of spring so that they may come to help us in the fight I know we will have to face when the winter snows have gone." He looked at Creidne again, sadness in his eyes. He was reluctant to send him out into the wilderness in such terrible and inhospitable weather, but the face of the storyteller was showing no such reluctance.

"Go to the villages yourself, those you can reach, speak for me, and with my authority, and above all, tell Ceolmhar that the queen is not to return here until I have the word that it is safe for her to do so. You will have a long and difficult journey, unpleasant for the most part with the weather the way it is, but it is necessary that someone I can trust bring this news to Ceolmhar. Will you do this for me?"

He looked at Creidne. Whatever doubts he had, Creidne did not speak them. True, he was disappointed that he would not tell his story at the feast, but at the same time he would be travelling away from the confines of the dún, and that fact pleased him. He accepted at once, much to the king's delight.

"Now that I know I have a worthy ambassador, I will enjoy this meal," he said laughing, his mood much lighter, now that the more serious side of the business was over.

"Will I travel alone?" Creidne asked. It was Blamad, not the king who replied. "Carriog here, will go with you, also Branvig, son of Ceolmhar, and Godrane, another young warrior, strong and without fear. In two days you will leave, but in the meantime you must tell no one what you are about to do. If any ask about the feast, act and behave as if you are going. It is important that no one knows of your journey, because we cannot be sure that the Druid hasn't got spies here in the dún, even in the king's house."

Creidne nodded. He understood. This was why they were eating and talking in the king's own room and not in the assembly hall where there were many ears to hear even the slightest whisper of gossip.

"I will be careful," Creidne replied.

Later, when they were alone, Blamad spoke to the king. "Why did you not tell me about the Druid?" he asked.

"Do not be offended my friend," the king replied. "I received word only a short time before we met, and I thought it best to tell you all at the same time. We've always suspected that he would someday go against us have we not? I always hoped that he would see reason, that he would make a treaty with us. I never thought that he would actually do it even though we suspected him."

"He has those Picts to keep under control," Blamad replied angrily. "Even the Druid cannot stop them raiding if that is what they want to do. They are worse than the Formorians, and I cannot imagine them fighting side by side. They hate each other more than they hate us."

"They will fight if the Druid tells them," the king said, and Blamad knew that this was true. The Grey Druid was a man of power. So called because of the grey clothes he always wore, he was now their enemy. A man who knew the old ways, a man who had learned much of the Danaan's secret magic. A cold, heartless, cruel man, without humanity, a man who spoke to the evil ones and was heard. Blamad suddenly began to understand fear.

"Have we any weapon against the Druid?"

The king smiled understandingly. "Much of the Druid's power comes from men's own fears, Blamad," he said. "He plays on their fear and so conquers them. He is a man like us, cold and brutal it is true, but a flesh-and-blood man who can die and feel pain, and any such man can be overcome."

The king's words gave Blamad some comfort, but he could not help feeling apprehensive. During the next few days before Creidne and the others left, he would not be able to put from his mind the image of the Druid. Even his dreams were troubled. Blamad's uneasiness grew.

CHAPTER TWO

Two days later, Creidne and his companions were ready to leave. It was a dark, bitterly cold morning, the snow fell heavily over the dún, while the wind swirled and shook the walls of the houses of the poorer people, howling and crying like a soul in torment.

The three horsemen waited for Creidne to leave the king's house. They were all wrapped against the driving snow, but were still cold and ill-humoured, the younger two especially, cursing and blaming Creidne for their present uncomfortable situation. Only Carriog, of the three, knew why they were leaving the dún at such an early hour and in such foul weather.

He looked at his companions in the dim early morning light, but he could see little of their faces in the gloom and through the snow, and because they were also half hidden by their hoods. The dún was in complete darkness, and there was no light or sound from any of the houses except the king's.

Carriog became aware of a shaft of light which came from under the door and spread itself on the fallen snow, a golden tunnel of light pushing aside the darkness holding it at bay, disturbed only by the shadows of the men who talked and moved beyond the door of the king's house.

Presently the storyteller came out. He had spoken to Blamad and the king who had thanked him once more for what he was doing, and now without delay, he took the reins of his horse from Carriog and mounted up.

The gates of the dún had been opened. The two sleepy guards who stood there impatiently swore silently, wishing the others would hurry up so that they could return to the warmth of their shelter.

Branvig, Ceolmhar's son, led the party out of the dún and was to lead them north because he knew the hidden ways and the quickest paths to Ceolmhar's dún.

They left as quietly as they could, walking their horses slowly so that they disturbed no one, or alerted anyone who might be spying for the Druid.

Once outside, the gates were closed behind them and they felt the full fury of the storm which lashed against them, driving wind and snow into their faces, covering them from head to foot in a blanket of white.

The forest was a long way off, but even in the darkness and through the worst of the weather, Branvig knew by instinct which way to go. Because of the storm which threatened sometimes to unsaddle them, they had to move slowly, bending down to escape the worst effects of the wind against their bodies. The dún receded into the shadows as they moved on towards the forest, now a dark outline ahead.

For hours they pushed their horses against the driving weather, hours when it seemed like they were getting nowhere, like they had hardly moved, such was the uniformity of the countryside they rode across. Still wrapped in darkness, which remained even with the coming of dawn, they pushed on, and by early afternoon had reached the outer limits of the forest.

The trees were densely packed together, and there seemed no clear path through, but Branvig led them along, skirting the foliage. He knew they could enter the forest where they would meet the old Nemedian road built many years before. The knowledge he had gained in childhood, when he had roamed this forest with his father, did not desert him now as he led the others through the darkness and the blizzard. He did not fear the forest as many others did, but remembered it as a place where he had spent many happy days. He was also glad to be returning to his father's house, and this thought alone made the journey bearable for him.

Behind him, Godrane looked out over the bleak countryside, and once again, for the sixth or seventh time, he cursed Creidne for having brought them out on such a day. He had left a girl behind in his bed, and as he thought now of her warm body and the smooth gentle touch of her hands, and the length of time he would have to spend away from her, he became doubly angry.

He swore audibly, but was not overheard because of the wind. His harp, wrapped in a blanket and covered by a leather case, hung over his saddle, but he swore that he would not give the storyteller the pleasure of hearing its beauty.

Carriog, strange and silent, with his dark face and penetrating eyes, his lean taut muscular body, was a man to himself. Creidne found himself wondering about the silent Nemedian who seldom spoke. Only once since they began their journey did he speak, but he was fond of dice, and his prowess was legendary among the warriors, as Blamad had found to his cost many times. Creidne wondered if all of Carriog's people were as mysterious as he was, but he shook his head. It was not possible. He did not notice the amused look on Carriog's face as these thoughts raced through his mind.

Finally Branvig led them into the forest at a place where a moment before there had seemed to be no entrance. They all felt relieved as the wind and the snow suddenly died away.

The forest was dense and quiet. The sight of the green breaking through on the ice-covered ground was welcome to their snow-weary eyes.

Reaching a small clearing, they dismounted. Carriog dug a place for a fire, while Godrane and Branvig saw to the horses. When they had put the feed bags to the horses' mouths they went to gather wood for the fire, helped by Creidne.

They returned to the clearing three times before they were satisfied that they had enough. Carriog meanwhile, had built a makeshift spit and on it he had impaled a hare which was now cooking slowly. The wood gatherers looked at each other in amazement. They had not been away very long.

Carriog however, did not seem to notice their stares, or if he did, he did not mind. He continued to feed the fire and watch the slowly roasting flesh. The smell made their hunger more acute and they sat watching him as he tended the meat.

Creidne, seeing that it would be some time before the meal was cooked brought Godrane and Branvig with him to gather boughs to make a rough shelter for the night. In a short time they had built a small but comfortable wattle shelter, big enough for four of them, on the floor of which they placed ferns which they had also gathered, to take away the chill of the ground when they lay down later to sleep.

Carriog, with perfect timing had the meat cooked by the time they were ready to eat. He tore off pieces of the carcass and gave each of them a share.

It was very hot and burned their fingers, but such was their hunger that they did not notice. Branvig filled their cups with wine, and they ate and drank quickly and in silence, each man lost in his own thoughts.

The burning wood crackled and echoed through the trees, as they settled into their first night in the forest. An owl shrieked somewhere in the darkness beyond. They were completely alone with only the fire to light the dark winter night, but they were out of the worst of the storm and for this they were grateful.

As they rested, sipping their wine more slowly now from their cups, Creidne began to speak. As he did, Carriog suddenly stood up and walked towards the hut. Creidne called after him.

"I want to speak to you," he said, anger in his voice. Carriog turned.

"There is no need," he said quietly and calmly. "I know what you will say. You may tell the others, but I will rest now."

With that, he turned and walked to the hut watched by Creidne and the others, none of whom knew what to make of the strange Nemedian who was to be their companion for the next few days.

"He's a strange one," Branvig said. "His people were great and powerful in their time, but they were not a friendly or happy race, if he is an example of their character."

Branvig was a young man with a light, likable character, carefree and easy to get along with. He had been fostered by the high king's father like most of the sons of the nobility who grew up in households other than their own, and it was more than three years since he had last seen his father. He had a ruddy complexion with copper coloured hair, and the older men said that he could easily be mistaken for Ceolmhar, his father, as a young man, such was the resemblance between them.

Creidne was looking at the hut. The Nemedian disturbed him.

"He has the Sight," he said to Branvig. "I am sure of it. I felt that he could read my mind as he spoke to me. It's not the first time I have felt that when I have been close to Carriog, and I can tell you that it is a strange feeling. I was almost afraid of him..."

"I too felt it," Branvig replied.

During all of this time, Godrane remained quiet and sullen. Creidne smiled a little, understanding the reason.

"I will tell you now, why it was so necessary for us to make this journey to Ceolmhar's dún, when only fools or low characters travel at this time, but when you have heard what I have to tell you, you will understand the reason why we are here."

He looked at Godrane.

"I know that you especially, resented having to leave your bed and the young woman whom you haven't stopped thinking about since we left, but it was the high king himself who picked you to escort me because he trusts you, and for that reason alone you should be honoured."

Godrane, like Branvig, was young, but inclined to be more serious, and unusually for a warrior, he was skilled in music. He also had a fondness for women and in this he was helped by his light skin and fair hair and deep blue eyes all of which he used to advantage, and also about which he was very vain.

Creidne went on to tell Godrane and Branvig what Blamad and the high king had told him, and the reasons they had not been told before. Their faces darkened as they listened to him, at first scarcely believing him, but realising as he went on that he spoke the truth. The sullen look went from Godrane's face as Creidne told them of the fear that the high king had for the coming spring, which would bring with it war, death and destruction.

Godrane had not expected to hear such dark and gloomy news, and like the other people in the high king's dún he had forgotten the Formorians, because they had not raided inland for so many years.

The Druid, however, was a different matter. The Druid frightened them. His power was immense, his magic said to be invincible, and there was no answer to it if he chose to use it. The Formorians were frightening Godrane thought, but not as frightening or as dangerous as the Druid.

Every village, especially those along the coast had a warning system, and the villagers learned at an early age how to defend themselves, and how to be vigilant.

Now Creidne was telling them of something new, something more sinister. Before, the Formorians had never made any attempt to settle. They came for plunder, making quick raids, returning to their ships before any assault could be made against them. They came in small numbers, each with a different leader and without a common plan. But now they were unified under a single leader, who brought them to the island to stay and to conquer.

Godrane and Branvig knew from what Creidne had just told them that when spring came there would be war with no mercy on either side. Whoever won would control the island.

The Formorians might easily be defeated, but if they were allied with the Druid they were the greatest threat that the high king and people ever had to face. It depressed them.

Godrane spoke to Creidne. "You were right when you said that I blamed you and resented you for my being here. I should have remembered that it is my duty to serve the high king, without question, and I should have respected you and your rank, but instead I insulted you and for that I am sorry."

"I thank you for that," Creidne said simply, pleased by the young man's action.

"I knew that you would understand."

"You have my support, Creidne," Branvig said quickly. "And my father's too, of that I have no doubt."

Creidne smiled.

"I know that I have Carriog's loyalty too," he said. They looked at him. "Carriog knew what I was going to say to you. He was with me when the high king asked me to come on his journey. Besides which he has the Power. There is more to that Nemedian than we know..."

Later as they sat quietly by the fire, their cups filled with wine, feeling the contentment of men with nothing to fear, Godrane took his harp from its coverings. Creidne smiled quietly to himself. Godrane played some airs while the others sat back listening as his fingers plucked the strings, drawing the melodies into their hearing. The sound hung in the cold night air, lingering before fading into the darkness.

Sleep began to overtake them, so they went to the shelter and lay beneath their blankets, leaving behind the cold, and their journey. Filled with wine and food, their spirits had been uplifted by the music Godrane had played for them, and they slept contentedly.

The fire was almost out when they woke in the early hours. It was dark and bitingly cold, much colder than the day before. They stirred from their sleeping positions and

Carriog went at once to rekindle the fire, and with an efficiency for which he was already becoming noted by the others, he had the wood blazing in a short time. Creidne watched the Nemedian. He felt a peculiar kind of relief that he was their friend and not their enemy. There was a commanding presence about Carriog, a feeling that he had not revealed his true self to them. He also felt, as he watched him, that he knew what was going on in his head, every thought he had.

Branvig called from a short distance away, where he had gone to gather more wood for the fire. His voice sounded urgent.

Carriog and Godrane drew their swords and ran to find Branvig, Creidne following with his dagger in his hand.

"Over here," they heard Branvig call, and in a few seconds they found him, crouching on the ground, gazing intently at the sword in his hands. Carriog crouched beside him, and Branvig handed it to him. For a few moments Carriog examined the weapon carefully, moving his hands along its surface caressingly.

The blade was curved, the handle studded with emeralds which lay in symmetrical and graceful patterns. He admired the workmanship, marvelling at the skill of the man who had made such a beautiful weapon. He turned to show it to the others.

"Is it a Formorian sword?" Creidne asked anxiously.

Carriog shook his head,

"They haven't the skill or the inclination to make a blade as fine as this," he said. He handed it to Creidne.

"Look at the workmanship," he said, lost in admiration. "Is that not the most beautiful piece of skill you have seen?"

Creidne took the weapon from Carriog, running his fingers over the handle, delicately and with care, one craftsman admiring the work of another.

"Perhaps they took it in a raid and lost it."

"No," Carriog said sharply. "They would not have come this way, it's too far inland."

Creidne looked at Carriog strangely, doubt in his eyes. He was sure that the Nemedian knew more about the sword than he was telling them.

"The barbarians are not as afraid of the forest as we are," he said. "They do not know our gods and so they do not fear them."

"They have their own gods," Carriog replied.

"They have nothing," Godrane said sharply, contempt in his voice.

"You are wrong there, my friend," Carriog said, startling them all by the tone of his voice. For the first time since they had met him, he had spoken with anger, and they were momentarily silenced by it.

"What do you know of their gods?" Creidne asked. Carriog looked at him but there was no anger in his look.

"The Formorians worship the gods of death and storms, the gods of darkness. Their gods are as evil as they themselves are. They take human sacrifice. They are the gods of dark roads and barren fields, gods who destroy and do not build, who take all, and give nothing. Gods of fear and terror who come from the darkest places in the Otherworld. You will know of their coming by the signs in the sky..."

"What signs are these?" Creidne was fascinated by the Nemedian's knowledge, and he wanted to know more. Carriog looked at him, and there was understanding in his eyes.

"When the sun is covered by great flocks of birds, black crows and ravens, when the wind rises with their coming and yet there is no wind, you will know that the gods of death and famine are about to announce themselves. When men feel terror in their hearts, when there is distrust and discord, then you will know that the hour of the dark ones approaches."

He finished speaking, and there was silence for a while.

"You are well acquainted with the ways of the Formorians," Branvig said, a sudden touch of coldness in his voice. Carriog looked at the young warrior, the son of Ceolmhar. He looked and saw and felt the suspicion the young man felt, but he was not angry. He took the sword from Creidne as he answered Branvig.

"My people passed down many stories about the Formorians," he began. "In the old days when we were strong, the Formorians came to the island and my people fought them in a great battle. We were victorious, and those Formorians who had not been killed were permitted to return to their island. A grave mistake as we later found out. The Formorians are cunning as well as cruel, and they have long memories. For years they waited, building up their strength, eager for revenge while my people forgot them, thinking now that the power of the Formorians was broken and they were in no more danger. The Formorians however came back once again to the island, only this time they were victorious and their revenge against us was terrible. Their king was a vicious and cruel man called Conann."

"I know of him," Creidne said, remembering the name from a story he had heard. Carriog nodded.

"He was as I said, a cruel and evil man, and those of our people who were still alive when the fighting was done, were bonded into the most cruel form of slavery Conann could think of, their women taken by the Formorians whenever and wherever the fancy took them. It was a time of great hardship and despair for my people, which they endured for many years until they could no longer tolerate the tyranny.

"Some of the young warriors rose against them. They even managed to kill the tyrant Conann, but they were not strong enough to overthrow the Formorians who killed any of our people they laid their hands on, even those who had not risen against them, making certain as my people had failed to do that we would never be a power against them. It was only after many many years, that they were finally driven back to their own island, but they have never been completely beaten and still they come in their ships to cause us annoyance and grief. If the gods do grant us victory over them, then we should remember our mistake from the past, and this time kill every one of them, women and children too. All of them should be put to the sword. All of them."

"Your words carry little hope," Creidne said wearily. Carriog had spoken more than was usual for him but his words had dampened their spirits and brought a common gloom over them.

He spoke again.

"The end has come, and the beginning. What is dark will be light, and nothing that is, will be," he said, mysteriously.

"What does that mean?" Creidne asked, but Carriog did not answer. Instead he held the strange sword closer, looking at it with a kind of reverence. His eyes were moist and he seemed about to cry, yet at the same time he was smiling, the first time they had seen him do so.

"This sword..." he said holding it away from his body. "This sword is not a Formorian sword. I give you my word on that. This is a Danaan sword, left here for us to find. A guide, a message to tell us that there are those who are with us, who will not let us fall into the hands of our enemies."

"A Danaan sword?" Creidne asked with amazement. "Are you trying to tell me that the Danaans, a people who have long since vanished from the face of the earth, have left this here for us to find?" He was plainly skeptical and from the expressions on Branvig's and Godrane's faces, they too felt the same.

Carriog turned, and he looked hard into Creidne's eyes. Creidne almost wilted under the stone hard stare.

"You, of all people, should know the legends. You are a man of learning, a scholar, with the knowledge and history of your own people and this island you live on. How can you not believe what I tell you? How can you doubt my word? Why can you not believe that there are Danaan people still on this island, in places where they cannot be disturbed by other men, as there are Nemedians like me, few and scattered though we are. You do not doubt our existence, why then should you doubt theirs?"

"There are still Danaans on this island?" Creidne asked, this time less doubtful.

"They have never left the island," Carriog replied quickly. "They live and breathe as you do, they hide from all men except those who serve them as I do."

"You serve the high king," Branvig said, a rough hardness in his voice. Carriog however, was not disturbed by his manner.

"I serve the high king as you say, but the Danaan king is my overlord. He is still more powerful than the high king. I will tell you something before you begin to doubt my loyalty. What is about to happen, what has already happened has been long foretold. First by my people, then later by the Danaans, even by your own seers and wise men. There will be famine, war and bloodshed, much suffering and grief before the time of destruction has passed. Many things which you could not begin to understand, will happen, and you will live to see such things that your grandchildren, should you live that long, will think that you made the entire tale from your head. They will not believe what you know to be true as you do not believe me now when I tell you."

He looked at each of them and was saddened by their suspicious looks, yet he knew that it must be hard for them to accept what he was saying.

"The high king has been looked upon with favour by the Danaan king who knows all and sees all. We are in his forest, this is where he sees us, and watches us. The spirits of the forest which your people fear, are sent by the Danaan to protect themselves and to keep men from coming too near to their places. They too fear what is to come, but they cannot change what is written, only the gods can do that."

"I do not understand," Creidne said, his mind confused, unsure of whether to believe Carriog or not.

"You will soon understand, Creidne," Carriog said gently. "You will all understand."

As he walked back to the campsite, Branvig and Godrane looked after him, and there was anger in their eyes.

"From now on, I'm keeping a close watch on that Nemedian," Branvig said. "That talk about the Danaans still being alive. Does he take us for fools?"

"I believe him, Branvig, " Creidne said, surprising the two warriors. "I agree that it's a peculiar tale, but there are legends about the Danaan people. When they were defeated in battle by our ancestors, some of the old manuscripts say that they were allowed to live in the lonely places, in the hills, in caves as lords of the underground and the dark forests. I have seen these writings myself and I have many times wondered about the strange Danaans who were skilled magicians, more powerful than the Druid. Take this forest, as Carriog has said. Our people have always feared it, avoided it if they could. The road which we shall travel was built long before we came, by the Nemedians, who were not afraid of the forest, yet we do and we are strong while the Nemedians are weak and few in number."

"Men have come into this forest, never to be seen again," Godrane said uneasily. "I do not like the feel of it. There is something strange about it. I felt from the moment we entered, something I do not understand." Branvig laughed.

"There is nothing to fear here," he said, putting his hands on his friend's shoulders.

"I ran through this forest many times when I was a boy. I hunted here and camped here. I've been through it many times, sometimes with my friends, but I never saw anything strange or heard anything to frighten me, except the sound of wolves, but nothing from the dark places."

"Do not doubt Carriog's sincerity or loyalty," Creidne said firmly. "He has served the high king too long, and too well to be anything other than a friend. This forest is vast and there are many places where even you have not been Branvig. Dark hidden places which even you are afraid to go to."

Branvig did not reply, but his manner suggested that Creidne had spoken the truth.

"Enough of this talk now," Creidne said, his voice a command. "I am hungry and we have delayed too long here."

They returned to the campsite. Carriog had made a broth with the remains of the hare, and some herbs which he had gathered while the others had been talking. It was steaming hot as he poured it into their cups, and they were grateful for it's warmth. They did not speak and there was a chilly tense atmosphere between them. As soon as they were finished they broke camp and prepared to move out.

"Godrane will go ahead along the road," Branvig said when they had mounted their horses. "Just in case..."

The snow had stopped falling but it was still very cold and they wrapped their cloaks tightly around their shoulders, holding their hoods ready to shield them if the snow came again.

It was an old overgrown road, hardly used anymore. On either side the trees were densely grouped together, in places almost covering the road completely, their branches overhanging downwards. The others had not known of the road's existence, but Branvig's knowledge of the forest served to make their progress easier and safer, since they did not have to travel over the open plain where they would have been exposed both to the weather, and to any of their enemies who might have been watching for travellers such as they.

The snow lay hard on the ground, the frost having iced the road, making it both slippery and dangerous. They walked their horses carefully, Branvig leading the way, Creidne and Carriog behind him, all of them alert for any strange or unusual sounds, their senses taut, their nerves jagged.

Only after they had been travelling for some time did they realize that something was wrong.

There was no sound in the forest. No bird sang, nor beast roared. Even the breeze had died. There was a strange eerie quiet, an unnatural calm and silence and they began to feel uneasy. Branvig looked back, but Carriog urged him on. "Keep going," he said. The horses became restless, reluctant to go on so that the men had to use their feet to try and spur them.

"I don't like this," Branvig said. There was a strange oppression in the air, and it seemed as if the sky itself would fall in on them. Carriog stood in his saddle, his eyes scanning the forest.

"There is evil near," he said fearfully. "Listen..."

Dismounting, they tied their horses to some trees close by. Looking up at the sky, they listened. There was no sound at all, only complete and terrifying silence, like the calm before a storm, though it was an evil and menacing calm. They drew their swords, feeling the nerve tingling excitement of men who are about to go to war, but they were not prepared for what did happen.

A great flock of crows and ravens suddenly appeared overhead, the sky blackened by their numbers. Fascinated, they stood and watched them pass over in a seemingly endless flock, noisy screeching creatures who were travelling in the same direction they themselves were travelling.

It was only when the birds had finally passed over, that they looked at each other, terror clearly written on all their faces. Godrane returned at that moment, and his face too bore the unmistakable signs of fear.

"I had a terrible feeling that something, or someone was watching me, and trying to strangle me," he said breathlessly. "I was already on my way back to you, when I saw them..."

He looked at Creidne.

"What are we to do?" he asked. Creidne spoke.

"Carriog was speaking the truth when he talked about the Formorian gods. I think that we will serve our course better if we follow his advice from now on." There was no dissent, though Branvig and Godrane still had misgivings about Carriog. Nevertheless Creidne was the high king's ambassador and his word was to be obeyed.

Carriog assumed command without a word, again seeming to read their minds since they had spoken away from him and out of his hearing, or so they imagined.

"The Formorians are on the march it seems, and the winter is not going to stop them," he said grimly. "From now on we will be doubly vigilant, though I doubt still that they have come this far, but it is best to be sure."

He spoke to Godrane.

"Go ahead again, and watch for anything unusual, no matter how slight or trivial. If something does not seem right, come back here at once and tell us, is that clear?"

Godrane nodded, saluted, and rode off again up the road. The others followed at a more leisurely pace, but they were not relaxed or calm anymore, their thoughts on the strange flock of birds which had passed over them such a short time before.

As they moved along the Nemedian road, they watched the trees, heeding Carriog's words that they hid many secrets, expecting at any time to hear their enemies rush out at them, but the forest was peaceful again and the day passed slowly and quietly and without any further incident or disturbance.

The noises of the forest were heard once more, this time gentle familiar sounds, soothing cries which brought some peace to the men as they passed through the dense, overhanging undergrowth. Carriog knew that their enemies would soon be following them, and he listened to every sound, and watched the sky with casual intensity, knowing as he did, the danger they faced.

To Branvig, going along this familiar road was both strange and exciting. He had come this way many times before when he had left his father's dún to go to the high king, and even the terrible fear he had felt earlier, had not entirely subdued the excitement he felt at the prospect of seeing his father once more. It had been a long time, and he looked forward to hunting with Ceolmhar again over the mountain heather.

It was growing dark, so Carriog halted them at a clearing which lay just off the road.

"We'll make camp here," he said, pointing to the trees which parted to form a natural archway which they would be able to use as a shelter. They dismounted. Branvig took the horses, while Creidne gathered wood, and Carriog waited by the road to watch for Godrane's return. When Branvig had fed the horses he lit the fire with the wood which Creidne had gathered, and he helped him to gather more. As soon as they had the fire lighting they sat down, Branvig filled two cups and they drank their wine slowly, watching the fire and waiting for the others to return.

They came a short time later. Godrane settled their horses while Carriog joined the others by the fire, gratefully accepting a cup of wine. When Godrane rejoined them, Branvig shared out the dried meat which was all they had to eat. It was tasteless after the fresh meat of the night before, but it killed their hunger and they laced it with wine of which they still had plenty.

Godrane for some reason was affected quickly by the drink, and he watched Carriog with growing hostility. The wine loosened his tongue, and in a little while he began to abuse the Nemedian warrior and his people. Carriog did not seem to notice Godrane's anger or abuse, and he continued to eat and drink quietly, without taking his eyes from the fire into which he had been staring for some time, lost in thought.

Creidne and Branvig tried to silence Godrane, and to make him stop his abuse of their companion, but Godrane pushed them away.

"He's a Formorian spy and he'll lead us into a trap, that's what he'll do. He's not to be trusted, I tell you. He's one of them..."

For a long time he continued to abuse Carriog despite the others, until, without warning, he could suddenly no longer speak. No sound escaped his lips. He turned to the others, his eyes wide with fear and terror. They all looked at Carriog who had not moved a muscle, nor taken his eyes from the fire but remained, goblet in hand, staring into the flames, an expression of utter indifference on his face.

"Carriog... what has happened?" Creidne asked weakly. Carriog slowly turned and looked at him directly, his eyes seeming to burn into Creidne's own. "He will be back to himself tomorrow when he has rested. He will sleep soon."

Carriog turned back to the fire and continued his meditation, leaving the others to stare and wonder at the power of their companion.

Godrane, as though driven by some secret force, got up from his place by the fire and walked to the shelter, his eyes heavy and weary, a terrible lethargy suddenly draining his energy. He lay down on the fern and was quickly asleep. Branvig and Creidne stared at each other for a long time, unable to speak, too overcome by what they had seen to understand. It was beyond belief, they had seen it, they had seen it happen, but they could not comprehend it.

"I've never seen anything like it," Branvig said finally. He spoke in a low tone so that Carriog could not hear, though he too now believed that the big Nemedian could read his mind. All the same, speaking quietly reassured him that his thoughts were his own, and those with whom he chose to share them with.

"I knew there was more to that Nemedian, I knew it," Creidne said, unable to put it from his mind. He was puzzled and shaken by what he had seen, and he wanted to satisfy his scholar's mind by asking the Nemedian how he had done it, but he knew that this was not the right moment. As if to confirm this, Carriog turned away from the fire and stared at him for a moment. He smiled, and Creidne knew for certain in that instant that Carriog could read their minds.

Carriog turned away again. The others stared at him as he gazed into the fire, but he neither noticed them nor paid them any attention. They sat quietly, neither one speaking, but their eyes kept returning to Carriog. The forest was deathly quiet, and a heavy frost formed on the ground around about the campsite.

"He's a powerful magician," Branvig said after a long time, never taking his eyes from the Nemedian's back.

"I've never seen anything to equal it," Creidne agreed. "Even the Druid himself would have been impressed. I'm sure of that."

"What are we to do?" Branvig asked, betraying his fear by the tone of his voice. Creidne looked at him and smiled. He understood the young warrior's fear. "We will do as he tells us, and keep Godrane easy, because he will cause trouble again with that reckless tongue of his, though I think perhaps that tonight he may have learned a lesson he will not quickly forget." He smiled at the thought of Godrane's astonished look when he had found he no longer had a voice.

Next morning, Creidne woke early and he left the shelter and went for a walk in the forest alone. There was a mist lying on the ground, which itself was hard with the overnight frost. The undergrowth was white, the blankets of the sleeping men also, and in places Creidne could see the intricate spider webs visible in the early morning frost. He rubbed his hands together in a vain effort to keep warm as he walked away from the campsite, pulling his cloak tightly round his shoulders as he did so. He passed the horses who looked at him with only a flicker of interest. Godrane usually fed them, and when they saw that it was not he who passed, they turned away.

The forest, for all the bad weather, was a pleasant place and Creidne felt a growing sense of peace and renewal as he walked, promising himself that he would come again when the war was over. It seemed so far away, another world almost, and he could not imagine death in such a beautiful and tranquil place, but as he walked, he became aware once more of the terrible silence, the evil unnatural silence, and he knew that even here in this seeming haven, that the war had already intruded, that the peace was fragile and superficial.

He remembered the birds which had flown across the sky only a short time before, and he knew that the forest itself would be spoiled and barren if their enemies came this way. It saddened him deeply and he shook his head angrily. He said a silent prayer to the gods that they would somehow spare this peaceful place, that war and evil would not fall upon it, but in his heart he did not think that his prayers would be answered. He turned slowly and with heavy heart, and feet, he returned to the camp.

The others were up. Carriog was by the fire building it up, while Godrane and Branvig were seated nearby, eating some of the cold meat they still had left. Godrane did not look up as Creidne joined them, but kept his eyes averted. He was ashamed of his behaviour towards Carriog especially, but also to Creidne and Branvig, and he did not know how to tell them he was sorry.

When Creidne sat by the fire, Carriog turned to Godrane.

"You will ride ahead today," he said without a trace of anger in his voice.

"Very well," Godrane replied without thinking, then suddenly realized that this voice had returned. He smiled at the others, and they too smiled. He went to say something to Carriog, but the Nemedian spoke first.

"It's time you were going." Godrane nodded. He went to saddle his horse, and was quickly on his way. Creidne spoke to Carriog.

"I have never seen a more powerful spell than that which you used against Godrane last night. Tell me, how did you do it? I did not know that you were so skilled in the magic arts."

Carriog was fixing the saddle onto his horse. He continued working as he spoke, a hint of mockery in his voice.

"I chose not to reveal my knowledge of the magic arts. And as to how I did it, that is something no man, apart from myself, will ever know. I will tell you this though. I am your friend, as I have been Blamad's for many years, and I am no friend to the Formorians. I do not have any dealings with them. I prefer my own company, to be left alone unless I choose otherwise. It is my way and that is how I prefer it. If I wish to speak then I will speak, otherwise I will keep to myself."

He looked hard at Creidne.

"I will tell you one last thing. Godrane has learned to feel shame and he is sorry for what he has done, so that is an end to the matter."

With that he mounted his horse and prepared to leave. Creidne and Branvig did likewise, and they returned to the road and resumed their journey.

CHAPTER THREE

In spite of the continuing snowfalls, most of the kings and chiefs reached the high king's dún for the Samhain festival.

Samhain, when winter began, was an important feast, a time when loyalties to the king were renewed. It was a time when the laws were regulated and enacted, a time when disputes were settled, because the high king was regarded by the other kings as the final arbiter and the most impartial judge, whose word and command was accepted by all without question.

At Samhain in the high king's house arms were not permitted and personal quarrels were put aside. All men enjoyed the hospitality and even personal enemies, who in other circumstances might resort to armed conflict, were able to sit side by side at the king's banqueting table in complete safety and without fear of molestation.

For the duration of their stay in the high king's dún, the only armed men permitted were the king's own personal bodyguard and his own warriors who, for the time of Samhain, were kept apart and out of sight of the visiting kings and chiefs.

There were twenty of these in the banqueting hall, awaiting the arrival of the high king. They were seated at two long tables, ten at each and facing each other. At the head of the room was another table, smaller and facing down between the two other tables. This was where the high king would sit. The walls of the hall were adorned with banners and brightly coloured shields, trophies of past wars. Behind the king's table hanging from the wall was his own standard, a sword and a harp. War and peace.

A huge fire blazed in the grate set into the stone wall, an unusual location since most fires at that time were situated in the centre of the rooms or houses of the people, but this was the king's own idea and it gave him space to see all his chiefs, and no man could hide from his gaze.

Over this fire a huge boar was being turned by two slaves, while other slaves were hurrying in and out of the hall with food and wine and meat in preparation for the feast which would begin as soon as the king arrived.

There were meats and freshly roasted birds and hares laid out whole on platters, one before each man, bread and fruit, jugs of honey and sweetmeats.

Along the walls the lamps had been lit and with the fire, and many men filling the hall, the atmosphere was hot and getting hotter by the minute and it was hard to realize that outside it still snowed heavily.

The chiefs and kings waited patiently for the high king to arrive, and not a morsel of food nor a drop of wine was touched until he sat at his place. Some of the chiefs spoke to each other, but most remained quiet, saving their energy for later, when wine would loosen their tongues.

Eventually the high king entered the hall, with Blamad following close behind. The kings and chiefs stood as he entered and remained standing as he passed between the two tables to his own. Only when he had seated himself and waved them to do likewise did they too sit down.

Blamad sat beside him, the only man to do so, the only man apart from the king's bodyguard who was armed.

As the king's champion, Blamad was permitted to take the first cut from the boar which had been removed from the spit and carried to the king's table. He rose, cut a piece of the meat from the flank of the animal, and put it on the plate set before him. The king took some of the meat also and the slaves then carried the boar to the other tables where the other kings rose and took their share.

A harper began to play as they began to eat, and, as they did so Blamad's keen and shrewd eyes scanned the hall, trying to read the faces of the chiefs as they set into the meal.

Some were eating greedily, quickly and taking as much as they could, while others were refilling their cups with equal rapidity. Some were listening to the music and when the harper finished playing there was a clamour of approval from these men and from the others. This was the signal for all to talk freely and there was now a general tumult in the hall as a score of voices began speaking at once.

The high king ate sparingly and drank even less, taking a sip or two from the wine set before him. His thoughts were with his queen, Morna, who was far to the north with Ceolmhar, but the presence of Blamad was some comfort. He trusted Blamad utterly, the only man he did, and he knew that he had the warrior's complete loyalty.

Alone of all the chiefs in the room, the high king was beardless, and this was regarded by some of the chiefs as a sign of weakness. Since he had become king he had grown increasingly careworn and tired, and he was at that time completely worn out and exhausted. It was only his need to persuade the chiefs of the danger they faced that kept him going, since he felt he needed a long rest and time to himself.

He had kept the peace against great odds, kept the Druid pacified, only to know that he had now lost the battle, that war must come, costly and destructive war with all its horrors — famine and misery, death and fear.

The Grey Druid's treachery had been a hard blow to bear and he still could not believe it had happened. He looked down at the men before him and found himself wondering whether he could make them unite against the Formorians and the Druid.

Some of them he knew would be hard to convince, some would not want to be convinced. They were as bad themselves as the Formorians, raiding each other's lands, stealing each other's cattle, and women. He thought once more of Morna. She was more worthy than any of the kings seated before him, and he wished that some of them could see things as clearly as she could.

For many years the Formorians had been raiding with increasing regularity, even coming up the rivers in their ships and raiding further inland. Nowhere had been safe from them, nowhere could a man lay his head to rest without having somebody to watch over him. Many of the coastal villages had been abandoned, their people moving inland while the kings and chiefs, bitterly divided amongst themselves, had been powerless to stop the Formorians.

Then, suddenly, two years before, the raids had stopped. Not a single raid in all that time, at least none worth mentioning. Never in living memory had it happened before. Never had the annals spoken of a year without a raid from the Formorians except in the time when Nemed's people had almost destroyed them.

Brian, king in the west and the brother of Morna, was the only defence against them at the moment. He had a large and well-trained army, and the coasts were regularly patrolled by them, but there were too many miles of coast and too few men to watch every mile. There were too, some fiercely independent Nemedian kings to the south of Brian's lands, and although they owed nominal allegiance to the high king, they remained independent and remote.

The king knew that the Formorians and Nemedians were bitter enemies and that was some comfort.

His thoughts returned to the hall and the chiefs before him. He put his cup down on the table and rose to speak. There was silence in the hall as he rose, and the kings looked at him expectantly.

"My friends," he began, looking at each of them in turn. "I want first of all to thank you for coming here to renew your allegiance to me. Now, this Samhain we celebrate today is like no other Samhain. It is a Samhain full of fear and foreboding, a Samhain of uncertainty, of betrayal. There will be war when spring comes. War, famine and death. This I tell you without pleasure, since I do not wish for war, but nevertheless it will come. The Druid has betrayed us and has allied himself with the Formorians, our enemies, who are even now threatening Brian, which is why he is not among you tonight."

There was uproar in the hall and some of the chiefs jumped to their feet in their excitement. The high king's guards had their swords drawn but there was no danger to the king, and no one had any intention of attacking him.

"Yes, my words are true," he continued. "There will be war in the spring. The Formorians have begun to build settlements. Brian sent word to me only a few days ago, and since then I have learned that the Druid has also taken arms against us. Blamad here believes that the Druid planned and organised this all the time he was talking peace. There is no one among you who will not be affected by the coming war. All will suffer. All will fall before this threat — unless we put aside our quarrels and unite against it. The Formorians intend to stay this time and our only hope is our combined strength, to match the forces they and the Druid will send against us. If we do not unite together then slavery is what is left for us. Death for the warriors, slavery for the rest. None of us wants that to happen, but I tell you there will be no separate peace with the Formorians. You cannot expect to see your neighbour destroyed and the Formorians to leave you alone. Sooner or later no matter what they promise you, they will come and destroy you. All of you know this. Most of you have experienced Formorian raids. You have had friends or family killed by them, so you know what to expect from them. It will not be mercy, it will not be life, but slavery. Or death."

He stopped for a moment, and was pleased to see that at least they were listening to him. He continued:

"The Druid knows our weaknesses better than the Formorians. That is why he thinks we will be easy meat for him. He is certain that we cannot oppose him, he is certain that he cannot be defeated and this certainty, this arrogance, may be his weakness. He wishes to be high king if he can, but he will not be a kind king if he succeeds, since he is not a merciful man. If he is victorious, he will take everything away from you and give it to those who serve him.

"There are those among you here who favour the Druid. This I cannot understand. You must know what he will do, what the Formorians will do if they overcome us. Remember this also. If you are for the Druid, then you are against me and you will find me, too, an unmerciful enemy."

Again he stopped speaking, and this time he could see that some of the chiefs were frowning, angry at his words, but this did not surprise him since he knew that some of them were supporters of the Druid, men who barely concealed their own ambitions for power.

"I will leave you in a few moments so that you can decide among yourselves what you wish to do, but I must implore you once again to unite against the common enemy, to put aside your quarrels which have made us weak — and to stand together against the Formorians. We can defeat them if we are united, but only then. Now, as custom decrees, I will leave you to debate it amongst yourselves. I ask you to remember that the threat is already real and that one of your number, Brian, is already facing the enemy."

He finished speaking, and for a few moments there was silence. Then Díele, one of the chiefs who favoured the Grey Druid, stood up. He was a dark-faced man, with a reputation for cruelty and greed, and he spoke to the king with no trace of respect in his manner.

"I have heard this kind of talk before," he said, resting his hands on the table and leaning his body forward. The other chiefs listened attentively, because they respected Díele's power.

"The Formorians have come many times before, and always we have defeated them. We are in no danger. My own lands are close to Brian's, my villages scattered along the coast, yet I do not fear the Formorians, or run home in a blind panic because a few raiders have landed along the coast. The Formorians will raid until there is none of them left. It is their way. It has always been their way, as it is with us when we raid. Have not our warriors won fame and respect from the gods because of their skill in battle? Have not our people always gone to war and raided each other's villages? Are we now to turn our backs on that heritage and cringe when the first report of an enemy is sounded? Are we to believe that an army which Brian has so often boasted about is not capable of stopping a few barbarians, that the forces which Ceolmhar keeps in his mighty fortress are not enough to stop the Formorians? Is the high king's strength so sapped by his women that he cannot lead the men he has against our enemies?"

This was a bitter insult to the king, and Blamad jumped up at once, his sword drawn, but the king stopped him.

There was a murmur of disapproval from the other chiefs, some angry because of Díele's lack of respect, others by Blamad's actions.

"Let him be," the king said quietly. "He is under my protection and must not come to any harm. Let him continue."

Blamad looked at Díele with bitter contempt, but Díele smiled triumphantly. He continued:

"The Formorians will not attack. There are too many of us, and only a fool would dare do such a thing, nor do I think that the Druid will attack. He wants peace, this I know. He has told me so many times and I believe him. He will make war noises but when spring comes, he will talk peace."

He looked at his fellow chiefs, and saw at once that he had their support. Only one of them, Aemrig, was not with him, but that was a small matter. Aemrig was not a powerful king, and had few followers. Díele quietly thought that Aemrig would be quickly brought into line by the others.

"I see no reason to send any of my men into another king's land to help against a few raiders which any reasonable force could destroy. I will not do it. Let each of us look after his own interests, and stand on his own two feet. If a man cannot do that, then he should not be king."

Díele sat down to a roar of approval, and it was evident that most of the kings and chiefs agreed with what he had said. Blamad looked at him with bitter anger as he rose to speak.

"I hope my lords that you will not be swayed by such talk, the talk of traitors and cowards, the talk men make when they are afraid," he said coldly. Díele jumped up and screamed at Blamad.

"I am no coward," he hissed, his eyes narrowed with fury. Samhain or not, he would have killed Blamad at that moment if he had had his sword. The high king stood up. There was a tremor in his voice when he spoke, and it seemed for a long moment that he might not be able to speak at all, such was the emotion he felt. "There has been enough arguing."

A few of the chiefs were ashamed as they watched the king and listened to his speech, ashamed that they had caused him such distress.

"You will, as custom decrees, talk about this amongst yourselves, then you will give me your decision. If you decide to do as I ask and unite against the Formorians and the Druid, I will tell you my plans. But if you decide otherwise I will from that moment regard you as my enemies for breaking your allegiance to me. At such a time you will leave here and you will no longer have my protection or support."

Without another word or backward glance he left, followed by Blamad. The guards also left, but remained outside to see that no one else left the hall.

Out in the cold night air, the king walked with Blamad. He was very angry and sad that the Samhain feast had come to such an abrupt and bitter end, and he was not at all optimistic about convincing the chiefs to do as he had asked.

It was still snowing, but neither man noticed it much, their anger still hot, their thoughts on the assembly inside the hall.

"I will kill that traitor Díele," Blamad said angrily, but the high king silenced him.

"That will solve nothing. They may yet decide to act with us. I know that Díele has always supported the Druid, but I was surprised that he behaved as he did. I did not realize he hated me as much as that..."

"He is a dangerous man," Blamad said. "Greedy too, he will follow the strongest man. He has always been like that and he will never change. He is too full of ambition himself — but if he persuades the others that there is no danger from the Druid or the Formorians, then you might have trouble."

They had stopped and were sheltering under the awning of one of the houses, watching the snowflakes fall on the ground before them in the darkness. There was complete and peaceful silence, belying the arguments which were no doubt going on at that moment inside the council hall.

Blamad looked at the king. Such a king they had, and did not realize it, and he regretted that he had to use the words he did, but he had always been honest and open with the king, and the king expected no less.

"Some of the chiefs already believe that you are not fit to be high king, that you are too peaceable, that you avoid war and battle and prefer to talk to your enemies. That is fine and noble and wise my Lord, but to men like Diele it is weakness; because to them there is only might and power. They understand only the sword, they recognise only the strongest as leader, and no other. They do not understand. I sometimes do not understand, but I would not question your authority. But see what I am trying to say."

"I do, Blamad. And it is refreshing to hear the truth spoken, and I know you always speak the truth. For that I am grateful."

They walked again, ignoring the snow which covered them, for it was a gentle and windless snow. In the near distance, the light from the brazier by the grates of the dún where the guards sat huddled, shone like a beacon through the darkness, the voices of the men too coming like a whisper to where Blamad and the king walked. "I have tried to change things, and perhaps men do not understand change, but I tell you Blamad, patience is not a sign of weakness, nor is tolerance, and if the moment comes when we have to fight, you will find out that I too know how to handle a sword."

Blamad smiled in the darkness. "I never doubted it Lord. Perhaps though, Brian will hold the Formorians and there will be no need for the chiefs to unite against them. Then Díele will have wasted his words."

"Brian will not hold out against the Formorians alone, this I know," the high king replied quickly. "If we do not send help to him soon, then he will certainly be destroyed." Blamad could not believe what he had just heard. Brian had one of the strongest armies on the island, and his dún was so well fortified that it had never been attacked, yet the king was telling him that unless the others went to his help, Brian would be overcome.

"The gods are against us at this moment Blamad, though I pray that at least they will help our argument in there."

It stopped snowing and the clouds gave way to a clear sky, star filled, and the bright Samhain moon made the night seem suddenly like day.

"Look at it," the king said, forgetting for a moment his anger and the chiefs. "Timeless and unhurried like the seasons, there before we were born, there long after we are all dead and forgotten. You know, what we do now seems very important and in a way it is, but one day others will look up at this same moon, at the stars as we do, and it will matter little to them what we have done. War is a foolish and wasteful business, Blamad. It takes our best men, destroys our villages and puts fear into our children. A foolish pastime indeed..."

Blamad looked at the high king in the full light of the moon. There was pain in his face and uncertainty, and Blamad was suddenly glad that he was only a warrior and not a king.

"There will always be war my Lord. Men will always fight and wish to conquer other men. Sometimes it is necessary to fight to survive. Our people have done it, others have done it, and when we are long dead men will still go to war. It will always be so unless men change, and I cannot see that happening. We have been safe here only because we have been strong, and it is our strength which commands respect. If we show weakness, then that day will be our last."

He spoke with such venom, that the high king, who was a gentle man, was taken by surprise. It was so unlike Blamad, he thought, and was saddened by what he heard. He looked at his trusted bodyguard and friend.

"There is much hatred in your heart, Blamad." Blamad did not reply.

A messenger came from the council hall at that moment, and stood before the high king.

"The others have made their decision Lord, and they ask that you return to the hall at once." The king nodded, the messenger turned and went back to the hall.

The king and Blamad looked at each other. Both of them were apprehensive though each man tried to hide his uncertainty from the other.

"We had better go and hear what they have to say," the king said. They walked back to the council hall, the guards opened the doors and the king and Blamad entered to silence.

As soon as he saw the faces of the kings and chiefs before him, Blamad knew what their decision would be. He could see it in their faces, see it in the eyes averted when he looked at them, and his anger grew. The guards came into the hall and closed the doors behind themselves, while Blamad and the king walked to the king's table.

"What is your answer?" the king asked as soon as he stood facing them. He too knew in his heart what their answer was going to be, but he still hoped that he was wrong.

He scanned the room but, like Blamad, saw how the others would not meet his gaze.

Díele stood up, and spoke for the assembled chiefs.

"We have spoken together as the law commands and we have decided that the danger cannot be as great as was told to you. Each of us alone we believe is capable of dealing with any nuisance raid from the Formorians. There is no need for an all- out campaign since the Formorians will be afraid to leave whatever small settlements they have made and I am sure, when spring comes, they will happily return to their own island where they will be safe. Brian is strong enough, his army is big enough to deal with any Formorian threat, and I will do the same in my own lands. There is no treason in what I say, only common sense.

"But you, my Lord, have been deceived by those around you, those who want to go to war for their own ends, those who seek only glory for themselves. There will be no war this coming spring. Of that we are all quite certain."

He looked at the king, mockery in his eyes, his confidence that the others would follow him breeding a further arrogance in an already arrogant nature. The king saw it, as did Blamad, against whom most of Díele's remarks were aimed.

The king looked hard at Díele. Though a peaceable man, his anger was now too much to restrain, and when he spoke again, there was a bitter edge to his voice, a penetrating anger which every man in the hall felt so that some looked away as if ashamed of what they had done, feeling in their own hearts that the king was right, yet afraid to go against their fellow chiefs.

"You have made your final decision and so be it." He looked hard at each man in turn.

"The laws of hospitality prevent me from doing with you as I would wish, as you deserve, but since you came here under my protection, you will have that same protection until morning, when you will leave this place. None of you will be permitted to leave this hall until then, but will remain here under guard until first light when you will be escorted out of the dún and sent on your way."

There was uproar as he turned to leave, but Blamad had signalled the guards, who pushed the chiefs back with the flats of their swords.

"Any man who leaves his place again will be killed," he said harshly. "I did not give my word to protect you, so beware."

Díele was livid with rage but he knew that Blamad would do as he said. He also knew that he would be the first one Blamad would kill, so he remained in his chair and did not move. Blamad let the guards out of the hall. When they were outside he locked the doors and doubled the guard, both on the hall and on the king's own house. In the meantime, all the attendants and slaves and escorts of the kings were rounded up and detained and no one was permitted any free movement through the dún until the coming of morning.

Blamad ran after the king, who was about to enter his own house. His face was careworn and drawn, and he could hardly speak.

"I wish to be alone, Blamad." When he saw that Blamad was about to protest, he added gently: "I shall be all right. In the morning, when I have rested, I will talk with you."

He went inside. Blamad called some of his guards.

"Keep close to the king. Permit no one to enter until I come in the morning."

The guards went inside the king's house and stationed themselves quietly outside his room while Blamad went to double the guard on the gates and the walls. He went onto the ramparts and looked out over the plain beyond the dún, and thought of Creidne and the others somewhere out there. Before he knew what he was doing he found himself praying to the gods, the first time he had done so for many years.

With the coming of dawn, the chiefs and their attendants were taken under heavy guard from the high king's dun, closely watched by Blamad and his men who had orders to kill anyone who tried to leave the formation.

Some of the chiefs, particularly Díele, were glad to be leaving the dún, but there were some among them who felt that they had betrayed the high king, and these men left with a deep sense of shame and tried not to look into the faces of those who watched them leave.

From his vantage point on the ramparts Blamad watched them go, and felt a bitter hatred for all of them. He swore that when the time was right he would make them pay for what they had done.

It took some time for the column of men and animals to leave the dún, but during that time Blamad remained where he was, watching and making sure that no one caused any trouble. Below in the courtyard before the gates, there was some commotion and the sounds of voices raised in anger.

Blamad looked down to see that one of the chiefs, with his followers, had refused to move and were instead standing unarmed and surrounded by Blamad's guards, who seemed likely to kill them such was their mood of anger and suspicion.

"Wait," Blamad shouted and he ran down the steps and came face to face with the chief.

"He will not leave," one of Blamad's men said. Blamad gripped the chief by the cloak angrily. He was a bigger man than Blamad, with dark red hair and beard, but he made no move to resist Blamad or to remove his hands from his cloak.

"Why have you not left with the other traitors?" Blamad said, spitting the words into the man's face.

The man smiled quietly and without a word or any effort, removed Blamad's hand from his cloak.

"Aemrig does not break his oath to the high king." He looked directly at Blamad.

"You are an angry man, and there is good cause for your anger. But that anger blinds you, and you see only enemies. I am loyal to the high king. I have always been loyal to him and no matter what was decided in the council hall, that will not change. I do not have the power nor the men the others have but what I have belongs to the king and him alone do I serve. I will not leave here without that being known. I am the king's servant, and I and my men are at his disposal."

Blamad did not say anything for a while. His anger however, cooled. As he looked into the face of the chief who stood almost looking down at him he remembered the name, and recalled that the king often spoke of Aemrig as a man he could trust.

After some moments, Blamad smiled.

"Come, we will drink some ale together and talk."

Aemrig smiled and allowed himself to be led away. His men relaxed as Blamad's men, on his command, put away their swords and returned to their posts. The snow was starting to fall again and the wind began to rise as the last of the chiefs disappeared over the horizon.

CHAPTER FOUR

A great fire burned in the hall as the slaves prepared the table for their master, the Grey Druid. They worked quietly and quickly, nervous in case he came and found them there.

The table was soon prepared, and the slaves withdrew. Apart from the fire which brightened the hall and threw many shadows, a few oil lamps flickered along the walls while, on the table itself a long candle set in the centre.

Also on the table were two wine goblets, a pitcher of water and a silver bowl, the whole atmosphere creating the impression that this was the house and table of a frugal man.

The house itself was large, two stories, made of wood and stone. The hall was spacious, with a high ceiling, across which great oak beams criss-crossed, supporting the upper structure, and from which hung many pennants and banners, captured trophies of wars and raids.

The floor was made of stone, rush-covered, yet giving the room a cold and cavernous feeling despite the warm fire and the lamps which held back the darkness.

The Druid entered. He walked quietly, flanked by two other druids who waited on him. He wore the grey gown from which he got his name, and which hung loosely over his spare body. He was tall and beardless, his cheeks sallow, almost cadaverous, and his lean angular features and dark penetrating eyes missed nothing as he crossed the room to his table, to eat.

As soon as he was seated, the slaves returned carrying a silver platter and jugs of wine and mead. The Druid watched quietly as they left the food and drink on the table before him, and withdrew.

He usually ate sparingly — never meat, sometimes fish, and it was fish which was placed before him now. He looked at the pink flesh of the salmon, freshly caught and steamed as it was put before him by one of the other druids. He ate a little, when Garweng, his attendant druid had first sampled it. It tasted very light, and he took some more. Garweng poured some of the wine into the two goblets, tasting it himself before handing the second goblet to the Druid, who nodded his approval. Garweng smiled, relieved.

It was an exacting task, trying to keep the Druid satisfied, but Garweng, who was a long time in the Druid's service, was as cunning as a weasel, and almost perfected in the art.

A small narrow-eyed man, who cringed when he was in the Druid's presence, he was a person of the utmost servility, whose head and shoulders had become permanently stooped because of this.

Although he usually anticipated the Druid's wishes, sometimes he, the Druid, overcome by the strange and frightening moods which occasionally overtook him, would not be pleased, and his anger at such times was fearful.

Garweng knew how and when to make himself scarce until such a mood passed, as it inevitably did but, while these moods lasted, the Druid seemed to be haunted by some unseen force. He would spend hours, sometimes days, alone in his room, away from everybody, pacing the floor, looking out his window to the distance as though he was searching for someone, or something.

At other times he would take his horse and ride hard over the plain, pushing both himself and the animal to the limits of their endurance, in a restlessness he could not explain himself.

Now, however, he was content, and expressed his approval.

"You have done well tonight Garweng," he said, his voice thin and harsh. "The salmon was delightful. The best I have tasted for a long time."

"Thank you, Master." Garweng poured some more wine into the Druid's cup which was almost empty. The Druid watched him as he lifted the jug.

"Has Diele sent word yet?" Garweng put the jug down.

"No, Master, he has not. Perhaps he has been delayed because of the snow... There have been more heavy falls in the past few hours and the roads are probably impassable."

"I am aware of that," the Druid replied coldly, his mood quickly changing. Garweng knew the signs. The Druid was impatient for news, and impatience in the Druid bred anger.

Garweng left the hall, ostensibly to see if the messenger from Díele had arrived yet, but in reality to escape from what he feared was to be another eruption of the Druid's feared temper. He stayed outside for as long as he dared, then returned, reluctantly, to the hall.

"There has been no word yet, Master." The Druid did not reply. He was lost in thought, thinking of Vitrig and his Formorians, who would soon have Brian at their mercy.

If Díele had done his work well, then there would be division in the high king's dún, and the chiefs would continue on their own, fighting and quarrelling as they had always done, and this suited the Druid's purpose well, since it meant that he would have no trouble disposing of them when the time came. Díele included.

He smiled coldly. Once the high king was dead, there would be no stopping him, he knew this. His lips widened into a smile as he thought of the fear and havoc he would unleash on the high king's people. They would soon know his real power. They would soon learn to acknowledge him as their new king, and not the weak mild-mannered man who now sat on the throne. They would have a real king, one with power, a king that no one would ever dare to challenge, not even Vitrig or his Formorians.

He thought about Vitrig. The Formorian had plans similar to his own. The Druid knew this, but he also knew that, against him, Vitrig was powerless. He would kill him when the first opportunity presented itself, after they had disposed of their common enemy.

There could be only one high king, one master and he, the Grey Druid, would be that master. His magic, and the Picts he commanded, would see to that.

The Picts hated the Formorians with an intensity matched only by the Nemedians' hatred of them, and this had been one of the Druid's great achievements, that he had allied the Picts and Formorians together for the war against the high king and his allies. It was an uneasy and fragile alliance, one which could easily break, and probably would as soon as they had defeated their common enemy.

He left the table and went to one of the couches which were set against the wall close to the fire, and lay down.

"Leave me," he said sharply. "Call me when the messenger from Díele arrives."

Garweng and the other druid left the hall. The Druid lay on the couch, staring at oak beams above. One of his strange, black moods was coming over him, and he felt heavily depressed, though he did not know why. He closed his eyes, and soon fell into a deep but troubled sleep.

Aemrig and Blamad drank together. The mutual anger between them had given way to a growing trust, and they sat by the fire drinking warm mead, letting the hours pass pleasantly.

They spoke of what had happened, and Aemrig, who knew the chiefs better than Blamad, told him that Díele had persuaded them that there was no danger at all.

"He's a very powerful leader. A good speaker too, and many of the others are afraid of him, because their lands border his, and they fear his revenge if they do not do as he says. If he is to retain his authority over them, he will come against me very soon, because I did not do as he commanded."

"The high king will not allow that to happen," Blamad replied confidently, Aemrig however shook his head.

"You are wrong my friend. The high king will be powerless to stop it. Díele will wait until the Druid attacks you here, then he will strike against me. He does not care who wins or loses this war. He is only interested in taking care of himself."

There was a knock on the door, and a warrior entered and stood before Blamad. He was weeping.

"What is it?" Blamad asked, a sickening fear beginning to rise in his stomach. The warrior did not answer immediately, and Blamad grabbed him and shook him violently.

"What is it man? Tell me..."

"The high king is dead," the warrior said sobbing.

Blamad's hands fell limply to his side.

"How?" he asked, his voice a mere whisper. "How..?"

"He was dead when we went to him a short while ago," the warrior replied. "After you left us last night, he told us that he did not wish to be disturbed, that he wanted to be alone. He said that when all the chiefs had gone, he would come to the council hall, but when he did not appear, our commander went in to see him, to know what he wished to do, and he found him dead, his servant too, stabbed many times both of them..."

The young man's voice was breaking as he spoke. When he finished he stood waiting, but Aemrig dismissed him, because Blamad was too choked to say or do anything. "We will speak with you later. Tell your commander that we will be with him in a few moments."

"There was a guard on him. How could it happen?" Blamad said incredulously.

He looked hard at Aemrig for a moment, and Aemrig felt the anger in that look, an anger which quickly disappeared as Blamad put his hand on his arm.

"I understand your anger, Blamad," he said quietly. "But I did not have anything to do with it. As to the question you have not yet asked me, I would say that the assassin was already waiting for the king when he entered his rooms last night. The guards could not have known that, they are blameless, I am sure of it."

"We shall see," Blamad said angrily. "For now, let us go and see the king's body."

They left the warm fire and the mead, going out into the grey snow-filled morning air. There was already a crowd gathered outside the king's house, and Aemrig was immediately struck by the fear and uncertainty in their faces. When they saw Blamad, they crowded around him looking to him for comfort, but at that moment he had none to give, his only thought to see the king's body and what the assassins had done to it.

They entered the house, and went to the room where the corpse lay. The king was lying lifeless across the bed where he had fallen, his tunic covered with blood, his eyes wide with fear.

On the floor the body of his servant was lying in a pool of blood. Aemrig covered him with a blanket, and he helped Blamad lift the king's body into a more dignified position on the bed, covering it too with a blanket.

When they had done this, Blamad called the slaves who had been waiting by the door to come and clean the room, while others were set to cleaning the bodies of the king and his servant.

Blamad had lost control of himself. The mighty warrior, king's champion and hero of many battles was completely disarmed and thrown into despair by the sight of the king's body.

Hardly aware of Aemrig who had taken command, he stood absently gazing at the corpse, his eyes filled with tears, and he cried as a child would for a dead father.

Aemrig ordered that the guard be doubled on the walls, and went to speak to the people who were assembled anxiously outside the king's house.

"The high king has been murdered," he said calmly. "We have not yet discovered by whom, but it is likely that one of the servants of the chiefs who departed from here this morning is responsible. You must remain calm and remember that Blamad and his warriors are here and they will protect you. The queen will be told, and those loyal to the high king. You have nothing to fear, so for the moment go back to your homes, see to your animals, while we prepare the high king's body for burial."

He dared not tell the assembled people, that the man they were depending on, the man to whom they looked for protection, was himself confused and desperate. He only hoped that the mood of despair which afflicted Blamad would quickly disappear so that he could take his rightful place as leader.

When he returned inside, Aemrig was pleased to see that the champion had indeed recovered his wits.

"I'm sorry," Blamad said. "Not the way for a warrior to behave."

"There is no shame in grief," Aemrig said truthfully. "You have lost a king, and a friend. I too feel as you do. I was not his champion or as close to him as you were, but I understand your sorrow. I have sent men out to find any of the chiefs they can, and bring them back, though I fear that it is too late already."

"You are a good man," Blamad said gratefully. "You have done well and I thank you for it."

Aemrig ignored the compliment. He sat on one of the chairs watching the slaves as they went about their tasks.

The king's body had been washed and dressed in battledress, and lay on the bed as a man sleeping before battle. His eyes had been closed, and his grey waxen face now looked calm and peaceful.

The servant's body had been removed from the room altogether to be prepared for burial.

"This was a well planned killing," Blamad said as he looked at the king, now that the ravages of his dying had been removed from his face and body. Aemrig nodded silently.

"It was most likely Diele who ordered it. His words have disunited the chiefs as nothing else could have done, and now, when they hear that the king is dead, they will quarrel even more about who is to be the new high king."

Blamad knew that Aemrig spoke the truth. Díele had for certain been responsible for the death but it was the Druid who had ordered it, that much they knew. Still one thing puzzled Blamad. "The Druid was so certain of victory, of capturing the high king and humiliating him, and yet he orders his killing. I don't understand it... I don't understand it at all."

"It's easy to see why," Aemrig said. "It was done to spread fear and panic. With the king dead, your leader is no more. I know that he was a peace-loving man, but he was a symbol to your people and they are going to need a lot of convincing that they are not going to be overrun by the Druid. Even you, if you forgive me for saying it, were temporarily paralysed by fear when you first heard the news, so how do you think that the other people in the dún feel?"

"I cannot tell them that we will not be overrun, since we do not know what magic the Druid has planned against us," Blamad replied. "Even the high king knew that there was a strong chance that the Druid would capture this dún. He said so before last night's meeting, that is why he was depending on the other chiefs joining with him against the Druid and the Formorians. He knew that even if they had all joined together, they would still be a formidable enemy. The Formorians we can defeat alone, but the Druid?..."

He left the words hang in the air, but Aemrig knew well what he meant. The Druid had magic, and it was this they feared more than the war. War they knew and could handle. They could rely on their strengths and skills against men like themselves, but against the Druid's magic they were fighting something powerful, unpredictable and frightening.

"You must try to calm their fears just the same," Aemrig said. "Tomorrow, when we bury the king, you must speak to the people and reassure them that they have nothing to fear."

"But they have," Blamad said quickly. "You know they have."

"I know it and so do you, but they do not have to know it yet, do they?"

Blamad did not reply. He was confused and, he confessed quietly to himself, a little frightened.

There was a knock on the door and one of the men whom Aemrig had sent out to search for the chiefs entered the room. He cast a quick glance at the high king's body as he approached Blamad and Aemrig.

"Well?" Aemrig asked. The man shook his head.

"Not a trace, Lord. The snow wiped their tracks, and the roads are all but snowed under again. In a day or two, there will be no travelling. We rode as hard as we could over the snow but still we could find no trace of them. They too must have hurried on their way." Aemrig nodded.

"Go and rest. You have done well."

The messenger left the room, again with a glance at the high king's body.

"They knew we would follow," Blamad said. "They all knew it."

"Aye Blamad, it would seem so. We will have to wait until spring now, to find them and punish them as they deserve, but I too must leave the rejoin my own people."

Blamad looked at Aemrig with surprise, so he explained:

"You heard what the messenger said, that the roads would soon be impassable, and besides, I too, will have to prepare my people for the coming war. My dún is not strong, the walls would burn under two flaming arrows, and my people are feeble from lack of action, so there is much to do. Tomorrow, after I have paid my final respects to the high king, I must leave."

"I understand," Blamad said, but the thought that Aemrig was leaving filled him with foreboding. The giant had proved himself a true and worthy friend, and Blamad had come to depend on him, but he knew that Aemrig must leave and prepare his own people for the coming struggle.

The following morning, they prepared to bury the high king. It was a cold dark, grey morning, and the snow clouds hung ominously in the sky. Since early light, the gates of the dún had been opened, and since that time, patrols had been ranging the countryside, watching for any sign of their enemies who might use the time of the king's burial as an opportunity to attack the dún.

A grave had been dug in the hard ground, close to the lake, and a large stone, which had been carried by slaves, lay close by to be put on later as a marker. The body of the king, and that of his servant were brought from the dún, and placed side by side on the snow. They were both wrapped in furs, and beside the king's body the slaves placed his shield and weapons as well as other gifts of food and jewellery which he would take into the Otherworld with him.

Blamad led the elders and the people of the dún to the burial site. The snow had begun to fall again in swirling patterns, covering the footsteps of the crowd even as they made them.

Aemrig watched the silent procession as it made its way across the snow-covered ground.

The slaves now lowered the king's body and that of the servant into two graves, which were side by side.

When they had finished, the slaves stood back, then Blamad began to speak.

"We have lost a friend and leader, and today we bury him and pay homage to his memory. Through treachery our king, still young in years now lies in a premature grave beside his faithful servant who died with him. At this moment, when our grief is greatest we ask the gods to watch over their spirits as they cross into the Otherworld. There is fear and anger among you, and this I understand. But you must remember only the king at this hour. A king who served his people well who gave them peace. A king whose hand was never raised in anger against any man, a great king who kept us from war. Remember him, and honour him now, as we throw this earth upon his body, and cover him with these stones."

The slaves began to fill the graves, and when they had done this, they moved the stones over the king's tomb. The people now began to return to the dún in silence. No one spoke, there was no need. All shared the same thoughts and foreboding. All feared what the morrow would bring.

CHAPTER FIVE

The messenger from Díele arrived at the Druid's dún. He went directly to see the Druid, as he had been instructed to do by Díele.

"The high king is dead, Lord. He was dead before Blamad or his people knew anything of it, and we were away from the dún even before the body was discovered."

"You are certain he is dead?" the Druid asked, unable to escape some small sense of doubt. The messenger nodded.

"There is no doubt about it, Lord. The word is already spread, and Blamad had men searching the countryside for those who were responsible."

The Druid laughed, a cold harsh, chilling laugh, humourless and terrifying.

"At last. At last the king is dead. My moment has come."

He looked at Díele's messenger. "Go and rest. Eat your fill and take some wine my friend, you have brought me the best news you could have."

The messenger left the hall, and the Druid turned to Garweng.

"Find Dubhghall, and tell him I wish to see him at once." Garweng went to do as he was bid, while the Druid sat in his chair unable to control the sense of triumph and elation he felt. In a while he would be high king, in a while he would have everything he had worked and planned for. It had been so easy. All that remained was to destroy the high king's dún, and Blamad, and then there would be nothing to stop his power.

He had decided to use the magic which had long been in his possession, to unleash the Power he knew was contained there, and which he had been afraid to use until now. He had learned much. He had studied the ancients' writings, had read them until he knew them by heart, and now he decided it was time to unleash that knowledge against Blamad, and the others who were in the high king's dún. A Power which would destroy them, but which would also show Vitrig and his Formorians that it was he, the Grey Druid, who would be high king.

He smiled coldly. The gods jealously guarded their secrets, but he had penetrated the darkness and discovered one of those secrets. He knew that the gods were watching him, he knew too that they were waiting to see how he would use the Power he had discovered, but he would show them that he understood the Power, could control it and make use of it. They would see, he thought. They would all see.

Garweng returned with Dubhghall, the leader of the Picts, the Druid's army.

"It is time to begin our march against the high king's dún," the Druid said. Garweng and Dubhghall glanced at each other.

"The high king is dead. Díele has done his work well, and now it is up to us to finish what he has started before Vitrig and his Formorians hear the news and come rushing for spoils themselves. You do not wish him to take the glory do you?

He knew the hatred there was between the Formorians and Picts, and he knew that the last thing Dubhghall would want was to give Vitrig any advantage over him. Garweng however, was doubtful that the Picts would leave their winter camp.

"Master, you know that I would not give Vitrig any chance to better me, but in this weather the men will grumble, and they will not like marching through snow and storms."

The Druid looked scathingly at him, then at Dubhghall.

"They will do as I command. Neither the snow, nor their own fear or laziness will stop them — is that clear, Dubhghall?"

The Pict shrugged his shoulders.

"For once I agree with Garweng, but you are master here, and if you say march, then we will march."

The Druid smiled. Dubhghall was a formidable warrior and a fearless fighter, but even he feared the Druid, just as the others did. To other men, Dubhghall was himself a man to be feared. A ruthless, merciless killer, his face was divided by a long scar which ran from his forehead to his chin, the relic of a sword cut which should have killed him, and would have killed a lesser man.

He was tall and dark like most of his race, but there was nothing pleasant about his look or manner, and his heart was cold, almost as cold as the Druid's.

"I have a plan for the high king's dún which I will give to you without you having to fight for it," the Druid said. "I promise you that. Your men only have to endure a few days of storm, then they will have all the plunder and women they want."

During the next few days, the Druid's dún was a hive of activity as the Picts prepared to march against the high king's people. The surrounding countryside was scoured for livestock and stripped bare by Dubhghall's raiding parties, who took also the men of the surrounding villages to be slaves for the army once it began to march. Whole villages were burned for resisting and many were left without shelter or food, to face the winter with little hope of survival.

In the dún itself, the smiths were working day and night forging weapons, taking turns at sleeping, never letting the fire die down, or the sound of metal against metal, cease.

The Druid was rarely seen during those days, and he remained within his own quarters, reading the manuscripts, studying the magic he intended to use against Blamad and the others.

The manuscripts were very old and priceless, and they contained many of the secrets which had been lost to all but a few like himself who were interested enough to study and search for them.

He kept the manuscripts hidden, even from Garweng, and no one knew of their existence except a few old Nemedian magicians, most of whom were now dead. He spent many hours poring over the ancient writings, and the lamps in his room burned long into the night as he increased his knowledge and understanding of the words before him.

Finally, their preparations complete, and with the Druid and Dubhghall at their head, the Picts began their march towards the high king's dún. They moved along the old Nemedian road. It was still a good road, and the Druid acknowledged the skill of the Nemedians who had built it many years before. They had been a clever race, he thought smugly, as he remembered the precious manuscripts he carried, some of which were Nemedian scrolls.

The snow was heavy in the open country, the wind sharp and biting, but they were able to make reasonable progress along the well paved road, though in some places the snow had drifted high, and they had to wait as the slaves worked to make a path through.

Some of the Picts grumbled as they stood in the biting cold, and they complained, saying only fools or madmen campaigned in mid winter, only fools left warm beds and soft women and good ale for a march through such a storm. The Druid however was relentless, and kept them going even when the snow fell without respite and the wind rose to a fury. He would not stop, he was driven by the force which impelled him to keep going.

Behind him, the men cursed him and called down every misfortune they knew on his back. Even Dubhghall, riding beside him, wondered what kind of madness drove the Druid, for it was surely madness which kept him going in such inhospitable and dangerous weather. He had never met a man like the Druid before, he had never known a man with such cold eyes or indifferent heart. They were all afraid of him, himself included, and he knew the Druid was aware of this.

He was a terrifying master, but he paid well and always kept his promises, and now he had promised them the whole island.

The storm rose to a fury and the army slowed to a crawl.
Some men became separated from the main column, lost in the wilderness, facing certain death. Some simply lay down and gave up, unable to face the fury of the storm, or their own exhaustion.

Finally, however, even the Druid had to admit defeat, late in the afternoon, when the slaves could not clear the road because the snow drifted almost as quickly as they dug it away.

"Make camp," he shouted to Dubhghall, through the wind. "Make camp," he called again.

The Picts immediately began to build shelters, cutting boughs from nearby trees, others lighting fires to warm their hands and faces. The wind increased and the snow covered everything, men, wagons, horses, the newly raised shelters and tents, and the tracks of the army, so that nothing was visible in a little while and all traces of the Druid and his men had disappeared.

Aemrig and Blamad stood by the water's edge, close to the dún which was behind them. A mist hung over the lake, and boats weaved and bobbed in the gentle breeze. In the distance a flock of geese disturbed the silence, the sound they made carrying far into the stillness.

Blamad and Aemrig looked over the lake.

"When will you tell Ceolmhar about the high king's death?" Aemrig asked. The water close to where they stood, rippled, and they could just about catch sight of a fish as it broke the surface for a moment.

"I'll have to get a messenger out soon," Blamad replied, still watching the spot where the fish had been an instant before. "The queen will have to be told and Ceolmhar warned about what has happened."

"At least we are spared war until spring," Aemrig said. "It gives us time to prepare, since who knows what the gods have planned for us!"

Blamad laughed.

"Since when did you put your trust in the gods?" Aemrig laughed also, but did not answer.

"I must leave now Blamad," he said a short time later. Blamad nodded. The sky promised more snow, and if Aemrig did not leave soon, he would have to winter in the high king's dún, something he could not afford to do, if he was to get his people ready for the war when spring came.

They returned to the dún, where Aemrig's escort was already waiting. Aemrig mounted his horse, and prepared to leave.

"Send word when you need me, Blamad. If it is possible, then I will come."

"I will," Blamad replied, gripping Aemrig's arm. "The gods keep you, and protect you on your journey." Aemrig smiled and kicked his horse gently. "We will meet again soon, Blamad," he said laughing as he rode away. "I feel it in my blood..."

When they were gone, Blamad called an assembly in the council hall. The entire population of the dún, that is the freemen, filled the hall. There was scarcely room to breathe, even though the hall was large and spacious, since never before had so many people crowded in between its walls.

This was the very room where the chiefs had gone against their king. Now, instead of gaiety, there was an air of despondency and gloom, and the armed men, silent and grim-faced, stood motionless waiting for Blamad to begin his speech.

He had left his sword and war cloak, as well as his helmet and shield on the table before him, and as he looked round at their faces, he saw that the older, more experienced men understood, and knew his thoughts exactly. He began;

"You all know why I have called you here." There was a nodding of heads and a general murmur of assent from the assembly. "Our king was murdered by Díele, of this we are certain, not by his hand, but by his orders. And by the order of one more powerful than Díele, the Druid. He has declared war against us, and we have to face the possibility that despite the winter he will attack us.

"I will not tell you lies. The situation is very serious. Brian has asked for our help because he is under threat from the Formorians, but we cannot send any help. And now that the other chiefs have refused to unite under the king's leadership, there is little chance that Brian will get any help at all.

"I speak with morbid words because I do not want any man to be unaware of the threat which faces us. However, despite this threat, despite the danger, we have the means to overcome our enemies.

"The winter is upon us, and this year winter is our friend and may keep our enemies from us until we have had time to prepare. Store whatever food you can, forge new swords and spears, prepare yourselves, so that when the snow melts, we will have enough provision to hold out until Ceolmhar comes to our aid.

"I am sending messengers to Ceolmhar tomorrow, to let him know what we face and to ask him to send help as soon as he can. The king was killed in order that we would become frightened and confused, and lose the will to fight, but we will not. We will prepare for the Druid, we will show him that we are not afraid, and with Ceolmhar's help, we will destroy the Druid forever.

"Have courage, friends, and remember that we have never been overcome before. We have never been defeated."

He was finished. The many faces which stared back at him were fearful and nervous, but he had said all he could to calm their fears. They had to know the truth, they had to understand that once the snows melted, their enemies would come down the Nemedian road, and try to take their dún, they had to find their courage and their will to fight.

No one spoke. There was no need, but no one moved or attempted to leave the hall. They remained, facing the weary warrior who was their leader until the queen returned, their chief on whose shoulders rested the fate and survival of them all.

They knew it, and Blamad knew it, and for the first time in his life, he was afraid. He would have to make whatever decisions were needed in the coming war and he did not know if he was up to such responsibility. He knew that there was no one else until Ceolmhar came, there was no one the people would trust until reinforcements arrived, he must hide his own fear and show them a strong and determined face, yet he felt anything but strong at that moment.

For a long time the people remained in the hall, standing, staring at Blamad, who stood quietly facing them, his own gaze unwavering. Somehow, from whatever reserve of strength or character he possessed, he began to exude a feeling of confidence, and they began to draw comfort from him.

Eventually, after what seemed a long time, and as if by some unseen command, they began to leave the hall until at last, Blamad was alone. He slumped into the king's chair.

His eyes glazed, and suddenly, dark shadows passed over him, echoes of what had been, screamed and passed through his mind. He saw ghostly feasts and phantom bards. He heard wild songs and gentle laments, mournfully sung by weeping harpists whose eyes held no light — whose loud, mocking laughter taunted him, until he saw clearly before him, standing like a demon upright, the figure of the Grey Druid. The figure walked to him and through him, laughing and mocking him as it did so.

He felt dizzy, and held the side of the chair to steady himself, but the images had faded, and he became aware of himself and his surroundings once more. He left the hall. Outside, the snow had begun to fall again, the long awaited storm beginning to rattle the dún as the wind rose to a fury. Blamad cursed the winter under his breath.

The Druid was in a rage because his plans had been delayed and upset by the bad weather. He lay on a pallet in his shelter, cursing and swearing, promising to inflict even greater cruelties on Blamad and the others because of the delay, as if they were responsible for the present situation, and not the weather. A solitary lamp flickered, and a brazier held a small fire which heated the shelter quite well. The hide shelter flapped as the wind rose again, flickering the lamp and scattering sparks from the fire.

The Druid swore again. Garweng stood beside him, and even in the dim light, he could see the Druid's face clearly. He knew from experience that the Druid was in a foul mood, and he knew also from experience that he was likely to be the one who would suffer the consequences of that anger.

"Leave me alone, I wish to sleep for a while," the Druid said, much to Garweng's relief. He left the shelter at once, glad to be away from the Druid, if only for a short time.

As he passed the shelters of the Picts he could hear the soldiers inside laughing and singing, and the sounds also of women's voices. He wanted to join them to be part of such pleasure, but he knew that the Picts would not welcome him into their presence. He knew that they feared him as much as they hated the Grey Druid.

He entered his own shelter. The other two druids with whom he shared the tent were speaking in hushed tones as he entered. They looked up at him, but again, there was no greeting. They too, hated him because he stood at the Druid's side, while they were little better than common servants.

One of them, Morc, a man with greedy eyes, and a sly servile manner, began to mock Garweng,

"Our master's shadow has returned." The second druid laughed. His name was Dichiu and he had been a druid in Ceolmhar's service before he had deserted to the Grey Druid.

He was the oldest of the three men, his hair already grey, but he was also the tallest and the strongest, attributes which increased his sense of frustration and anger, because he believed that he, and not Garweng, should have been the Grey Druid's assistant.

"You may mock me," Garweng said. "But you would do well to guard your tongues, or else the master will tear them out if I tell him that you speak ill of him."

He spoke smoothly and quietly, without anger, yet they felt the threat in his voice and they were afraid.

"He would not believe you," Dichiu said, a tremor in his voice as he spoke.

Garweng smiled coldly. "He will believe me. He will if I tell him, because he trusts me. Now both of you, on your knees before me, and beg my forgiveness, or I will tell him that you conspire against him."

He stood before the other two, and though he was dwarfed by Morc, their gazes wavered under his.

"On your knees," he roared, and this time, without taking their eyes off him, they slid to the floor and knelt before him.

"Well..?"

Morc and Dichiu glanced at each other, and with great effort of will, Dichiu spoke. "I intended no offence," he lied, cursing Garweng silently, cursing himself for saying the words.

Morc too apologised, his eyes cold with unconcealed hatred, but Garweng was enjoying himself.

"Remember before you speak to me again, that I can have you destroyed whenever I wish it." He left the shelter and went out once more into the night. Morc and Dichiu, by now ashamed of their own weaknesses before him, cursed him, and swore vengeance.

Meanwhile, Garweng was walking through the encampment, through the heavy falling snow, dreaming that one day, he would take the Druid's place. He looked and was, a solitary figure, loved by no one, hated by all, even the master he served so well.

The Druid had woken, and for a few moments sat on the edge of his pallet, collecting his thoughts. Then, reaching underneath, he pulled out the metal box which he had hidden there. He lifted it onto the pallet, and from round his neck, suspended on a chain, he took a key. The box itself was ornate with many carvings and strange images engraved on its top and sides.

When he opened the box, a strong fragrance filled the tent, a strange perfume which the Druid enjoyed for a few moments before he took the manuscript out. The box contained many strange herbs and potions, and other manuscripts, but the Druid was interested only in the one which he now held on his knees. It was written in a strange tongue, but the words he understood, and he ran his fingers delicately over the ancient vellum, and carefully opened one of the pages.

He read the script for a few minutes, and as his eyes scanned the page a smile crossed his lips. He had found what he was looking for, and he knew now for certain that it would make him the most powerful man on the whole island.

He read and re-read the words carefully until he knew them by heart, then laid the manuscript on the bed beside him. Taking some herbs from a pouch in the box, he mixed them together and put them into another, smaller pouch. Then he returned the larger pouch and the manuscript to the box, locked it and put it once more under the pallet.

Garweng returned a few moments later, followed by Dubhghall.

"The snow has eased a little," the Pict said. "If it continues like this, we may be able to get the slaves working to clear a way through for us."

"You are impatient for battle?" the Druid asked coldly, a thin smile crossing his face. Dubhghall nodded. "I cannot stand being confined in this desolate place for much longer."

"Have patience, my friend," the Druid said, his mood suddenly light, which surprised both Dubhghall and Garweng.

"The time for waiting is almost over, and soon you will get plenty of chances to use that axe of yours."

Dubhghall looked at him strangely.

"Pardon me for saying so Master, but this is still not campaigning weather, even if it stops snowing. The countryside is buried under snow, and we will not be able to form proper battle lines. The high king's dún is heavily fortified, the walls are strong and formidable. We would have to wait for the snow to melt before we could attack such a defence..."

The Druid did not interrupt Dubhghall as he spoke, but he let him finish and gave the appearance of being completely interested in what the leader of the Picts had to say. Only when Dubhghall had finished, did the Druid begin to speak, a rare act of humility on his part.

"You are right Dubhghall, when you say that this is not campaigning weather. In the normal sense I agree with you, but what if I told you that you could take the high king's dún without fighting, what would you say then?"

He watched Dubhghall very carefully as he spoke, measuring him as he waited for an answer. There was doubt in Dubhghall's voice when he did reply.

"How could such a thing be possible, Master..?"

Garweng listened but said nothing, expecting the Druid to become angry at Dubhghall's words, but the Druid merely smiled.

"I have a way into the high king's dún, a sure way which will not fail," he said triumphantly. "There are Powers which can overcome even the strongest opposition, and with these Powers I will soon rule the whole island. I have at my command such magic which, were I to reveal even part of its Power, would terrify you and drive you mad. When we reach the high king's dún, you must follow my instructions carefully, and do what I tell you without deviation. Otherwise you too, will feel the weight of the Power on you, and you will die like the rest. Do you understand me?"

Dubhghall nodded. His doubts were gone, and he could feel the Power emanating from the Druid. Garweng felt it too, and a new kind of fear rose in the pit of his stomach. Unlike Dubhghall, he knew what Power the Druid already possessed, and it terrified him to think that he had at his command even more awesome Power than he had ever before used.

The Druid spoke again. "I want you to bring your men within arrow distance of the high king's dún, arrow distance mind you, no closer. Do not attempt to approach any closer than that, and do not send any patrols out when you have established your camp. Remain where you are, and if any of Blamad's men come out to attack you, defend yourselves, but keep your distance from the dún. Watch and be ready. One of my druids will come to you, when the time is right for you to take the dún.

"When you have reached the place where you are to wait for me, dig your men into the ground, make shelters for yourselves and your animals. This is very important. If you do not do this, then you will be destroyed. Is that clear?"

Dubhghall nodded silently. He did not know what to say. The Druid had never spoken to him in such a way before, but now he was beginning to understand what kind of a man he really was, and he was fearful.

"What is to happen?" he asked, his voice trembling. The Druid smiled thinly, pleased to see that Dubhghall appreciated his Power at last and was suitably afraid.

"You will see soon enough. You need have no fear. If you do exactly as I have ordered, you will come to no harm. Tomorrow, you will take your men to the high king's dún, and begin your preparations. In three days from now, I will join you, and do what I have to. Be sure that you have all your preparations made by then. Remember, if you disobey any of my orders, you will know the real meaning of fear, this I promise you."

He dismissed Dubhghall, then turned to Garweng. "We too must leave at dawn. You will tell Dichiu and Morc to be ready at first light."

"I will do so Master," Garweng replied quickly. The Druid waved his hand lightly, indicating that he wished Garweng to leave him alone.

When Garweng had gone, the Druid sat down once more on the pallet. A sudden weariness came over him, and he lay down and fell quickly into a deep and peaceful sleep.

CHAPTER SIX

The sounds of trumpets, calling the men to arms, woke him at dawn.

The slaves had taken advantage of the lull in the storm and had cleared the road enough for the Picts to march once more.

Now, though the snow was falling again, they were already camped at the places the Druid had indicated, and as Garweng stood watching the Druid, he could also see the outline of the dún through the falling snow.

The Druid walked up and down, pacing the ground almost like a sentry, sometimes stopping to look at the dark shape of the dún in the distance. He spent some time doing this, and the others were getting cold and impatient, but the Druid was unmindful of their presence, or the blizzard which blew over them. At last he stopped, and called Dichiu to his side.

"I have marked this spot carefully. Gather what wood you can find, and leave it here. I will return in a short time and tell you what to do then."

Dichiu went to do as the Druid had commanded, while the Druid called Garweng and Morc to follow him.

Some distance away he repeated the same procedure, and once again he selected another spot, repeating the same instructions to Morc, who went to gather the wood as commanded.

Again the Druid walked on, this time followed by Garweng alone, and when they reached the third location, the Druid repeated what he had said to the others. He left Garweng to gather wood, while he himself went to find the fourth location. When he had found what he was looking for, he began to gather wood himself. It was tiring and heavy work, and because he was unused to physical exercise, he was soon breathless and perspiring.

When he had gathered enough wood, he went to see that the others had done the same, and smiled when the saw that everything was ready. The landward side of the dún was cut off, and the lake was the only means by which Blamad or his people could escape. There was little chance of that though, since Dubhghall's Picts were patrolling the shoreline, watching for any sign of the boats being taken out. Satisfied that everything was ready, he took the pouch from under his cloak and opened it, throwing some of the powder onto the wood he had just collected.

He went to each of the other druids in turn, and after praying together to the gods of air, fire and water, they lit their fires. When they had done this, he told each of them to return to where Dubhghall and his men were waiting, that he alone would remain in the open for the final part of the spell.

He returned to his own pile of wood and lit it. The wood, though it had been lying in the snow for days, crackled and blazed instantly. The Druid watched the growing flames with satisfaction, and he looked at the grey sky through the snow, then he began to shout.

"DARK WINDS, BRINGERS OF FEAR, CARRIERS OF RAIN AND SNOW, LISTEN TO ME YOUR SERVANT WHO SPEAKS TO YOU AND CALLS TO YOU FOR HELP."

He threw more powder onto the fire, and a blue column of smoke rose from the flames and remained stationary over his head, in spite of the wind.

"LISTEN TO YOUR SERVANT, WINDS OF THE NORTH. LISTEN AS I PLEAD WITH YOU, AND CRY FOR YOUR HELP. CARRY THIS CLOUD I HAVE MADE, OVER THE DÚN, AND DISPERSE IT OVER MY ENEMIES, THAT IT MAY BRING FEAR AND DESTRUCTION TO THEM. MAKE ME STRONG AND GREAT IN THE FACE OF MY ENEMIES, AND LET THOSE WHO WOULD CHALLENGE ME SEE MY POWER AND BE AFRAID. LISTEN TO ME OH GODS OF

DEATH AND DESTRUCTION, AND DO AS I ASK, EVEN AS I CALL TO YOU..."

From the other fires, columns of smoke also rose, and they too hung in the air, regardless of the wind.

The Druid held his hands aloft and he called once more to the gods to answer his prayer.

In the dún, Blamad was watching the strange activity from the ramparts. For the past few days they had been aware that the Picts were close to the dún, but they made no attempt to approach or attack, and this made Blamad wonder and become increasingly concerned that something more sinister than an attack by the Picts was imminent.

He sent out raiding parties, but each time they were driven back. Yet still the Picts would not follow them, but it was not until he saw the lean figure of the Druid that he knew that something evil was about to fall upon himself and everyone else in the dún.

He dispatched more raiding parties, this time with orders to take or kill the Druid, who was accompanied only by the other druids, and therefore an easy target, or so Blamad thought.

The wind suddenly died, and the snowfall, and a deathly stillness filled the air. The gates of the dún were opened, and the raiding party set out. The Druid was now standing alone by the fire, the strange column of smoke hanging in the air above his head. As he watched the horsemen leave the dún, an evil sound escaped his lips, but still he did not move, instead looking back to the sky, showing by his actions his contempt for the approaching horsemen, and his indifference to the danger they seemed to pose for him.

"They will soon know my Power," he whispered quietly.

As he spoke, the wind suddenly rose once more, the snow began to fall again, but this time only between the fires and the dún. Behind the fires, where Dubhghall and his men waited, the snow did not fall, nor did the wind rise.

Peals of thunder filled the air, followed by flashes of lightning which illuminated the grey sky. The wind rose and in a matter of moments a raging blizzard had blown up. The four columns of smoke began to move, carried by the wind towards the dún. Swirling and tossing on the wind and lit by the unnatural storm, they seemed to assume grotesque and monstrous shapes, now demons, now raging animals, the thunder sounds adding voice to the twisting forms.

Through the falling snow the unnatural smoke advanced. More thunder sounds filled the air, more lightning dispelled the darkness, and through the eerie light the approaching horsemen seemed to see the very Storm God himself unleashed against them, unrestrained and un-stoppable.

As the cloud passed over them, ethereal demons seemed to envelope men and horses alike. Ghostly eyes stared, phantom hands stretched out to touch them until their horses screamed and would go no further, throwing their riders to the ground, bucking and crying their terror as they ran away through the cloud, riderless. The terrified men, still trying to fight off the ghostly demons who assailed them from every side, heard the mockery of their tormentors carried on the wind. Furious storm sounds filled the air, ghostly wails and shrieks which unnerved and unmanned the warriors, who could not move despite their torments, the unseen demons standing between them and the Druid who was within their reach.

The storm intensified. Every element, earth, fire, water was in turmoil yet the Druid stood motionless, unaffected by the wind or the terrible demons he had conjured up. Even the lightning which flashed and struck down trees and lit the landscape with its eerie light, passed over the Druid, moved around him almost as if it was in fact protecting him, even as it menaced everything and everyone else.

The horseless riders, who a few moments before had come out to kill the Druid, were now released from the spell which restrained them and they began to run back towards the dún screaming in terror, lashing out at the demons which followed them, stumbling and falling all the while waving their hands trying to ward off the evil which pursued them relentlessly.

The clouds passed over them, over the lake, over the walls of the dún, covering everything, every man and animal, every bird and insect, even the fish in the lake under whose waters a silent but equally horrifying pandemonium was taking place. Men and animals began to scream and attack each other in blind panic, the guards threw themselves from the walls of the dún to escape the demons which flew at them and covered them, while others, in their terror to escape, killed those who stood in their way.

The wind increased yet again, the snow was followed by hail which battered the houses, breaking through the thatch roofs, hurting or killing those who were unfortunate enough to be struck, adding further panic to an already grotesque and demonic nightmare.

Blamad held himself against the wall of the dún, blindly groping his way, weeping uncontrollably as he did so. He tried to blot out the terrible screams, both human and demonic, tried to keep his eyes averted so as not to see any more of the monstrous demons who seemed now to be everywhere and whose ghostly arms reached out to envelope him. Harsh mocking laughter filled his ears despite his efforts to keep out the sounds, and the unnatural light which illuminated the cloud, carried demons who assailed him. Sword in hand, he lashed out at anything or anyone who approached, and already he had killed three of his own people he had mistaken for demons of the most disgusting and grotesque form who wished to swallow or destroy him.

He screamed every time someone came close, his sword hand rose and he swung it without thought, without seeing who it was he struck, unmindful that those he killed were his friends and companions.

Suddenly he could take no more. He cowered against the wall of a house, covering his head with his hands, dropping his sword to his side in a vain attempt to ward off the legion of demons who attacked and taunted him, swaying to and fro, until one of this own men, maddened as he was, rushed at him with his sword. Blamad did not see until it was too late, and he had no time to rise or defend himself, as the great dark demon charged towards him. He knew no more, as the sword struck him and he fell down unconscious, blood pouring from his neck.

The dún and its people were beyond help. The wind died, the terrifying cloud disappeared, the snow and hail also. There was a sudden and eerie calm. The people stood dazed and uncomprehending, unable to move, unable to think or do anything. There was no recognition in their eyes for each other, and they waited for whatever fate held for them, like strangers together, driven beyond endurance into the madness the Druid had sent over them.

Out beyond the dún, the Druid had been joined by the other three druids who had approached him warily, terrified of the Power they had seen unleashed.

It was some time before he became aware of them and acknowledged their presence, then he turned to Dichiu.

"Go to Dubhghall, and tell him that the dún is now his to take." Dichiu nodded and left. The Druid turned to Garweng. "Get me some wine." He sat on the ground, utterly weary, the strain of the past few minutes showing on his face. His strength was sapped and he was thoroughly exhausted.

Garweng poured some wine from the skin into a goblet, and gave this to the Druid, who was too tired to notice whether Garweng had first tasted it. He took the wine and drank it gratefully, then held the goblet up for another fill.

He saw the fear in Garweng's eyes and Morc's, and he smiled to himself. Nobody would forget what had happened this day he thought. The word would spread quickly through the countryside that the Druid had used a strong and powerful magic and had destroyed the high king's dún and its people. After this day, no man would dare to stand against him.

He alone knew what had happened inside the dún, and it gave him immense pleasure to know that he had Blamad and everyone else in the dún at his mercy.

Dubhghall had watched the storm from the safety of his shelter as the Druid had ordered, and his own fear and terror had been great when he had seen the Power which the Druid had unleashed.

He had watched fascinated as the Druid had stood and remained rigid, even during the worst of the storm, and he had listened terrified to the screams coming from the dún, terrifying sounds which drained the blood from his face and made him shiver. He had seen the horsemen scattered, their horses making sounds he had never heard horses make before, their riders running blindly any where they could, killing each other or running over their companions who had fallen.

He had been terrified. Even in the safety of his shelter he had been terrified in spite of the Druid's word that he would be safe, while a few of his men, overcome by their own fear had run out of their shelters into the open, trying to escape from the unnatural and deathly storm. They had been quickly overtaken by the madness which hung in the air, and their screams too were frightful as they ran demented out of sight.

Dubhghall was still perspiring when Dichiu reached him with the news that the Druid had given him.

"My Master says that the dún is now yours to take."

He noted with some satisfaction, that Dubhghall was afraid. It was the first time that he had seen the mighty Dubhghall afraid, and this somehow lessened Dichiu's own fear.

"What kind of sorcery was that?" Dubhghall asked, a tremble in his voice. Dichiu shook his head.

"I do not know. I have never seen magic like it, nor do I ever wish to see it again..."

"No matter," Dubhghall said uneasily. He looked towards the dún. A feeling of helplessness and despair passed over him, and he shivered again.

"Tell the Druid that we will take the dún as he commands."

Dubhghall ordered his men to march to the dún, but there was no haste among the Picts to leave their shelters to go where only a short time before there had been such horror, and the men had to be pushed and threatened before they began to do as they had been ordered.

As they neared the dún, they could see that the gates had been opened by the people inside who had tried to flee from the terror. Almost as a body, the Pictish army stopped and watched as some of the people from the dún wandered aimlessly through the gates, heedless of the Picts their enemies, their minds and senses gone, their wills destroyed, their humanity stolen by the Druid's magic.

By the gates also, lay the bodies of those who had jumped from the walls, or who had been thrown by their companions, grotesque figures whose faces still bore the signs of terror they had felt in the last moments of their lives.

Dubhghall, sensing that his men were still reluctant to enter, rode up to the head of the column, axe in hand.

"Clear those bodies away from the gates," he shouted. His voice spurred the Picts to action, and they began to do as he commanded. They ran shouting, trying to still their own fears and drive away whatever evil spirits still lurked there.

As they entered the dún, Dubhghall was horrified by what he saw. Many of the people were already dead, but those who were still alive stood before the Picts unmindful of the danger facing them. Others still clung to the walls, crying and moaning, the terror still on them. Others lay on the ground, or crawled like snakes, afraid to lift their heads in case the demons came for them again, warriors as well as women and children, and it was this sight which maddened Dubhghall. He raised his axe and began to swing it at the people within his reach, decapitating the first two he struck. The rest of his men were suddenly filled with the same bloodlust, and they too began to hack and cut and thrash at the helpless and unheeding people who stood, or sat, or lay waiting for death.

The Picts killed everybody, sparing no one, neither man woman nor child, keeping only a few of the best looking women for later. Dubhghall's axe was soon covered with blood, and it ran down the handle onto his arms. He was so maddened by the sight and smell of blood that he did not notice or care. Yet it was a hollow victory, and the Picts felt no joy or triumph in what they had done, when the heat of anger went out of them.

When they had killed everybody, the Picts began to loot the corpses and houses of their enemies. Dubhghall went with some of his men to the high king's house to look for Blamad, who was known to him by sight. He went straight to the council hall. The hall was quiet, and little of the noise and confusion of what was going on outside, penetrated its walls.

"You have done well," a voice said at the doorway. Dubhghall looked around to see the Grey Druid standing behind him.

"Your men are rewarding themselves I see," he continued, a hint of contempt in his voice.

"We are all seeking our own rewards," Dubhghall said defensively. "Besides, the thought of plunder makes them fight harder. Men expect plunder at the end of a battle, they need an incentive to fight..."

"It was hardly a battle," the Druid said, still with mockery in his voice. His tone and attitude reminding Dubhghall that he had taken the dún not through bravery in battle, but by magic, that the Picts had merely killed what was left of the people, who had not even resisted them, but stood waiting for death. Dubhghall was also subtly reminded of the Druid's Power, and when he spoke again, there was more respect in his voice.

"What magic did you use against the dún, that causes men to do as these have done?"

The Druid smiled. "You were impressed?" Dubhghall nodded.

"So you should be. I am the most powerful magician in the island, and there is no man who can stop me, or match my Power. Because of this, there will be no end to our conquests, no shortage of reward for you, for that is what you want, is it not?"

Dubhghall did not reply. Instead, he asked another question.

"You have never used this magic before?"

"I have only recently learned its power, and there is a limit to how often it can be used. The gods guard its use jealously, and I fear to use it too often."

"You... afraid?" Dubhghall said, doubtfully. "This I do not believe."

The Druid laughed.

"Yes my friend, I am afraid. Do you think that I fear no one. Do you think that I am immortal or greater than the gods? I tell you, I fear the gods whose Power I have used, and I fear the Power and the hold they have over me. I am only a man like you, and I must fear those who are more powerful than I."

He looked round the council hall. It was strange, he thought. He had come here many times in the past, he had sat with the king and the other lawmakers, they had feasted and celebrated the changing seasons, they had made new laws, and settled disputes. But all of that was a long time ago, a time gone forever. His moment had come, the moment he had long waited for, the moment he had feared would never come. Now, as he walked around the hall he felt exhilarated and triumphant as he finally sat in the high king's chair, the fulfilment of his ambition.

"We have broken one king. But this is only the beginning. Ceolmhar will never submit. He's too stubborn. He's a born warrior, not like the one who was king here."

The Druid spoke about Ceolmhar with respect, because Ceolmhar was a fighting man, but he had no such respect for the memory of the high king who was too gentle for the Druid's taste.

To the Druid gentleness meant weakness and it was the one trait he despised in any man.

"We will winter here, and when spring comes, we will turn our attention to Ceolmhar. In the meantime, Vitrig will take care of Brian."

"I don't trust the Formorians," Dubhghall said venomously. "They will not settle for being second best, but they will want to be kings themselves."

"I know all of this," the Druid snapped. "But it suits me to allow them to think that they will overcome us once we have beaten our common enemy. When the time is right, I will see about Vitrig, and then he will know who is to be king — he or I..."

"I have no doubt that it will be you," Dubhghall said, certain now that there was nothing, no power or king capable of stopping the Druid, and he was suddenly glad that he served the Druid and was not his enemy.

Blamad's body lay where it had fallen. He had not yet been found by the looting Picts who were still looking for him. His neck was bloody and red where the sword had cut into his flesh, and a pool of blood darkened the snow where he lay.

His dead eyes stared mutely at the sky, and the snow had already, with the natural progress of nature, begun to freeze his body. For a long time, in the relative seclusion of the place where had fallen, his body remained undisturbed and undiscovered, as the Picts looted and plundered throughout the dún.

Suddenly, his body seemed to change, slowly and imperceptibly at first, beginning to fade and become transparent, until in a little while, it had disappeared completely. Only the bloodstains still visible on the snow betrayed the fact that he had lain there at all.

The Picts reached the place a little while later, but they paid little attention to the blood on the ground as they passed quickly by to tell Dubhghall that there was no trace of Blamad anywhere in the dún.

"Have they searched everywhere?" The Druid asked angrily when Dubhghall told him the news. "He was here within the dún. I know for certain he was here."

"My men have looked everywhere, and they cannot find him. There is not a corner of the dún they have not looked into, even the pig pens, but there is no trace of Blamad. They searched all the boats at the pier as well."

"He can't have just disappeared," the Druid said, little realising that was precisely what had happened. He was angry, more than angry, he was uneasy, and the thought that Blamad might have escaped his magic, unsettled him. He dismissed Dubhghall.

"Search the entire dún again, and this time make certain yourself that your men look everywhere."

Garweng and the other two druids entered the hall. "The Picts cannot find Blamad's body," the Druid said angrily. "They say they have searched everywhere, but I do not believe them. I want you to look also. Be thorough. Blamad cannot have escaped, so he must be here somewhere."

As they left, the Druid sat in the king's chair, pensively. Where was Blamad, he asked himself uneasily. He had been seen just before he had sent the cloud over the dún, and Díele had said that he was in the dún, so where was he now?

He could not help feeling uneasy. No one had left the dún except the horsemen, and they had all been destroyed, but still Blamad could not be found. Perhaps he was still alive, having somehow escaped the cloud. That was impossible, he thought, but nevertheless he had Dubhghall put a guard on the hall. And himself.

The Picts who were delegated to guard the Druid, looked at him with sullen resentment because they had lost the chance of plunder, and the sight of the Druid lost in thought in the king's chair did not lessen their anger.

CHAPTER SEVEN

Blamad lay asleep in death. There was no measure of the length of time he remained so, when he woke, to find a young, very beautiful young woman standing over him. She was the most beautiful woman he had ever seen, with long golden hair which fell down onto her shoulders, and the white mantle she wore. She smiled gently when she saw he was awake. He could not take his eyes away from her, but she did not seem to mind his gaze and she too stared at him.

He sat up to find that he was by the side of a lake, across which, in the distance, he could see the dim outline of mountains, not quite obscured by the clouds, hanging low in the sky.

There was no trace of snow on the ground, and it was also quite warm, but Blamad did not seem to notice this. He felt entirely peaceful and without care, as he stared at the young woman who now spoke to him.

"I have been waiting a long time for you, Blamad." Her voice was velvet-smooth and silky. It had an hypnotic effect on him which he found hard to resist.

She went to edge of the lake, her long cloak touching the water, then she turned to look once more at Blamad, her eyes seeming to speak to him.

"How did you know my name?" he asked. He looked away from her, at his surroundings, as the memories came flooding back. He recalled the dún, and the terrible fear he had felt. "Where am I? I do not remember coming here..."

The young woman smiled. "Are you sure you do not know?"

"I do not know you," Blamad replied. "And yet I feel that I do know you. It's very strange. There is a feeling of utter peace here, that the war is very far away. I cannot explain it..."

He looked at her again. She really was the most beautiful woman he had ever seen. Even Morna, the high king's wife, who was very beautiful, looked plain beside this young woman.

He tried to guess from her face how old she was, but in her youthful countenance there was nothing to tell him what he wanted to know. Not one of her features he could describe clearly, because it seemed to him that the closer he looked at her, the less of her he saw. He suddenly began to understand what had happened and where he was, and he was surprised that he had not understood sooner, surprised also that he was not afraid. He moved towards her.

"I see now that you understand," she said, smiling, touching his arm gently with her hand. "You are a mighty warrior Blamad, and you have earned the right to speak at the council of kings. You have taken the champion's portion many times, and your name is spoken of with respect, even by your enemies."

Her grip on his arm though gentle, was firm. "Now that you know that you have crossed over from one life, and are preparing to go into another, where you are eagerly awaited, you have no need to be afraid. Come, it is time now for us to leave."

She led him by the water's edge, the strange water which made no sound even as it lapped the sandy shore. "See what you have left behind..." she said, pointing to the water. In the reflection he saw the high king's dún, and the Picts, what they had done, and what they were doing even at that moment, yet he was curiously detached. He saw the Druid speak with Dubhghall, but he could not hear what they were saying, though he noticed that the Druid was sitting in the high king's chair. He felt no anger, merely curiosity at the sight of his enemy. He looked on as an idle spectator, no longer part of the old world, no longer wishing to be part of it. He glanced at the young woman, who was still smiling.

"You have left the cares of men behind and now you will know only happiness..." Blamad was calm and unafraid, ready to meet whatever came his way.

"Alfred told me many times about the maiden of death," he said after a while. "A beautiful maiden who takes men to the Otherworld. You are she."

"Yes, Blamad, I am she." He smiled.

"I always had my doubts, but Alfred used to tell me I should not mock the gods, that my blasphemy was the scandal of the court, but he exaggerated of course. He was always exaggerating."

"He is a good man," she said. "A man held in much esteem by the gods."

Alfred was the high king's counsellor, a wise man, old in years, but very experienced and with a clear, sharp mind much valued by the king and the queen, with whom he had gone to Ceolmhar's dún to winter.

The young woman looked at Blamad, and her eyes were suddenly sad.

"You know Blamad, the gods do not punish you for lukewarm belief. Even during those times when you felt that you did not believe, they knew that somewhere inside you, deep down and hidden, even from yourself, was true belief which could never be erased, no matter what you said or did. I tell you now that you have earned your place in the Otherworld because of your bravery, your skill in battle, and your service to the king. Look there..."

She pointed out over the lake. A small two-masted boat was approaching the shore. Blamad watched as it moved through the water with ease on a straight course towards them though there was no breeze, and no crew aboard that Blamad could see. When the boat reached the shore, it stopped and remained stationary, lying in the shallow water without listing, a fact which Blamad noticed with awe.

The young woman went aboard first, then beckoned him to follow. As soon as he stepped aboard, it began to move again, away from the shore. There was no wind, but they moved through the water quickly towards the mountains which Blamad had noticed earlier. As the boat neared them, Blamad could see a gap between the peaks, and a long gorge, through which the lake joined the ocean.

The young woman had not spoken to him since they had come aboard. She stood by one of the masts, staring straight ahead, her eyes fixed on the horizon, her body erect and rigid in spite of the swell of the lake, no longer aware of Blamad who made no attempt to speak to her.

He reached out to touch the wood of the boat, to reassure himself he was not dreaming. Everything was real, except for the deathly silence.

A mist suddenly came down over the lake, yet the boat did not slow down or alter course, but continued ahead towards the gap between the mountains. Blamad felt cold, and wrapped his cloak round his shoulders as the mist moistened his hair and beard. The boat was approaching the gorge, and the noise of the ocean beyond reached Blamad's ears, the smell of salt air filled his nostrils. Grey rocks looked out of the water, and the mist became heavier, then suddenly, the boat stopped. The woman turned and looked at him, and he saw that her eyes were sad, tears already forming and beginning to fall.

"We are to return," she said simply, and turned away from him again. The boat, by whatever force was guiding it, was turned round and began to sail back to the place where Blamad had woken and had first seen the young woman.

As they approached the shore once more, Blamad saw that someone was waiting for them, an old man, wearing a long flowing golden coloured robe. In his hand he held a long golden staff. Though he was old, he stood erect, his body strong in spite of his age, and Blamad felt the power of his eyes bore into him as they approached the shore. When they disembarked, he greeted them warmly.

"Welcome," he said, his voice clear and strong. He was taller than either Blamad or the woman.

"I am sorry to interrupt your journey." There was amusement in his voice as he spoke, and Blamad felt at ease immediately. The old man led them to the trees nearby.

"Sit down, please," he said gently, but at the same time, Blamad felt that it was a command, and he did so at once. The young woman however, remained standing a little way off, and the old man looked at her for a moment.

"You may return now," he said firmly. "There will be no passenger for you today."

She bowed to him, and without a word to Blamad, returned to the boat, went aboard and sailed away again. They watched her sail away over the lake, Blamad trying to catch a last glimpse of her. The old man, who knew Blamad's thoughts, smiled indulgently.

"We will talk now," he said. "Many strange things will happen soon, things which have been spoken of, and expected since the beginning of time, when there were few men in the world. Since the time of Nemed, even beyond, such things were spoken of and foretold, but now the signs tell us that this is the expected time, the time of death and destruction, the time of fear, when evil is turned loose in the world. Men have released forces they do not understand, and there are dark days ahead for your people, yes and for your enemies too. The gods in their wisdom have seen all of this, they have seen what is to happen. That is why they have allowed you to return to your own people, to help them in their coming trial. You have been called here, but the queen and your people need you more and that is why you are being permitted to return...

"You did not cross the sea to the Otherworld, but you will have only a short time back with your people, and you will return to us when your work is done. You must see that the queen is protected, because she carries with her the future for your people, the high king's child, a child he did not know about, a sign for the future. The Druid fears her, and even now he plots to capture her as soon as the winter snows melt, but you will see that she comes to no harm."

"When the time of war and death has passed, she will be the one to lead your people, but now she needs your protection.

"In a very short time you will be in your own world once more. You will not see me again until it is time for you to return to this place..."

The old man finished speaking, but Blamad could only nod dazedly at what had been said to him. It was almost too fantastic to believe, yet it was happening and he could not deny it.

The old man smiled briefly, then Blamad fell into a deep sleep. His body became transparent again and disappeared, reappearing on the forest floor in the snow. The old man stood over Blamad's body, watching it as the sound of a horse approaching reached his ears.

Godrane rode into view and saw the body lying in the snow, but he could not see the old man, though the horse sensed his presence. The old man moved his lips silently, and the animal was quiet at once. Godrane bent down to examine Blamad, his sword in hand, afraid somehow that it might be a trap, but when he turned the body over and saw who it was, he dropped the sword, took his cloak from round his shoulders, and covered Blamad's body. The others meanwhile arrived.

"It's Blamad!" Godrane said excitedly. "It's Blamad lying here in the forest."

Carriog jumped from his horse and bent down to look at Blamad, feeling his chest, listening to his breathing. "He's alive," he said looking at Creidne. "But he's frozen through. Gather some wood and make a fire. Quickly..."

Taking some wine from his saddle, he held it to Blamad's lips. "Drink," he said in a low voice.

Blamad opened his mouth, and a moment later opened his eyes, Carriog noticing the terrible scar on his neck as he took his arm away.

Branvig and Godrane had gathered the wood and lit a fire, and Carriog lifted Blamad, and brought him closer to it, putting him down on the ground as gently as he could.

"Welcome back friend," he said, gripping Blamad's arms. Blamad smiled weakly.

"How long have I been here?"

"We have only this moment found you," Carriog replied.

"And the other man, did you see the old man?" Blamad asked. Carriog looked at Godrane.

"There was no one else," he said, positively. "No one else at all. You cannot have been here for long, because there was no snow on you when we found you, and it's been snowing for a long time. Can you remember how you came to be here in the middle of the forest?"

He asked the question quietly, so that the others could not hear. Blamad looked at him, but Carriog's face was impassive.

"I was on a strange journey," Blamad said aloud. "A journey from which I did not expect to return, but as you see I have returned, alive, if not altogether well."

The old man who was still close by though invisible to all including Blamad, smiled benignly and disappeared once he knew that Blamad was safe and with his friends.

Blamad sat up, and the others saw the pain in this eyes, the traces of fear, something they had never seen before, and they knew that something terrible had happened to him. After a few moments, he told them everything.

"The high king is dead," he said quietly, remembering what had happened. "He was murdered after the Samhain feast. The chiefs and kings refused to unite against the Formorians, and Díele persuaded them that there was no danger. It was him they listened to, not the high king. Only Aemrig has remained loyal to the high king."

"Anyway, the king was found dead by his guards the following morning, dead in his bed, stabbed many times. They must have been waiting for him when he left the council chamber. I had spoken to him before he retired, and had guards posted outside his quarters, and outside the council hall where all the chiefs had been detained until the following morning after the king had ordered them to leave the dún.

"They were gone before we discovered him, but there is no doubt that it was Díele who ordered his death, Díele, whose men did it."

"We buried the king and his servant who was also killed, then Aemrig returned to his own dún. It wasn't long afterwards that the Druid came with his Picts, a very large force, though they made no attempt to attack the dún. Instead they dug themselves into hollows and holes, and for a couple of days they remained like that without making any attempt to attack us. When I saw the Druid however, I knew that something unpleasant was planned for us, so I sent a group of horsemen out to kill or capture him, but before they could reach him, he had conjured up a terrible magic from the fires he and his fellow druids lit close to the dún.

"From each fire a terrible blue smoke appeared and spread over the air, over the horsemen. It was terrible to watch. Men and horses went mad before our eyes, but we in the dún did not have long to wait, because the cloud soon passed over us, and we too, went insane with fear..."

He shook his head, remembering that terrible time, and in his head he could still hear the screams of terror, the haunting laughter of the demons as they overwhelmed him. The others watching, were terrified by the look of pain on Blamad's face.

"Guards threw themselves from the walls, others began to hack and kill each other in their desperation to get away from the horror which had come over us, but there was no respite, no shelter or refuge. We were all trapped by the evil cloud and it passed through us until we were all affected.

"I too went through the dún as frightened as the rest, I held myself close to the walls and struck anyone who came near me. I could see demons everywhere, horrible creatures who slithered towards me and mocked me, whose slimy hands caressed my face, whose foul breath almost choked me, but I could not escape, I could not protect myself. They were everywhere, and in the end I gave up trying, and lay down by the wall of a house and covered my head with my hands.

"I don't know how long I lay there, but I heard something scream at me, the scream getting louder, and I could not help my curiosity, so I looked up and that is when I was struck by the sword and I knew no more, until I woke by the shore where the young woman told me the rest..."

The others listened to Blamad's story with increasing fear in their hearts. They could see that he had been through some horrible experience, and there was also a large killing wound on his neck which had almost healed, but was still plainly visible. They were afraid, but their curiosity was greater than their terror.

"This woman you speak of, who is she?" Creidne asked. Before he answered, Blamad took some wine.

"I was coming to that. I woke up as I said, in a strange place, by the shore of a lake, with this young woman standing over me. She was very beautiful, so beautiful that I could not take my eyes from her. It was so calm and peaceful there, no snow, no wind, even the water lapping the shore made no sound.

"We talked for a while, and I began to understand at last where I was, and what had happened, and this seemed to please her, because she smiled and went to the water's edge and looked out into the distance. In a little while, a small boat came, empty, but steering a straight course towards us. We boarded it together. It took us across the lake towards a gorge through which we would pass into the open sea, the ship all the while moving of its own accord. The woman stood by the mast, silent, while I sat behind, my curiosity keeping me alert. We were close to the gorge when she looked at me and told me that we were returning to the place from which we had embarked. On the way back, as she had done on the way out, she remained silent, never saying a word to me, never looking at me, though I had a strange feeling that she knew exactly what I was thinking..."

"Were you afraid?" Godrane asked quietly.

"Indeed I was, Godrane, at first anyway, but when I realized that no harm would come to me, that the woman wished only to look after me and protect me, I lost my fear. When we reached the shore again, an old man was waiting for us, and he told me many strange things about what had happened, and what is to happen. Then he returned me here to the forest, but he told me that my time with you was short, that I must soon return to the shore and the boat, when I have done what I have been destined to do here."

"You crossed to the Otherworld, Blamad, you crossed over..." Carriog said, genuine awe in his voice. The others too, looked at him fearfully.

"No, my friend, I did not fully cross over. Otherwise I would not be here. My time has been extended, but only until we have overcome the Druid and his evil. After that I will return, and then I will cross over."

He spoke so quietly and with such calm, that it was difficult to believe such an incredible thing had happened to him, yet here he was, the wound clearly visible on his neck, the mere fact that he was in the forest at all proof enough that something strange and frightening had happened to him.

"Are you really telling us that you met the Maiden of Death?" Creidne asked, a look of doubt in his face, which Blamad saw at once. Creidne thought perhaps that Blamad's mind had been unhinged by what had happened to him, and this explained the strange story. Despite the evidence of the wound he was doubtful.

Blamad was angry. He was unused to having his word questioned, and he bared his neck from Creidne to see.

"Look at this. Is it not a killing wound, a wound of death? Why should I tell such a story, I who have always doubted the gods? Why should I do such a thing, and how do you explain that I am here in the forest here before you, when you left the dún while I was still there?"

The others could not meet his stare. Only Carriog looked back at him, and there was sympathy and understanding in his look.

"Tell me what happened at the dún," he said gently.

"They are dead," Blamad said. "Most of them anyway, except for a few of the women the Picts kept for amusement. They had an easy victory, the Druid made it so for them. The old man told me what had happened, and he told me that it was my duty to protect the queen now that she is pregnant."

He shivered violently, and Carriog put his own cloak over his shoulders, but Blamad's words had struck the others like a thunderbolt.

"The queen with child?" Carriog asked, scarcely able to mouth the words.

Blamad nodded. "So the old man says."

"This old man you speak of, did he tell you his name?" Creidne asked.

"He gave no name," Blamad replied. "He told me only what I have already told you. I was too surprised and confused to think of asking his name."

He saw the doubt still in Creidne's face, while the others too looked at him strangely. Only Carriog accepted his word without hesitation.

"I can see that you do not believe me," Blamad said bitterly. Creidne and the other two shifted uncomfortably, half afraid to put their thoughts into words, still afraid to offend Blamad who was their leader after the high king, also their friend, yet they could not help it, the story he told was so incredible that it took some believing. It was Creidne who spoke their thoughts.

"You have told us a story so strange that it is hard to imagine such things happening, a story made stranger by the fact that of all the people in the dún, you are the only one to escape and survive. Do you not think it strange?" he asked, the implication clear in his voice, that perhaps Blamad had been too overcome by his fear of what had happened, and so had run away. Blamad's eyes narrowed and it was clear that he was extremely angered by Creidne's words. He shifted on the ground, and with some effort, and a little help from Carriog he stood up, directly before Creidne.

"I do not think it strange," he said crisply, almost spitting the words out. "It happened, and if you do not believe me then I cannot help you, but soon you will know that I have spoken the truth. As for now I am going to Ceolmhar's dún, the rest of you may do as you wish."

Carriog spoke. "It would be better if we all remained together until we reach the safety of Ceolmhar's dún. Leave all quarrels aside until then. We will need to be strong and united on the journey ahead."

Blamad was about to protest, but Carriog looked at him strangely, the way he had once looked at Godrane, and Blamad, like Godrane before him, could not speak.

The others agreed to do as he suggested. Blamad however, was still bitterly angry. He would not allow any of the others near him, or help him onto his horse, one of the pack animals they had given him, except Carriog, who stayed by his side when they had mounted their horses, and who watched him carefully as they set out, for any sign of weakness or fatigue.

When darkness began to fall, they stopped and made camp for the night. Blamad and Carriog stayed apart from the others. No one spoke, and there was an air of gloom and foreboding in the camp, each man silent and lost in thought. Creidne was confused. He had known Blamad for a long time, and he had always liked him and trusted him, but what he had just told them was too incredible to be true. He found it so difficult to understand, yet in his heart he knew that Blamad was not a coward who would run away at the first sign of danger. Still, Blamad was the only one who had survived from the high king's dún. What was he to think? He regretted what he had said to his old friend, but at the same time he felt that he had been right to say it.

The hours before sleep came were long, awkward and silent, each of them overcome by grief and despair, and it seemed to them, that whatever had happened at the high king's dún, however Blamad had escaped or why, a bond had been broken between them, a trust destroyed, which nothing would ever put right.

Godrane had the first watch, and he sat by a tree, his cloak wrapped over his shoulders against the cold night. He threw some more wood onto the fire, and watched idly as it caught fire and crackled, sending sparks into the night air.

CHAPTER EIGHT

The night was well advanced when a strange sound began to fill the forest. It was a gentle sound, barely audible, and the more Godrane strained to hear it, the less he succeeded. He lay back against the tree, but as soon as he did, it started once more, and this time he recognised the sound of a flute being played very quietly, and very well. He sat back against the tree, listening to the music which was sweet and gentle, soothing and calming, and without realising it, began to fall asleep.

From the depths of the forest, figures began to move towards the campsite, quietly and without effort, men well used to the forest paths, and the darkness. They looked at each of the sleeping figures, their leader smiling as he did so.

He was a young man with a slight beard, like Godrane in appearance because of his blonde hair, but there was no hostility in his look or nothing sinister about his smile, as he waited for the rest of his men to join him.

They began to lift each of the sleeping men and carry them into the darkness, gently and with great care, without apparent effort, but strangely, their activities did not disturb the sleepers, who remained completely unaware of what was happening to them.

There was an air of gaiety about the column, a disregard for precaution which suggested that they feared no one, or that they knew there was no danger within the forest for them. They walked with supreme confidence, their torches showing the way. They did not stop to rest, and for hours they continued to walk without haste, until they came to the deeper part of the forest, to the place where most men feared to go, the place which was said to be haunted by evil spirits, and about which there were so many stories and legends. The marching men, however, had no fear, and they continued into the dark places without hesitation.

After many hours they came to a glen, hidden deep in the forest, almost completely overgrown and hidden, unknown to anyone except themselves.

A path, heavily covered with bushes led down to the glen. The leader of the marchers ordered his men to hold these aside while the rest of the column passed through. They had some trouble persuading the horses to go down the sloping ground, but after some gentle coaxing, they followed their captors down. When everyone had entered, the leader and the rest of his men concealed the path once more, and followed the others into the glen.

Again they marched for some time until they came to a solid rock face, before which they stopped. The leader went to the rock, touched a spot lightly with the palm of his hand, speaking a strange tongue as he did so. Nothing happened for a few moments but then the rock opened, revealing a large cavern beyond. He stood aside while the rest of his men entered the cavern, and when they had done so, he too went in, uttering some strange words once more, causing the rock face to close behind him.

They moved down the long cavern, still carrying their sleeping burdens, and leading their horses. Some ran ahead and lit the torches which were set at intervals along the walls, and in a short time, they came to a junction where three other caverns met. The young man spoke.

"You know what to do," he said to those who carried Blamad and his friends. They moved into one of the caverns while the others, who had their horses and weapons, moved into another.

Blamad and his companions were taken to a room, which was well lit, and in which five beds had been placed, ready to receive them. They were laid gently on the beds, and the men who had carried them withdrew at once, while the leader went to each bed, examining the five men carefully. When he was satisfied that all was well, he too left the room, closing the door gently behind him as he did so.

On a table in one corner there were five cups, and a large gold decanter filled with wine. There was no other furniture in the room, which was well lit by the two oil lamps hanging on the wall.

Although there was no fire, the room was not cold, and the five men slept peacefully. It was many hours later before any of them began to waken from the deep sleep they had fallen into.

Creidne woke first. Slowly, unbelieving, he rose from his bed and looked about the room.

"By the gods this is a strange place," he said aloud, waking the others.

"Where are we?" Branvig said, sitting up on his bed, rubbing his eyes, trying to shake off the strange weariness which lay over him. There was a tremor in his voice, but Creidne was reassuring when he spoke.

"I do not think we have any cause to be afraid," he said smiling.

"I agree," Carriog said, and when the others looked at him, he pointed to the decanter and the five cups on the table.

"If they wished to kill us, then they would not have put us in warm beds, nor left wine for us to drink, would they?" Branvig smiled, seeing the logic of Carriog's words.

"But how did we get here?" Godrane asked, still not satisfied that all was well.

Carriog looked at him strangely.

"You were on watch. Don't you remember anything?"

"There was a strange sound, now that you mention it," he replied, suddenly remembering the music. "A beautiful sound in the forest. Every time I tried to listen to it, it went away. I sat back against the tree, and that is all I remember..."

Carriog smiled quietly, and seemed satisfied by what Godrane had said, but it was obvious from his manner that he knew more about the strange sound than he was telling.

"This wine is excellent," Branvig said. He had filled his cup and taken a mouthful, and now he filled each of their cups in turn. The wine was as good as Branvig had said, mellow and smooth, and Creidne especially, appreciated its quality. Blamad did not speak, but emptied his cup. He was suspicious, and something nagged at him, uneased him, but he did not confide his unease to the others with whom he was still angry.

Creidne went to the door, and was surprised to find that it was not locked. He called to the others.

"We are not prisoners after all." He peered out into the corridor. There was no sign of life, though there were many lamps lit along the walls.

"I think we should explore this strange place," he continued, and the others readily agreed, their curiosity intense about the strange cave they had been brought to, and the people who had brought them.

They went out into the corridor, and as they walked, they could feel themselves going slowly deeper into the cavern, deeper underground. Because it was so well lit, they had no trouble finding their way, until they heard a sound which made them stop.

"Listen," Carriog said sharply.

It hung on the air, barely perceptible, the same elusive sound which Godrane had heard in the forest, the sound which had lulled him to sleep. It came from somewhere deep within the cavern, but they could not tell from which direction, and like Godrane they found that the more they listened to it, the less they heard.

They tried to follow the sound, led by Carriog, whose heart was thumping with excitement because he knew where they were and who they were about to see. The sound never grew louder, but neither did it fade, and they knew they were going in the right direction, guided by someone or something which knew their whereabouts.

Presently, there was a glow ahead, and when they came nearer they saw that the passage widened into a great hall, lit by many lamps, which flickered though they could feel no breeze.

A great many people were in the hall, all of them watching as Carriog led the others into view, hundreds of eyes watching with amused curiosity, the uncertain and hesitant entrance of the five men among them.

The hall itself was immense and the five stared unbelieving at the sight before them. Many of the people wore gold necklaces or chains, or other richly ornamented clothes, and on the many tables before them, they could see that all the cups and wine jugs were also made of gold. They were speechless with amazement, Carriog included who, though he knew whose cave this was, had never before seen the power and wealth now before his eyes.

They were not afraid, and this too was strange. They felt only curiosity, and had for the moment forgotten the world beyond the cave and the reason for their journey. The young man who had led them to the cave came over and welcomed them.

He was dressed in a long tunic of almost pure white, belted at the waist with a thin gold chain. His hair was shoulder length, and golden coloured, and it was banded with another, finer gold chain. Though he was unarmed and dressed in the household fashion, he exuded power and command, something they all felt at once.

"You are welcome here Blamad," he said warmly, placing his hands on his shoulders. Blamad smiled but could not say anything, and from the touch of the smiling young man before him, he could feel power and strength enter his own body.

"You know my name?" he asked at last. The young man smiled, but ignored the question. Instead he turned to Creidne and the others.

"You are welcome storyteller. There is one here who is anxious to meet you. You, Branvig son of Ceolmhar, and you Godrane, of the quick tongue, are also welcome."

Carriog had remained apart from the others, and the young man now went over to him, his welcome for the giant Nemedian being especially warm and sincere.

"Greetings once again friend." He gripped Carriog's hands, and although he was smaller than Carriog the young man seemed to dominate him.

"You have done your part well, and the king is well pleased with you, though he will tell you this himself tonight when he comes to the feast."

"Thank you for your welcome," Carriog replied. The others looked at him with amazement, but the young man did not permit any questions.

"My name is Rory. It was my companions and I who brought you here, for what reason you will learn in a little while, and the answers to many questions. For now, you must be content just to sit with us and be happy, since there is much to enjoy here. Come."

He led them to a table full of food and wine, and even though they were hungry, their looks of surprise amused Rory.

"It's all right," he said laughing. "You do not have to eat all of it."

The people who had gathered to watch their arrival, were for the most part like the young man, golden haired, and youthful-looking in contrast to their own dark looks. In the fire glow Blamad and the others could see that, whoever they were, their hosts were very rich indeed, because without exception, they were all ornamented and bejewelled with gold and precious stones.

As soon as they were seated, servants came and filled their cups, and once more, they saw that everything before them, cups, jugs, even the plates from which they would eat were made of gold. They was a feeling of wealth and plenty in the hall, a feeling that all was secure and well protected, a feeling of absolute power, which made them forget the Druid and the war.

As they began to eat, Blamad noticed one table which was set apart from all the others. It was at the top of the hall, and a solitary gold cup was the only object on it, while on the wall behind, many banners and trophies hung, reminding Blamad painfully of the high king. Nevertheless he gazed at the weapons, the swords and axes, javelins, the highly decorated shields and banners, lost in admiration and a little envious.

"I've never seen anything like it," he said to Carriog. He pointed out two spears which hung on the wall, crossing each other. They were highly ornate, the blades as well as the handles, and he spent some time just staring at them.

"They are good spears," Rory said, reading Blamad's thoughts. "Though they have not tasted blood for many years, they are the finest weapons ever made, finer even than your smiths can make."

Blamad smiled, but he knew that Rory spoke the truth. It was plain to see, even though they were dust covered, that here was the work of craftsmen.

"Why do you live in this cave?" Creidne suddenly asked. Rory turned to him, and smiled.

"You are a clever man, storyteller," he replied amiably, "and the thought is already in your head who we are, and why we live here, but it is not for me to tell you. Listen."

From the far end of the hall came the sound of a harp. The music was soothing and gentle, peaceful and hypnotic, both on the newcomers and the cave dwellers alike. It was the sweetest, most haunting music they had ever heard, which carried them into another world, a peaceful world they had thought was gone forever.

They flew over stormy seas on the backs of giant birds, watching beneath them the angry sea crashing against the rocky coastline. They saw also the dark, anger-filled skies, heard the roar of thunder race across the horizon and listened to the sounds of many voices crying and wailing. They saw battles, heard the noise of men driven to desperation, then suddenly all was still and quiet again, once more the sound of the harp soothing them, an awareness of the hall, and the wine they drank, returned with their senses. They looked at each other as if to comfort themselves, but the music had stopped. There was a sound at the other end of the hall, and Rory stood up quickly.

"The king approaches..."

Flanked by four bodyguards, each of them carrying a spear similar to the ones on the wall behind the solitary table, the king approached.

He was a young man, bearded, and he wore a long mantle, white like Rory's, belted at the waist. He looked neither right nor left, but kept his eyes fixed ahead as he went to the solitary table and sat down.

There was total silence as the king accepted a cup of wine, offered by his personal servant. Rory left Blamad and the others, approached the king's table and bowed. The king gave no sign that he was aware of Rory's presence as he ate the food which had been put before him. After a short delay however, he looked up.

"I have brought those whom you asked to see Lord," Rory said, his voice quiet and subdued, showing none of the command or power he had displayed earlier. The king nodded.

"Thank you Rory." The voice was quiet and melodious, but again, Blamad and the others were struck at once by the power and force of the king, whose presence dominated the hall.

"Bring them to me now. We will talk for a while."

Rory went back to Blamad and the others.

"The king wishes to speak with you now." It was clear that the king commanded great respect and fear, and Blamad and the others rose and followed Rory to his table.

Though they wore light sandals, their footsteps echoed throughout the hall as they went before the king.

He knew all their names, but it was to Creidne that he spoke first.

"I am proud to welcome you here," he said gently. "Your fame goes before you, and I have heard it said that there is no one wiser in the laws of his people than you are. I have also heard it said that no one can tell a story like you can, so I have long waited for this moment. I welcome you and your companions here where you will have our protection for a while."

"Thank you, Lord," Creidne replied, flattered by the king's greeting. "I accept your welcome on behalf of my companions."

The king looked at each of them but his eyes rested fondly on Blamad, whom he regarded with a special interest.

He stood up from the table and he went round and took Blamad's hands in his own. There was a murmur from the hall as he did so, this simple act which surprised his people, a rare thing for their king to do, and they recognised that a special honour had been done to Blamad.

"You are especially welcome here Blamad, you whom the gods have honoured."

He returned to his place at the table, but remained standing, and spoke to his people.

"You see before you a man justly known for his skill and bravery in battle, a man who stood at the side of his king and defended his honour, a man whose loyalty is beyond reproach.

"He has returned from a journey no other man has ever returned from, he has seen what no man living has seen..."

He paused for a few moments. All eyes were on Blamad, who was himself staring at the king, wondering how he knew so much of what had happened to him. "He has seen the Otherworld, and has returned. He has returned because the gods have marked him with a special favour to do their work for them."

He paused again, Creidne and the others were staring at Blamad, but Blamad ignored them and continued to look at the king.

"A great evil is loose over the world, an evil which has already taken many men from this life into the next, an evil which is spreading everywhere, and which will continue to grow unless it is stopped soon. There will be much bloodshed, and a great battle.

"We enter a time of change and destruction, a time we have waited for, which was foretold, the time of our release, the final time."

There was a clamour from the general body in the hall, and many voices were raised. Rory too, was deeply moved, and his face showed a mixture of relief and expectation as he heard the king's words.

The king raised his hands, and there was silence.

"The time is not yet upon us," he said softly. "We are in a time of preparation, and much has yet to take place before what has been foretold will happen. We will give these companions what help we can, we will offer them the full hospitality of our home, but the time of our greatest help, the time of our own deliverance, has not yet come."

He looked at Blamad and his companions.

"You have only to ask for our help for it to be given to you. At the moment of your greatest need, when all seems lost, when there is no hope; at that moment you will find that we have not forgotten you. You have the word of Oengus son of Boann on that." Blamad gasped.

"Oengus son of the Dagda, the god of the Danaan people, long vanished from the face of the earth. It cannot be."

The king smiled.

"As you can see, I am still here. We have vanished from the face of the earth, but not from the earth itself. We are now the dwellers of caves and dark places, lords of all beneath the earth, our share of the island, given to us when we lost the great battle, and the island to your people. The gods have been kind to us, they have not deserted us, nor have the allowed us to vanish entirely from the affairs of men. We have become almost gods ourselves. Our magic was always strong and powerful, and now we can move unseen in your world and observe what is happening."

He paused. They were confused, he could see that, and a little afraid, so he wanted to be gentle with them, to take his time, to let his words be understood before he continued.

"It was we who guided you through the forest, though others more powerful than we, guided you Blamad. It was meant that you should come here for shelter, until it was safe for you to continue your journey."

"The Druid will soon let his evil loose over the forest, and you would have all died before you had a chance to reach Ceolmhar's dún. That it why we brought you here. It is a powerful and dangerous magic he possesses, a magic he discovered from a book. This book which belongs to our people contains many secrets, many things which in the wrong hands would be dangerous if they knew how to interpret the signs, for the book is not written in a way that ordinary men would understand.

"Only a man skilled with knowledge such as the Druid could understand the signs and use the book to make magic as he has done. Like the cloud of fear he had unleashed against the high king, and which he now sends over the forest, which causes men to go insane, and makes them easy to destroy.

"It is powerful magic, but not infinite. If it is used too often or too lightly, it can destroy him who uses it. This the Druid must know, so he will have to be careful.

"Do not be despondent because of what I have said, but remember that when your need is greatest, we shall help you, not before. We are not permitted to interfere in the affairs of men, until the gods judge the moment to be right.

"You will know the time yourselves when it comes, and when it comes, we will be at your side to help you."

"Your words are dark and heavy, and there is much to fear in what you say," Creidne said. "There is little hope then for all of us."

"Not so my friend," the king replied. "I can see a little of the future, that which I am permitted to see, and I will tell you what I know so that you will understand. Although there are dark days ahead for all of us, there is still hope, much hope that the evil which threatens you will be defeated."

"I had a vision a little while ago, and in my vision, the three goddesses came to me, the goddesses who foretell the coming of war. They told me of your journey, and of Blamad's return from the land of the dead. They appeared in the guise of crows, and the news that they gave me was evil and unpleasant at first.

"The great queen spoke first, and she told me about the death of the high king, and your coming, also of the great battle which is to come, a battle which will decide forever the fate of your people, as our fate was once decided. There will be much death, and misery will be every man's lot until this evil time is destroyed. A terrible blood price will be owed for the victory which will eventually be yours.

"Macha and Babh warned about the Druid and his evil cloud, which makes men tremble and takes away their courage. They warned that men will need much courage if they are to live through what is to come, until there is peace once more..."

He finished speaking, and there was total silence as he sat back and took a mouthful of wine.

"The darkness is falling and we are helpless," Creidne said, his voice trembling, his heart heavy. Everyone in the hall looked to the king, who looked at Creidne and his companions with infinite sadness and pity.

"There will be darkness, that is true. But the light will come again, and that was the real message the goddesses brought. It was told long before the coming of your people, that such a thing would happen. It was written and told by our bards that a terrible evil would be loosed on the world one day, but that it would be overcome. You must not lose faith now. You have my promise already, that all will be well in the end."

"I have spoken of your people many times in my tales, and I have already told of their greatness, but now I see it for myself," Creidne said to the king. "Such wealth you have, the gold, the jewels, your weapons, the skills of your people in magic, all of these things I have seen, yet still cannot believe, though my eyes tell me that it is true. I am still confused, and I cannot understand, yet what has happened to me and my companions, but I do believe what you have told me. Your words, though I am still trying to understand them, give me comfort and make me ashamed that I thought a great wrong about my friend Blamad, a wrong for which I hope he will forgive me."

He looked at Blamad, an expression of utter misery on his face, which moved Blamad at once.

"There is nothing to forgive," he said generously, and they embraced. There was a murmur of approval in the hall, and the king himself was smiling broadly. "Good, good," he said, glad to see that the quarrel had been put aside and forgotten. "This is how it should always be between friends. There has been enough talk of war and other gloomy things, so let us now enjoy the wine, and our warm fires, and forget the world outside for the moment."

More servants appeared at an unspoken command, carrying trays of salmon, freshly cooked, still steaming hot, and the king waited for the servant to place it before him.

"Sit here with me," he said to Creidne and the others, again showing by his actions a high degree of favour to them. Chairs were brought, and they sat at the king's table and shared his food.

Rory remained standing behind the king, and the four bodyguards relaxed, though they still kept their spears at the ready.

"You will like this," the king said, cutting off a piece of flesh for each of them himself. They ate silently, savouring the fresh clean light taste of the fish.

"This is the best of all food," the king said as he lifted some more of the delicate flesh to his mouth. "Better even than beef or venison. Some of the old ones say that a man gains knowledge by eating the flesh of this fish, but I am not so sure that it is so."

He laughed loudly, his humour light, the cares of the future forgotten for the moment.

"I have never tasted any better," Creidne said truthfully.

"Good, good." The king sat back in his chair, replete and content, wine goblet in his hand, his face flushed, glowing red from the wine and the fires burning around the hall.

"Now we will have some music..." At once a harper began to play. They could not see him, though the sound came from somewhere within the hall, and though it was light and gentle, it seemed to cover everyone, making them drowsy, bringing down a heavy sleep on them.

For a long time they remained so, calm and peaceful, lulled and soothed by the music, until suddenly it changed, and they were once again within the hall, where there was much noise and celebration, laughing and singing. Creidne and the others, affected by the wine and the music, and gently warmed by the benevolent magic of the Danaan king, joined in.

They drank freely from the jugs of wine which were constantly being replenished. They danced and sang, laughed and told stories, danced and sang again, united with the Danaan people. They forgot the high king, had no remembrance of the dún or the forest, or the dark sinister crows which had flown over them carrying the evil over the countryside. They heard only the music. Their senses were numbed, and they were for the moment, at peace and content with life, a fleeting moment given to them by the Danaan king who watched them quietly.

There was deep sadness in his eyes as he watched the scene before him. Only Rory and the four bodyguards remained, like the king, aloof from the dancing and singing. The king smiled sadly. There was so little time left, it was almost upon them, the time of their deliverance from the caves and the dark places.

The prophecies had been clear, and already much of what had been foretold had come to pass. In spite of the promise of delivery of his people from the bondage in which they had languished for so long, he could not help feeling some regret and foreboding about what was to happen. Soon, very soon, they would go to the Otherworld, and this world would no longer see or remember the children of Dana.

The music somehow matched itself to the king's melancholy mood, and the harper now played a plaintive air, which brought tears to the eyes of the listeners. Each person present was suddenly alone with his or her own sorrows or regrets, and for a few long, seemingly endless minutes, they relived every sorrowful moment of their lives until once more the music stopped, and they were all again aware of their surroundings. The Danaans began to sit down, quietly and with slow, vague movements, trance-like and silent they returned to their places as the feast came to an end.

Creidne, Blamad, Godrane, Branvig and Carriog sat before the king once more. None of them could speak, each man still feeling himself in that far-off world the music had conjured them to, uncertain and unsure, vulnerable and afraid, but the king knew their thoughts and understood their fears.

"It has a strange quality, has it not, my friends? It lifts mens' hearts and provokes many dreams and emotions."

"It was magic," Branvig said, mesmerised by what he had heard, but the king laughed.

"Not magic, my young friend, but one of the marks of a good harper. It is said that a man is not regarded as such until he can play the three emotions, and produce what our good friend Fiachre has done for us."

"He has made us cry, he has made us sing, and most important of all, he has made us laugh. He makes us soar on the air until we are back in our youth, and we see once again what is past and gone, our friends, our own youth and innocence, our dreams unfulfilled perhaps, all the things we hold dear and remember with love. Through a dream-filled sleep he has given us these things, filled us with joy and laughter, sadness and regret, and brought us back here once more to reality. Truly it is the mark of a great harper that he can do these things."

He looked away from them for a moment, as he too remembered something from a long time ago — then he spoke again, and this time his voice was suddenly filled with fire and power, and thunderous emotion.

"You have heard the music of Lugh, of the sea god Manaanan, the music of the Dagda the greatest of our people, the Dagda my father, who ruled wisely, whose harp was the sweetest maker of music in the whole island. It is from the Dagda that the skill of Fiachre comes, it was the Dagda who showed men the three ways of playing the harp, whose skill it was which lulled the Formorians to sleep with his music when they came to destroy him; it is music without age, as the Dagda himself is without age, on whom the weight of years has never fallen, nor the cares of age or uncertainty. He rules as he has always ruled, wise, supreme and powerful, our god and protector."

Creidne and the others suddenly felt Oengus's power; they understood at last, that they sat before a powerful god, and there was fear in their hearts as they realized it, but Oengus, reading their thoughts, soothed them.

"You have nothing to fear from us," he said simply. Rory left his place behind the king, and he came over to where Creidne and the others were standing.

The Danaans seemed to read each other's thoughts, and to be able to communicate without having to speak. Even the servants, who moved always by unspoken commands always appearing at the right moment with wine or food, or whenever something was needed by the king. So it was now with Rory, as the king spoke again;

"You have had a tiring day," he said to Creidne. "It is time to retire. Tomorrow we will talk again..."

His voice though soft and quietly spoken, nevertheless carried an edge of authority which they felt unable to oppose. They rose, bowed to the king, and followed Rory from the hall, which was now strangely quiet and subdued though some of the Danaans still lingered on their couches.

The fires burned low, the lamps were dimmed, and the king sat with Carriog, who had remained at his request.

"You have been a good friend to your companions," he said. "You have served us well, although you have not understood all that was asked of you. You are special to us because you are like us. Your people were masters of this land as we once were, and like us, they lost everything. Like us, you have the Power but you know as we do, that there is a price on that Power, and that price must soon be paid. Do you understand?"

Carriog nodded quietly. "I have felt it for a long time, that my time was almost upon me."

"You have no fear of death?" the king asked. He knew Carriog well, and he remembered the Nemedians as a proud race of men.

"I don't fear death," Carriog replied calmly. "As long as it is honourable. I pray that the gods permit me to die with the blood of my enemies on my hands."

"I am certain that the gods will hear your prayers. But for the present, I would like you to lead your companions through the forest to Ceolmhar's dún. In a few days, it will be safe for you to do so. There will still be many dangers to face before you reach the mountains, but I have faith in you, and you will have the protection of the Dagda himself.

"You know, we will have a long hard winter, and the spring will bring with it only death and misery, so you must try to convince those you meet of the dangers which will face them as soon as the snows melt. Tell those who will listen, that they must go to Ceolmhar and put themselves under his leadership, including those of your own people who still live in the remote places. They must help, or be destroyed. Have no doubt about that my friend, they will be destroyed."

Carriog looked at the king. He knew that he spoke the truth, he knew that there was no other way to stop the Druid or the Formorians, but he doubted whether his own people would consent to put themselves under the leadership of a man not of their race.

"You must convince them to do so," the king said, reading Carriog's thoughts. "You must persuade them, for all our sakes."

"I will try Lord," Carriog replied quietly. "I will try..."

They remained within the safety of the cavern for some more days. During the time, the Druid sent his evil cloud over the forest, covering everything with a blanket of terror and death. Every living creature, every bird in the air, hunter and hunted, every animal which roamed beneath the dense green cover, down to the smallest insect was affected and maddened by the evil presence in the cloud.

Chaos great and small, carnage, destruction and death followed terror through the forest. Screams and screeches, bird calls, grunts and growls and roars rose high into the air in a crescendo of madness and insanity, while all the time, locked away in the safety of the Danaans cavern under the forest, Blamad and his companions remained safe and unharmed.

The Druid, maddened by Blamad's escape from the high king's dún, was afraid that he was hiding in the forest, trying to make his way to Ceolmhar's dún, which was true, though the Druid was not aware that the Danaans had revealed themselves to help Blamad and his friends. He sent the evil cloud over the forest to try to stop Blamad, even though it was dangerous to use it again so soon after destroying the high king's dún. The Danaan manuscript had been clear in its warning that the magic was not to be used too readily, but his hatred for Blamad was such that he chose to risk using it again.

Within the cavern, Blamad and the others were allowed complete freedom to move about without guides or supervision, though they had no doubt that the Danaans knew every move they made.

Nothing was hidden or locked away from them. The Danaan people trusted them, yet it amazed them how casually the Danaans left their valuables lying about as if they were mere trinkets and not the most precious treasure they had ever seen before. Gold ornaments, drinking vessels, torques, chains, bracelets, all made from the purest gold were everywhere to be seen and touched, jewel-encrusted cups, diamonds of every shape and size, enough to make each of them rich beyond imagination. Creidne thought ruefully, as he gazed at the immense wealth at his fingertips, that the high king had been a pauper compared to the Danaans.

There was a mundane side to the life of the Danaans in the caves, and in spite of their capacity for magic, their people lived and went about their business in a way that seemed very ordinary to their visitors, and in a manner so like their own way of life before they had come into the forest.

They came across a bakery, and they watched the freshly baked bread being taken from the ovens and placed on trays to cool, the fresh, rich, ungodlike smell, filling their nostrils and making them hungry.

They saw also weaving rooms, and a workshop where craftsmen were making strong leather shields, though they saw no weapon maker, something which intrigued Blamad who was very curious about this, yet it was Creidne who was most interested and fascinated by everything he saw within the cavern. He noted everything, listened to everything, his eyes and ears alert to every sound, absorbing as much as he could of the life of the cave, noting every detail, storing everything for the day when he would tell the new high king and his chiefs of his time with the Danaans, and the wealth and riches he had seen. There would never be another storyteller like him after that he knew, his fame would soar, and he would be the greatest storyteller who ever lived, and the Danaan king had told him that they would see many more wonders before too long. His mind was racing, soaking up every scrap of information, restless and savage in its curiosity, and greed for knowledge.

They came to a door, and when Blamad tried it, he found it was locked, the only locked door they had encountered. He tried to open it without success.

"There must be something really valuable in there," he said to the others. "Why else would they lock the door when they leave so much gold lying about?"

"It's very strange," Creidne said.

"Not so strange," a voice said from behind them. Rory had come up to them without being heard.

He took a key from his tunic, and opened the door for them.

"See for yourselves, what treasure is behind this door." He stood aside as Blamad led the others in, then he too went inside and lit the lamps on the wall by the door.

There was a musty smell of age and decay in the room, and they had to hold their nostrils for a few moments until they became used to it. As the lamps were lit, what they saw was not what they expected. Along the walls, neatly arranged in racks were weapons of all shapes and sizes, spears like those they had seen on the wall in the great hall, leather shields, each one bearing a crest, lying on the floor beside the spears. The crests were dust covered, but still clearly visible, though their colours were faded.

Single headed and double headed axes, such as those which Blamad favoured lay side by side, fierce efficient weapons which he spent a long time looking at and admiring. There were long swords and short, close quarter swords, daggers of all kinds, some with highly decorated and ornate handles, but most plain and practical, weapons for fighting men, not for show. Some of the older weapons were made of bronze, but most were iron, and all were still usable.

"Why do you keep these locked away?" Blamad asked. He was holding one of the axes he so admired, feeling the smoothness of the handle which seemed to fit his hand perfectly.

Rory was amused by Blamad's actions, and he saw how much he admired the weapon he was holding.

"When we came here, we put all our weapons into this room, all except those which hang behind the king's table, and those which his bodyguards carry, though they only carry them for ceremonial purposes, since no one here would even think of harming the king. We have no need for weapons any more, at least we did not need them until now..."

"I've never seen weapons as beautiful or so well made," Godrane said. He was holding a sword in his hand, the sword they had found in the forest.

"We left that for you to find. And through it, we were able to watch your progress. The king has said that each of you may take the weapon of your choice from this room."

"I will take this sword," Godrane said quickly, holding it close to his chest. His actions amused the others and they laughed.

"You may have it, and gladly," Rory said. Blamad took the double headed axe he held in his hand which he still caressed lovingly, while Carriog too took an axe. Branvig took a sword as Godrane had done, but Creidne, who was not a fighting man, took one of the daggers, purely as a souvenir. When they had made their choices, Rory blew out the lamps and led them from the room which he locked once more.

He led them along the corridor, into a part of the cavern they had not been to before. There were guards standing at intervals, and before the door to which Rory now led the others.

"The king's private quarters..." He turned the handle and opened the door and led them inside. The king was seated at a table, looking at a map when they entered.

"Ah my friends," he said cheerfully when he saw them. He rose to greet them. "It is almost time for you to resume your journey. Tomorrow it will be time for you to leave us, and return to the forest. I shall not see you again before you go, but remember what I said to you at the feast. When your need is greatest we will come and help you, when you feel that you have no other hope or choice, call us to help you and we will be there by your side. It must be when you have no other hope, since the gods will not permit us to hear you unless you are in mortal danger."

"The Druid's evil has passed over the forest, and so you are safe from danger, but after what has happened, you would be wise to go carefully and with caution, since there may be something of the Druid's evil loose in the forest. I bid you a safe and successful journey. May the gods guide you and keep you safe until we meet again, and may you never forget your friends here who will watch you and keep you in our thoughts until that time when we do meet."

He turned and went back to his map, sitting down once more, indicating that the audience was over, and there was nothing more to be said. Rory nodded to Creidne, and they followed him out into the corridor.

They said nothing. The prospect of resuming their journey pleased them, yet they felt a stirring sadness having to leave the warm and friendly caves, and the equally warm and friendly Danaans.

They feasted that evening, a hearty but subdued meal, the hall strangely quiet, with no music or sounds of celebration, their moods sombre and quiet, and it was with a mixture of foreboding and anticipation that they finally retired to their beds for their last night among the Danaans.

CHAPTER NINE

They were woken early the next morning by Rory, and after a light breakfast of bread, meat and wine, they were led to the entrance of the cave, where their horses had already been brought.

The entrance was open, and armed Danaans stood outside, watchful and alert, nervous and edgy. The snow was falling quite heavily, and Blamad and the others were surprised to see it again, having forgotten about snow and the winter during their few days in the cave.

"We have filled your saddle bags with food and wine for your journey," Rory said. He was clearly uneasy because the cave was open, all the Danaans were, so their farewells were brief.

"I wish you well on your journey," he continued, gripping Carriog's arm. "We will meet again, I am sure of it."

"I hope so," Carriog replied. The others had already taken their horses outside and mounted up, and now Carriog followed them.

"The gods be with you all," Rory said, and with that he went inside once more, and the cave was quickly closed, leaving the five men staring at the grey rock face, feeling suddenly very alone and vulnerable. It was bitterly cold and they had to wrap their cloaks around themselves to keep the worst of the wind from their faces.

"Let's be going," Carriog said taking a last look at the cave. "If we are to make any progress at all, we had better go now."

They rode through the glen in the direction Rory had told them. The trail was snow covered and difficult to pass through, but after some hours they reached the place where Rory and his men had led them into the glen.

Coming out through the hidden path, they were once more in the forest proper, moving towards the Nemedian road still some hours away.

The forest was quiet, and they saw no animal life. It was as if they were the only creatures left alive. The snow covered ferns and broken twigs were muffled as they snapped under their horses' hooves, and although it was daytime, there was a sinister darkness, a cold joyless light to the day. The strange, uneasy silence spurred the five men to reach the road as quickly as they could, which they did towards noon.

Strangely there was little snow on the road, and when they had rested themselves and their horses, they took advantage of the relatively clear trail to gallop their horses to make as much time as they could while daylight lasted.

With the coming of darkness, they left the road, and made camp among the trees. The Danaans had provided well for them, and each of them found bread, meat and wine in his saddle bag. The wine was light and delicate, the same wine which with Fiachre's harp had brought them into another world when they had feasted with the Danaan king.

They did not light a fire for fear that there might have been Picts or Formorians near, but the good food and wine took away some of the cold, and in spite of the snow, they were able to sleep soundly and peacefully.

Next morning early they resumed their journey. Towards mid morning the forest began to thin, and they came to open country for the first time, a sure sign that they were close to Ceolmhar's country.

In the high open country, the wind blows hardest, especially the winter winds, snow carriers, which blow down the mountains over the treeless plains below, swirling and tossing everything in their path. It was a grim inhospitable country where few people lived.

The five horsemen, with no shelter to shield them, took the full fury of the wind and snow which froze them even through their warm cloaks and tunics. However, they still felt that the worst part of their journey was over.

They entered a valley, lush green, with heavy growths of fern and other plants waist high and in places impenetrable. A river meandered through the greenery which was devoid of snow, either settled or falling, but although this was strange, the riders did not have time to stop or wonder about it.

They went down the loose rocky slope into the valley, which they reached after a careful descent. The floor was soft and muddy, but there was a track of sorts along which Carriog was resolved they should go. They checked their bearings, making certain that their weapons were within reach and easy to take hold of in case of ambush, and when they were satisfied, Carriog led them along the track.

For the rest of the day they travelled without incident, and at dusk they stopped and made camp. This time, they felt safe enough and secure to light a fire, and Carriog, in his expert way, went to hunt game. Godrane and Branvig gathered wood for the fire, while Blamad and Creidne saw to the horses.

The fire was soon blazing and the four men sat down to wait for Carriog's return. As they sat, Branvig looked at Blamad's face in the fire glow, his eyes distant yet bright, his mood gay, yet melancholy.

"I'm sorry for the way we treated you Blamad," he said, his voice full of remorse. "You did not deserve such treatment. I should have known that you would never have betrayed the high king. I should have known it."

Creidne and Godrane seemed about to say something, but Blamad spoke first.

"It is over now, and best forgotten," he said generously, his voice quiet and sad, his manner calm and dignified, as if he was already gone from them. "It was a strange story and perhaps took more than faith to believe it, but we should look to the future, not the past."

He smiled to show that he was not harbouring any hatred towards them, and this smile alone cheered Branvig and eased his troubled conscience.

"This is a peaceful and easy night," Godrane said, looking up at the star filled sky. There was no snow in the valley, but it was still bitterly cold, though the wind was gone, the cruel biting wind which had tormented them earlier in the day. They huddled round the fire, contented and at peace, watching the wood burn, the sparks rise in the darkness, listening to the crackle and snapping as the flames ate into it.

Carriog came back carrying a hare, newly killed, which he threw to Godrane. "Skin it for me." Godrane caught the hare and he went to do as Carriog had commanded.

The Nemedian sat by the fire, rubbing his outstretched hands together before the flames.

"There is hardly any snow here in the valley, hardly any at all. I thought it strange when I was hunting, then I remembered that we've seen no snow at all since we came into this valley."

"It is strange," Creidne agreed. "But then perhaps not so. Perhaps the Danaans have done this to help us on our journey."

Carriog was doubtful;

"Maybe so, Creidne, but they seldom venture beyond their forest," he replied. At that moment, Godrane returned with the skinned hare, and with a quick movement which he was becoming adept at, had the hare spitted and turning on the fire in less than a minute.

Soon the smell of cooking flesh filled their nostrils, and while they waited for the food, they filled their cups and drank some wine, at peace and contented.

"Fresh meat," Godrane said eagerly as he turned the spit. "I like the Danaans, but eating salmon all the time is tiring."

"You're too fond of your belly," Blamad laughed, but he was stopped from saying any more by Carriog, who put his fingers to his lips, indicating silence.

"What is it?" Blamad asked.

"Listen," Carriog replied, his fingers still close to his lips.

They listened. Faintly at first, but getting louder, they heard the sound of a wagon coming in their direction. Whoever it was, would surely see their fire in a little while, so Blamad quickly doused the flames, scattering wood and ash and the still cooking hare into the undergrowth. Then with the others he went to the road, two of them, Blamad and Carriog on one side of the track, Branvig, Godrane and Creidne on the other.

Someone swore in the darkness and they heard the sound of a whip cracking, but still the wagon lumbered on slowly until it drew level to where the five men waited in ambush. Blamad and the others leapt from their hiding places, tumbling the occupants from the wagon to the ground. There were only two of them, a man and woman — an old man at that — but both of them struggled wildly, and it took some effort to bring them under control.

"Curses on you pirates," the old man said screaming, at the same time swinging wildly at Blamad and Carriog who tried to hold him, to keep him still.

"Let me go or I'll tear you apart with my bare hands."

Blamad laughed as he tried to hold the old man.

"Take it easy, old man, or you'll hurt yourself," he said, but his words only made the old man angrier.

"Old man is it? Old man? I'd take care of you quickly enough if that black giant who's holding me wasn't here. Let me go."

Creidne and the others had taken the girl, who had given up her struggle, seeing how futile it was for her to fight three men, and together with her captors, she watched the struggle between Blamad and Carriog and the old man, her father.

"Let me go," he screamed once more. "Let me go before I lose my temper."

"Lose your temper?" Blamad laughed. "You seem to have lost it a while back. Who are you, and why are you travelling alone at night in this wild and desolate place?"

The man was suddenly quiet, as he realized that whoever it was who had ambushed himself and his daughter meant them no harm, at least for the moment.

"My name is Maron," he said defiantly. "I'm a smith, the best there is I can tell you without boasting, and this is my daughter, Aobhne. If any of you even think of laying a hand on her, I will kill you..."

Blamad and Carriog released him, while Creidne and the others released his daughter.

"You have no need to fear us," Blamad said. "We are not pirates or bandits, but travellers like you. Come with us, our camp is close. We have food, and wine, and we will have a fire again in a little while."

The old man hesitated for only a few seconds, then he nodded his acceptance of Blamad's offer. Godrane and Branvig had gone ahead and they had the fire lighting once more, the hare over the flames almost cooked and none the worse for wear after what Blamad had done to it.

"Sit close and warm yourselves," Blamad said. Maron and his daughter sat by the fire, and gratefully accepted a cup of wine from Carriog. Maron looked at him strangely, not afraid, but rather curiously as if he was trying to remember something.

"We spoiled your supper," the woman said, pointing to the half cooked hare. The others laughed.

"It's of no consequence," Godrane said lightly. Creidne however looked at the woman, and he felt a strange sensation rise within himself, an excitement, something he had not known before. She was dark, her long hair shadowing her face, blue eyes looking crystal and moist by the firelight, more than once flashing in his direction. Her voice, when she spoke, was soft and clear, and he waited impatiently for her to speak again.

"Who are you?" Maron asked sharply, noticing how Creidne and his daughter looked at each other, and angry for some reason because of it.

"I asked you the same question," Blamad said smiling. For some reason he liked the man though he was sharp and cranky.

"Aye, you did, and I gave you an answer."

"My name is Blamad, and my friend's name is Carriog."

Maron looked at Carriog once more.

"A Nemedian?" he asked quietly. Carriog nodded, as the man smiled.

"I've always liked your people," he said warmly, the first trace of humour coming into his voice. "Too few of them left for my liking. Good traders they were, the best. Generous too with their wine, and their women, I can tell you."

"Father," Aobhne said angrily, but Maron smiled.

"Well it's true," he said defensively.

"Thank you for your kind words," Carriog said quickly. He too was smiling in the darkness. Maron, despite his seeming abrasive manner, was not a hard man to like. Blamad introduced him to the others;

"That is Creidne the bard, who sits beside your daughter, and the others are Godrane and Branvig, the son of Ceolmhar."

Maron nodded to each, but he was thinking hard, and in a moment it came to him.

"These are names I know," he said quickly. "So, what I have been hearing these past few days along the way is true."

"What have you heard?" Blamad asked. Maron took a mouthful from his cup, then held it out for Creidne to fill again. He was still watching Creidne carefully and with suspicion.

"I am a smith as I have already told you. Travelling these roads since before any of you were born. I go in safety, always have, because no one wishes to harm a man who might be of some use later, besides I have nothing of value, nothing worth killing for."

Creidne looked at Aobhne when he said this, which Maron noticed, but he let it pass.

"Anyway, in all the dúns, in the inns and villages along the way, there is talk that the high king is dead, that the Druid is Master now. Strange sights and happenings are spoken about, and I myself have seen the sky blackened with great flocks of birds who seem to spread a sinister quiet over the countryside. We've come across burnt or deserted villages, animals and men gone mad with fear, and everywhere we go doors are closed against us. You are the first people we have seen for two days."

"Have you seen any Picts or Formorians?" Blamad asked. Maron took another mouthful of wine, then shook his head.

"There were some Picts in a place we stopped at two days ago, the last time we saw anyone, a small, run down inn. They caused no trouble, and they were left in peace."

"Picts this far north," Carriog said uneasily. "That is not good for us."

"Why are you on the road?" Maron asked, shrewdly, already half guessing the reason.

"It is true that the high king is dead," Blamad replied. "His people too, and that is why we are trying to reach Ceolmhar to tell him what has happened and to tell him also that the Druid and his Picts are on the march. We also need to tell him about the terrible magic the Druid possesses which causes men to fear and go mad."

"By the gods, I heard rumours, but I did not believe them," Maron replied, genuinely shocked and frightened by what Blamad had told him.

"Those Picts I saw..."

"They are hunting for us, trying to stop us from reaching Ceolmhar's dún," Carriog said, the first time he had spoken.

"They are grouping, preparing for the time when they can attack Ceolmhar's dún. Only the winter stops them now, the winter and the snow, which for once are our friends." Carriog was unable to conceal his own sense of gloom, a feeling which the man was quick to catch.

"It is very strange, but for some time, I have had a premonition that something evil was about to happen. I don't know why, but I have been uneasy. I'm afraid, not for myself, because I am an old man and I have led a long and full life.

I'm afraid for Aobhne though, and what will happen to her. Will the Druid overcome Ceolmhar..?" Carriog shook his head.

"I do not know old man, but Ceolmhar is a strong and powerful chief, and there are others besides the Druid who know the secrets of magic. To go to Ceolmhar and to winter there with the queen will give us time to prepare and to find a solution, and besides, if only to be safe for the winter, it is the place to go to."

Maron looked at his daughter, and it was clear that their thoughts were one.

"You have skills which will be greatly valued by Ceolmhar," Blamad said. "Skills which will not protect you from the Formorians, who care only for death and destruction. They will not respect you, and your daughter also will be in great danger. Travel with us to Ceolmhar's dún and be safe. There will be little work for you if you go south, only uncertainty, but Ceolmhar will have enough work for fifty smiths this winter."

Maron sighed, but the decision was not a hard one to make. "To tell you the truth, I'm fed up with this life," he said. "My bones are stiff and I'm not as young as I used to be, besides, how will Aobhne ever marry if she has to follow me the length and breath of this island? We will go to Ceolmhar's dún with you."

"Good," Blamad said smiling. "You have made the right decision, and one you will not regret, I promise you."

They had taken Maron's wagon from the road and concealed it among the undergrowth with the horses, and now, they prepared to enjoy the hare which was at last cooked, and which Godrane took from the spit. Blamad divided the meat into seven portions, taking first choice as the high king's champion, while the others took their share from the rest, Creidne taking two pieces, one for himself and one for Aobhne, much to Maron's disgust.

They ate in silence, and drank more wine from the skin which Carriog carried on his saddle, each of them content and happy now that they were able to rest and enjoy the food which Carriog had caught for them.

After some time, Godrane took his harp from its cover, and began to strum the strings idly, not really playing a melody, for a moment reluctant to do so.

"I'm not sure that I should play this again, after the music we heard in the Da..." but Blamad looked at him so sharply, and with such anger that he stopped speaking. Maron, however, caught the look and wondered what the young man had been about to say which angered Blamad so much. He promised himself that he would try to find out later.

"Play something for us," Blamad said commandingly.

Godrane began to play. His music was sweet and happy, gay, carefree, light and pleasant to the ear. They sat back to listen, relaxed and content.

To Blamad and the others, having heard the sweet magical music of the Danaans, Godrane's music, although beautiful, was without the power and tranquillity which the Danaan music possessed. Blamad understood Godrane's reluctance to play and he was sorry he had spoken to him so sharply. His only fear was that Maron would find out where they had been.

They were content however, and in this their first night in the outside world again, they reflected on what had happened to them since they had set out from the dún. Creidne and Aobhne, their mutual and instant attraction now openly acknowledged, sat apart from the others, and conversed quietly, unaware any longer of their companions, who watched them with amused detachment. Even Maron was no longer angered by Creidne's interest in his daughter. Even if he wasn't a warrior he thought, he was still the high king's bard and a man of rank, and as such he was a suitable match for his daughter. She was the daughter of a smith, and a smith was held in high regard by men of all ranks, because he alone had the skill to forge the weapons the warriors needed, he it was whose skill meant the difference between life and death on the battlefield. In that sense she had rank enough for Creidne.

He had lived a long and full life, had enjoyed many years of travelling, and with the help of the gods, still had many years left. He still had his strength and that, he thought happily, was all that a man could ask for.

Maron smiled as he remembered his own carefree youth, and he lay back against the tree, supremely content and happy now that they had found safety, with the promise of shelter and position when they reached Ceolmhar's dún.

He listened to Godrane's playing. For a warrior, the young man played well enough. He had a gentle touch, his fingers moving lightly over the strings capturing the melody and strumming it for them to hear. Yes, he thought, he was content and he thanked the gods who had brought him this way to fall into the hands of his new companions.

"Your father does not like me," Creidne said quietly. "I have seen the way he looks every time I try to talk to you."

Aobhne smiled, and even in the dark, away from the light of the fire, he could see her white teeth flash. She put her hand on his and indicated the others, who were listening to Godrane's playing.

"He's not looking at you now," she said, smiling because in many ways he was so childlike and innocent. She guessed rightly that he had little experience with women, because he was still ill at ease with her, though she was perfectly aware of his feelings towards her, and she had made hers for him plain to see.

"If he was angry, he would not permit us to sit away from the fire alone," she said.

"Do you think so?" Creidne asked quickly. She laughed again, "You're such a child, storyteller. You speak of life in your stories, yet you know so little about it yourself. My father is a strong-willed man, old now it is true, but he still has the strength to protect me, and I tell you that if he did not wish us to be together, then we would not be so."

"I have had little time to be among common men," he replied. "It's true that I have spent most of my time in the king's household, but I know life, I know about death and fear, about desire and grief, but I have never thought about it seriously. I never asked myself if I was happy or whether there was more I wanted. I thought I had everything, I thought I was content and without want until I saw you, then I knew that I had nothing..."

She did not smile this time, but she was happier than she had ever been. He had told her how he felt, and in such a way that there was no doubt that he was sincere.

"I do not ever want to be parted from you Creidne," she answered.

"We shall not part Aobhne, this I promise you. We shall never part."

CHAPTER TEN

Next morning when they woke, the ground was covered by a dense mist. It was cold and damp, the dew crystallising on the leaves of the trees and the fern surrounding them. It was a calm morning however, peaceful and still, a good hunting morning Blamad thought, but today they had other things on their minds.

After a quick breakfast, they started out again. This time Carriog and Godrane went ahead together while Blamad and Branvig followed the wagon to which Creidne had boarded and tied his horse, much to Maron's annoyance, thinking him a lovesick fool who should have known better.

The heavy wagon left furrows in the muddy track as it passed, but there was nothing they could do about it. By mid morning it began to rain. A slow steady drizzle continued to fall for the rest of the day. The heavy wagon slowed them down considerably, and on more than one occasion, they had to pull it free when it became entangled in the muddy ground.

In the afternoon, they passed through a deserted village, where Carriog and Godrane had stopped and were waiting for them.

"We've searched everywhere," Carriog said to Blamad. "Every house is deserted. They've taken everything with them."

Blamad dismounted, and together with Carriog, entered one of the cabins to have a look for himself.

"They were frightened away," he said looking at the bare cabin where nothing remained except the fire space. Every single other item of value had been taken by its owners. "There is no other explanation for this sudden departure. I think it would be better if we did not delay here too long."

"I agree," Carriog said. He had a strange uneasy feeling, that there was trouble ahead, or close by.

"Let us get out of here." Blamad followed him out and they mounted their horses.

"Did you find anything?" Creidne asked, but Blamad shook his head. "Nothing at all, Creidne. And that is what worries me."

Carriog and Godrane went ahead once more, while Blamad and the others followed more slowly, their progress delayed by the heavy cart.

They had only gone a short distance when a great flock of crows passed overhead, almost blackening the sky with their numbers. Carriog and Godrane came back to rejoin the others.

"I felt that there was evil close," he said, dismounting. "I knew it when we were in that village."

The endless flight of birds noisily passing over them, the sinister sight and sound they made unnerved them as they looked at each other anxiously for comfort. A deathly stillness hung over the valley, nothing stirred or moved, nothing made any sound or called in the undergrowth. The only sounds were the birds flying over, heading towards Ceolmhar's territory, as they were.

"What does it mean?" Maron asked. He turned to Blamad, and for the first time since he had joined them, there was doubt and fear in his eyes.

"Why do I feel so afraid?"

"You are not alone in your fear, old man," Blamad said. "We have seen these birds before. They mean that the Druid and his evil are not too far behind, and that there will be trouble ahead for all of us."

Carriog spoke.

"We will go ahead, Godrane and I." Blamad looked at him, a question in his eyes.

"We have to go on, Blamad," Carriog replied, reading Blamad's thoughts. "We have no other choice but to continue our journey."

"Be careful," Blamad said, accepting that what Carriog had said was the truth. They had no other choice but to continue, since the Druid would find them anyway if they turned back. Their only hope, the only hope for their people, was if they reached Ceolmhar's dún, where at least they would find shelter for the winter, and a respite to allow them to find a way to beat the Druid and his evil.

There was a foulness in the air which they could almost touch. It was as if life itself had disappeared from the valley, life and goodness, and they felt themselves helpless and alone, friendless and without refuge as they went further along their journey.

They kept their weapons drawn, and they spoke little, their nerves taut and jagged. Even the horses felt it. They were restless and difficult to handle, but kept going in spite of their own fears and instincts which told them otherwise. Suddenly up ahead, quite clear in the still air, they heard the sound of metal against metal, as well as the sound of many voices shouting.

"Get the wagon off the road," Blamad roared. Just then Carriog and Godrane came rushing up to them.

"Picts coming this way. Into the undergrowth quickly."

"Get down old man" Blamad ordered, but Maron remained where he was. "I'm not leaving this wagon for any man," he said defiantly. Blamad grabbed his tunic and pulled him to the ground.

"We have no time to argue," he said, throwing the reins to Aobhne.

"In there, through that gap!" This time she did not argue, but with Creidne's help she drove the cart to the place which Blamad had indicated, while Godrane and Branvig pulled the gap closed to hide the entrance. Flecks of snow began to fall. Blamad lifted Maron off the ground where he had remained lying, muttering and cursing his anger against Blamad.

"I'm sorry, old man, but our lives may depend upon it." They moved into the undergrowth on the opposite side of the road from where they had left the wagon. Maron did not argue, but his silence was a sign he accepted that Blamad had acted correctly.

They pushed their way through the thorny bushes which pricked their faces, and tore at their hands and clothes. They could hardly see where they were going, but it did not matter so long as they escaped from the Picts.

Aobhne and Creidne followed, and before long had caught up with the others, though they did not stop moving until they were some distance from the road.

The snow was falling quite heavily now, and they were freezing and soaked. They had little food, just some dried meat which Carriog produced from another bag on his belt, just enough for each of them to banish the worst of their hunger.

They spent a long cold, sleepless, miserable night, and by the light of dawn, were thoroughly dejected.

The snow was ankle deep even in the depths of the forest, added to which a cold bitter wind blew.

"All our food is in the wagon, Blamad," Carriog said. "But after what we saw yesterday, I don't think there's much hope of finding any game here in this place."

"We'll find something Carriog, I have no doubt," Blamad replied, trying to sound cheerful, something he hardly felt at that moment. Although they had taken their horses with them, the forest was too densely overgrown to ride them, and they had to lead them by hand and force a way through for them.

After about two hours pushing their way through the undergrowth, and just when they were beginning to feel that they would never find a way out of it, they reached the road once more.

"At last," Blamad said. He mounted his horse, but as he did so, a scream came from the undergrowth, followed by another and another still, until they found themselves surrounded by a large force of Picts. They had no time to defend themselves, before they were pulled from their horses and restrained. Only

Maron tried to resist but he was quickly felled by a heavy blow to the head, and fell to the ground bloodied and senseless, while Blamad, Carriog, Godrane and Branvig were held prisoner. By some amazing stroke of good fortune, Creidne and Aobhne managed to slip into the undergrowth while the Picts' attention was on the fallen Maron. Because they were not warriors the Picts had not restrained them as closely as they had the others. Creidne by twisting his body, managed to free himself, push his guard to the ground, overcome the other guard who held Aobhne, and almost before the rest of the Picts were aware of it, made their escape into the undergrowth.

"After them!" the leader of the Picts shouted, and a group of his men ran into the forest.

"Thought you'd fooled me, eh?" He said, laughing, as he stood over Blamad and the others who were forced to kneel on the ground, their hands tied behind their backs. He was a giant of a man, dark-skinned as were most of his companions, with several scars on his face and arms. He carried in his hand a double- headed axe such as that which Blamad favoured. Over his shoulders was a heavy fur cloak, which was so bulky that it seemed likely to engulf him at any time.

"We found your wagon and we knew that you'd have to come out somewhere close to this place, and so we waited for you. The Druid will be very pleased to see you all. He has a special welcome for you..."

The Pict leader looked at Blamad whom he recognised.

"You disappointed the Druid by not waiting for him at the high king's dún when we called," he laughed. "But we will make amends for that when you meet him next time..."

He ran his hand across his throat, imitating a knife cut.

They were taken, tightly bound hand and foot, back down the road to the Picts' campsite which was in a clearing by the river. It was large but crudely built, though there was evidence of more permanent buildings being constructed, from which Blamad and the others surmised that the Picts intended to winter here. There was much activity with many people coming and going, flocks and herds of animals gathered together and once, the sight of a smith working to fashion weapons.

They were led to a hut, roughly built but secure, one of the few wooden structures yet built in the encampment, and set apart from the rest. They were thrown inside and the door locked behind them.

The hut was bare of any furnishing whatever, and the only light they had came from under the door which did not quite reach the ground.

Maron lay unconscious, but the others, tied as they were, could not help him or check to see whether he was in fact still alive. Blamad knelt beside the old man and looked down at him. His head had been split open and the blood still oozed from the wound but not so much as before, a good sign, because they knew by his laboured breathing that he was still alive. Blamad leaned down close to the old man's ear.

"Maron, listen to me, Maron..." There was no response.

"He's out cold, but at least he's still alive," Blamad said to the others. Carriog nodded.

"He took a heavy blow to the head. It's a wonder he still lives..."

"We're beaten now," Godrane said despondently.

"We are not beaten," Blamad said harshly, his voice seeming to thunder in the quiet and confined space of the hut.

"We are not beaten. Remember, Creidne has escaped, and that was the point of our journey to see that he got to Ceolmhar's dún safely, that is what matters, not whether we live or die. Our lives alone are not important, our survival will mean nothing if Creidne fails in his mission. Remember that. There is still hope for us, there is always hope while we have life, and besides, the Druid does not have us in his claws yet. They will not harm us, these Picts, since it is plain that the Druid himself wishes to dispose of us. They will have to bring us back to wherever he is, and who knows what opportunity may arise to escape. Have courage my friends, because all is not yet lost."

Godrane leaned back against the wall of the hut, his fear diminished by Blamad's words, his courage restored. Blamad tumbled himself back to the wall of the hut to rest, and for several hours they remained quiet, trying to conserve their energy for the time when they might need it.

The old man still lay without moving, though from time to time he moaned, and once he called his daughter's name, until at last, he began to stir.

It was dusk and there was little light in the hut, so they could not see whether he was awake or not, while Maron, who was in fact awake, was still stunned and groggy and unaware of his surroundings or the fact that his companions were within inches of him.

He sat up, and his movement was caught in the reflected light of the campfire which crept under the door of the hut.

"By the gods but my head hurts," he said sharply.

"Maron, it's me Blamad, can you hear me? I'm here behind you..."

It took Maron a few moments to realize who was speaking to him. His head hurt badly, and when he touched the wound he almost fainted with the pain, and a dizzy sensation made him sway.

"Maron, I'm here behind you. Are you all right?" Blamad called again. "Can you untie us? We cannot help you because we are bound."

The old man said nothing, but slowly he got to his knees. His head spun, and it took some effort for him to keep his balance, but he finally managed to get to his feet. He leaned against the wall of the hut for support while the others watched for him anxiously in the darkness. He moved to where Blamad was kneeling, following the sound of Blamad's voice as he guided him.

"Let me see your bonds," he said finally. He knelt down beside Blamad, who turned his back so that the old man could just about see his hands. "They're very tight, but I think I can manage it..." He went to work on the knots, and because he was still groggy and dizzy it took some time for him to loosen them enough for Blamad to undo them himself. When he had done so, he gripped the old man gently.

"Sit my friend. You have done enough. We'll tend to your wound in a moment or two."

Maron sat down, utterly spent and exhausted while Blamad untied his friends. Carriog who was skilled as a healer, went to look at Maron's wound.

The old man winced under Carriog's touch, gentle though he was.

"I'm sorry Maron, but you have a deep wound there which must be seen to."

Tearing some cloth from his tunic, he tried as best he could in the dim light, to wipe away the dirt covering the wound. The old man swore, but Blamad and the others laughed, because they were glad to see that he was well enough to protest. When Carriog had finished tending the wound, they began to talk about escape.

"We are free now and if anyone comes to the hut, we'll have the advantage of surprise."

It was Carriog who spoke.

"What about my daughter?" Maron asked, suddenly remembering that she was not with them.

"She escaped," Blamad said soothingly. "She and Creidne were not captured and they ran into the forest."

"Good, good." He tried to smile but it caused him too much pain, but he was happy nonetheless.

It was night. Outside, the camp had grown quiet as the Picts settled down. The activity of the day had given way to fireside talk and singing, the fires lighting the night, the light from them dispelling some of the darkness in the hut where the five lay waiting for an opportunity to escape.

It was a long time however, before they heard the sounds of footsteps approaching the hut, and as soon as they did, they resumed their former positions, and held their hands behind them as if there were still unable to move.

"Remember, let whoever it is, come right into the hut before we make any move," Blamad ordered. He sat back against the wall close to the door, his legs under his body, in the position they had left him earlier.

The lock on the door was removed and a moment later two Picts entered the hut. Although they had their swords drawn, they were clearly not expecting any trouble from their captives whom they believed to be still tied, and in Maron's case, unconscious.

One of them stayed by the open door close to Blamad who could see that it had been snowing heavily. Meanwhile the other Pict approached Maron.

"This one's had it I'm sure," he said, using his foot to turn Maron over. The other Pict laughed, and looked down at Blamad who was closest to him, his sword point close to Blamad's face.

"You will soon wish you were dead," he said grinning, but he got no further as Carriog's massive arm wrapped itself around his neck, twisting it, and with a snap, breaking it.

The other Pict turned round, but Blamad, Godrane and Branvig all jumped on him, and quickly stifled any cry of alarm he might have made. Maron meantime, rose from the ground and went to the body of the Pict who had used his foot on him.

"Now who has had it?" he said viciously and kicked the lifeless body at his feet. "Now who has had it?"

None of the others restrained him in his anger.

They stripped the Picts of their weapons, two swords, two daggers and one axe which the Pict by the door had dropped. Blamad claimed this, while the others divided the rest between them.

Carriog went to the door, and opened it a little more to see what was happening outside. As Blamad had observed, it had snowed heavily, and it was beginning to snow again.

The hut was, as they had earlier noticed, separated from the rest of the camp, with no special guard or precaution taken against them escaping, the Picts obviously believing that such a thing was impossible.

"It was very thoughtful of them to put us away out here."

"The Picts are too confident that we will not escape, and they've left no guard on the hut," Blamad said with contempt. "But we had better move fast in case these two are missed."

Carriog looked outside again, and when he was satisfied that it was safe for them to go out, he gave the signal for them to move. Before they left, Blamad took the cloaks from the two dead Picts, and these he put over Maron's shoulders to keep the worst of the cold from him.

They slipped out of the hut and went behind it, away from the main camp. Silently and carefully they walked away from the hut and the camp, passing as they did, some sleeping Picts, once even disturbing a dog who scented them and barked ferociously but incredibly, no alarm was raised.

The snow was falling heavily and with the exception of Maron, the others had no cloaks to protect themselves. They were freezing, but they paid scant attention to the cold or to the fact that the snow had soaked through their tunics. They were so glad to have escaped from the Picts that they would have endured any hardship, gone through any pain or suffering as long as they were free.

It was hard for them to move through the snow without their horses, but they were thankful to be alive. Carriog led the way, moving confidently as if he knew the way, though there was no moon to guide them, no familiar landscape. They walked, sometimes ran until the coming of dawn found them at the other end of the valley, far away from the Picts, tired, breathless, and soaked to the skin, but happy.

They stopped to rest in a small clearing, surrounded by the forest, and they felt safe and secure. The Picts were far behind, and unlikely to follow and this confidence eased their anxieties, as well as the falling snow which they knew would hinder any pursuit.

"The gods were with us last night," Blamad said wearily as he sat on a tree stump. It was gnarled and twisted into a grotesque shape, but he found a comfortable niche on it. The others too had found resting places for themselves.

"The Picts will not follow us here," Carriog said positively. "We were just unlucky to meet that last band."

"I'm hungry," Godrane complained suddenly, and the others laughed, even Carriog, but not Maron.

"I'm hungry too, but I don't see the humour of it," he said sharply. Blamad laughed.

"Forgive us, Maron, but it's just that Godrane is always hungry, always complaining about it. Last night he was a prisoner of the Picts, this morning he has just escaped with his life, and all he can think about is the fact that he is hungry."

"Foolish if you ask me," Maron replied sharply, his ill humour caused not by the other's levity, but by the absence and lack of news of Aobhne. He could not get the thought of her from his mind.

"There's little in the way of game in these parts," Carriog was saying, "but have patience all of you and we may find something."

They set off again, still tired, still wet and hungry, but their hearts were lighter, the tension of the night before, gone.

They began to climb to higher ground, and the loose stones and rocks hurt their feet and tore at what remained of their boots which were tattered and frayed from the snow and the hours of walking they had done.

As they climbed higher, a cold easterly wind blew across the hills, adding to the miseries of their journey, driving the snow against them, closing the passes and the valley behind, heavy unremitting snow which showed little sign of stopping.

Towards evening, they reached the top of the hill, and began to descend to the other side. They reached a sheltered hollow among some rocks, where they decided to rest for the night, by now totally exhausted, their spirits low, and in need of sleep.

"Build a fire with whatever you can find," Carriog said. "It will be safe enough here. I will see if I can catch anything on the hill."

He left them to gather wood while he went in search of game. While he was gone, the others gathered as much wood as they could find in such a place. Blamad found some boughs which he chopped down to make a rough shelter for the night. These he placed over the hollow, securing them down with heavy rocks he found close by.

Branvig and Godrane soon had a fire blazing, and when Blamad had finished making the covering for the shelter, allowing a space for the smoke to escape through, they went inside to wait for Carriog's return.

Maron was exhausted, and he could hardly keep his eyes open. He was cold too, and shivering, even the fire gave him no comfort, and when Carriog returned some time later empty handed, he sighed and allowed himself to drift off to sleep.

"Nothing?" Blamad asked, unable to believe Carriog had failed to catch anything.

"There's not a sign of life anywhere," he said grimly. "It's as if everything has been lifted from the earth and taken away, no birds, no pigs, nothing."

"What are we going to do?" Godrane asked anxiously, but for once, no one had an answer.

CHAPTER ELEVEN

Far away to the west, in a windswept encampment where the wind and the rain had not let up for two weeks, the leader of the Formorians sat impatiently by his fire, listening to the reports which his men brought him.

The Druid had taken the high king's dún, the high king himself was dead, while he, Vitrig, was held up by continuous bad weather. The list was endless, yet he was helpless.

It was still only a little past midday, but the lamps had already been lit as the grey winter day could not fully displace the night, and the darkness was intruding once more.

"The gods curse him," he shouted angrily, his voice terrifying those who stood before him.

"How did he do it, how?"

"There is talk of magic, Lord," one of the messengers said warily. Vitrig looked sharply at him. The man explained:

"In the villages it is all that men talk about. Some have been abandoned because the people have heard of the Druid's terrible magic and what it will do to them, so they have fled into the wilderness."

Vitrig was furious.

"What kind of magic can overcome the high king's dún?" A terrible thought flashed through his mind. "The Druid is using us, letting us keep Brian and the other chiefs quiet, while he runs ahead and takes the spoils for himself. He thinks to fool us while he builds up his power, but I know now what he is up to, and I will stop him before it is too late."

He saw the danger clearly. The Druid was already too powerful, and if by this magic he was said to be using was able to conquer the high king, then he was a danger which had to be stopped, and quickly. Unchecked, he would turn on the

Formorians when they had served their purpose for him. He dismissed the messenger.

"Well?" he asked the men who remained. "The Druid has taken a step ahead of us and, by all accounts, it is a powerful step indeed. What do you suggest Gomrik?"

Gomrik was Vitrig's second in command, a man noted for his cruelty, even among his own people. Younger than Vitrig by many years, they shared the same strong physical appearance, but whereas Gomrik's hair was still dark and full of growth, Vitrig's was thin and grey.

Gomrik was a vain, ambitious young man, whose dark eyes and willing manner hid a cunning and jealous mind, and he would gladly have killed Vitrig and assumed the leadership himself if he had been sure of support among the Formorians.

"I think perhaps, that Cruachain will know something of this magic," he replied.

Vitrig nodded. "Send for Cruachain."

"The Druid is a dangerous man, Lord," Gomrik said quietly. "We should kill him the first chance we get."

"All ambitious men are dangerous," Vitrig replied causally, though the look he gave Gomrik suggested that he was not as ignorant of Gomrik's true feelings as Gomrik perhaps thought he was.

Cruachain entered the tent. He was Vitrig's Druid, skilled in the magic arts himself though no match for the power and might of the Grey Druid. His knowledge however, was immense, and it was for this reason that Vitrig kept him in attendance, though he had little time for men of knowledge, believing as he did that the only real men were warriors.

Cruachain was a medium-sized man, bent slightly from a fall he had suffered as a boy. In his middle years now, his lined face and tired eyes betrayed a life of unhappiness and frustration, which service in Vitrig's household had done nothing to diminish.

He stood before Vitrig, head slightly bent, an attitude of submission which Vitrig found irksome.

"The Grey Druid had used a magic which has given him the high king's dún without having to fight," he said watching the druid's face as he spoke.

"It is said that this magic causes men to fear and to lose their reason. What do you know of such a magic?"

Cruachain, as was his habit, did not reply at once, being a man who considered every aspect of a problem before answering, but his silence angered Vitrig who was in no mood for Cruachain's caution at that moment.

"Well?" he roared. "Have you no answer for me?"

"Noble Lord, there was such a magic. It was known to the Danaans who were, as you know, the greatest magicians ever to have lived. This magic was said to ride on a cloud which was released by fire. Everything this cloud passed over, every bird and animal, every insect in the ground, every man who came under its influence went mad with fear because it conjured up within each creature its own fear, that which it was most afraid of, and tormented them until they went insane." His words had a profound effect on the Formorians as he paused for a moment.

"Go on," Vitrig commanded. "Tell me more."

"The knowledge of this magic was thought to be lost when the Danaans disappeared but there were stories from time to time, that some men at least, the Nemedians, had come across this secret and it is perhaps this which the Druid now possesses. If that is so my Lord, then the Druid is a dangerous adversary."

"So, I was right," Vitrig said harshly, a dark angry look on his face. "He will use this magic against us when the moment suits him, when we have done his bidding long enough. Is there any magic to counter this?"

"There is a limit to its use, or so the legends say," Cruachain replied. He had never seen Vitrig so angry before, or so afraid.

"The Druid cannot use this magic too often, or the gods will be angry. It is said they will turn its power on the one who does not heed the warnings. There are still some Nemedians who may know of a magic to stop the Druid, but I do not know where to find them..."

"I do not have the time to go chasing Nemedians," Vitrig said impatiently, "but you have given me some hope. Now tell me what the signs say, I'm impatient to be away from this place, and I do not want the Druid to have it all his own way."

Cruachain took a pouch from inside his tunic, and scattered the contents on the ground. He looked down at the bones carefully where they had fallen, and smiled.

"The signs speak of a victory for you Lord. A great victory. There is a battle, but you have scattered your enemies. A woman stands by your side, a woman of great beauty who will bring much trouble for you, a woman with whom you should be careful. The spectre of death follows her and surrounds her. The signs also say that you must act now, if the victory I have seen is to be yours."

"By Tethra, did you hear that?" Vitrig was well pleased. He was smiling. Gomrik smiled too, though his dark eyes watched Vitrig shrewdly, and he remembered the Druid's words about the woman, and his talk of death.

"You have done well. You may go now. Later I will speak with you again. I shall need some of your magic."

When he had gone, Vitrig poured two cups of wine, one for himself and one for Gomrik.

"Let us drink to the future. You have served me well Gomrik, and I shall reward you well for it, after all, we do not want to leave everything for the Druid do we?"

He laughed harshly, cold humourless, vindictive, but this time Gomrik did not even make a pretence of smiling.

"I seek only to serve you," he said, but in his heart dark malignant thoughts lurked.

"In a day or so, when we have made our preparations, we will march against Brian and destroy him. I will leave the preparations to you..."

A few days later, the Formorians left their camp in the care of a small garrison, while the main body of their army marched inland towards Brian's dún. Since they had first landed, they had been constantly attacked by Brian's men, but each attack had been beaten back. Yet Vitrig was well aware that Brian's army was formidable, and he warned his men that such an army would be more difficult to overcome than a few scattered bands of raiders, which was all they had so far encountered.

The Formorians movements were noted by Brian's scouts who kept Vitrig's camp under constant observation, and word was sent back to Brian that the Formorians were at last on the march.

The Formorians moved slowly over the rain soaked plain, the heavy wagons which followed the main force having more than once to be pulled from the mud.

Gomrik had gone with a second force to flank Brian's dún, and prevent any reinforcements from reaching him.

Vitrig knew that there was little hope of Brian leaving the safety of the dún to come out and fight on the open plain, he would not have done so had he been Brian, but he sent Gomrik on his way just in case.

It was at dusk the following day, when they came within sight of Brian's dún. It was protected by thick, fortified walls and steep mud embankments. Vitrig rode ahead with some of his captains to survey the defences.

The walls were made from strong oak beams deeply embedded in the ground, rising to a height of twenty feet, heavily guarded by archers, who waited for Vitrig and his men to come close enough to be within reach of their arrows, but Vitrig kept himself and his men well out of range of the men who watched him.

Beneath the walls and running the entire length was a ditch, six feet wide, and equally deep, and only at the gate was there any direct access to the dún. A bridge crossed the ditch leading to a double set of gates, which opened into the heart of the dún itself.

He looked at the defences with a great deal of interest, and as he tried to decide on his method of attack, one of the archers from the dún loosed an arrow which landed before him, missing him by several feet. Rather than being angered by this, he laughed at the impudence of the man whoever he was, but he had seen enough and since it was already getting dark, he returned to his own camp.

The Formorians had already begun to set up their tents and build their battle shelters. The rain continued to pour down. It was miserable and cold, but from what his messengers had told him the Druid too was suffering the discomfort of bad weather — snow and ice, and storms, and this cheered Vitrig who bore the Druid no love at all, and who was uneasy because of what the Druid had already accomplished. The lamps were lit, and in a small brazier, a fire took the worst chill from Vitrig's tent. The wind howled and lashed the rain against the covers, the lamps flickered and sometimes almost went out, the cries of men and animals as the Formorians tried to organise their camp under the growing storm carried on the wind. Vitrig sat on his pallet spent and exhausted, his mind tossing over the problem of taking Brian's dún. He ignored the noise outside, the storm, the cries of his men as the plan he had already half formulated in his mind finally took shape.

Gomrik entered the tent some time later.

"Everything is settled," he said. He took off his helmet, and shook the rain from his cloak.

"The men are sheltered and the animals fed. I've posted a heavy guard on the perimeter, just in case Brian is foolish enough to attack us."

Vitrig smiled, and indicated a cushion.

"Sit down," he said amiably. "Take some wine."

Gomrik helped himself to the wine which was on a small table beside the pallet, and some fruit which lay beside the jug.

"The walls are strong, too strong for a frontal assault," he said when he had eaten. "They're well protected too. I almost took an arrow when I went to see them." Vitrig laughed, remembering the impudent archer who had fired at him.

"I was thinking about the walls, and that is why I brought those wagons with me," Vitrig said.

"Brian thinks that we will attack the walls, wear ourselves out, then he will sortie against us and finish us off. We will not attack the walls however, at least not directly."

"What are you going to do?" To Gomrik's way of thinking, there was no other way to attack Brian other than by assaulting the walls, though that was clearly impossible. Vitrig smiled.

"The wagons are our weapons, the wagons and the barrels of tallow I brought along as a precaution."

"Tallow?" Gomrik asked. Vitrig smiled.

"Yes Gomrik, Tallow. The wagons will be brought up to the walls, and against the gates, and our archers will fire the barrels. The flames will be such that even those walls will catch fire, and to prevent Brian or his men from fighting the blaze, our archers will be lined up to keep them pinned down. We will lose few men, and it will force Brian to come out and fight us, where we have the advantage. Between us we will crush him, and then Cruachain's prophecy will have been fulfilled."

"What about the ditch surrounding the walls?" Gomrik asked.

"I've thought of that too. I've had slaves felling trees since we came to this place. They will be used as bridges to allow the wagons to be brought up against the walls. It does not matter if the slaves are killed, they are expendable anyway, but they will make it possible for our archers to light the walls."

It was a simple plan if it worked, but as Gomrik said, getting the barrels of tallow there walls would be a formidable task, because Brian's archers would pick off any man who came too close, and they would be alert and watching for just such a move.

"When do you propose to attack?" said Gomrik. Outside the weather was foul and the wind had risen, driving the rain against the shelters. Vitrig listened to the storm for a moment, his eyes blazing with fire and hatred, exuding a kind of triumph and determination.

"Tonight. We attack tonight."

"Tonight? But listen to that storm. You cannot attack in such weather. Our men would be destroyed. The walls will not light, there is too much rain..."

"On the contrary Gomrik, this is the perfect night for such an attack. Brian's men will not expect it, and because there is no moon, we will have the cover of darkness to get the barrels close to the walls unobserved. The Druid is not the only one to have the power of magic. Cruachain has made a magic which will light any fire even in such weather. You will see it soon. Have faith, and Brian's dún will be ours."

It went as Vitrig had predicted. Under the cover of the storm and the dark rain-filled clouds, the Formorian slaves were forced to carry the trees they had felled towards the ditch which surrounded the dún, while others led the wagons forward.

The slaves were forced into the ditch to carry some of the barrels close to the walls while others crossed by the makeshift bridges they had thrown across the ditches. The tree trunks were slippery from the constant rain, and some of the unfortunate slaves, weighed down by the heavy barrels, stumbled and fell into the muddy water below. They could not scramble up the other side because the embankment was too slippery from the constant rain, and the more they tried to raise themselves out of the water, the further back into it they slipped. Men screamed and drowned, alerting Brian's men on the walls, who began to rain a hail of arrows down on the unfortunate slaves, many more of whom fell, but others succeeded in crossing safely and leaving their barrels by the walls. However they were forced by their Formorian captors to get into the ditch and lift the barrels which had fallen there by means of ropes which were passed down to them. Other slaves hauled these up and by this method, despite the loss of many men, all the barrels were at last put against the walls.

The Formorian archers began to keep Brian's men pinned down, and two wagons were dragged to the bridge and left by the gates. This time, the Formorians suffered no casualties.

Vitrig watched while this was going on, Gomrik by his side.

"You see, I told you it would work," he said triumphantly. "Now, if the tallow does its work, with Crauchain's magic we shall have Brian within our power before too long."

The archers were lined up still firing over the walls attempting to keep Brian's archers from harming the Formorians, but now Vitrig gave them the order to fire the barrels. A hail of fiery missiles lit the night sky as the archers loosed their first volley against the dún. The defenders within laughed mockingly, believing that the Formorians were conducting futile tactics but their laughter died away when the first of the barrels caught fire, and the flames shot skyward, then another and another still, until all of the barrels had been ignited, the flames spreading to the walls in those places closest to the pitch. The gates too were quickly aflame, the fire leaping high into the sky, uncontrollable and unchecked by Brian's men who could not now raise their heads above the leave of the walls without inviting another stream of Formorian arrows down on their heads. They could not believe what was happening.

Within the dún there was great panic and confusion as the flames took hold, and some of the fiery missiles passed over the walls into the dún itself catching the straw roofs of the houses, adding further to the panic and fear.

Brian knew that the Formorians had brought a great army, but he knew too, that he had a strong fighting force within the walls of the dún which should have been to his advantage, but the Formorian leader had done something unexpected, had used some kind of magic and now the advantage was with him, while they could do nothing except watch helplessly as their dún was burned about their ears.

He called a council of war to decide what to do, and went to the Great Hall to preside over it.

He was a light haired man, tall and muscular with bright clear eyes. He was a steady, unspectacular commander, a warrior in the second rank compared to men like Blamad or Carriog, but there was no denying his bravery or zeal, even if he lacked the breadth of vision which was needed at that moment.

It was a sombre meeting as the warriors gathered before him, the scent of defeat already in the air, unmistakable and felt by all.

"The Formorians have set fire to the walls and there is nothing we can do to stop them," he said gloomily. "They are using magic against us, a magic which allows even soaking wood and straw to ignite. Our men cannot even look above the walls to see what is happening without being killed. We will have to face them soon, and we must be ready for that moment. The walls will not hold them back, but we are men, warriors trained to fight, and whenever we have to fight the Formorians, we will show them that we have not lost our courage because of what has happened here this night."

He stopped speaking for a moment as a scream from close by filled the hall, followed by another.

"Courage my friends," he said. "We will try to fight our way out and past the Formorians. We'll move inland and try to join up with the high king who will help us as soon as he knows the danger we face."

A warrior ran into the hall, breathless and black with smoke. His eyes were wide with fear, his voice filled with unbelief, as though he had seen the Dark Ones himself.

"The walls are ablaze, Lord," he said quickly. "Many houses too. We cannot stop the fires because their arrows keep coming over the walls killing anyone who is not under shelter."

As if to reinforce what the man said, the smell of smoke filled the council hall, and the screams from outside became more frequent.

"Gather everyone together," Brian ordered quickly, a tremor in his voice, a fear he tried to hide, though the other men present caught his mood.

"We'll see what can be done about these fires."

He led his men outside, but they had to move close to the buildings, some of which were completely ablaze, to try to reach the ramparts. There was smoke everywhere, flames, people running trying to escape from one fire, only to run into another. On the ground men and women who had been caught by the Formorian arrows lay dead, their bodies burning, some already blackened and charred by the flames and the heat.

Brian and his commanders reached the ramparts, and they climbed up to try to see what was happening beyond. As he climbed he could feel even through the thickness of the wood the heat from the flames beyond, but he was unable to look over the top, because when he tried to do so, a hail of arrows was loosed at him. One of the men standing beside him was struck by a flaming arrow which went through his eye, and he fell screaming down to the ground below.

Brian and the others went back down, and stood under the shelter of the steps. The man who had fallen was dead, his body struck by two more arrows.

"We have to stop the fires somehow," Brian said desperately. "If we do not then we are lost, because there is already too much panic and fear among our people. Get anyone who can walk to carry water to the walls, and put out those fires within the dún. Hurry, there's little time left..."

As his men went to do as he commanded, Brian went to find Deirbhne his wife. Like all the women in the dún she was indoors, huddled together with the women of her household, who looked to her for comfort and guidance. They rose and left as soon as Brian entered the room.

As he looked at her his heart was filled with joy and fear. She was so beautiful he thought, her long fair hair and clear blue eyes, a smile which could melt the hardest heart. He thought her the most beautiful woman he had ever seen.

She was as tall as he was, graceful and slim, and he was filled with a sudden surge of pity and dread, as he thought of what the Formorians might do to her if they captured her.

She for her part saw by the grim look on his face and the clearly defined fear in his eyes, what way things were going outside.

"Is it that bad?" she asked tremulously, her voice soft and smooth. He nodded, coming closer and holding her for a moment.

"They are using magic. They have set fire to the walls and we cannot stop them, though we are going to try once more. There are too many archers firing against the walls, and stopping our men from firing back, so I fear the worst, that is why I have come to you. Soon you may have to leave here, get away to some safe place until we drive these savages back to the sea. I don't want you to fall into their hands."

She looked at him, her eyes blazing. "I will not leave," she said angrily. "I will fight with you and our men, but I will never leave while you are still here. Never."

Brian could help smiling. It was some comfort to him to know that she was not afraid, and he drew strength from this, but nevertheless he knew that if it came to the worst she would have to go, despite her protests.

"We will try to stop them as long as we can, but the flames and the confusion are causing panic. I only hope that the high king got my message."

"He will know what is happening," she said quietly. She squeezed his hand, and for a few previous moments, they were at peace together, silently comforting and encouraging each other.

CHAPTER TWELVE

As dawn approached, the Formorians continued to fire arrows against the walls of the dún. They came from all sides, from Gomrik's men as well as Vitrig's, and in spite of all their efforts, Brian's men could not stop the fires nor fight back against their unseen enemies who gave them no peace throughout that long and bitter night. Even the rain did not help Brian, though it fell throughout the night, as the flames, reinforced by Cruachain's magic — ate the walls and the gates of the dún and burned the buildings within.

Hardly a building now escaped the attention of the arrows, and when one landed on the roof of the stables, the horses inside went mad with fear and panic, broke their bonds and smashed their way outside, running through the crowded, smoke filled dún, trampling those who did not get out of their way quickly enough.

Panic now spread throughout, and voices were heard calling for Brian to surrender to Vitrig. Brian angered by this, ordered that anyone who spoke of surrender to be killed, because he knew that Vitrig was not a merciful man who would kill them all if they did surrender, and he wanted to stem any sign of panic at once.

In the first light of the new day, it was plain that they could no longer remain within the dún, that they would have to think soon about leaving.

Brian called his warriors together, and he sent others to gather the women and children.

"It is better for us to leave this place, to go out and face our enemies, die like the warriors we are if we must, rather than be burned here like sheep." They looked at him fearfully, trying to find some comfort but he had none to give them, the time for comfort long gone.

"We will sortie against the Formorians and while we do so, the women and children will try to make their escape. Get as far away as you can, it won't be easy I know, and some of you will die, but we must try because it is our only chance. The gods protect you all, and with their help, we will meet again on a better day."

They heard a roar from the outside as part of the wall collapsed, but still the Formorians did not attack. Wave after wave of arrows now began to fall down into the dún, no longer flame carriers, but seeking human targets. Men and women began to fall under the deadly hail. Some of the warriors held their shields over their heads, but still the arrows found their targets, this new terror adding to the terror of the flames and smoke. "Open the gates," Brian screamed. "Open them quickly."

Deirbhne had joined the women, and with an escort of warriors, she intended to lead them out of the dún to safety when the moment came to do so. She had said a quiet and dignified farewell to Brian and now as he prepared to lead his men out against the Formorians, she could only look at him with a silent prayer on her lips.

The gates of the dún were pushed back, and when they had been fully opened, Brian and his men could see just how much they had been damaged. In a short time they would have collapsed anyway, so they had taken the last chance of surprise.

"Kill the Formorians!" Brian shouted as he ran past the flaming gates, over the bridge, past what was left of the wagons, away from the dún, trying by their actions to save the women and children.

They pushed past the Formorian archers whom they killed without mercy, but these were only the first line, and Vitrig, who had been warned that Brian had sortied, had left his tent, where he had gone to rest, and came up to take command himself. He also sent a messenger to Gomrik, ordering him to join him as soon as possible.

As Brian's men advanced, screaming and raging after their night of terror, Vitrig ordered his second and third lines of archers to fire directly into the advancing men who were an easy target for the arrows, since they ran in close formation, and in the heat of their anger without any plan or coordination.

Brian was struck in the leg by one of the arrows, and fell to the ground in agony. Without thinking, he pulled it from his leg, almost fainting with pain as he did so. Another arrow struck the ground beside him, and around him, his men were falling as more and more arrows found their targets. He struggled to his feet, ignoring the hands which tried to help him.

He began to walk towards the Formorians, limping and in considerable pain, the blood flowing down his leg from the wound he had received. His men were lifted by his courage, and even Vitrig, who saw him coming, felt admiration for his bravery.

Deirbhne meanwhile, was trying to lead the women and children from the dún, but the crush was too great as Brian and his men tried to fight their way towards the Formorians, the space so narrow to move between the flames, that she could not get beyond the gates.

Children screamed and panicked, or fell under the crush of their own people, or the Formorian arrows which continued to rain down on them. Coughing the smoke from their lungs, they tried to avoid the flames which were everywhere around them, the heat from which scorched and drove them on.

It was at this time that Gomrik and his men came up behind the dún. He sent half of his men to round up the women, while the rest he sent against Brian and his men, who were now trapped between the two forces of Formorians.

Gomrik's men drove Brian and his men further from the gates of the dún, pushing them forward with fanatical determination, allowing neither their enemies, nor the bodies of their dead, nor the embankment, to halt or impede their progress as they cleared the entrance to the dún.

Brian, caught between the two forces, fought a vain battle, and defeat was inevitable. He was wounded yet again, captured and dragged before Vitrig, with scarcely twenty of his men, all that were left alive, the rest having died in the battle or been butchered.

The women and children were brought into the Formorian camp. Deirbhne led them, proud and unafraid, her head held erect, and Vitrig watched her approach with great interest. There was fire in his eyes, as he saw the proud manner of the woman who led her people, and whom he guessed correctly, must be Brian's wife.

Gomrik rode beside Deirbhne, and he was looking at her with the most impatient lust, at the same time laughing at her, and telling her crudely what he would do to her later when they were alone. She pretended not to hear him, but she kept her eyes fixed ahead, yet there was fear in her heart as she walked, though she hid it well from everyone.

"You there, what is your name?" Vitrig called, when she was close to him. Gomrik frowned at Vitrig's interest in the woman, and dismounted and stood by her side, as if to signify his ownership of her. Vitrig ignored him, and looked at the woman. She looked at him defiantly, and he thought that he had never seen a woman as lovely as she was, her fair hair down on her shoulders, her eyes looking at him with the most vivid hatred, which only made his interest in her more intense.

He lifted his hand and struck her hard on the face. Vitrig did not believe in being gentle with women no matter how beautiful they were.

"I asked you your name," he said harshly. Tears formed in her eyes, and her cheek was red from the slap.

"My name is Deirbhne," she said softly.

"So Deirbhne," he said, taking her in his arm and smelling her softness, feeling an intense desire for her at the same time ignoring the sullen look on Gomrik's face.

"You will stay with me for your own protection," he said laughing. Brian, who was tied with the other warriors, tried to rise and rush at Vitrig, but was knocked to the ground.

"Take him away from here," Vitrig ordered. "But don't harm him. I want that pleasure for myself later."

Brian was taken away, while Vitrig brought Deirbhne to his own tent.

"Remove your clothes," he said when they were inside. This time, Deirbhne did not argue. Silently, and with head bowed, she took off her clothes, letting them fall to the floor.

Vitrig gasped when he saw her naked, her firm perfectly formed breasts, her shapely hips, the way she stood, even in her shame, with dignity. Despite his lust he was impressed.

"Over there," he ordered, his voice thick with emotion. She went to the place he had indicated, the fur covered bed, and she stood quiet and unmoving.

"Lie down." Again she obeyed without protest. He quickly disrobed himself, impatient to have her, his lust increased by the sight of her body lying helpless, and at his mercy.

She did not resist, knowing that to do so was futile, and when he had finished with her, she lay quietly crying, trying to hide herself from the gaze of the barbarian. Several hours later, when he had taken her many times, Vitrig's lust was finally satisfied, and he began to feel hungry. He could hear the sounds of laughter from outside, the screams of Brian's women, his own men singing.

"We will eat now," he said. He rose, and quickly dressed, but Deirbhne remained where she was, not knowing what to do.

"Get dressed..." She rose from the bed, ignoring his grin, her own fear and shame numbed, and put her clothes on, almost without knowing what she was doing.

He led her outside. The Formorian camp was celebrating their victory. By their fires the Formorians were drunk, or singing. Some were taking Brian's women, whose screams still filled the night air, laughing at the tormented wails of their helpless victims.

Vitrig gripped Deirbhne's hand and led her to a large tent where the Formorian chiefs were celebrating.

The sight that greeted Deirbhne when she entered the tent filled her with fear and pity for her friends, some of whom were being raped even as the feast went on, their humiliation witnessed by everyone, their tormentors making wagers as to who would endure the longest.

She lowered her head in shame, but Vitrig laughed when he saw what was happening, and at the look on Deirbhne's face.

"Perhaps I should share my good fortune with them, and show them your body," he said, taunting her. She shuddered.

There was a cheer from the other chiefs, when Vitrig's presence became known. Envious eyes watched the woman beside him, though none dared show open envy, because he was a cruel and vicious man, and none of the chiefs dared cross him.

Deirbhne sat beside him at a table set apart from the others and close to the fire quiet and inwardly angry, the memory of her recent humiliation still strong in her mind.

Vitrig drank some wine and offered her a cup, but she refused, also the food which was put before her. Vitrig grunted, but said nothing. If she wanted to starve he thought, then so be it.

He drank several cups of wine, and ate some roast pig, which was still hot, his appetite strong after his time with Deirbhne. The food was good and he ate until he could eat no more, much to Deirbhne's silent disgust.

The Formorians, who had quietened down when Vitrig had entered the tent, now resumed their celebrations under their chief's amused and detached gaze.

He looked at Deirbhne sitting quietly beside him. She was staring straight ahead, her eyes fixed and unmoving, her emotion betrayed only by her constant swallowing as she fought to contain her rage and grief and pain.

Vitrig smiled. She was everything he had dreamed she would be when he first saw her, and he felt a fire in his belly as he remembered lying beside her naked. He would have her again later, he promised, he would have her many times before he was finished with her.

He drank more wine, and for a time watched his men as they ate and drank and played with Brian's women, but gradually such scenes began to bore him, and he signalled one of his guards, and whispered something in his ear. The guard nodded, and went outside.

"Now we shall have some real amusement," he said looking at Deirbhne, his voice harsh and threatening. She looked at him, but he only smiled.

Brian was dragged into the tent and brought before them. He was flanked by two guards who dropped him on the ground at Vitrig's feet.

He was bloody from his wounds and in great pain, but this he tried to hide as he looked up at Deirbhne, who looked at him with horror in her eyes. She almost rose to go and help him, but Vitrig's hand held her back.

He looked down at Brian, grinning with triumph.

"Your wife is warm and comfortable. She helped me pass many pleasant hours today."

Brian's eyes blazed with anger, but Deirbhne looked at him and with her eyes, she signalled him to stay calm. Vitrig however caught her look, and since it was his intention to provoke Brian, he began to fondle her, moving his hands under her dress, holding one of her breasts.

There was silence in the tent. All the other chiefs looked on with fascinated anticipation for what would happen next.

Vitrig's hand roamed over Deirbhne's body, slowly and deliberately, but all the time, he was watching Brian whose anger was becoming unbearable. He was bound, but he felt like throttling Vitrig who continued to mock him and torment him.

Finally, Vitrig removed Deirbhne's dress from her shoulders and lowered it to her waist. There was a gasp from some of the chiefs when they saw her semi-naked. Gomrik sat open mouthed, astonished by her beauty, angry that Vitrig had taken her from him.

Vitrig fondled her breasts again, as she hung her head in shame. Brian, overcome by grief and anger, rose to his feet and charged at Vitrig even though he was tied, but Vitrig was ready for him, and he kicked Brian hard in the groin.

Brian fell to the ground screaming with pain as the Formorians laughed and cheered their leader.

"Take him away, and be sure that he does not see his wife, or anything else again." Brian was dragged away. Vitrig sat down, and filled his cup once more. Deirbhne pulled her dress back over her shoulders, her eyes dead, her humiliation complete. Vitrig had established his ownership over her for all to see.

There was a piercing scream from outside which silenced everyone, then another and a short time later, Brian was brought back before Vitrig. His eyes had been torn out, and two bloody holes gaped at them, two rivers of blood ran down his contorted face.

Deirbhne screamed, but Vitrig silenced her with a savage blow to the head. There was silence in the tent. Even the Formorians no longer laughed.

Vitrig looked down at Brian, who lay before him sobbing with pain and anguish. His legs and clothes were covered with blood, his hair matted and twisted, a pathetic sight, a cowed and beaten man, at last his will and strength gone.

"Turn him loose for the wolves," Vitrig ordered. "Now, everyone will know that Vitrig is master here."

Deirbhne looked at Vitrig with utter hatred. She felt dead in all but name, and an angry coldness came over her as she looked at Brian's ravaged face, his bloodied and torn body.

From that moment, she became detached from her surroundings, numbing herself against pain, her only thought now, to kill Vitrig. She knew, as everyone else present did that Brian would not survive for long alone in the wilderness, blind and unarmed, and she prayed that death would come quickly to him, because death would be the only mercy left for him.

As she watched them take Brian away, she knew that she would not rest until she had avenged him. If she had to endure Vitrig's lust she would, until the right moment came her way, then...

She whispered a silent prayer to the gods to be merciful to Brian. Vitrig ordered the celebrations to begin again, but curiously, there was little joy among the Formorians, who respected bravery in a man, and who believed that Brian, who had shown great courage in battle, should have been given a better death.

Seated down the tent and watching Vitrig with utter hatred, Gomrik swore that he would not wait much longer to take what he believed was his by right.

CHAPTER THIRTEEN

A long way from Brian's dún, Creidne and Aobhne had finally reached the mountains. They had seen no more of their enemies since their escape, and they were surprised at the ease with which they reached Ceolmhar's territory.

They had travelled almost without pause since their escape, putting as much distance as they could between themselves and the scene of the ambush in which their friends had been captured.

At first Aobhne had wanted to go back to see if there was anything they could do for her father and the others, but Creidne had explained the hopelessness of such a course. He told her that Blamad and the others would not be pleased to see them return, since the whole point of their journey was to ensure that he, Creidne, reached Ceolmhar's dún safely and having seen them escape, they would not want him to return and endanger his own life.

"You would leave them with the Picts?" she had asked, unable to believe that he would, but he nodded his head.

"It has to be. They will find a way to escape, I am sure of it. Carriog has magic like you have never seen, and Blamad is a clever warrior. They will find a way out."

She had looked at him curiously, with a mixture of disbelief, even dislike, but she began to see the logic in what he said. It was true they would not have been able to help her father and the others, there were too many Picts, but her conscience still troubled her, and for a long time she had thought about her father, and what the Picts might have done to him.

The sky was full with snow, and already the higher parts of the mountain were white and impassable. The air became colder and fresher, and they breathed it deeply and gratefully, feeling at last that they were safe from the Formorians and the Picts, and as Creidne looked round the lonely mountain where there was so little sign of life, animal or human, it reminded him of the Danaans and the time he had spent among them which now seemed so long ago.

"This is a very desolate place," Aobhne said quietly. She was afraid, and shivered with cold in spite of the heavy cloak wrapped round her shoulders, and Creidne's arm. He hugged her to him gently.

"It has much to recommend it though," he said. He felt safe on the mountain, at peace in the solitude, but his tranquillity was rudely interrupted as Aobhne cried out:

"Look!" A lone horseman was watching them. He was a good distance from where they stood, but made no move to approach them.

"It's one of Ceolmhar's men, I am sure of it," Creidne said gently. "Have no fear, Aobhne. Up here we have no enemies."

She leaned her head against his shoulders. She felt safe with Creidne, even though he was not a warrior. There was an air of command in his manner, a confidence which few men possessed, and she knew that he would not allow her to come to any harm.

"I'm tired," she said wearily, but Creidne held her firmly. "A little while longer," he said gently. "We can't be too far from Ceolmhar's dún."

He led her higher, moving towards the horseman who watched them approach and pass beneath where he sat watching, but he kept his lonely vigil, never once moving all the time Creidne and Aobhne saw him. Creidne had no doubt however that word of their coming had already been sent ahead to Ceolmhar, otherwise the horseman, whoever he was, would not have permitted them to pass without challenge.

Now that he was close to Ceolmhar's dún, he began to wonder what he was going to say to the queen about the high king's death. There was much to tell, but first they had to get past the patrols which guarded the mountains for Ceolmhar.

"Stop!" a voice suddenly commanded, and they looked behind to find that six horsemen had come up behind them without betraying their presence.

Their swords were drawn, and all of them were grim faced and unfriendly.

"Who are you?" one of them said, coming closer, but his look of suspicion faded when he recognised Creidne.

"Welcome, Lord," he said, putting his sword away. The other horsemen did likewise.

"I did not recognise you at first, or our greeting would have been kinder. We have been watching you for some time now, and because there are few honest travellers at this time of year, we have to be careful."

Creidne smiled. He felt relieved that they had been found at last by Ceolmhar's men because both he and Aobhne were almost at the end of their endurance, both were tired, hungry and mentally exhausted.

"There is danger in not being watchful," he replied, "and you have to protect your lord."

The young warrior looked at Aobhne and Creidne introduced her.

"This is Aobhne. We have shared many hardships together."

"I am Dara," the young warrior replied amicably, noting how possessive Creidne was about the girl.

"I was fostered by the old high king, that is how I recognised you my Lord. I have listened to your stories many times, and when I felt lonely for my own people, they made the hours easier to bear."

"I bring grave news to the queen," Creidne said sombrely, keeping his voice deliberately low so that the other horsemen would not hear what he was saying.

"The high king is dead, his dún destroyed, and everywhere there is death and evil."

Dara almost swooned when he heard Creidne's words, but quickly steadied himself. His face however, was filled with grief, and he barely whispered his next question.

"How could such a thing happen?" he asked, his voice quivering. "The high king had a powerful army."

"The king was murdered," Creidne replied. "In his own bed. It happened after the Samhain. Blamad, Carriog, Branvig son of Ceolmhar, and Godrane who was your friend, are the only ones who still live, and myself of course, but Blamad and the others have been captured by Picts, along with Aobhne's father."

"I am sorry to hear it," Dara said to her. Aobhne nodded tearfully, remembering her father's face.

"But do not be too despondent, because if they have any hope of escape, then Blamad and Carriog will be the ones to do it."

Dara's words echoed Creidne's words earlier, and this somehow comforted Aobhne, who smiled at the young warrior gratefully.

"We will take you back to see Ceolmhar at once." He signalled one of his men, who came and dismounted from his horse. He gave the reins to Creidne who jumped up, then helped Aobhne up behind him, while the warrior jumped up behind one of his companions.

They set off for Ceolmhar's dún, Dara leading the way, only the two warriors who shared the same horse following, the rest going back to their silent vigil on the mountain.

"The Formorians are everywhere," Creidne said. "Picts too, even further north than I have ever seen them. They mean to attack Ceolmhar when spring comes, I am sure of it."

"Ceolmhar will not like the news you bring him," Dara said gloomily, "but the news that his son was still alive a few days ago will please him."

They did not speak after that, but climbed steadily upwards. Ceolmhar's dún was hidden deep in the mountain, accessible only during the summer months when the snow was melted, and by one twisting road. There was another, secret way, known only to the people of Ceolmhar's dún, and it was by this path that Dara led Creidne and Aobhne to their final destination.

Hidden between giant rocks, the path was invisible even from close up. Their journey along this path took more than an hour until, at last, they came within sight of the dún.

It nestled against the sheer rock face of the mountain, and from the ramparts, which were partially hidden by the half-grown trees which Ceolmhar's father had planted many years before, the sentries could see over most of the surrounding countryside.

The walls of the dún were made entirely of stone, there being plenty of that material lying about on the surrounding ground, and although the stones were of different shapes and sizes, the builders had neatly arranged them, interlocking them together to make a straight, sturdy and formidable wall, some ten feet thick.

The gates of the dún were open, and people were moving in and out, some herding cattle, others carrying wood or exercising horses, people behaving normally, unaware of the terrible things which had happened to the high king, or the danger which now threatened them.

Aobhne was amazed by the size of the dún. It was bigger than any she had ever seen and it stretched along the rock face for a good distance, further than she could see.

Flocks of sheep grazed on the sparse grass which was snow speckled, and already shorn under the continuous assault of the sheep. Curious faces watched the travellers as they entered. An occasional greeting was called to Dara, who quickly returned the compliment with a wave of his hand, and it seemed to both Creidne and Aobhne that this was a strong, safe, secure dún, which would be hard for anyone to take, even the Grey Druid.

There was no fear on the faces of the people, and their own fear left them, the uncertainty, and they smiled and relaxed, feeling safe at last. Creidne smiled at Aobhne.

"Our troubles are now over," he said, gently, trying to reassure her, though he knew that they were only beginning.

They were brought directly to Ceolmhar's house, a large, two-storied building in the style of the high king's house, enclosing a courtyard.

Aobhne was taken by Ceolmhar's servants to the women's quarters to refresh herself and rest, while Creidne was taken to the great hall to see Ceolmhar, who was waiting impatiently for his arrival.

Ceolmhar was close to sixty years old, a great age, but he had the physique and constitution of a man ten years younger and, if his hair and beard were grey, his mind was as alert as ever, his sword arm as strong and as skilled as it had always been.

"Welcome Creidne," he said rising, when Creidne was brought to him. "Come, sit here by the fire and take the chill from your bones."

He saw at once how tired and careworn Creidne was, the fear in his eyes.

"Tell me your news," he said quietly, fearing the worst.

The lamps had been lit and a slave left a jug of wine and two cups on the table beside Ceolmhar, who dismissed him, and poured the wine himself.

Creidne began his story. He started from the time when Blamad had come to his room in the high king's dún, and he told him everything, leaving nothing out, including his doubts about Blamad, and the Danaan king's praise of him. When he came to tell him about how the others had been captured by the Picts, Ceolmhar's face turned pale.

"Is Branvig alive?"

"I think so," Creidne replied. "They would have killed us at once if that was their intention, but I heard one of them say that we were not to be harmed, that the Druid wanted us for himself."

Ceolmhar said nothing more. He motioned Creidne to continue his story, which he did without further interruption. When he had finished, he saw that Ceolmhar's eyes were moist, that the old warrior was crying, but fighting hard to control his grief.

"What you did was right," he said gently. "Your news was too important for you to be taken also."

He looked into the fire, at the burning logs, his eyes absent and vacant, his thoughts on his only son Branvig. For a long time there was silence, and neither man spoke but after a while, Ceolmhar looked quietly at Creidne who, although tired and weary, had waited patiently for him to say something.

"The queen will have to be told," he said, "but you may leave that to me."

Creidne nodded gratefully. Telling the queen that the high king had been killed was something he had been dreading, and he was grateful now that Ceolmhar would do it.

"You should rest now. I will speak with you later. The queen I am sure will want to talk to you, so you should be rested and refreshed before you see her." Creidne went with one of Ceolmhar's slaves who had been summoned, to his quarters, while Ceolmhar braced himself for his talk with the queen.

Queen Morna was in her room playing chess with Alfred, her adviser, when Ceolmhar entered. She looked up, and at once noticed the dark expression on Ceolmhar's face.

"What is it?" she asked fearfully. She was not yet twenty, but had been queen for two years. She was a tall, dark haired woman, and her clear blue eyes gazed intently at Ceolmhar, her foster father.

"The high king is dead," he said as gently as he could. He took her hand in his, and felt her grip tighten on his own as his words sank in.

"When?" she whispered.

"Some time ago," he said. "At the Samhain feast. The dún is destroyed, all the people dead. Creidne is here, tired and lucky to be alive. The high king sent him with Carriog and Branvig my son, but they have been captured by the Picts. I have sent Creidne to rest, but you will see him later."

Alfred made to rise, but the queen motioned him to remain where he was.

"I will be all right," she said quietly, giving him a silent smile, then she turned to Ceolmhar once more.

"Tell me all of it." He told her everything, as Creidne had told him and she listened without comment, until finally, when he was finished, she looked first at Alfred, then back to Ceolmhar, their thoughts as one.

The Formorians would attack Ceolmhar's dún, when spring came, of that there could be no doubt.

"So, what we have expected for a long time, has come," she said sadly.

"But the Druid is also against us," Alfred said gloomily. "And this we did not expect, nor the magic he uses."

He was an old man, white haired, well past the time when most men died, but his mind was still alert and active, a man of much wisdom, who had been the queen's adviser since before she had become queen.

"Yet we knew that one day the Druid might turn against us," she said. "The King often spoke to me of this. It was his one wish to make final peace with the Druid, even make him a member of his council, but he was happy to have even an uneasy peace. The Druid is a dangerous man."

"There is much danger for all of us now," Ceolmhar replied, "but most of all for your brother Brian. He it was who warned the high king about the Formorians, and now his lands are the ones they will have to cross to take the island."

"We will have to warn him," the queen said urgently, but Ceolmhar shook his head. "It is already too late for that. Creidne told me there are Picts everywhere, Formorians too, spreading themselves over the countryside, watching all the roads and passes, those which have not been snowed under."

"What are we to do?" she asked, her grief momentarily clouding her judgment. "Are we going to wait for them to come to us?"

Ceolmhar looked at Alfred, and there was sadness in the eyes of the two old men who loved the queen, and who wished they were able to help her in her sorrow.

"There is nothing we can do yet," Ceolmhar replied. "We are safe here, and the winter will give us the respite we need to prepare for the war which will come with the spring. The Druid or the Picts cannot attack us here on the mountain because we are too well protected, and we control all the passes."

"The Druid uses magic, Lord," Alfred said quietly. "We must find an answer to his magic or he will take this dún as he took the high king's."

The queen suddenly rose from her chair.

"I will talk with you later," she said, her voice quivering, and she left the room under the gaze of two men.

"She is very angry," Alfred said when she had gone.

"She has every right to be." Ceolmhar stared into the fire, lost in thought, remembering half forgotten things, pieces of his childhood, strange thoughts which had nothing to do with his present situation. At last he spoke.

"What do you think of it all?"

Alfred spoke slowly and deliberately, his voice soft and frail, somewhat hesitant.

"There will be war, Lord. We have two powerful enemies against us, one of whom has a magic which drives men wild, and from what Creidne has told you, this dún and a few other isolated places are the only ones where they have no control."

The room was deathly quiet, and only the sound of the logs burning on the fire disturbed the silence.

"What about Brian?" Alfred did not reply for a moment, but Ceolmhar saw the pain in his eyes, the sorrow on the face of the man who was his friend.

"I'm afraid that it may already be too late for Brian. If they could destroy the high king and his dún, they could destroy Brian."

"I agree," Ceolmhar said, "but the queen must not be told. She has sorrow enough to bear at this time."

He smiled sadly, resting his back against the wall of the room, adjusting the couch under his body to make himself more comfortable.

"This is not the first time you and I have seen war, is it, my friend?"

Alfred nodded. "I fear you are right. We were used to it then, sometimes, I think, too used to it, but I fear now for the younger ones. There has been too much peace, too much tranquillity. They will find it hard to have courage against a man as cruel and as savage as Vitrig. The Druid is not a merciful man either; there's too much hatred in his heart, and a man like that is very dangerous..."

He paused for a moment.

"I have had many harsh words with the Druid," Ceolmhar said. "In the council I have argued with him, and gone against him more than I care to remember. Once I thought that he was going to take his dagger out to me, he became so angry."

Alfred frowned. He knew what would happen to all of them, if the Druid took Ceolmhar's dún. It was a thought he put from his mind very quickly.

Morna, lately a widow, sat and remembered her husband the high king. She spent hours alone, remembering what had been, her youth, the time when her father had brought her to the high king's dún, and she had seen the man who was to be her future husband for the first time. He had been such a gentle man, kind and without the coarseness of many of the warriors, a man who held the respect of his people in spite of his gentle ways because he had brought peace to them, and for years the spectre of war had not hung over them.

It was so long ago, she thought, suddenly feeling very angry. Anger was replacing her grief, and she swore silently, cursing the Grey Druid with all her being.

He had never fully submitted to the high king, never committed himself to the king's cause, and there had always been about him an air of suppressed menace. She had urged the king more than once to take stronger action against the Druid whose danger she had long been aware of, but the king had preferred diplomacy and tact, patiently hoping to win the Druid over. A forlorn hope, she thought, a fatal mistake for which the king had paid with his life.

There was a knock on the door, and on her command, Creidne entered. Morna rose to greet him.

"Come in, my friend," she said, glad to have someone to talk to again, especially someone who had been lately with the high king. She indicated a chair.

"Sit here, and tell me your news." He sat down.

"You look tired. Have you not rested enough?" she queried. He nodded.

"I am well enough," he replied awkwardly, not knowing what to say to her. "I am sorry to be the bearer of such bad news..."

She smiled lightly, her eyes moist, and for a moment he thought she was going to cry.

"Ceolmhar tells me that you have had a very hard time getting here," she said, controlling herself. "Tell me about it."

Creidne told his story. When he had finished, Morna looked at him, a frown on her face.

"The Danaan people still alive?" she asked, doubt clear in her tone. "Is that what Blamad said to hide his own cowardice? He was the only one left alive after the attack of the high king's dún, a strange thing, do you not agree?"

Creidne felt a surge of anger when she spoke about Blamad in such a way. She was wrong as he had been wrong, the shame of which he still felt, but he would have to prove to her, as it had been proved to him, that Blamad was to be trusted.

"You need have no doubt about Blamad, or his courage," he said coldly, his own anger barely suppressed.

"You forget that I too was with the Danaans in the forest, I too saw their king and heard his words, but more than this, something which convinced me for certain that Blamad had spoken the truth."

She looked hard at Creidne, felt his anger, then some of her own anger left her. After all, she had always liked Blamad, and she knew that the high king had placed a high value on his friendship and trust. It was because so much trust had been put in Blamad that she was so bitter and angry because he had survived and the high king had not. This was why she could not accept the explanation which Creidne had given her.

"What is this thing he spoke of, which convinced you he was telling the truth?"

Creidne hesitated for a moment or two. It was after all, a delicate subject to broach.

"Well?" she asked again, and this time Creidne told her.

"He told us you were with child," he said, watching the look of shock as it spread over her face.

"He told you that..?"

Creidne nodded.

"The god or whoever it was who spoke to him on the other side, told him that, as proof of the truth of his words, that you were with child and by this knowledge you would know he spoke the truth in all else he said."

She looked at him beseechingly, not knowing what to say or do.

"The high king himself did not know this," she said quietly, her eyes moist again. Her eyes were full of tears, her mind confused and disturbed.

"What is to become of us, storyteller?" she asked wistfully. He did not answer, he had no answer, because he too was confused and uneasy, he too felt the terrible foreboding come over him once more, so that he did not know what to say or do. What had happened was so strange, so unbelievable, that it took some time to accept, and while Creidne had begun to accept what he had seen and heard, Morna, still overcome by grief and anger, had not.

Creidne who was a wise man, a man of learning, did not share many of the superstitions and fears of his friends, but somehow in that dim light, with only the small fire keeping back the darkness, he felt fear, real fear such as he had never known before in his life. It was all around him, real, tangible, waiting and menacing, and when he looked at the queen, he saw that she too felt it.

"Even now, Lady, when I feel terror, I know that there is hope that someday, somehow, the evil will be overcome and destroyed. There are many dark days ahead, days of fear and fright, days when we will think that all is lost. There will be much sorrow before we win, but win we shall, I know it, because the Danaan king said we would, and this Brian will also know because they will have already moved against him."

His words had a shocking effect on her, and for a moment she forgot that she was a queen, and cried openly and without shame.

"I'm sorry," he said quietly, "but it is better that you know it now."

"Will he be able to stand against them?" He looked at her sadly, the answer plain to see in his eyes, and she turned away for a moment.

"Nothing is impossible," he said, trying to soften the blow. "Blamad knows what is to happen. He spoke much with the Old People, and they returned him to us. When our need is greatest, when we have no other hope, then they will help us. That is what the Dagda promised. You must believe it, and have hope."

She looked at him and smiled, her grief spent, her thoughts once more on the future.

"You are a good friend, Creidne. You were always so, and your words have given me peace and taken the pain from my heart, but what you have said has also made me realize that we must try to destroy the Druid and the Formorians ourselves. We cannot wait for any help. It must be ourselves."

He smiled.

"That is what the Danaan king said, it is the reason why Díele was ordered to kill the high king. The Formorians and the Druid are afraid of the united leadership. They know that if all the chiefs united against them they would have no hope of winning any more battles, even with the Druid's magic."

Creidne looked into Morna's eyes and what he saw was the old determination, the will to fight, the same strength of character he had always known she possessed. He was glad to see her angry, glad to know that, by her anger she was putting the pain of her grief to one side, and preparing for the ordeals to come. She would need all of her strength and wisdom, all her courage if she was to come through the darkness, they all would.

"We will overcome this evil," she said firmly.

"Aye, Lady. That we will."

CHAPTER FOURTEEN

Aemrig, the only chief who had remained loyal to the dead high king, was tired. The past few days had been exhausting and perilous for him. On his journey home, he had constantly expected Díele's men to attack him, and prevent him reaching his own dún, and it was with some surprise therefore, that he reached home safely.

Since his return the defences of his dún had been strengthened, and the smiths were busy forging new weapons in anticipation of war.

Aemrig's dún lay on the coast, built round a sheltered harbour and enclosed from the landward side by heavy forest. The walls were built not for defence against attack, but against wild animals. Now his scouts were scouring the forest, watching and waiting for any sign of intruders, as well as patrolling the coastline in case the Formorians were foolish enough to try and attack from the sea, despite the severe and prolonged storms which had kept Aemrig's own ships sheltering in the harbour.

After a long night's rest, he woke to a cold hard frosty morning. There was no wind and the snow-covered ground was crisp and hard.

Muireann, his second in command, woke him and brought him some bread and wine. He was a young man, still beardless, but a strong, hard warrior who was utterly loyal to Aemrig, whose nephew he was.

"There are Picts in the forest," he said quietly. Aemrig drank his wine.

"How many?" Muireann pulled back the cover from the window and a beam of sunlight entered the room.

"Too many to count," he replied. "They're coming from the south and there's another group coming in from the west."

"Díele," Aemrig said bitterly. He rose from the couch, put on his boots and sword and went outside. The cold air hit him as he stepped outside, almost taking his breath away, and he pulled his cloak tighter around his shoulders.

"Show me," he said. Muireann led him to the ramparts and together they scanned the trees.

"About three miles in that direction," Muireann said pointing, though it was impossible to see anything except leaf, branch and sky.

"They've stopped and made camp, and it's my guess they will move up at first light tomorrow and attack when they have both got themselves into position."

Aemrig thought about this for a moment. Muireann was probably right, he thought. The Picts would wait for Díele's men to get into position before they moved up to the dún, and the attack, when it came, would be a two-pronged one.

"Raise the alarm, but quietly," Aemrig said. "We don't want panic. The forest is our greatest protection, and Díele will not be able to dispose his men as he would wish, so we have some advantage, that and our knowledge of the forest."

Muireann went to do as Aemrig had commanded, and for the rest of the day Aemrig's men prepared for the expected attack. After dark Aemrig and Muireann sat together planning their defences for the attack which they fully expected at dawn. They knew that the dún could be defended, because there was little room in the dense forest for an attacker to bring up enough men at once without being picked off by Aemrig's archers, who were long practised and expert at holding the path leading to the dún.

They spent a long and restless night at their posts in case the Picts decided on a night assault, and next morning at first light every man was at his post and prepared, but the hours passed and there was no attack. Aemrig's scouts were sent out to find out what was going on, and although they reported much activity in the enemies' camps, there was no sign that the Picts were planning to attack the dún. Darkness came again, and Aemrig ordered his men to stand down, leaving only a token guard on the walls.

"Something is wrong," he said to Muireann, when they were alone. "I don't like the feel of this. They have the men and the means to destroy us, yet they do not attack."

"Perhaps they are waiting for the Druid." Aemrig shook his head. "The Druid is with the Picts, I am sure of it."

Something stirred in Aemrig's mind, although he could put no substance to it. He looked at Muireann.

"Do not think me mad, but we must get away from here at once..." Muireann looked at him, a question in his eyes, but he trusted Aemrig and respected him.

"I may be wrong, but I think that the Druid is going to use some kind of magic against us. I seem to remember Blamad telling me that he was said to have found a great magic which no man could resist. I cannot explain it Muireann, but I have this thought which tells me to get away from here, to take everyone and go now."

"I will get the people ready," Muireann said quickly. He knew Aemrig was not a man to panic easily and he trusted his judgment completely. "And I will tell the captains to have their ships ready for sailing, though I do not know what they will say to that, because of the storms."

"I will talk to the captains. You get everyone else ready."

Aemrig had four ships whose captains came at once when Muireann told them what Aemrig was planning to do.

"I do not wish to go against you, Lord," one of them said, "but the sea is high and not at all suitable for sailing. We risk being swamped if we take ship in such weather. It's madness to even think of doing it, with respect, Lord."

Aemrig nodded.

"I understand, captain, but we face a worse fate if we remain here. Believe me, I do not ask you to do this thing lightly."

Somehow from the tone of his voice, although he had not told them the reason for this apparently foolish scheme, they knew that Aemrig, a courageous and fair-minded man, must have a sound reason for asking them to embark at such a time.

"We must go tonight, without delay," Aemrig said, trying to hide the urgency in his voice. "Tomorrow may be too late. We must go tonight."

The very tone of his voice and expression on his face eliminated any further doubts from their minds.

"So be it, Lord," the captains said, and they went to prepare their ships, wondering what had frightened their leader so much that he would take them onto the wild seas on such a terrible night, yet determined to follow his orders and obey this apparently foolhardy whim of his.

The four ships were provisioned lightly. They were small, two-masted vessels, used mainly for fishing and trade. Aemrig had reckoned that there was just about enough room on the four vessels to take the people of the dún. No baggage was permitted. The people boarded with only what they wore, and their weapons. Important equipment like the blacksmith's anvil and tools, were also taken aboard.

Throughout the night, and with the urgency which the shortage of time caused, they embarked the people of the dún. Some provisions were loaded and, most importantly, water.

Some of the people screamed and did not want to go, but Aemrig's men put them aboard, having little time to argue or coax anyone, and as each ship was filled it took to sea, driving out of the shelter of the harbour into the full force of the storm. The high waves seemed certain to submerge the overcrowded ships, tossing them like tiny pieces of wood, but miraculously each ship got away safely, until only one was left. It was only then that Aemrig boarded, reluctant himself in the end to leave because not all of his people had embarked and he did not wish to go himself while others remained. It was Muireann who persuaded him that his duty was to the majority and this in the end he accepted.

A few of the people from the dún had refused to go, despite threats and pleadings, and they remained on the pier, mostly old men who preferred to take their chances in the dún, rather than risk the uncertainty of the storm-tossed sea rising and raging beyond the harbour.

They stood silently, watching as Aemrig's ship slipped its anchor, unfurled its sails and began to move out to the open sea.

It was a sad moment for all those on board as they pulled away from the shore. Muireann, who stood on deck beside Aemrig, knew that his leader was feeling the weight of sadness in his heart, because he too felt it. At that moment their thoughts were not of the raging ocean they would soon face, or the Druid and his evil magic, but on the homes they were leaving, and the forest and the life they had known.

They left the shelter of the harbour and were hit by the full fury of the storm, which lashed their ship, tossing it time and time again almost swamping it, but Aemrig's men were skilled sailors and they rode the waves, and steered their ship through the heavy seas into the storm and before the wind.

The ship was small with not enough shelter below decks for everyone, so most had to remain on deck to suffer the wind and spray, the cold and ice. At dawn it began to snow hard, adding to their miseries. It was a dark, sinister morning and Aemrig realized for the first time, the size and magnitude of the waves which constantly pounded the ships. He was afraid that because the ship was overloaded, it would flounder, and he wondered if he had made the right decision to leave, but they sailed safely throughout the day and into the night, their second on board ship.

During the night they spotted campfires along the coast. Aemrig had ordered that the ships be kept in darkness so as not to be seen from shore, but in such a storm it was unlikely that whoever was behind those lights, friend or enemy, would take to the sea.

Most of the people on board had become somewhat used to the stomach-turning movement of the ship, tried to sleep and in some cases succeeded, but others, overcome by the damp and cold, by fear and uncertainty, died quietly on deck, and were quietly and without ceremony put overboard into the raging sea.

At dawn they saw the mountains in the distance. Aemrig knew this was where Ceolmhar had his dún. It was a welcome and cheering moment, and their spirits rose, the sight of land a welcome relief after the stormy journey they had endured. They also came within sight of the other ships which they had not seen since they had set out on their journey. They were scattered and distant, but still visible in the calm clear morning, because the wind had died and the snow had stopped falling. After hoisting full sail, Aemrig's ship cut the distance between it and the others, and together they sailed on.

A couple of hours later they reached a cove. They sailed the ships as far in as they could, beaching them in the shallows when they could go no further. The warriors scrambled off first, to make sure that the land was safe before they allowed women and children to disembark.

A thick forest lay several hundred feet from the beach, which was quite sandy and free of rocks. Beyond the forest, they could see the mountain which was their final destination.

The warriors ran to the trees and fanned out, going deep into the gloom to make certain that their landing had not been observed, and when they were satisfied, they returned to the shore to give the signal for everyone to come ashore.

They gathered wood, and as the people landed, they lit fires and sat on the beach to rest for a while. They were glad to feel the earth beneath their feet once more, even though the ground inland from the beach was snow-covered and rock hard.

A strong breeze blew in from the sea, bitingly cold, but the people hardly noticed it, so grateful where they to be on dry land once more.

After some time, Aemrig spoke to them.

"Many of you are wondering why we left our dún so quickly and with such risk to ourselves to cross the sea in such a storm, something which even the Formorians did not dare to do, but I tell you this. The Druid was planning to attack our dún, but not with his army. Do not ask me how I know this. He would have used a powerful and terrible magic against us, a magic which would have destroyed us all and given us no chance to fight back. You must believe what I tell you is true. When we reach Ceolmhar's dún we will have time to rest and reflect, but we will be safe, and when the time comes, we will have an opportunity to strike back at the Druid, our enemy."

Such was his standing with his people, and so much did they trust him, that not one word of dissent was raised against him. He had ordered it because he believed that they were in danger, and that was enough for them. As his captain trusted him, so too did his people.

They left the ships beached, put out their fires, and started out on their journey towards Ceolmhar's dún in the mountain.

They entered the forest, a party of warriors going ahead to cut a path through the thick undergrowth. For several hours they moved silently and steadily, until they came to more open country approaching the mountain.

They began to climb the bare cold rocky landscape. The wind was chilly, the air thin, and there was no shelter or cover in case of storm or attack, but from somewhere they found the strength and will to keep going, even though they were all starving and exhausted. As Aemrig had guessed, Ceolmhar's scouts soon spotted them, and word was brought back to Ceolmhar that a large column of people was on the mountain and heading for his dún.

Ceolmhar sent a strong force of men down to find out who the intruders on the mountain were, but once again Dara, who led them, recognised the leader and knew that the people before him were not enemies.

Aemrig and his people were escorted back to Ceolmhar's dún where a large crowd had gathered to watch the strange and bedraggled group of people come among them. Some were ready to fall down with exhaustion, all were extremely tired and in need of sleep, and while Dara took Aemrig and Muireann to see Ceolmhar, his men saw to the rest.

"You are tired and it is plain that you need rest," Ceolmhar said when they were brought before him. "You are not the first visitors we have received this last while. Creidne is here... The Druid used a powerful magic to destroy the high king, and there is evil throughout the land. No one is safe and it was fortunate you left your dún when you did."

Muireann looked at Aemrig, and there was admiration and gratitude in his eyes when he spoke.

"We left our dún because Aemrig had a premonition that the Druid would use a magic against us. Surely the gods gave him that message, Lord."

"It seems so," Ceolmhar said gravely. "Because you would surely be dead if you had not left the forest. Dead or mad."

"Then we have much to be grateful for," Aemrig said. Ceolmhar saw how tired he was, how much in need of rest, and he decided that both men must sleep first. They would talk later.

"I will send for you in a few hours." He called a slave. "Show them where they will sleep, and see that they are not disturbed."

Aemrig and Muireann followed the slave, leaving Ceolmhar staring into the fire. So... he thought, another attack from the Druid, but closer to his own dún, too close. Ceolmhar was disturbed. The Druid was not letting the winter stand in his way, and if he kept going as he was, he would be on the mountain in days rather than weeks. The thought terrified him.

CHAPTER FIFTEEN

Stung by pain and terror, unable to see, Brian stumbled through the forest. Full of despair and anger, he cried out for the gods to end it all for him as he tripped and fell yet again.

He heard wolves howling, but could not tell how near they were. He was hungry and thirsty, his thirst almost greater than the pain from his wounds, and he was frozen through, without his cloak to protect him against the cold night air and the hard, frosty ground.

He did not know how long he had been wandering in the forest, he did not even know if it was day or night, but he guessed that it must have been a long time, because his wounds did not hurt as much as they had done before. He did not know either whether he was going round in circles, but felt that he could not endure the pain or the hunger or the cold much longer.

He knew that he would have to rest and eat soon if he was to survive, but without his sight he was helpless. He couldn't find food, couldn't get his bearings, and when he stumbled again he lay there for a moment, wondering if it really was worth it to get up again. A wolf howled again, this time much closer, and Brian's heart jumped. It was a terrible thing to be blind he thought, blind and helpless. If he could see the wolves then he would have some chance of survival; but sightless, he was certainly dead.

He thought of Deirbhne and he cried again. His mind saw her beauty, heard her voice and he remembered their times together, then he recalled what Vitrig had done to her, the humiliation he had made her bear and he cursed the Formorian, his voice rising high above the trees, spending itself in the air above.

"I'll kill you, Vitrig..." he shouted over and over again, his anger mounting because he knew that he would never kill the Formorian chief. He would never avenge himself or Deirbhne for what had been done to them both. He picked himself up, and began to walk once again, tripping over some tangled briars, the thorns from which cut into his hands and face, adding more pain to his pain, and this time he remained on the snow-covered ground and cried.

Blamad and his companions had stopped to rest for the night. They were weary but relaxed, in high spirits, their escape from the Picts having restored their morale and confidence. Maron had recovered his senses as well as his foul temper, and had complained and moaned the whole day about being hungry, about the cold, about everything it seemed to Blamad, who was not sure whether to be sorry or glad that the old man had found his acid tongue again.

The snow on the ground had hardened into ice, and it was bitterly cold. They were eating berries they had collected earlier, and were huddled round the fire which burned brightly, keeping some of the cold, and the forest creatures at bay.

For a long time they sat in silence, but were happy to be in control of their own destinies once more. Suddenly there were noises in the forest close by, the sound of a twig breaking and leaves rustling, the sound of a voice cursing.

"What is it?" Maron asked, but Blamad silenced him.

"Someone is approaching our camp," he whispered. "Someone who is either very brave or very foolish."

Carriog doused the fire, and they all drew their weapons and withdrew into the cover of the trees to wait for the intruder.

After a few minutes, Blamad saw the dark outline of the man as he entered the camp site, and with a sudden leap brought him to the ground and held him, but the man beneath him did not struggle or make any attempt to free himself.

The others came back into the clearing, and Carriog lit a torch and held it over Blamad and his captive.

"By the gods, it's Brian," Blamad said horror stricken when he saw Brian's disfigured face, the eyeless sockets, the blood and dirt, the destruction of what had been a king's perfect body.

He jumped away, and with Carriog's help lifted Brian gently from the ground. They sat him against a tree, while Branvig lit the fire once more. Carriog looked quietly at the sightless man, probing his wounds, learning from Brian's reaction to his touch that he was still in great pain.

"Brian..." Blamad said gently, putting his hand on the man's shoulder. "Can you hear me?"

Brian turned to Blamad.

"I've been wandering for a long time," he said wearily. He rested his head in his hands and cried bitterly. Carriog lifted his face, and wiped away the caked dirt and blood. From his pouch he took some ointment which he had made himself from herbs and roots, and gently eased this onto Brian's wounds.

Brian cried with pain, but Blamad held him firm while Carriog finished what he was doing.

"It will not take long," Carriog said gently. "In a little while the pain will ease and you will sleep."

He took off his cloak and put it over Brian's shoulders. Brian was shivering, and it was plain to see that he would have to have proper care soon or he would die. Blamad got some of the berries, and gave these into his hands.

"I wish we had more," he said. Brian ate the berries greedily, sighing when he had finished them.

"Who did this to you?" Blamad asked.

"I kept thinking about the wolves, that they would get me, that no one would ever know what had happened to me," he replied with some agitation. He turned to Blamad. "We thought we could hold them, we had as many men as they had, and a good strong dún, but they used fire against us, and magic. They took Deirbhne. The flames, the flames..."

He became more agitated, and kept shaking his head, calling for Deirbhne as he did so. Blamad rested his hands firmly on Brian's shoulders in an effort to keep him calm.

"Rest easy Brian," he said gently. "You are with friends now. You will come to no more harm."

Blamad looked at the others. There was sadness and anger in their faces, and he supposed that his own face must look the same. He certainly did feel very angry, and vowed revenge on the men who had done this to Brian.

"So, this is how Vitrig means to fight," he said bitterly.

"They have destroyed him," Carriog said quietly. "More surely than if they had killed him."

Blamad was doubly angry because he knew what Carriog meant. Even if Brian could still see, he would never again be king, because the law said that no man who was deformed could be king.

Even the great Nuada had to leave his throne when the Formorians cut off one of his hands, but Nuada had been able to see, and when he had a silver hand made for himself he was allowed to lead his people and become king again.

"It is well that we will reach Ceolmhar's dún tomorrow," Carriog said. "Brian will need rest and care for some time if he is to recover. The cold and his wounds have broken his body, and I fear that his mind may also be affected."

"It's a terrible thing they have done to him," Godrane said bitterly. Blamad looked at him sharply.

"It's no more than I expected from the Formorians."

The night passed slowly, and at first light they continued their journey. Carriog and Godrane supported Brian between them, each of them having put his cloak around Brian's shoulders.

Brian's mind was away from them, and he did not speak at all on the journey. Blamad's anger had not subsided, and he swore that somehow he would find those responsible for Brian's terrible injuries and kill them himself.

They walked for hours, knowing they were so close to Ceolmhar's dún, and they did not stop to rest, because they knew that Brian needed urgent care which they had not the means to give him.

In the afternoon they were met by a patrol who had been sent to keep watch on the mountain by Ceolmhar, who hoped that by some chance, his son Branvig might escape from the Picts.

Blamad and Branvig were recognised at once.

"You are welcome here Branvig, son of Ceolmhar," Dara said, for it was he again who led the men. "Your father will be overjoyed to see you again. He has heard of your captivity from Creidne."

"Creidne is here?" Blamad asked smiling. Dara smiled also.

"Yes, he is," he replied. "He came a few days ago with a woman," and this time it was Maron's turn to smile. A tear came to his eyes as he realized that Aobhne was safe and well and he would soon see her.

Dara looked at Brian's ravaged face and frowned.

"Formorian hospitality," Blamad said angrily. Dara shook his head sadly. "The queen will be doubly sad to see her brother like this. She has much grief to bear these days."

Godrane and Carriog held Brian who seemed not to notice anything of the commotion around him, or be aware that they had come to the end of their journey.

"It's a terrible thing to see a king so badly mutilated," Dara said. "Yet, there will be more of such things I fear, because now there is talk of war everywhere. Do you know Aemrig?"

"I do," Blamad replied, remembering his friend. "He was the only chief who remained loyal to the high king."

"Well he too is here, with all his people," Dara replied.

"The days ahead will be dark and filled with danger, but look here, we should get Brian back to the dún, where he can receive proper attention."

Dara dismounted.

"Put Brian on my horse," he said. "I will walk back to the dún with you."

Godrane and Carriog lifted Brian onto Dara's horse, and when he was astride the animal, Godrane jumped up behind him, and took the reins, at the same time holding Brian steady.

"Follow me," Dara said, and he began to lead them by the secret path towards Ceolmhar's dún. He saw how much Brian was hurt and so he sent one of him men ahead with the news to the dún, that suitable arrangements be made for their injured friend.

They reached the dún a little while later, and Brian was taken at once by some of Ceolmhar's slaves to a specially prepared chamber where the physicians were waiting to look at his wounds.

Blamad and his companions were led by Dara into the great hall where Ceolmhar sat waiting for them by the fire, Morna by his side, her face careworn and troubled.

As soon as they entered the hall, Ceolmhar rose to greet them all warmly, especially his son Branvig, whom he had begun to think he would never see again, and whom he now embraced long and hard, much to Branvig's embarrassment. "I cannot tell you how happy I am to see you here," he said, his eyes moist and tearful. "I thought for a time that you were dead, but you look well in spite of everything."

"The gods were on our side, Lord," Branvig replied quietly. Ceolmhar nodded happily. "They must have been, for you are all safe and alive."

Blamad and the others were desperately weary, but they had to wait until Ceolmhar got his fill of his son before they could sit down and rest and it took several minutes for Ceolmhar to remember them.

"Sit down my friends, have some wine." He greeted them all after some time with apologies for keeping them waiting, Blamad about whom he had heard so many strange tales,

Carriog, the giant and silent Nemedian who never seemed to lose his serene sense of calm. Then there was Godrane, the young warrior whom he did not know, but guessed from what Creidne had told him that this young man must be he, and the old man who stared at him boldly and with such a lack of respect had to be Maron, Aobhne's father, a difficult man by all accounts. He smiled at each of them.

"You are all welcome here in my house. Now, tell me your news."

Blamad looked at Ceolmhar, then at the queen, who had not spoken a word, or acknowledged their presence, a fact he put down to her grief, not knowing that she harboured a deep suspicion about him, and could not bring herself to say anything to him, despite what Creidne had told her.

Blamad sensed that something other than grief might be the cause of the queen's coldness, but did not think that he might have been the cause of it, since he could not have known how he had offended her, but seeing her aloofness, he hesitated before giving her more terrible news.

"We found Brian," he said quietly, and there was a terrible silence in the hall as he spoke. "Blinded and turned loose in the forest by the Formorians, half demented and nearly dead..."

He was deliberately blunt, seeing no point in concealing anything from her, since she would have found out later anyway.

"Where is he?" she asked, looking at him with ferocious anger and hatred.

"We left him with the healers," he answered, unable to meet her stern gaze.

"And Deirbhne?"

"What about Deirbhne?"

She was crying now, almost overcome by this latest grief, and he felt inside that she could not take any more.

"She was taken with the other women as far as we could tell," he replied. "It was hard to find out since Brian's mind has wandered and he has been delirious most of the time since we found him."

Morna clenched her knuckles until they were white, and she turned to Ceolmhar.

"She had better be dead. I am going now to see Brian, I will come back later."

She left the hall without another word. Ceolmhar looked after her with an expression of utter sadness.

"Do not take her words to heart Blamad," he said gently. "She has had to bear much sorrow these last few days and, in her grief and anger, says many things she does not mean."

He put his arm on his son's shoulder.

"Tell me your news," he said. He led Branvig towards the fire for a few moments of private conversation. Blamad and the others left the hall, Maron to find his daughter, Blamad, Carriog and Godrane to find a bed to rest on.

As they left, a familiar figure walked towards them.

"It's Aemrig," Blamad said, and rushed to greet his friend.

"I was told that you were a prisoner of the Picts," the big warrior said smiling and gripping Blamad's arms.

"I'm glad to see you here, all of you," he said to Carriog and Godrane. "Tell me your news."

Blamad told him everything, and when he had finished, Aemrig's face was grave. "We too had to leave our dún," he said. "I cannot explain it, but I had a strange feeling of unease. I knew that the Druid was planning to use something evil against us, so we took to the sea. When I heard what had happened to the high king and his dún I was glad that I obeyed my instincts."

He laughed suddenly.

"The journey was a nightmare, Blamad. I was never a good sailor, and I can tell you that after two nights in such stormy seas I was glad to get my feet on dry land once more."

Muireann approached, and Aemrig introduced him to the others.

"I heard what happened to Brian," he said. "A terrible misfortune. How is he now?"

"His mind is gone, which in a way is just as well," Blamad replied. "He has so many injuries, as well as having his eyes torn out, and the rough time he had in the forest before we found him. I'm surprised that he's still alive."

"He was a great warrior," Aemrig said quietly, unconsciously using the past tense.

"Aye," Blamad replied, almost chocking. "A great warrior."

A slave came over to them with news from Ceolmhar.

"Lord Ceolmhar will see you tonight in the council hall," he said quickly, and left without a reply. Blamad and Aemrig looked at each other.

"A war council," Aemrig said absently. Blamad did not respond.

Ceolmhar was waiting for them later, when they entered the council hall. The others were already there, Carriog and Branvig, who were talking quietly together, while the queen sat, watching Blamad and Aemrig enter. Godrane and Creidne were seated to the queen's left, while Alfred, the queen's adviser, stood waiting for Ceolmhar to sit.

He motioned Blamad and Aemrig to their places at the table, then sat down himself. When they were all seated, slaves came and left trays of meat and fruit on the table, with jugs of wine and ale.

A fire roared in the huge grate, and the heat made the room very comfortable. Tallow lamps hung from the walls, their flames flickering light around the room, throwing shadows along the walls. When everything had been left on the table, Ceolmhar dismissed the slaves.

"We will serve ourselves," he said to the assembled group. He gave the signal to eat. They ate silently, each of the warriors making up for their time in the wilderness, much to Ceolmhar's amusement.

Morna had to be urged again and again to eat by Ceolmhar, but in spite of this, she ate and drank very little. When the others were finished, Ceolmhar spoke.

"We are gathered here tonight under dangerous circumstances. You all know what has been happening, and from every traveller who has passed this way the news has been the same. There will be war soon, and by spring the Druid will have tried to take this dún, which by all accounts is the only one which does not already owe him allegiance.

"We have a great and powerful friend on our side, a friend who will keep us safe until we are ready. I speak of the winter, and the snow which will keep the Druid's army from marching and away from the mountain. Yet we must be prepared for attack even before that time, because the Druid might not wait until spring."

He paused for a moment, seeing in their eyes the expectant fear, the tension, above all, the relief they felt at having escaped from the Druid and his magic.

"The Druid is our real enemy my friends, our greatest threat. He possesses a magic so powerful that it destroyed the high king and his dún, and it is only by good fortune and his own instincts that Aemrig is here with us. The Druid's magic is strong, but it has a weakness, and the weakness is that he cannot use the magic too often or it will destroy him. There is time for us to find a way to counter his magic, to prepare ourselves to meet him on equal terms. There must be somebody somewhere, who knows the Druid's secrets and a way to counter them."

"There are such men, who have that knowledge," Carriog said suddenly. "I myself as you know, possess some power, but my power is minute compared to the knowledge these wise men possess. In the remote places where the last of my people live, there are men who understand such things. I've heard the older people speak of such men."

"Would you be able to find such a man?" Ceolmhar asked. "And would they help us if you asked them?"

"If they are still alive, I will find them, and if I find them, and ask them to help us, they will do so," Carriog replied confidently. Ceolmhar smiled. It was unusual to find the usually reticent Nemedian so boastful. "Then that is what you must do. Find such a man, and bring him to us. My son Branvig, and Godrane will accompany you."

Carriog did not reply, but accepted Ceolmhar's command with a slight bow of his head.

"We have only a little time to prepare for what is to come. We cannot stay by our fires this winter, but we must prepare and prepare well. Blamad and Aemrig will train our young men, make warriors of them, because they are slow and lazy and fond of pleasure. It's the curse of peace, that it makes men soft and weak. The Formorians would have no trouble overcoming us now if they attacked because we are so soft."

The others laughed because they knew that Ceolmhar did not mean what he said, that his warriors were formidable fighters, tough and almost without equal.

"I will see to the walls and other defences," he said almost as an afterthought. "The Formorians, if they get this far, will pay a high price in blood for this dún."

"When that time comes, I will not stand idly by," the queen said, her voice hard and sharp, her eyes shining in the fire glow with a relentless and bitter hatred.

"I too intend to fight."

"That is impossible," Ceolmhar said firmly. "You will have to protect the child you are carrying."

She looked at him sharply, then at Creidne who kept his head down.

"Creidne told me, but you must not be angry with him. It was his duty to tell me. If the Druid found out that you were carrying the high king's child, he would make a greater effort to kill you, perhaps even use another magic against the child, which we could not prevent. You will remain here, away from any battle, out of sight if this dún is attacked."

His voice was sharp and filled with command, perhaps more than he intended to sound, but she was a strong-willed woman, and he wanted to be sure that she would do as he had commanded, which was by no means certain. She looked hard at the man who was her foster father, but she saw the equal if not stronger determination in his eyes, the look which told her that he would not change his mind. She looked at the others, and it was plain from their faces that they too, agreed with Ceolmhar. For a few moments more she said nothing, but finally admitted defeat.

"I will stay here," she said quietly. There was a sigh of relief from the men when she gave her answer.

"It is well," Ceolmhar said gently. "The people will find courage in your presence. Tell me, how is Brian?"

"The healers have said that his time in the forest has let poison into his blood, and they say he will not live. It is well he will not live, because his mind is gone, and he is not Brian anymore, only a broken man who was once a king. He is but a shadow now."

As she spoke, she kept her head lowered, but her trembling voice betrayed the emotion she felt, that and the tears which fell onto her lap, though she tried to hide them.

"There will be a blood payment for this," Ceolmhar said bitterly.

She rose from her seat. "If you have finished, my Lord, I would like to return to Brian."

Ceolmhar nodded.

"Of course." She left the room, and when she had gone, Ceolmhar continued. "In a day or so when you have rested, you will look for this Nemedian magician of yours," he said to Carriog. "For the moment however, you must all rest, and recover your strength for the hard days which lie ahead."

CHAPTER SIXTEEN

During the next few days while they rested, Carriog and Godrane were able to see something of the life of the dún. Blamad had already begun drilling the young men preparing them for war, staging sword fights and javelin throwing contests, sharpening men whose skills had become dull, keeping them working from early morning until well into the afternoon and in the process, sharpening his own skills and reflexes.

One day they went to watch Ceolmhar while he held court, where disputes were brought before him to be settled.

They were brought by Alfred, who motioned them to be quiet when they entered the hall. Two men were already standing before Ceolmhar. One of the men was addressing him, at the same time pointing angrily at the other man, his tone and manner devoid of respect for the king who looked, and was annoyed by the man's manner. One of Ceolmhar's guards hit the man sharply on his back with the shaft of his spear and reminded him sternly whose presence he was in. The man reddened and bowed to Ceolmhar.

"I am sorry, Lord," he said quickly. "I meant no disrespect."

"Continue," Ceolmhar said coldly. The man told his story.

"This man killed my brother with his knife, and when we went to him to demand the fine due in such a case, he laughed at us and refused to hear of it. We tried to take what was our due, but when we did we were taken here to you. I ask you now, Lord, for justice, and the payment which is due to us."

Ceolmhar looked at the man for a moment, then the younger man, the one accused of the killing.

"What do you have to say?"

"I killed his brother, it is true," the man replied. "I do not deny it, but I killed him in a duel, and since our laws say that no fine should be paid in such a case, I did not pay."

"I will speak of the law," Ceolmhar said sharply, once more offended by the lack of respect shown to him.

He turned to the other man, the accuser, whose face now showed fear.

"You did not say that your brother was killed in a duel."

"It was no duel, Lord," the man replied quickly, highly agitated. "He was goaded into fighting by this man, but it was no duel, and my brother was no match for him."

"Is this how it was?" Ceolmhar demanded of the other man, who did not reply.

"Is that how it was?" he asked again, his voice angry and fierce. A voice answered. It was Alfred, who left his two companions and walked closer to Ceolmhar.

"It happened as the older one says. His brother was no match for him. I saw it happen, but I am too old and slow, and was not able to intervene in time."

The accused man looked at Alfred with bitter hatred, but it was clear that his case was lost. Ceolmhar thanked Alfred for his testimony, and Alfred returned to Carriog and Godrane.

"You will pay this man five cows and a barrel of ale," Ceolmhar said to the accused man. "You may count yourself fortunate because the fine would have been greater if you had not been attacked by this man and his family. Settle this matter between you quickly, and let that be an end to the quarrel."

The two men bowed, their acceptance of Ceolmhar's judgment unquestioned.

A man and a woman now stood before Ceolmhar. The man was the woman's uncle, and the case concerned the payment of money for the woman's marriage, a common dispute at that time.

She was a young woman, not beautiful, but good looking, small in build, stubborn and able to look after herself, as her presence before Ceolmhar showed.

"What is your dispute?" Ceolmhar asked, though in fact he knew, since he knew everything which went on among his people.

"I was given by my uncle in marriage, my father, his brother, being dead. He is my guardian and head of our household, but he has refused to give me that share of the bride price which is rightly mine."

Ceolmhar nodded. The woman stood back while her uncle stepped forward to give his side of the story.

"Lord Ceolmhar, I am in all but name the father of this woman," he began. "My brother, her father, is many years dead, killed honourably in your service. I have been her guardian since that time, and I have given her all that was expected of me, and more, and I have always regarded her as my own daughter."

He too now stood back, while Ceolmhar spoke with his council who were sitting either side of him, and with Creidne, who whispered something in his ear.

They spoke quietly like this for a long time, before Ceolmhar finally gave his judgment.

"The law is clear on this matter. Where a woman's father is alive, then he would give the full bride price, but when her natural father is dead the woman is entitled to half the bride price, and that is my judgment."

Once more Ceolmhar's decision was accepted without protest. Alfred turned to leave.

"Ceolmhar is a wise and fair judge. He is seldom wrong," he said when they were once again outside. Carriog and Godrane were fascinated by the way Ceolmhar was able to make such judgments.

"I am glad that I do not have to make such decisions," Carriog said. "I would surely give the wrong one."

Alfred and Godrane both laughed.

"It is true that you were not made for the council hall, Carriog," Alfred said lightly. "Intrigue is not part of your character, nor yours either, Godrane."

He smiled at the young warrior.

"You are too honest and open with your feelings."

"You know us too well," Carriog replied. There was a great deal of respect between the old man and the Nemedian warrior, and they had spent many evenings in the past together, playing chess or talking about the old days, and the Danaans, or the Old People, as Alfred called them.

Alfred had a special regard for the Nemedian, whose people, like the Danaans, had been scattered and overcome. There were he thought, many traits in the Nemedian character which more of his own people would have done well to emulate, and they were he knew, solid, quiet, above reproach and courageous without exception.

His thoughts were interrupted by the arrival of Blamad and Aemrig who had finished drilling their men for the day, and who had come to join them.

"How are the young men faring?" Alfred asked, greeting them.

Blamad smiled.

"They will be formidable fighters when the Druid comes. They have character, and they are eager and willing."

He was smiling as he spoke, pleased that Ceolmhar's men were good fighters who only needed a little battle experience to become the best, but Alfred was suddenly serious.

"Will we really be able to stop the Druid and his magic? Or are we wasting our time..?"

"It is true that there will be more suffering and death before there will be peace again, but it will come," Blamad replied quietly. "The prophecies will be fulfilled."

He remembered the words of the old man by the lake, when he had been taken from the ship. His sadness increased, and his eyes grew misty, but the others did not fully understand, not even Alfred.

"I am not afraid to die," Aemrig said quickly and firmly. "If I can destroy Formorians, then that is the death I would welcome."

He put his hands on Blamad's shoulders. Alfred smiled. It touched him deeply to see these two warriors showing such a tender side of their character. He knew that it was something he would not often see, and he was glad that he had seen it at all.

"You are a brave man, Aemrig. But you are wrong to believe that death is good even if it comes fighting against your enemies. Death is always the wrong choice. It is better to live, to give your strength and knowledge to your people, to help the young ones grow strong in mind as well as body. I abhor death, and I hate war, there is no glory in it for me. Perhaps it is because I am old, but I see things more clearly now, and I do not like what I see around me. Even an old man such as I finds life precious, perhaps more precious than you do. I do not look forward eagerly to death as you do."

They did not know what to say. Alfred's words, coming from another, would have offended them, but out of respect for him they remained silent, and because they believed as warriors in the glory of battle, where to die fighting was for them the ultimate honour. They said farewell to each other, and went to their separate quarters, each for different reasons sombre and subdued.

Two days later, Carriog, Godrane and Branvig left Ceolmhar's dún. They rode west, leaving the dún quickly behind, avoiding the roads and villages, all the while using the cover of the forest or the flat, empty, uninhabited plain, where few men wandered at that time of year.

It was snowing again, but when they stopped to camp for their first night they did not light a fire, for fear of drawing attention to themselves.

They set off at first light, and sometime during the morning, they saw smoke ahead. They rode onto higher ground, drawing their swords and axes, at the same time praying to the gods to be with them as they made their way more cautiously.

Down ahead on lower ground, they saw the burning village, from which many columns of smoke were rising into the air, but there was no sign of life.

"We shouldn't linger too long here," Carriog said grimly. "There's likely to be Formorians or Picts close by."

They stayed on the higher ground and rode on. For the rest of the day they did not stop, but kept moving, constantly alert, watching the horizon or the sky for smoke, or the telltale sign of birds taking to the air.

It began to snow more heavily during the afternoon, so they had to slow down until they were barely moving. The wind rose to a gale, swirling and driving the snow into the faces of the men and horses, and they knew that they would have to find shelter soon of some description or they would certainly die, exposed and in the open as they were.

They found a cave just before dark. They almost missed it in the storm, but Carriog's keen eyes spotted it even through the snow and the semi-darkness.

It was a small cave used by hunters and there was a pile of wood at the back, neatly stacked, and the remains of a fire on the floor which was black and charred within a circle of stones, around which the hunters must have huddled when they sheltered there.

Branvig lit the fire, and the sight of the flames cheered them. Godrane led the horses to the back of the cave, and put the feed bags to their mouths, while Carriog poured three cups of wine.

"There's enough wood here for days," Godrane said, when he rejoined them.

"Just as well there is," Carriog replied, pointing to the entrance, which was becoming blocked with snow. The wind howled as the storm grew more ferocious, bringing with it even more snow, but they were warm and comfortable, with wood enough to keep them warm for longer than they would need.

"We will be safe here for a day or so," Carriog said. "The way that storm is blowing, we won't be able to leave here for a while. Now, let's see what we have to eat."

He took the provision sack and laid it on the ground. There were dried meats, some cereals as well as two containers of water, but Carriog put these aside and lifted the wine skin. It was full. This meant that they had two, a thought which cheered him. They might be stuck here for a while, and the thought of being stranded without any wine made Carriog shudder. Having satisfied himself that they were well provisioned he put everything back into the sack, except for some of the dried meat which he gave to his companions.

With darkness the storm increased its fury, and the blizzard which fell during the night completely blocked the entrance to the cave and the paths leading to it. The whole countryside beyond was also covered by the same blanket of snow. Nothing moved, neither man nor animal, and there was, for the moment, peace throughout the whole island because the warring factions could not leave their dúns or winter camps.

Godrane played the harp, his music helping to while away the long, idle hours. The others rested by the fire, content and at peace, refreshing themselves for the journey ahead, safe and warm, and secure with their fire, their food, and above all, their wine.

On the third morning, the storm eased. It was still snowing but lighter than before and the wind was dead. Carriog and the others pushed the snow back from the cave mouth, and for the first time since the storm began, they emerged into the open. The air was crisp and fresh, but the ground was soft with snow which still continued to drift.

"We'll never get the horses through that," Godrane said. Carriog agreed.

"We may have to spend a few more days here." His face however, suddenly brightened.

"I have a fancy for fresh meat," he said, feeling the urge to stretch his legs, to feel the heat of the chase, the satisfaction of snaring his quarry.

"Branvig can remain here with the horses, and you can come with me," a suggestion to which Godrane readily agreed, being in the same mood of restlessness as Carriog.

They clambered over the snow, moving further up the hill, to a cluster of trees standing stark against the grey snow-filled winter sky. As they climbed, there was utter silence, the only sound in the stillness being their boots as they broke the snow beneath their feet.

"See if you can gather more wood, while I try to find something through here," Carriog said. "Don't go too far, because I won't be long. By the look of that sky, there will be more snow."

It fell only lightly now, but everything on the ground had already been covered by the storms of the past few days. Nevertheless, Godrane managed to find an armful of wood, which he brought back to the cave. He made four journeys in all, and when he returned with the last of what he had gathered, he helped Branvig carry it inside.

When they had finished, they both stood at the entrance savouring the clean fresh air which tasted good after their time in the confines of the cave, but they soon felt chill, and so they returned to the warmth and safety of the cavern.

Carriog did not return for a long time, but when he did, he was carrying two hares, one in each hand, a smile of complete satisfaction on his face.

"A feast for tonight," he said gaily. He threw the hares to the ground and knelt before the fire to warm his frozen hands while Godrane and Branvig took the animals and skinned them, then hung them over the fire.

When the meat was cooked some time later, Carriog cut one of the hares into pieces and divided it between himself and his two companions. He cut the other hare also, but this one he put into the provision sack to keep for the next day. They ate the freshly cooked meat greedily, savouring every mouthful, drinking cups of wine to wash it down. When they had eaten, they sat back against the wall of the cave resting, listening as Godrane played a slow, lazy tune on his harp, a gentle sleep-inducing tune which soon had its effect.

The sun was shining when they rose, and a shaft of light crept along the floor of the cave like an orange snake moving slowly towards them. The air was not so cold and some of the snow had melted away from the entrance.

"We might leave today," Carriog said looking out. As he watched, a large piece of snow fell from one of the branches of the trees up hill, while at his feet the snow had already turned to slush.

They ate a quick breakfast, fed their horses, then walked to the crest of the hill, to where Carriog and Godrane had gone the day before. They moved slowly because the snow was slippery and sometimes gave way under their touch, but they soon reached the crest. Down below, they could see bare snow-covered barren countryside, and far beyond that the mountains which led to the ocean, the same mountains which Carriog knew hid some of his own people, and where he hoped to find a man who knew the old Danaan magic, which might help them defeat the Grey Druid.

They moved slowly downhill again, trying hard to keep their own footing and that of their horses, aware that they were now coming into dangerous country, filled with wild lawless men, as well as Picts and Formorians who would undoubtedly be hunting for them, but until they reached firmer ground they did not dare to mount their horses or move any quicker than they did.

They were in open country now, with no protection, no cover to shield them from ambush or attack, and on the snow-covered landscape they made an easy target for any scout with keen eyes who might be watching.

Finally, they were on level ground and on Carriog's command, they mounted up and began to move with more pace.

As they rode across the bleak, desolate countryside, Carriog spoke to them.

"Over there is where the Crom Cruach used to be," he said, pointing to small hill which they had passed without comment.

"Such an evil god; the curse of my people, who served a long and bitter slavery to him. He demanded human sacrifice, and they gave it to him. He was a god who took all and gave nothing in return, only misery, like the Formorian gods who bring only tears and death, famine and desolation, darkness and despair. Samhain was a sorrowful time then for my people, a time of tears and sadness, a time of loss and sorrow, when men walked with fear in their hearts. An evil time."

"Your people are few now," Branvig said quietly. Carriog kept his eyes ahead.

"The Danaans were stronger than we were, they had the magic, but they, too, fell. We had no chance against such powerful magic as they possessed, and so they took what had been ours and made it theirs, until it was in turn taken away from them."

"Yet you were friendly with the Danaans, and they with you," Branvig said, puzzled by the obvious affection he had seen between the Danaans and Carriog, an affection which he thought strange between people who should, after what had happened, have been enemies.

Carriog laughed, not a bitter laugh, but the laughter of a man who remembered too well the past.

"What you say is true Branvig," he replied more seriously. "Yet fate is a strange thing, and the gods move men's hearts in ways which may seem strange to mortal men, but since they are not mortal, they do not do or think as we do. Anyway, the Danaans and my people share a common destiny now. We are both outcasts in our own land, conquered people who have had to give way to another, stronger people."

"Even when they ruled the island as we did, they treated us well and were generous to us, and they permitted us to live in peace, and without fear. Only the druids and magicians suffered, because the Danaans killed all of them, or those they could find, because they feared their power which might rival their own, and be used against them one day. Those who survived fled to the mountains, to the hidden places, and they carried with them their secrets so that their knowledge would not be lost. The Danaans knew that they had not killed every magician or druid, but when they were satisfied that we were no threat to their power, they left us in peace."

They continued on their way, and for the rest of the day, rode in silence, taking refreshment in the saddle, trying to put as many miles behind them as they could before the coming of darkness.

At dusk they stopped to rest for the night, but because they were out in the open, and easy to see for miles in any direction, they did not light a fire. They were fortunate that the wind had died because there was no shelter, no cover in case of storm, yet still it was bitterly cold, and they pulled their cloaks tight around their bodies, their cowls over their heads trying to keep warm.

In the morning they continued on their way, and in a few hours reached the mountains which led to the coast, and where the snow was heavier.

It was late morning, close to noon, when they saw smoke rise above the rocks ahead. They halted, but Carriog was smiling.

"Have no fear, my friends, we are close to one of my own people's villages. Approach slowly, and whatever happens don't draw your weapons. Our coming has already been noted..."

CHAPTER SEVENTEEN

As Carriog spoke, a group of armed men appeared from behind the rocks above them, another appeared to their right, yet another to their left. Finally, six horsemen rode up behind them, cutting off their retreat. They did not hurry, but followed Carriog's pace, each with his sword or axe held in his hand, ready in case of any sign of trouble from Carriog or his companions. They were not as tense as they might have been because they saw that neither Carriog nor his companions made any attempt to draw their weapons or to escape.

By keeping their quarry between them, the men surrounding Carriog and his companions were able to steer them in the direction they wished to take, though in fact Carriog knew quite well where he was going. Soon they came within sight of the dún, which like Ceolmhar's, was surrounded by a large stone wall. The gates were open however, and a large group of men watched their approach.

When they were several yards away from the waiting men, Carriog and his companions stopped their horses and dismounted.

"Follow me." Carriog said sharply. "But say and do nothing."

He began to approach the waiting men.

"By the gods, it's Carriog," one of the waiting men said. He was tall and dark, like Carriog, and they could almost have been mistaken for brothers. On his cloak was a gold brooch, and when he saw it, Carriog became hesitant, and bowed his head. The other man extended his arms and embraced him.

"Welcome back, old friend," he said warmly. "It's almost a lifetime since you were last with us, but you have changed little." He held Carriog at arm's length, and looked closely at him.

"You're a little heavier than I remember, but you are still the same Carriog."

"You too have grown a little, Eornan," Carriog replied smiling.

While this exchange was going on between Carriog and Eornan, Godrane and Branvig looked at each other in bewilderment. They could not understand what was being said between the others, but the sight of Carriog smiling was a strange and unusual thing for them to see.

"You are king now," Carriog said, his voice and manner deferential and full of respect.

"I have been king for three years now," Eornan said quietly. "Times are hard for us, my friend, and we are a forgotten people. Soon I think, we shall be only a memory as the great Danaans are now."

"That will never happen," Carriog said, his confident manner returning. "But I will talk more about these things later in private."

He turned and indicated his two friends to come forward.

"These are my friends, Godrane and Branvig, son of Ceolmhar, young men as you see, but brave for all that, wise too in their own way. They have come to help me in what I must do."

They bowed to Eornan, who acknowledged them, Carriog translating what he said.

"Eornan bids you welcome. He and I are friends since childhood, this is my home dún, though I have not been here for many years. Eornan, my friend, is also now our king."

They followed Eornan and the other Nemedians who crowded round Carriog, greeting him and plaguing him with many questions which he tried vainly to answer.

Eornan led them to his house. It was a large wooden structure with a straw roof set in the centre of the dún. There were several rooms, and they were taken to the largest,

Eornan's own chamber. It was a large dimly lit room, in the centre of which a large fire burned, the smoke rising through a hole in the roof to disperse in the air outside.

They sat on couches around the fire, while a slave filled their cups with mulled wine which they accepted gratefully.

The room was spartan, almost completely without decoration. Only Eornan's standards and weapons hung from the walls and, alone of all the men who followed them, Eornan himself was unarmed.

"You have news of importance for us Carriog, or you would not have made such a long journey at this time of year," Eornan said. As he spoke, Godrane and Branvig stared at him, fascinated by his manner of speaking, the first time they had heard the Nemedian language, and although they did not understand one word of what was being said, they were nevertheless interested spectators.

"I bring grave news," Carriog said. "The high king is dead, murdered at the Samhain feast on the Druid's orders. The Druid has made himself high king, and he has called the Formorians to help him. There is turmoil everywhere, there is death and fear and distrust. Brian's dún was destroyed by the Formorians, while he himself is now near death, blind and half mad. Only Ceolmhar remains against the might of the Druid and Vitrig. Only Ceolmhar, and you."

Eornan and the other Nemedians listened to Carriog's words with growing concern, and it seemed to them that the past was once more repeating itself. They remembered the stories of how Nemed himself had fought against the Formorians, how Escalon and his people had destroyed the Formorian king, only to be destroyed themselves, their people scattered and dispersed, fugitives in their own country, men without power or influence. They had these memories to remind them, and they had the more recent memories of the Formorian ships sailing up and down the coast. And in the plain below their mountain they had seen armies of men march by, and now that Carriog had come with his own grim news,

Eornan felt more strongly the sense of doom which had affected him lately.

"The Druid used a powerful magic to destroy the high king and his people," Carriog said. "An old Danaan magic, a cloud which took away men's courage and made them afraid. I heard it myself from Blamad, what this magic can do."

He paused for a moment. All eyes were on him, and no one tried to speak.

"Ceolmhar and the queen have asked me to come to you to ask your help."

"Our help? How can we help since we are few in number and would be of little use against so many Formorians?"

"There are those of our people who remember the old ways, the magic; the Danaans did not destroy all our knowledge. Ceolmhar is a brave man, and a good leader, but he fears for his people if the Druid should send his magic over his dún, a magic against which he has no defence. He needs brave warriors, and he needs a magic as powerful as the Druid's, if he is to save his own people, and those who do not wish to be slaves of the Formorians. I have come on Ceolmhar's behalf to ask for your help, and to find out if there are still men among our people who possess such knowledge..."

Eornan shook his head gravely. It was clear to see that he sympathised with Carriog but there were other things also on his mind, doubts and uncertainties, and these he spoke now to Carriog;

"I will help you however I can, but you know the way of our people, a way we have followed since we lost the mastery of this land to the Danaans. We do not leave our dúns, we do not interfere with the affairs of men beyond our own lands, and we keep to ourselves. We are afraid — yes, my friend — afraid to leave the safety of our own places, afraid to provoke reaction and retaliation, afraid of being submerged by those who are now masters of the island. We have become recluses, and no longer have any part or say in what men do."

"I cannot understand why this should be so," Carriog replied quickly. "After all I am accepted for what I am. Nobody objects that I am a Nemedian, no one said that I should not serve the high king, or stand by his side."

"You are a fortunate man, Carriog, that you have friends among people other than your own, but I wonder how it would be if too many of us started to appear in their dúns and villages? There would be alarm, and fear, and from fear my friend, comes hatred, and from hatred comes death. No, we are better served by staying where we are, and protecting ourselves and what is left of our people. But you may have something when you say that we should not isolate ourselves completely."

He turned to the other Nemedian who had entered the hall with them, the members of his council, who had sat listening to Carriog's words in silence, but with the same growing sense of alarm which Eornan had expressed. Eornan now addressed them.

"Our brother Carriog had come a long way with the news you have just heard. You have heard him speak of many strange and terrible things, of magic and strange manifestations, many of which we have seen and heard ourselves.

"We have for a long time now been an unimportant people, alone and isolated, forgotten but I fear that this may not be so for much longer. What have you to say about this?"

One of the elders spoke. He was old but there was anger and fire in his eyes when he stood up, his anger directed at Carriog, whom he regarded as a trouble-maker for bringing such news to their dún, to disturb and frighten their people.

"Why should we leave the safety and shelter of our own dún to go and help men we do not know, men who have never been our friends? Carriog speaks of the might of Ceolmhar's enemies, yet he expects us to march with him, to almost certain death. Is it not clear to all of you, that soon there will be a new master on this island, a new king? There will be new laws and, if we do not oppose the Druid, the Formorians will leave us alone and in peace. We will gain nothing by going to Ceolmhar's aid, only our own destruction."

He sat down to a roar of approval from the assembly, and it was quite clear that all the elders agreed with what he had said. Eornan rose to speak again.

"Your words have some truth in them," he said gently. "And no man here will deny their sincerity, but I fear that we will not be passed over in the coming war. The Formorians are our traditional enemies. Have you forgotten that it was the Formorians who once enslaved us, and took blood sacrifices and child hostages? How can you speak of living peacefully with such men when they have it in their hearts to destroy us? They are not the Danaans or the high king's people, both of whom left us in peace to live as we always did in our own ways.

"The Druid is not a merciful man, this we know, and there is not a man here who needs to be reminded of the ways of the Formorians, who once almost destroyed us all. I tell you all here and now, that even if we do not go to Ceolmhar's aid we will still have to fight, because the Formorians will come to us eventually."

"They will leave us be!" the elders shouted back, again to the approval of the assembly. Carriog now stood to speak, and there was immediate silence in the hall.

"Eornan has spoken the truth," he said quietly. He looked at the assembled warriors and was suddenly reminded of the feast in the high king's dún, when Blamad had told him of the high king's efforts to convince the chiefs of the dangers they faced, and then Díele's treachery. And now here he was, trying to convince his own people just the same way.

"You will do well to heed Eornan's words. When spring comes and the snows melt, an army will come here. It may be the Druid's Picts, it may be Vitrig and his Formorians, it may even by Ceolmhar and his army, but be sure of this; an army will come.

"You have seen the Formorian ships, you've seen their armies on the march, and when the time is right they will come and when they come it will not be to talk, you can take my word as a warrior for that. The time for talking is past. It is time now to prepare for war, because everywhere the Druid and the Formorians are gaining control. Everywhere their evil spreads, submerging everything in darkness and fear, the same darkness and fear which will follow you here."

The elder who had spoken before stood up once more, but this time he spoke quietly and with dignity.

"Perhaps what you say is true. Perhaps an army will pass this way when the snows melt, but even if such an unlikely thing was to happen we have the most natural defence anyone could hope for. The pass below, the narrow path where only a few men at a time can pass through. We can hold off a multitude there with only a few men. That is the only approach to the dún, and unless the Formorians plan to scale the cliffs or have discovered how to fly, then they will not come close to this dún." There was laughter at this, laughter which provoked Carriog's temper.

"You are a fool!" he shouted, forgetting himself, and to whom he spoke. Immediately there was uproar in the hall, and men drew their swords, shouting angrily and pointing them at Carriog and his two companions, who had remained quiet and in the background throughout.

Godrane and Branvig however, although they could not understand what was being said knew well enough from the attitudes and tone of voice of Carriog that something was wrong and, when they saw the assembled men before them drew their weapons, they too did likewise.

Eornan stood before Carriog, his face contorted with anger.

"Enough of this. How dare you draw your swords in my council hall, and in my presence..."

The warriors immediately put away their weapons and, at a signal from Carriog, Branvig and Godrane did the same.

Eornan turned to Carriog, still furious, his voice when he spoke, cold and hostile.

"You have abused our hospitality by your behaviour," he said. "There was no cause for you to speak as you did, since every man has a right to speak his mind, and no man may call him a fool for doing so."

Carriog bowed low. He knew that he had done wrong, and he was genuinely sorry. He was also aware that he had perhaps ruined any chance he might have had in persuading the Nemedians to help Ceolmhar.

"I am sorry," he said to the elder to whom he had spoken so sharply. "In the heat of the moment I forgot myself. I spoke angrily only because I know what is to come, and I do not wish to see my own people destroyed. If I offended you with my words, then I am truly sorry."

The elder accepted Carriog's apology at once.

"I understand your motives. Even if I do not agree with what you say."

Eornan was pleased once more, and smiled.

"Good, that's settled. We should not quarrel with each other, but enough for now. We will talk of this later when Carriog and his friends have rested and refreshed themselves..."

The meeting was thus brought to an end. Eornan took Carriog aside when they left the hall. His face was grave as he spoke, and there was concern in his eyes both for Carriog, and for his people.

"You must moderate your words and actions, otherwise you will not make friends. The elders sympathise with you, but you must understand, that it will take them time to get used to the idea of leaving this dún, and going to fight for a people they find strange. Let them think about it for a while, otherwise you will get no help from us at all."

Carriog was chastened by Eornan's words, and realized that he had acted too impatiently, like a young and untried warrior.

"You are right, Eornan. But there is so little time, with so much to do. We are fighting for our very existence whether we know it or not, and if the Druid sends his evil cloud over this dún then we shall all be dead, and that will be the end of it."

Eornan smiled. Although he and Carriog were the same age, and had been boyhood friends, kingship had made Eornan a wiser man.

"There is much to be done Carriog, but it will be done, and done in time. Now to take some of the sorrow from your shoulders, I have some news which will cheer you. There is a man who knows the old ways, a magician who came to us many years ago from one of our other dúns. His name is Fenan, but we call him Old Fenan because he must be almost a hundred years old. He lives in a remote place a few miles south of here, and avoids other people as much as he can. He will know the men I shall send to him, and will listen to them. Whether he chooses to come back with them or not is up to him. He cannot be forced to come if he does not wish to, but he is a man who knows many secrets, a very wise man indeed."

Carriog smiled. He felt some of the despair which afflicted him go away, and he began to think that at last there might be hope, a way to defeat the Grey Druid and his magic.

Eornan left him and returned to the council hall.

"Do you think that this Old Fenan will come?" Branvig asked, when Carriog had told them everything. Carriog shrugged his shoulders.

"I really don't know. He's a stubborn old man by all accounts, and he likes his solitude, but perhaps Eornan's words will have some effect on him, though I really don't know. Let us go for now, and rest awhile. I feel very tired all of a sudden."

Deirbhne lay in the darkness, her eyes wet from weeping. She stifled her sobs in case the sleeping Vitrig woke. It was the same every night, and she had not grown used to his touch. Even the very presence of the barbarian repelled her, and her spirit recoiled at the thought of him. Hope was the only thing which kept her alive, hope that someday, somehow, she would find the opportunity for revenge on Vitrig for what he had done to Brian, and for her own humiliation.

She thought about Brian. In her mind he was well and alive, though she knew that this could not be so. Vitrig stirred beside her but did not waken. Deirbhne looked at him fearfully, but his eyes remained closed. She looked for the dagger, but as usual he had hidden it. He still did not trust her, and since he had taken her he had been careful not to leave any weapons lying around for her to find.

Every night after they had eaten in the communal hall which Vitrig's men had constructed in what remained of Brian's old dún, he had brought her back to his own quarters. Whatever rude comforts there were in the Formorian camp, Vitrig had them, and whatever he had he shared with Deirbhne, whose continuous stubbornness and sullenness puzzled him.

From the first days when he had merely lusted after her body, he had found to his astonishment that he had become attached to her, and found himself wanting to be in her company. He tried in many small ways to be kind to her and show her a more tender side to his nature, but she remained cold, aloof and impossible, responding always with indifference to his lovemaking.

He always ended the night cursing her, swearing that he would teach her to show more respect, but always he would try during the following day to win her again. So it had been this night, and as she did every night, Deirbhne once again searched for the dagger. She could not find it so after some time, she lay beside Vitrig and stared at the ceiling. She would wait. Someday the moment would come, but until then she would wait.

Díele was a contented man, happy with his future. Not for many years had such an opportunity for riches presented itself to him, not since the old days, when each chief raided his neighbours, before the high king had stopped them.

Since the high king's death, Díele had increased the size of his lands. The Druid had given him some of the king's lands, but he had also taken Aemrig's lands for himself so that now, only the Druid was stronger than he was, only the Druid had the power to stand against him, but since he served the Druid, he was content. He was impatient, however, for winter to be over so that he could join the Druid in the march against Ceolmhar's dún, where he anticipated a further increase in his wealth and power.

Díele's only worry was the Formorians. He did not trust them, nor did he like them, and he had warned the Druid about them, but the Druid only smiled and told him not to be concerned. Sometimes Díele did not understand the Druid, but he was too clever and wily to turn away from, or disagree with the man who had given him so much wealth and power, and he had to admit that he was afraid of the Druid, who was a strange and terrifying man. There was an air of menace about him, a feeling of power which made even men like Díele afraid.

The Druid rested and kept very much to himself. Since Blamad's second escape, the Druid's mood had varied between anger and depression, and even the news that Vitrig had taken Brian's dún had not lifted his black mood, because he learned also that Aemrig and his people had escaped and gone to Ceolmhar.

He spent days reading through old manuscripts, leaving Garweng to run the dún for him. The Picts would not obey any order given to them by Garweng, who had to speak to

Dubhghall before they would do as he asked. Dubhghall had smiled, but commanded his men to do as Garweng asked, or suffer his anger.

It was a time of waiting, a time of rest and preparation, a time when men reflected on the year just past, and the war to follow, the dark time when spirits wandered abroad, when men lay huddled within their cabins and by their fires. The quiet peace before the storm of war, before the Storm God released misery and devastation once more in answer to the Druid's command.

CHAPTER EIGHTEEN

The winter finally set in hard. Heavy snowfalls left the whole island covered in a deep blanket of white, closing every road and pass, filling valleys and cutting off the mountain dúns.

Eornan's dún like many others, was cut off, and the men he had sent to talk to Old Fenan, the magician, had not returned. Eornan's fear was that they had been caught in the open by storms, and if such a thing had happened, he feared for the old man's life. Carriog and his two friends were glad to be able to rest at last. For Branvig and Godrane it was a strange and exciting time, as they began to understand the ways of the Nemedians and to respect them. Although they could not speak the language, they found they were still able to make themselves understood, and to understand much of what was said to them. They absorbed everything, watched everything in the dún, especially in the evenings in the great hall when the Nemedian bards told tales in their lyrical tongue. The Nemedian music was gay, yet somehow sad, like the Danaan music they had heard in the forest. Sometimes Godrane played his harp and sang the songs of his own people and he especially, of the three friends, found peace of mind and contentment in the Nemedian dún.

Carriog spent his days brooding. He saw little of Eornan during the day, but every night they spoke together, mostly about what would happen when spring came. Every evening Carriog spoke to the elders about the coming war, though he had learned to moderate his manner and to speak calmly and without urgency, something he hardly felt within himself, being impatient and anxious to continue his journey.

The elders listened to him with polite disinterest, and they wished that Eornan would turn Carriog away from his purpose, but Eornan, who agreed with Carriog, allowed him to speak each evening, in the hope that he would change the minds of the elders.

Branvig and Godrane spent their evenings drinking in the great hall with the other warriors, their nights with the Nemedian women. Godrane, whose reputation among his own people for his love of women was well known and smiled at, found through his music and his own easy manner, that the Nemedian women needed little encouragement to share his bed.

Carriog alone of the three men, spent his nights in solitude. Brooding about the Druid, and the Power he threatened to unleash when spring came, there was little he or any one else could do while it still snowed, and while the roads and passes were blocked.

Three weeks went by, each day following the one before without change, until at last the storm abated and the snow stopped falling. The sun broke through the cloud, low and weak in the sky, but they were all cheered by the sight of it.

Over the next few days, the snowed thawed a little, and Eornan was at last able to send out patrols and hunting parties to the nearby woods to search for fresh food and game.

The thaw also decided Carriog, that he could hardly bear to endure the confinement of the dún much longer, and so he went to his friend Eornan.

"I must go and find Fenan myself. I must go. If I stay here any longer, wondering what is happening in the world outside I shall go mad."

"I cannot permit you to go," Eornan said, aghast at the idea that Carriog should go out into the wilderness at such a time. "This thaw will not last, it's only a temporary respite. You will die if you are caught out in the wilderness. My men have not returned, so how do you think that you could reach Old Fenan, since if it was possible to return with the old man they would have done so already?"

Carriog was unmoved by Eornan's words.

"I must go. I must try to find Fenan. I am useless here, wasting time, a parasite. I must go. I will leave the others here, then if I fail, they can follow my trail when the time is right, but I must go. I must..."

Eornan saw that he would not be able to persuade Carriog away from his course, and he knew that his friend would in all probability go on his own, perhaps at night when they slept or at some other quiet time, but go he would. With these thoughts in mind, Eornan gave his reluctant blessing.

"If at any time there is danger, then you must come back here at once. Ceolmhar would not appreciate your death. Nor would I."

Carriog took Eornan's arm. There was genuine affection between the two men, a deep bond of friendship which had been nurtured through a shared childhood and survived many years of separation.

"Thank you," Carriog said warmly. "I will be careful."

"I'm a fool for letting you go," Eornan replied. "But you'd better go now, and tell your friends."

Carriog went to find Godrane and Branvig.

"But we must go with you," Branvig insisted, when Carriog told them what he was about to do.

"Eornan is right. You cannot go out into the wilderness alone. What if something happens to you, what if you are attacked or injured, lying alone without any hope of rescue? You cannot think of leaving us here."

"You will stay," Carriog insisted firmly. "I will do this alone. Old Fenan will certainly not talk to three strangers, but he might listen to me since we are of the same race. If I fail, then you will still be able to try, but for the moment you will remain here."

"I do not agree with this," Godrane said quickly. "We were sent by Ceolmhar to find someone together, yet now you tell us that we are to stay here, but I say that we will go with you."

"You will stay," Carriog said with such a tone of menace that they knew he meant it. Carriog walked away, leaving the two young men staring after him.

"What do we do?" Godrane asked. "We cannot leave him to go alone."

"We will go and talk with Eornan," Branvig said. "He will know what to do."

They went to find Eornan. Somehow by signs and other means he told them that Carriog would indeed travel alone, that they would not be permitted to leave the dún until he returned.

Next morning Carriog set off on his journey. Eornan had given him precise instructions as to where Old Fenan lived, and he tried once more to dissuade Carriog from his journey. Carriog, however, was determined to go.

"Then the gods go with you," were Eornan's last words to him. Carriog rode out of the dún and immediately headed south, towards the hills where Old Fenan lived.

It was a clear sunny day, cold still, yet it might have been mistaken for spring if not for the snow on the ground. There was no sign of animal life, and Carriog had the countryside to himself as he rode quickly away.

He rode until dusk, when he found a hollow at the foot of a hill. He was sheltered well enough from the bitingly cold wind which rose in the darkness, and before he lay down to sleep he gathered some boughs and put them on the ground, covering them with the spare cloak which Eornan had given him. When he had done this, he lit a fire and fed the horse, then sat down and pulled his cloak about his body. He took some dried meat and drank from his wine skin, resting against one of the rocks, feeling a growing contentment now that he had escaped from the confines of the dún.

He was not a man who could settle easily into routine life, and it was this restlessness which had made him leave the dún many years before, and go into the high king's service.

He had served two high kings, the one lately killed by Díele, and his predecessor, who had been a noted warrior. A warrior's court he had kept and while Carriog had served each of these kings without favour, it was to the old warrior king's court that his mind kept on returning.

He had seen changes since that time. The Formorians came every year, and the high king fought them every year. Blamad had grown and come into the high king's service under the watchful eyes of Carriog, who had consoled him when the Formorians had killed his father during one of their raids.

Blamad had held his father's head in his arms as he lay dying, and it was Carriog who had suppressed the young man's fury and grief. They had become friends, slowly at first, but with the passing of time they had become closer than brothers and they had remained so over the passing of many years, and through a score of battles and raids.

Carriog sighed. He was free once again, free from the dún, out in the saddle, out in the open countryside he loved so much. There was deep satisfaction in such a thought for the Nemedian as he fell into a contented sleep.

It was late when he woke. He cursed his own laziness as he jumped up, brushing the snow from his clothes. The fire had long since gone out, and his horse looked at him curiously. He laughed.

"I am sorry, my friend," he said addressing the animal. "I'll feed you right away."

He stroked the horse's mane as he put the feed sack over its neck. The horse ignored him and began to eat. Somehow, this simple act of normality made Carriog feel lighter, and he began to sing as he took some of the dried meat out to eat. It was a cool, calm morning the bright winter sun lying low in the sky as the sat on a rock, chewing.

"There'll be an early spring..." he said absently, looking at the sky. When he had finished eating, he took the feed bag from the horse's mouth, and mounted up. The countryside through which he now moved was barren, rocky and treacherous underfoot for horse and man alike. Tufts of heather forced their way between the rocks, vivid purple, more so against the grey stone and snow. They were moving steadily uphill, but there was no sign of life still, except when some gulls passed overhead.

In the afternoon Carriog reached the place where Old Fenan lived. A steep hill, seemingly without any way through, but Eornan's instructions had been precise. Carriog dismounted and went to look for the path he knew was close, a narrow path between the rocks, partially covered by dense bushes, which seemed to be growing everywhere. When he found the path, Carriog drew his sword and led the horse through the gap.

After some time walking he saw a cave, so he tied the horse to one of the bushes and advanced cautiously. The snow had cleared from around the entrance, but there was no sign of life, no sound, and this unnatural quiet unsettled Carriog, who remained where he was, hidden and alert, waiting for some time to be sure that there was no danger.

When he was satisfied that it was safe to approach the cave, he raised himself from his hiding place and walked, sword in hand, towards the entrance.

The five bodies were dead some time and the stench was overpowering. Several rats ran further into the darkness as Carriog lit a torch. When he saw the bodies, he retched and ran outside, dropping the torch as he did so. He leaned against a rock and inhaled deeply. He knew that he would have to go inside once again, so he inhaled deeply once more, and drew his cloak over his face.

He found the torch he had dropped and relit it. Everything had been destroyed, everything tossed and scattered about. He saw Old Fenan's body, the gaping chest wound alive with maggots, the rats which with growing boldness, even in Carriog's presence, feasted and gorged themselves. Tears welled in his eyes as he saw what had been done to the old man and his companions, and to his hope of finding someone to oppose the Druid. He cried bitterly.

"Why," he called over and over and over again. "Why now, when I was so close?" He felt total despair fall over him, as he slumped to the ground, hugging the wall of the cave, ignoring the rats which scurried at his feet, some of them sniffing him as a potential meal. He did not know how long he remained like that, but finally decided that he would be safer away from the cave. Before he left, he searched through the confusion for Fenan's manuscripts which, as he expected, were gone. He swore silently, then he left, leaving Old Fenan and the others to the rats and the maggots. He went back to where he had left his horse, remounted and rode quickly away from the hill, down over the rough, slippery wasteland until he came to a river. He was unmindful of the danger of driving his horse so hard over ground which was as dangerous and uncertain as this was, but fortunately they reached the river safely.

It was almost dark now as Carriog dismounted and sat by a small tree which grew close to the water's edge. He was exhausted and utterly without hope. He did not eat, but drained the wine skin so that he fell into a deep sleep.

It was a sleep filled with dreams, a restless sleep in which it seemed that the future passed before his eyes as he lay against the tree, spent and exhausted.

In his dream, the river by which he lay was turned to blood, and he heard many voices crying in the distance, voices pleading and soulful. Many horsemen appeared on the horizon, coming closer all the time, and behind these, Carriog saw the evil cloud rise up from the ground and begin to swirl and turn in the air above. Then the cloud too began to move closer, the voices crying louder and calling for mercy. The whole sky seemed to be filled with the foulest desolation as out of the cloud came a terrifying group of animals and monsters, which spread themselves over the whole countryside, devouring and destroying everything in their path.

Dwarves, horrible deformed and grotesque, leapt out at him, waving battle axes, swinging them wildly, screaming as they did so. They were followed by foul beasts whose very touch corrupted everything, blood dripping from their mouths, the stench from their bodies utterly foul and evil.

Carriog was terrified, and he felt the utter helplessness of one who is powerless to stop a calamity. He began to feel that they were all doomed, that the Druid would surely overcome them all with powerful magic, such as was being shown to him in his dream. He cried out for mercy. They were beyond hope, beyond saving, the evil was too powerful.

He tried to rise, but the beasts and animals and dwarves kept coming at him, screaming and passing over him, around him and through him in a crescendo of rising terror, taunting him, probing him, terrifying him.

There was no escape from them, and the more he tried to rise the closer they came, until it seemed that he would go insane with fear.

Suddenly he was calm, and the darkness lifted. A voice spoke to him, a gentle voice which soothed his fears as he tried to listen to it, and as he did so the cloud grew smaller and smaller, the horrible images retreated and disappeared.

He saw green fields once more, heard the voices of men as they planted crops in the barren ground, saw groups of warriors as they came into view over the hill, their voices clear and open, even from where he sat. Each one was mounted on a white horse, while behind them, the sun rose in an orange glow and spread itself where the white horses trod, the light of life following in their path.

The dwarves and other creatures fell back before the warriors, who continued to march forward until the evil ones were driven to the edge of the sea and the darkness also. Still the warriors came, and the cries of their enemies were drowned as they disappeared beneath the waves, and the warriors roared their victory.

The voice in his dream gently reminded him of the Danaan king's message, telling him softly not to lose hope, or to fall into despair. The big Nemedian began to find his courage once again, and he woke calm and relieved. Around him all was peaceful, but he knew for certain that what he had seen had not been a dream, that a little of the future had been shown to him, to give him courage.

He was reassured and he remounted his horse, which had remained quietly where he had left it the night before.

The terrible nightmare was gone. The cold and the coming war no longer bothered him as he rode back towards Eornan's dún at peace with himself, content in the knowledge that whatever happened to him personally, the evil would, in the end, be overcome. With that thought in mind, he began to sing.

CHAPTER NINETEEN

Vitrig the Formorian slept peacefully, sated once again after another night of lovemaking with Deirbhne. He never tired of his moments with her, in spite of her passiveness and sullen silence, and now he slept soundly, unaware that Deirbhne was wide awake and alert.

There was a fire in her eyes as she lay there waiting, a look of triumph as she clutched the dagger in her hand, out of sight under the covers.

When she was certain he was asleep, Deirbhne took the dagger and with a firm rapid movement, she slit Vitrig's throat. He woke quickly, horror in his eyes as the dagger jabbed the sight from them, and he was still alive when he felt the pain between his legs as she castrated him, but his mute screams of agony were unheard by all except himself.

Deirbhne did not speak as she watched him die. She lifted the dagger and stabbed his chest repeatedly, to be certain that he no longer lived. Her hands were covered with blood which ran down the handle of the dagger, but she didn't care as she spent her anger and fury on the now lifeless body.

She wiped the blade on the bed clothes, rose from the bed naked, wiped the blood from her hands and arms before dressing herself, as she considered the next move. She knew that she would have to get out of the dún as soon as possible, before dawn certainly, when Vitrig's guards came to call him, as they always did. If she was still in the dún when that happened, she would be killed without mercy.

She finished dressing, putting the dagger in her belt. She did not know how it had come to be among her clothes, perhaps Vitrig had overlooked it, but she was grateful that it had been there. She had taken her revenge on the barbarian for what he had done, and she still felt the elation she had first felt when she had slit his throat.

Her surroundings did not interest her. Her one thought was flight. She found her cloak and put it round her shoulders then went to the door. She opened it. There was no sign of any guard outside, but she knew that they were within earshot. Quickly she went out, closed the door quietly and for a few moments remained still, watching and waiting before she crossed the clearing to the shadow of one of the buildings close to the wall. A dog barked somewhere, so she stood hard against the wood, rigid and quiet, but there was no sign of alarm. The walls of the dún, burned by the Formorians, had only been rebuilt in a crude fashion, with rough stakes loosely hammered into the ground, a wall not built to stand a siege, but simply to keep out wild animals.

Deirbhne felt her way along the wall in the darkness, until she came to a place which was wide enough for her to squeeze through. Once outside, she eased herself down the embarkment, up the other side, then ran as fast as she could to get away from the dún.

For most of the night she ran, ignoring the animal sounds she heard, her terror of the Formorians' revenge greater than her fear of any wild creatures. She was cold and tired, damp and hungry, but she pressed on, knowing that the Formorians would soon come looking for her.

She had to rest however, since her feet would carry her no further, and at first light on a cold, damp morning, frosty and still, a strange quiet hung over the forest which she had entered some hours before.

Everything was strange and beautiful, the sense of freedom she felt, intense. She sat against a tree and took a deep breath of the cold morning air, savouring every second of it. She was so at peace in those few moments that she felt if the Formorians had captured her then it would have been worth it, so good did she feel, with the added knowledge that she had killed their most powerful leader.

She started to run once again, and for the rest of the day she continued on her way, stumbling through the forest, sometimes losing her footing, but never daring to stop.

The forest was quiet and peaceful and she heard none of the sounds which had disturbed her during the night. Along the way she found some mushrooms in a dark place. She picked, and ate them.

When evening came, she found a place to hide among the dense bracken. Wrapping her cloak around her body, she lay on the hard ground, covering herself with the boughs she had gathered, which concealed her from all but the most vigilant and observant eye, as she fell into an exhausted sleep.

Deirbhne was woken by the sounds of voices. She raised her head carefully, afraid to disturb her cover, afraid to make a sound and reveal her hiding place. There were six men, and they were coming in her direction. From their voices she knew they were Formorians, but in the dim light she could not see their faces.

She lay down on the ground, feeling terror rise within her, as the men neared her hiding place. She knew that if they were seriously looking for her they would find her in spite of her efforts at concealment, but the six Formorians had long since given up any hope of that, and in their hearts they believed her to be already dead, eaten by the wolves which were numerous in the forest. Their search consequently was casual, and they were only continuing their journey because they feared to go back to tell Gomrik that they could not find the woman.

They came closer and Deirbhne held herself hard against the ground but, to her utter relief, they passed within inches of where she lay without spotting her. After a few minutes, the sound of voices died and the forest was still once more. She remained there for more than an hour, but finally pushed the cover aside, dragged herself to her feet, wiped all traces of the forest from her clothes, and began to run once again, this time in a different direction. She knew, however, that there would be more Formorians in the forest, so she moved now with extra caution.

Carriog returned to Eornan's dún. The news he brought back made the king very angry, and more determined to help his friend.

"When the time comes, we will give whatever help we can," he said bitterly. "Be sure of that. Old Fenan deserved to die quietly in his old age."

"The Druid must have known about him," Carriog said. "None of his manuscripts were there. Whoever killed him took everything."

"We will find a way to destroy the Druid, have no fear." Eornan spoke however without much conviction, and Carriog was not fooled by his friend's pretence, but he smiled just the same.

"Your friends wanted to follow you, so I had to lock them up for a while until they saw sense. I'm afraid that they are very angry with both of us." Carriog laughed. He saw that Branvig and Godrane were acting out of loyalty to the high king by their actions, and he was glad.

"I will speak to them. They are good warriors, headstrong and impatient it is true, but good men just the same. They will understand that I had to do it alone, but we must go back to tell Ceolmhar what has happened."

Eornan nodded. There was no reason for Carriog to remain in the dún now and by going, he would give him the opportunity to talk to his people without the reproachful glance of Carriog to annoy or anger them.

"I will convince the council that they must help you, but for now, see your friends and make your peace," he said quietly.

Godrane and Branvig were incensed when they saw Carriog. Branvig stood before him, his face almost touching Carriog's, for once his fear of the Nemedian gone.

"We were kept prisoner here while you were away, held against our will. My father will hear of this."

Carriog, who understood the young man's outrage, tried to mollify his anger.

"It was better that you remained here, while I looked for Old Fenan," he replied without anger or impatience. "There was no point in three of us being killed on a mission where only one man was needed. I meant no offence or insult by my action."

Carriog explained all that had happened, and some of the anger went from their faces, but nevertheless enough of it remained for Branvig to hold to his promise to tell Ceolmhar.

"We should not have been kept here, no matter what your reasons. We should never have been held against our wishes."

"I am sorry," Carriog said to both of them. He left them alone and it was only when he had gone, that they realized that it was the first time that he had ever apologised to them.

The following morning they said goodbye to the Nemedians. Eornan spoke to the two young men before they departed.

"Don't be harsh with your friend," he said to them in their own tongue, the first indication they had that he understood their language. "He believed he was doing the right thing, and he did not wish you to come to any harm. When the time comes, we will join you in your fight. I am sure of it. For the moment the gods go with you, and keep you safe on your journey."

Somehow Branvig doubted that Eornan could convince his people to help Ceolmhar, but he wished him well nonetheless. They left Eornan's dún, and were escorted down to the lower country by a party of his men, who left them at the base of the hill and returned once more to the safety of their dún.

Carriog and the others rode hard for the rest of the morning, leaving the hills far behind, and coming once more to the forest. Only then did they relax, only then did Carriog speak to them.

"I am sorry once more, that I left you in Eornan's dún," he said. "But, as I said before, it was better that I went alone, because the Formorians were always close."

"I still say that you were wrong to treat us in such a manner," Branvig replied sharply. "We too are warriors, who deserve a warrior's respect. You have not shown us that respect, so I tell you that if we are to remain together, if we are to be friends, then you must never do such a thing to us again. Do you understand?"

He spoke with such authority and command that Carriog was surprised. He had never before heard the young warrior speak that way, and he was impressed.

"You are indeed a king's son," he said, smiling. "I will try to remember that I do not know everything."

This broke the tension, and the three of them smiled. They shook hands to show that they were friends once more.

"I will consult you in everything from now on," Carriog promised. "I was wrong to have acted as I did, and I am sorry."

The rest of the day passed quietly enough, and when evening came and brought with it a frosty darkness, they made camp in the forest.

They ate the fresh meat the Nemedians had given them, and drank the overpowering mead they were so fond of, which livened their veins and made their blood flow more quickly, after which they slept soundly. Next morning, they rose and continued on their journey.

Deirbhne was exhausted. For days she had been running and, apart from the mushrooms, had not eaten anything. She was thirsty also, in spite of the snow which she put to her mouth, and her lips were cracked from the cold.

She longed for a mug of warm mead and a bed, and the longer she continued the more her spirits fell. She had almost given up hope of ever finding Ceolmhar's dún, and her initial elation at having killed Vitrig and having escaped from the Formorians had given way to a deepening despair. Still she kept going, in spite of a growing sense of futility, and since she had lost her sense of direction she might have been going back towards the Formorians for all she knew.

As darkness fell she stopped to rest. She slumped down against a tree, her head resting against the bark, and began to drift off to sleep. She had not been there for long, when she was woken suddenly by a hand which clamped itself firmly over her mouth. Terrified, she could not scream, but a voice spoke to her out of the darkness.

"Do not say anything when I take my hand away. Do not scream," it said gently, yet with command, and in her own tongue. She nodded, and the hand slowly left her mouth. She turned to see Carriog standing before her but, strangely, her fear was gone.

"Who are you?" she asked. He looked hard at her for a few moments.

"It is I who should ask you that question," he replied.

"My name is Deirbhne," she said, but before she could continue, the others came out of their hiding places.

"There is no one else," Branvig said. He recognised Deirbhne.

"By the gods, I'm glad to see you." He embraced her and held her close, much to the amusement of Godrane and Carriog.

"I though that you might have been captured by the Formorians."

"I was," she said quietly, remembering what had happened, anger in her eyes. "I escaped after I killed their leader," she added almost as an afterthought, but her words hit Carriog like a thunderbolt.

"You killed Vitrig?" he asked, unable to believe it. She looked at him, a question in her eyes.

"My name is Carriog," he said quietly. "I served the high king."

"I have heard of you," she replied.

"That is Godrane, my friend," he added, pointing to Godrane, who remained in the background.

She nodded quietly in his direction, then turned back to Carriog.

"Yes, I killed Vitrig. He tore Brian's eyes out and made me his mistress, and I swore that I would pay him back for that, and I have. He knew what it was like to be sightless and without his manhood before he died..."

She cried suddenly, pulling away from Branvig who held his arms out for her.

"We knew of Brian's misfortune," he said to her gently. "We found him in the forest, near to death, but I'm afraid that his mind was gone, and he was no longer the Brian you knew."

"Is he still alive?" she asked, scarcely able to believe it. She held Branvig's arm tightly.

"He was alive when we last saw him some weeks ago. He was weak and close to death because of what had happened to him, but he was still alive."

"Brian alive..." she said quietly, smiling. Branvig looked at the others, then he put his arm around Deirbhne's shoulders, and led her away to where they had made their own campsite.

"I expect you're hungry," he said, and she nodded.

"I've only eaten some mushrooms in the past few days."

When they reached their own camp, Branvig filled a cup with mead, and gave it to Deirbhne who took it eagerly.

"I'd almost forgotten what this tasted like." He filled her cup again, while Carriog took some of the bread and meat they had, and gave these to her to eat.

"The Formorians are in the forest," she said. "They passed me yesterday, but missed me because I hid in the undergrowth."

Branvig told her of their adventures. His news about the high king's death came as a shock to her, and she asked about Morna. Her own husband maimed and deprived of his senses, the high king dead, but the full implication of what she had heard did not penetrate her mind. She only knew that she was glad to be alive, glad to have the three warriors to guard her, and keep her safe from whatever harm lay ahead before they reached Ceolmhar's dún.

"How many Formorians did you see?" Carriog asked. She looked at him again. There was something strange about him, a power she felt, even though he spoke quietly and with perfect friendliness.

"I saw only six. But I am sure that there were many more."

The Nemedian disturbed her for some reason, and she realized suddenly that she was afraid of him, of his strange eyes which seemed to be able to read her thoughts.

"Why do you think there were more?" he asked again.

"They would hardly send only six men to find me," she said haughtily, unable to control her impatience. Carriog smiled.

"No, they would not, you are right. You must rest now. Tomorrow we shall reach Ceolmhar's dún, and the night is already well advanced."

Carriog's voice carried the same tone of command he had used before with Godrane, a tone which while gentle, nevertheless accepted no argument.

They lay down to rest, Branvig taking the first watch. The rest of the night passed quietly, and morning found them rested and refreshed. Deirbhne felt much better after her first peaceful sleep for many days, and was eager to set off at once for Ceolmhar's dún, but Carriog insisted that they eat a leisurely breakfast and feed the horses before they set off.

Branvig gave Deirbhne his horse, while he jumped up behind Godrane. Carriog led the way as they set off for Ceolmhar's dún and safety.

They soon reached Ceolmhar's lands, and once again, Ceolmhar's scouts brought news of their coming to him. Ceolmhar sent a group of his men down the mountain to escort Carriog and the others back to the dún.

Deirbhne was taken to the women's quarters, while Carriog and his two companions went to see Ceolmhar, to report on their journey.

Alfred was with Ceolmhar, and when they had greeted them, Carriog told them what had happened from the time they had set out until they had found Deirbhne in the forest. When he finished speaking Carriog bowed slightly to indicate that he had no more to say.

"You bring us terrible news, terrible news indeed," Ceolmhar said grimly. "Though I am happy that Deirbhne has been saved. Nevertheless, with the old man dead, where are we to find another who knows the Danaan magic?"

He turned to Alfred, the queen's trusted friend and adviser.

"Deirbhne has killed Vitrig, which is a blessing, but this Gomrik who rules the Formorians, what is he like, do you know?"

Alfred nodded.

"Yes Lord, I know him. In many ways he is more cruel than ever Vitrig was, if that is possible, but what he has in viciousness he lacks in flair and vision, and so may be an easier adversary to overcome. Yet I would not underestimate him."

Ceolmhar nodded. Soon there would be war and, with luck, and with the help of the gods Vitrig's death would have unsettled and disturbed the Formorians.

Deirbhne, meanwhile, sat with Morna, and the two women talked of what had happened to them and their people. Morna spoke of the high king and about the Druid's terrible magic, about Brian and how he had been brought to the dún. At the mention of Brian's name, Deirbhne began to cry.

"When did he die?" she asked softly. Morna rested her hands on Deirbhne's lap. "Soon after he was brought here, when Carriog and Branvig went to find the Nemedian magician. He was weak and out of his mind. It was a miracle that he lived as long as he did."

"I was fortunate to meet Carriog and Branvig," Deirbhne answered absently.

"You both were, Brian and you," Morna replied. "Your three companions are blessed by the gods."

Deirbhne was gazing into the fire, her thoughts far away, in another time.

"So much has happened," she said quietly.

"They gave Brian a hero's funeral," Morna said after a short silence. "Ceolmhar himself gave his own sword for Brian to take with him to the Otherworld. We will visit the grave whenever you wish."

Deirbhne did not reply, and she appeared not to have heard Morna, but continued staring into the fire.

"You know that I killed Vitrig?" Deirbhne looked suddenly at Morna, a strange look which somehow made her seem fragile and vulnerable.

"Yes, I know you did," Morna replied, unable to hold back her own tears.

"When I did it I felt good, after all the things he had done to me and Brian, but now I feel cheated. It's as if I have become as savage and monstrous as he was. I cannot shake the thought from my mind. It has begun to disturb me."

She looked into the fire, her thoughts far away once more.

"That's not true," Morna said quickly. "You could never be as evil as he was. If we are to destroy the Formorians and the Druid, there are things which we shall have to do which we will not like, but they will have to be done. You should speak to Blamad. Ask him what happens to a man who falls under the spell of the Druid's magic. See then if you are as savage as Vitrig was."

Morna's voice when she spoke about Blamad, was surprisingly harsh, and Deirbhne looked at her questioningly.

"You do not like Blamad anymore?"

Morna's feelings about Blamad were still confused, and she avoided his company and did not usually mention his name.

"It's a long story. I will tell you another time."

"Where is the woman!" Gomrik screamed. Vitrig's body lay grotesquely on the bed, his blood staining the furs and the floor. He had almost fainted at the sight of Vitrig's severed manhood, and the mutilation of the rest of his body, but with difficulty he controlled himself.

The woman had certainly gone to work on Vitrig he thought, and he wondered how she had caught him off guard.

"We have searched everywhere throughout the dún, but the woman is gone," the guard said tremulously. He was afraid of Gomrik, afraid that he would take his anger out on him, though it wasn't his fault that the woman had escaped, but such a distinction would not matter to Gomrik who was even more unpredictable than Vitrig had been.

"Find the woman!" Gomrik screamed, his voice echoing throughout the house. "Find her, or all your heads will lie in the snow for the crows to pick at!"

The men left to look for Deirbhne. They did not realize that Gomrik's anger was not because Vitrig was dead, but because the woman had escaped, and he had wanted her for himself. He looked down at Vitrig's torn and bloodied body, his eyes filled with contempt.

"Now, my noble Lord, see where your greed and lust has brought you. I knew the woman would kill you if she got half the chance." He laughed. "You became too foolish in the end, and she destroyed you."

He laughed loudly. He was leader of the Formorians now, king at last. He laughed again as he thought of how he would enjoy the woman when his men found her. He would enjoy her as Vitrig had enjoyed her, and then he would kill her.

A few days after she had come to Ceolmhar's dún, Deirbhne finally met Blamad, whom she had been impatient to see. They walked together out of the dún. It was a calm day and a light breeze blew over the mountain, taking what heat there was out of the sun. Traces of snow lingered on the ground, but there had been no fresh falls for a week, though the elders, who knew of such things, spoke of more to come.

They walked in silence, going down the path which led from the dún, until they came to a ledge overlooking the plain below. There was little about the day to suggest that it was mid winter, and both Deirbhne and Blamad wore light cloaks to keep off the breeze. Deirbhne had rested, and some of the vagueness and distance had gone from her eyes, but Blamad still bore about him an air of gloomy melancholy.

"Morna tells me that you know of the power of the Druid's magic." Blamad nodded.

"She does not believe me," he said, a deep sadness in his eyes and voice. "She still believes that I am a coward, that I ran away from the Druid."

Deirbhne smiled quietly. Her instincts had been right. Morna disliked Blamad and now she knew why.

"Tell me about it," she said gently. She laid her hand on his for a moment and he looked into her eyes and smiled, very quietly, very softly.

There was something mysterious about Blamad, something she could not define. He looked the same as ever, his smile was as winning, yet there was about him an aura of sadness, of separation. She shivered. It was as if he belonged to another world, she thought. Blamad pointed down over the plain.

"Imagine all of this filled with blood," he said, waving his arms in a half circle. "Imagine those rocks there as creatures rising from the ground, pulling at you, dragging you down, and spreading their slime over you. See those trees there? Imagine them rising from the ground, their branches extended, trying to crush you, their roots like giant claws gripping and strangling you so that you could not breathe or do anything about it, as they dragged you into the very holes in the ground from which they had come a few moments before. Watch your friends scream and throw themselves from the walls of the dún, or attack you with axes or swords, and feel yourself doing the same thing in spite of yourself. Every fear you know assaults you at the same time, every secret terror which lies hidden deep within yourself, every shame, all attacking you together, with no respite, no release. After a time you scream, your mind becomes numb with terror and you will do anything, kill anyone, to escape the demons who chase you, the demons who will not leave you alone. It's horrible."

He bowed his head, perspiration running down his forehead onto his beard, terror in his eyes. For a moment she thought he was going to cry, but he did not.

"Yet you survived," she said gently. He looked at her.

"I did not," he said, looking directly into her eyes, which questioned his, but he did not answer for a few moments. Then he began to tell her everything that had happened.

Her eyes widened as he told her. She could hardly believe what he was saying, but she herself had seen so many strange things, and so much had happened to her, and she had known Blamad for too long to doubt his word, so she believed he was telling the truth. It was a strange truth, but she believed him.

"Then the Danaans are going to help us?" He nodded.

"In spite of their help many will die. It was written a long time ago that this would happen, and nothing will change what has been preordained."

"What about you, Blamad?" She felt a tender love for him, a filial love for this man who was part of their world, yet was a man apart, and she wished that there was something she could do to help him, to ease his own sorrow and loneliness. Blamad smiled. It was a sad smile, filled with regret and resignation.

"I shall see Brian again soon," he said simply. She squeezed his hand.

"Thank you for talking to me. You have made it easier for me to accept what has happened to me and to Brian, and I begin to hope at last."

"There is much to be done yet," he replied.

They walked back to Ceolmhar's dún, arm in arm, at peace with themselves and with each other.

CHAPTER TWENTY

Spring came early. The snows melted, the days grew longer and warmer, new-born lambs skipped and ran through the pastures, flowers forced their way up and out into the ever warmer air.

Ceolmhar's scouts were busier now, keeping the plain below under constant watch but there was still no sign of the Druid.

Ceolmhar, however, knew that the Formorians were in the forest close to the mountain. His men avoided the forest, but they ranged over the plain, visiting the villages and other settlements asking for news. Everywhere men were waiting for the expected attack, and some villages had already been abandoned, their people having fled into the wilderness far to the north. Most were still occupied, their people hoping that somehow the Formorians would ignore them, yet they all knew in their hearts that the Formorians would come to the mountain to destroy Ceolmhar and anyone else who stood in their path, that this respite was only temporary.

In Ceolmhar's dún itself, frantic efforts were being made for the coming war. The walls had been strengthened, and the smiths were working day and night under Maron's stern and particular control, forging new weapons and tempering old ones.

Maron had been made chief smith by Ceolmhar. His skill was without question, but his brittle manner caused many arguments in the forges. Blamad had to tell the old man several times to hold his tongue, while to the other smiths he offered the excuse that Maron was an old man, set in his ways, and that behind his gruff manner he really was a likable rogue. The other smiths grumbled and accepted the old man's presence, but under protest.

After the first few days of spring had passed, the Picts were finally ready to begin their march to the mountain, and Ceolmhar's dún. Gomrik had sent word to the Druid that he would be marching soon, and this news, as well as the news of Vitrig's death which Gomrik's messenger brought, stirred the Druid out of his long period of lethargy.

It had been a long, dreary winter, and the Druid's elation at having killed the high king had given way to gloom and depression during the long months of enforced idleness. Now, with the news he had just received, he was ready to begin his final assault against Ceolmhar and those who still held out against his power, and he commanded Garweng to call a council of war.

"There will be a battle soon," he said to all his captains, when they were assembled before him. "The final battle. You all know what you have to do, what will have to be done once victory is ours. The Formorians have already begun to march, hoping no doubt to beat us to our prey, but they will not."

There was something totally evil about the way he spoke those words, that the others who were present felt a cold fear come over them.

"You, Garweng, will ride to the forest. Tell our men there that we will soon be on the march. You Morc, go to Díele and tell him the same thing, while Dichiu will go to Gomrik, and tell him that we shall met him on the plain before we begin our attack on the mountain. We will march in a day or so, as soon as our men are ready. Now go and tell the news as I have commanded."

The three druids left the tent with the other captains and leaders. Only Dubhghall remained.

"Are all our preparations made?"

Dubhghall nodded. "We have been waiting only for your word, to begin," The Druid smiled, a smile very close to warmth.

"Then, we shall steal some of Gomrik's thunder."

Dubhghall laughed loudly. The news of Vitrig's death had come as a shock to him, but it was a shock not out of concern for Vitrig, only in the manner of his death. He was glad that Vitrig was dead, because Gomrik, whom he knew and had once crossed swords with, was not half the man Vitrig had been, and he would cause no trouble when the time came to push him aside.

A few days later the Picts began their march towards Ceolmhar's dún. The Druid, mounted on his horse, watched as his men marched past, thousands of them, some carrying javelins, some with short, close quarter swords; some, like Dubhghall, carrying by their sides double-headed axes, sharp fierce weapons which, in the hands of an expert, could take a man's head off with one blow. Each man carried on his back a leather shield.

They marched silently past the Druid, followed by five hundred archers, more lightly equipped than the other soldiers. They wore neither shield nor armour, but instead carried over their shoulders their bows and quivers of arrows, deadly marksmen all, who were greatly respected by their own men and feared by their enemies.

Behind the archers came the chariots. There were only several dozen of these, two-man teams, but they were fast, mobile, deadly against lines of foot-soldiers, who seldom could resist their combined onslaught.

Lastly came the baggage wagons and the horsemen who were flanking and protecting the entire column, their numbers spread out either side, before and behind the main group.

Dubhghall rode up and joined the Druid.

"We are ready, Master." He wore a leather helmet which came down over his eyes, and a breastplate, also of leather. His sword hung from his waist, while on his saddle was the double-headed axe he was so fond of. He looked so fierce and proud that even the Druid was moved to admiration.

"It is time to begin," he said and, with Dubhghall by his side, rode to the head of the column.

The countryside was lush and green, with many flowers growing in the fields, daffodils in abundance, and violets, carrying the scent on the breeze. The sun was strong, and it warmed the earth and softened the ground, melting away the last traces of winter.

The breeze fanned the Druid's face as he surveyed the plain before him. Mile after mile of unbroken flatness, ideal marching ground for his men, an ideal battleground also. He smiled. He knew that there would be no battle, there would be no need for battle. His enemies had retreated into the mountain, thinking themselves safe behind the rocks and the walls of their dún, laughing at him he was sure, but they would soon know how safe they were, they would soon feel, as the high king had felt, the power of his magic, and would understand what real terror was.

Dubhghall had sent scouts ahead as a routine precaution, though he, like the Druid, did not anticipate any trouble and the scouts, as expected, returned to the main column with the news that the countryside was quiet.

"The villages are deserted, the smaller dúns too," their leader said. "In some places, the fires were still burning as if the people had just fled."

"They have seen our coming," the Druid said coldly. "This is good, because they will spread fear and panic by their words and with each telling, that fear and panic will increase..."

The Picts were well disciplined, and they marched in an orderly line, which was unusual since they had once been as wild as the Formorians, and had always fought in an undisciplined mass. Their time with the Druid, however, had taught them much, and they had accepted the new discipline, out of fear because they had seen his Power, and they knew that it could destroy any army sent against them. They knew also that once the Druid had destroyed their enemies they would have enough plunder to satisfy each of them, a consoling thought which helped them forget the harsh discipline he imposed.

They came close to the forest by nightfall, but the Druid ordered them to make camp on the plain, in a place where they could not be surprised, and from where Ceolmhar would be able to see his campfires, and realize just how many men he had.

The Druid did not think that Ceolmhar would be foolish enough to attack his army but the forest was not to his liking. It made him uneasy and for some reason, the Power of his magic was not as strong there as in other places. Some other power ruled the forest, there was no denying that, and he wondered if the legends were true, whether the Danaans still lived in the dark places as the bards said they did. He had always dismissed the idea that they still existed and, though he was not a fearful man, there was always a nagging doubt in his mind, an uneasiness when he entered the forest. He knew of the hidden places where men were said to have vanished completely from the face of the earth, the dark places, the haunts of the dead and spirits, the thick overgrown glens and hollows, so forbidding and sinister. He shivered at the mere thought of it.

His slaves erected his tent, and prepared his meal. Dubhghall ate with the Druid, who drank only a little wine. Dubhghall, with some impatience, took the wine jug from the slave and put it on the table before him. The Druid seemed not to notice, but in fact he saw every move, and it gave him some quiet amusement to see the Pict's impatient weakness. The lamps were lit and the dim light flickered as the breeze entered the tent when the flaps were opened. The two men ate the cold meat which had been put before them in silence. Dubhghall hated dining with the Druid, who always ate like a child. His own appetite was enormous, and he found the spartan fare of the Druid's table almost too much to bear.

"Gomrik will not be pleased that we have begun to march so quickly," the Druid said, disturbing the silence.

"Gomrik's a fool," Dubhghall said contemptuously. "A fool who will never be the man Vitrig was."

"But Vitrig allowed a woman to kill him. He did not die a warrior's death."

The irony of the Druid's words was not lost on Dubhghall.

"It was no ordinary woman who killed Vitrig. But the wife of a king, who knew the warrior's art, as the wife of a king should. She and the high king's wife are the same kind of woman, and I would like to meet her if the gods permit."

"You wish to have her for yourself?" the Druid asked casually. Dubhghall nodded, and the Druid smiled indulgently.

"Then you can have her when we take Ceolmhar's dún."

Dubhghall was dumbfounded. The thought that the queen would be his when they had taken Ceolmhar's dún was almost too much to contemplate, and he felt elated, impatient to do battle, to get the conflict over so that he could enjoy the queen. His mind was filled with many fantasies, and he did not notice how coldly the Druid looked at him, and with what contempt.

"We have not yet taken the dún," he reminded Dubhghall. "You must curb your impatience for a while. Gomrik will be here soon. You may think that he is not the man Vitrig was, but he has a cunning way about him that is more dangerous than all of Vitrig's skills. He will bear watching, this Gomrik. Keep your men away from the Formorians, make certain that there is no fighting, and tell your men that the penalty for those who disobey this order is death. Later, when we have destroyed Ceolmhar, we will settle with Gomrik and his Formorians. Now, leave me alone for a while, I wish to rest..."

Dubhghall finished his wine, and left the Druid's tent to go to his own. He ordered one of his slaves to being him another jug of wine and some food, because he was still hungry. When the food and wine had been brought to him, Dubhghall relaxed and thought about the queen, and the time he would have with her, and he became suddenly impatient once more for the battle to begin.

Gomrik was firmly in command of the Formorians. Nobody had challenged him, and there was no doubt among the Formorians that Gomrik was their leader.

His men was all fighters, seasoned veterans, and they saw in him the same recklessness, the same lack of caution they themselves possessed. The Formorians were not heavily armed, nor did they wear armour as the Picts did. Their heads were bare, and their long hair hung loose, sometimes being caught on the wind, rising kite-like, into the air. They were however, fierce fighters, utterly fearless and brave. They scorned the Picts, their allies, for their armour and for the protection they sought by wearing helmets. They relied on their own skills and courage in battle, and they sang as they marched over the countryside towards the mountains and Ceolmhar's dún. They anticipated, like the Picts, an easy and confident victory over Ceolmhar and his people. Foraging for food along the way, preferring to travel lightly, raiding villages and hunting game when they needed to eat rather than bring their wagons, which Gomrik knew would only have slowed them down.

As they moved over the countryside, word of their coming spread from village to village and a growing number of the people in their path took to the wilderness to avoid death or slavery at their hands.

Since Deirbhne's escape, Gomrik had thought of nothing else but finding her. He swore that he would have her if she was alive, though he was beginning to doubt she was. He felt a stirring in the pit of his stomach as he thought about her. Perhaps she had survived the forest, and was safe in Ceolmhar's dún. That thought cheered him because he knew that if she was there, then he would possess her soon.

Ceolmhar would soon be just a name, one which would quickly be forgotten, but he, Gomrik, would be remembered as the greatest Formorian king, the only one to have conquered the whole island. He would destroy the Druid and kill Díele as soon as he had destroyed Ceolmhar. He hated Díele even more than he hated Ceolmhar, and he distrusted him, because a man who betrayed his own king was not to be trusted.

He looked at his surroundings. He knew that they were close to the place where the Druid said they would meet. He had thought to beat the Druid to Ceolmhar's dún, but the Druid was wily and had anticipated him, yet it didn't matter. He would settle with the Druid also, when this war was over.

Ceolmhar was standing at the table, his face grave and pale, the others gathered round him. The room was gloomy, reflecting their common mood, and there was uneasiness and a sense of fear present as they waited for him to speak.

"The situation is serious my friends. The Druid has reached the edge of the forest, and by late afternoon tomorrow, he will be at the mountain. The Formorians are on the plain and they too, will be here soon. There will be no escape in a while if they join forces and, because of this, and the fact that I believe that the Druid will use his magic against us, I must ask you what are we to do?" He stopped for a moment, saw the fear in their eyes, and tried to reassure them.

"We are not meeting here to panic, but to decide what to do, if there is something we can do against the Druid's magic. Can anyone tell me if there is?"

"Why not attack them while they are unprepared?" Alfred said, but Ceolmhar shook his head.

"It's impossible my friend. Already they outnumber us, and they are far from being unprepared. Their archers are camped behind their main lines, but they have horsemen roaming the countryside watching for any of our people, and killing anyone they find."

Blamad stood up. All eyes were on him. With the passing months, they had grown to accept that there was something special about him, that he had been marked by the gods. Only Carriog was close to him now, only to Carriog did he confide or speak his thoughts, and he no longer tried to make the queen understand what had happened to him in the high king's dún.

"If we stay here then we shall be destroyed, that is certain," he said. The others agreed.

"Well then, we should go down there and fight."

Alfred shook his head. "But Ceolmhar has already said that such a thing is impossible."

Blamad smiled.

"I do not mean that we should simply go down there and throw ourselves at them. The Druid's magic can only be used in a limited way. He will send his Power over this mountain, meaning to destroy us, but if we are not here then the magic will have been wasted, and he will not be able to use it again for a time. That is when we attack, because he will think we are dead, or mad or whatever."

Ceolmhar smiled. It was a perfect plan, and like all perfect plans, so simple, but here was one minor problem.

"What about the others, the women and children? Where are they to go? The queen is heavy with child, and cannot be expected to run down a mountain. What is to happen to her?"

"Go to the forest," the queen answered suddenly. Ceolmhar turned to her.

"If the warriors go down as Blamad says, then the women and children could go to the forest and hide there until the battle is over. There are many safe places there, much cover, and there will be no Formorians or Picts because they will all be trying to take the dún for their plunder. While the warriors fight we will be safe, and if anything goes wrong and our men are beaten, then we will have a ready hiding place."

"But there is so little time," Alfred said, concerned for her safety. "We will be cut off by tomorrow at the latest."

"The queen is right," Ceolmhar said. He looked at each of them. "It's perfect. No matter what happens, the women and children must go to the forest, the men elsewhere to hide until the Druid has sent his magic over the mountain. Go to it, now."

"I will leave at once," the queen said. "I am perhaps a little slower than usual, but I shall be all right."

They smiled at her attempt at humour despite the seriousness of the situation.

Ceolmhar spoke to Blamad.

"You will take some men, go to the plain below and, with as much noise and distraction as you can, draw off any Formorians who might be lurking there. Be sure that the paths are safe for the women and children. Lead any watchers on such a chase so that the women and the others can reach the forest without being observed."

Blamad nodded.

"I will go with Blamad," Carriog said. Together, they left the room. Ceolmhar turned to the others.

"You all know what to do. Aemrig and Muireann will lead the women to the forest. You may take thirty men to go with you, I'm sorry that it can't be more, but take the best men, so that you will be easy in your mind."

Aemrig was about to protest, when a hand restrained him. It was the queen.

"There will be other battles," she said, simply and quietly, so that the others did not hear. She knew that Aemrig wanted to go with Ceolmhar to fight the Formorians but she also knew that his place was with her and the other women. Aemrig obeyed the command of her hand, and his protest remained unspoken.

It was quite dark now and from the plain below the lights from the fires in the Druid's camp and in that of the Formorians lit the night sky. Ceolmhar's people had been hastily assembled. There was a lot of noise and confusion as hundreds of voices spoke at once, babies cried, people argued that they did not wish to go, that the night was too cold for old people and children to be outside, or that the Druid would not dare to attack so strong a dún as Ceolmhar's.

They did not understand the Power of the Druid's magic, because Ceolmhar had kept them ignorant of it to save them from panic, but now Aemrig's men and the sight of their swords convinced the waverers that they should not argue. Each person was allowed to take some small personal possession, but all the livestock, all the food and wine, stored over many months, was left behind. They took with them only some bread, a little wine and a good supply of water.

Deirbhne accompanied the queen. Aemrig made Muireann personally responsible for the queen's safety, and the young warrior remained constantly by her side, much to her amusement, though she was in fact, quite pleased.

Creidne meanwhile, took charge of Maron and Aobhne. They had married, and Aobhne too was now with child, though the old man still had not quite accepted the idea of Creidne as a son-in-law. He grumbled also about having to go with the women and old people, but this time his arguing did not help, and he was prodded along like the rest by Aemrig's impatient men.

CHAPTER TWENTY ONE

Blamad had done his work well. He had drawn off the spies who were, as Ceolmhar had guessed, at the foot of the mountain, by a movement with the seeming intent of attacking the Druid's camp.

Aemrig and Muireann led the women down the mountain. As they descended, they could see the lights from the Druid's camp in the distance, and Aemrig silently thanked the gods that the Picts and Formorians had not sealed off the mountain yet, or the forest.

It was difficult for those who carried heavy packs and for the older people, and those women who, like the queen, were pregnant, but the fear of what the Druid would do spurred Aemrig and his men, and they kept everyone moving as quickly as they could, ignoring the cuts and bruises and falls they suffered.

Deirbhne and Alfred walked beside the queen, each of them taking one of her arms and with careful steady steps, they made it safely to the lower ground.

When everyone had reached the base of the mountain, Aemrig moved them out, leaving half of his men to follow as a rearguard in case of attack, while Muireann and the others led the queen and the rest to the forest a short distance away, which they reached without incident a short time later.

Blamad had, by moving in a wide circle, returned to the dún, having lost his watchers who had gone straight to the Druid's camp. Ceolmhar was waiting for him, with the rest of his men.

"Well?" he asked. "Did it work?"

Blamad laughed. "They've gone running to the Druid's camp like yelping dogs. Aemrig and the others have reached the safety of the forest."

"Good," Ceolmhar said smiling, his anxiety about the queen laid to rest. "It's time we began. The Druid will send men to investigate your little escapade."

They started down the mountain. It was a bright, still night with a slight frost, and they were aware that whatever sound they made might have carried to the Druid's camp, but the Druid's men remained unaware of Ceolmhar's descent. They too moved towards the forest, which they entered from a different direction, and a long way from where Aemrig and the women had entered. They moved quietly and quickly into the darkness until they found a place to rest and hide.

Guards were posted throughout the forest to watch for any sign of Picts and Formorians, while Blamad, Carriog and Ceolmhar stayed close to the edge of the forest to watch whatever happened, because they knew that with the coming day, the Druid would use his magic against the mountain.

They settled themselves on the forest floor. The trees were closely grouped together, providing cover and shelter, but it was an uncomfortable place to rest, and they were pricked by the thorn bushes which grew everywhere around them, making proper rest impossible.

Dawn came bright and clear, a calm, peaceful morning, belying the evil and destruction which lay a short distance over the plain, and which would soon approach the mountain.

Nor far away, Gomrik sat in the Druid's tent.

"I have done as you asked," he said, a hint of mockery in his voice. "My men are in position, and an ant could not get off that mountain now without us knowing about it."

He laughed, at the same time taking the wine jug from the Druid's table, and helping himself to a cup.

"Help yourself," the Druid said with heavy sarcasm. Gomrik glanced at him with barely concealed hatred. He was still tired after his long march, and he had hardly time to rest. He knew that the Druid thought of him as a lesser man than Vitrig, but the Druid would learn his mistake soon, when it was too late. He needed him and his magic to overcome Ceolmhar but, once that was accomplished, he would personally kill him, with his own hands.

"You have done well," the Druid said. "I have already set the fires at the places needed, and it needs only my magic to destroy the dún and everyone in it. When the cloud disperses, you can take your men up to the dún, which will then be yours for the taking, but remember what I said. Wait until the cloud disperses, or you will feel the Power." He laughed.

Just then, Díele entered the tent.

"Greetings," he said heartily, but his greeting was not returned. He saw in Gomrik's eyes a look of pure hatred, a look which frightened him because, for all his bluster, he was not a brave man.

"My men are in position and ready to do as you command," he said to the Druid.

"Go back to your men, and wait until the cloud I shall shortly unleash is dispersed," the Druid said coldly. He smiled, thinking at the same time, that Díele's days were numbered, that before this day was over, he too, would be just another memory.

Díele nodded, turned and left the tent, much subdued and fearful. When he had gone Gomrik pointed after him.

"I don't trust that vermin. I will kill him the first chance I get."

"After we have taken Ceolmhar's dún, you may do whatever you wish with him," the Druid said indifferently. Díele meant nothing to him, and he too, had nothing but contempt for the man who had betrayed the high king, even if that betrayal had served his own cause perfectly.

They left the tent and went outside where Dubhghall was waiting. Neither he nor Gomrik spoke to each other, or made a sign that they acknowledged each other's existence. The hatred between the Formorians and the Picts was intense, and it was almost a miracle that they were fighting together side by side against a common enemy, only the Druid's overwhelming Power keeping them together. Gomrik went to rejoin his men.

"I will enjoy taking his head," Dubhghall said bitterly. The Druid did not reply. He mounted his horse, and rode with Dubhghall to where Garweng was waiting by the first fire. The Druid dismounted, and without speaking to Garweng, lit the fire, threw some of the powder from his pouch onto it, remounted his horse and, again without speaking a word, rode away with Dubhghall to the next fire. After he had repeated this four times, he spoke.

"You know what you have to do." Dubhghall nodded.

"Then let us begin." Dubhghall took the reins of the Druid's horse and he led it away, behind his own.

The Druid stood before the fire and threw the remaining powder onto it. A blue column of smoke rose into the air and hung above his head while, over the other three fires, similar columns of smoke had also risen. The Druid raised his hands into the air.

"BE WITH ME NOW, YOU GODS OF THE ELEMENTS. BRING SUCCESS TO US OVER OUR ENEMIES, AND LET THEIR HEARTS BE FILLED WITH TERROR. LET THEM TREMBLE BEFORE YOUR MIGHT AND GIVE US THE VICTORY WE ASK FOR..."

He listened for a few minutes, but the smoke remained stationary over his head, so he looked to the sky once more, perspiration running down his face, even though it was quite cold.

"LISTEN TO ME YOU SPIRITS OF EARTH, FIRE AND WATER. HEAR MY VOICE AND BRING DEATH AND

DESTRUCTION TO MY ENEMIES, AND LET THEM FEEL YOUR POWER..."

He remained motionless, still staring at the sky. The cloud suddenly began to move towards the mountain. At first there was complete silence, and a deathly stillness hung over the surrounding countryside but without warning, the sky darkened, and a heavy peal of thunder shattered the silence, followed quickly by terrifying flashes of lightning.

It began to rain heavily, and the sun was hidden by ominous black clouds which swirled across the sky, angry storm-filled clouds. The wind rose to a fury, sweeping those who had not found shelter off their feet and blowing them away like the lightest leaves or twigs from the trees, which themselves were bent and buffeted by the power of the storm.

The thunder pealed constantly, while the dark clouds turned the day into night, a darkness lit only by the lightning, which flashed and showed the Druid standing in the open, erect and unaffected by the storm he had unleashed, or the wind and rain which seemed not to come near him, protected by the very force which he had conjured up, and which was turning the surrounding area into a devastation.

He stood with his hands aloft, as the smoke from the fire began to move more rapidly, joining with the smoke from the other fires, each of them meeting and merging into one gigantic blue cloud, which did not swirl or disperse in spite of the wind and rain.

The cloud moved with its own force and speed, and it slowly rose up and began to cover the mountain, every rock and stone, falling into the most secret and obscure places, leaving not an inch of the whole mountain uncovered.

Whatever life was there was affected by the cloud. Birds in the air, the animals hiding from the noise of the storm, the smallest insects crawling on the ground, everything was driven to the insanity of terror, which the Druid had sent to destroy Ceolmhar's dún. Ceolmhar, watching from the forest with Blamad and Carriog, thanked the gods quietly, that they had taken Blamad's advice and come down off the mountain.

After a long time the storm spent itself and the blue cloud disappeared. The sun broke through once more, the wind died, the rain stopped, and the birds in the forest began to sing again. It was as if there had been no storm, with everything calm and peaceful once more. Only the wet grass betrayed the fact that there had indeed been a tempest a short while before.

The Druid still had not moved, remaining with his arms extended for a long time after the cloud had dispersed, but finally, and without returning to full awareness, he lowered his arms and bowed his head.

Dubhghall and Garweng approached him, and Garweng brought his cloak. The Druid looked at them, his senses slowly returning, and he smiled thinly.

"Now it is up to you," he said to Dubhghall. "If you want your queen, you'd better take your men up that mountain before Gomrik beats you to it."

Dubhghall left without a word, and ran to where his men were waiting.

Gomrik meanwhile, had watched the cloud disappear, and when he saw Dubhghall rush towards his men, he knew that the Druid was trying to get to Ceolmhar's dún ahead of him. He screamed at his own men, who still remained in their shelters.

"Get yourselves out of there at once!" he roared. "If you want the Picts to have all the spoils don't hurry, but if you want your share of plunder and some of Ceolmhar's women, then get out now, and up that mountain!"

He didn't have to say anymore. The Formorians emerged from their shelters with renewed eagerness, and with a sudden and uncontrolled rush they charged up the mountain.

It took them some time, but soon they approached the dún, the gates of which were, as they expected, closed against them.

As they came nearer, they heard sounds such as they had never heard before, terrifying sounds which made them stop in a body. Gomrik rode up behind them, anger in his eyes when he saw that they had stopped running.

"What is the matter," he roared impatiently, but then he too heard the sounds, and he too, felt a sudden terrifying fear for a moment. Suddenly he laughed.

"It's only a cry of fear," he said to his men. "The Druid's magic has worked for us. There is nothing for you to be afraid of. Now break down those gates and take this dún, before the Picts get here."

His men rushed against the gates, which they were surprised to find were not locked. They swung them open and emptied themselves inside, but there was no battle, no expected orgy of death or rape. Instead of finding Ceolmhar's people, all they found were crazed animals, still penned and tied, but totally demented and maddened by the cloud.

The sight unsettled and unnerved the Formorians, so Gomrik quickly ordered the animals to be killed at once. A pack of dogs, rabid with fear, rushed at the men from behind one of the buildings, snapping and snarling at those Formorians who could not get out of their way quickly enough, because of the onrush of men behind them. The dogs attacked the men nearest to them, bringing them down, sinking their teeth into flesh, refusing to let go until they killed, their strength increased by their fear.

There was panic and confusion as the dogs raced among the massed Formorians and the Picts who had, by now, entered the dún, snapping, biting and killing, the screams of hurt or dying men adding to the hysteria.

Gomrik shouted at his men, raised his sword and killed several dogs himself, but it was a long time before the men were able to kill the rest of the maddened animals, and order was restored. Gomrik surveyed the carnage. Ten men had been killed by the dogs, and many more were injured to varying degrees. He ordered all the animals in the dún to be killed and, though the Formorians knew the value of good livestock, they did not hesitate, because they were still terrified after what had happened and they were afraid that other animals too might attack them.

Gomrik meanwhile went with some of his men to find Ceolmhar or anyone else, but after a fruitless search through the king's house he realized that there was not a man or woman in the dún.

"Wasted," he shouted with rage. "This whole thing was a waste of time. There is no one here."

He did not know how Ceolmhar and the others had escaped, but they had, and he had been robbed of victory, a victory which had lain within his grasp. Some of his men had begun to loot the houses in the dún, but he gave an order that nothing was to be burned.

"We may have to live here for a while," he said sombrely. Dubhghall and Díele joined him at this moment.

"So much for your Master's magic," Gomrik said scornfully. "Where are Ceolmhar's people? This is the last time that I will listen to anything he has to say, and you can tell him that for me."

He was almost incoherent with rage, so much so, that Dubhghall kept his hand on the hilt of his sword.

Díele was terrified. He was completely afraid of Gomrik, more so than he had been of Vitrig, because Gomrik's rages were so fierce and unpredictable that he became another person, a man possessed, and Díele, who knew that the Formorian hated him, was afraid for his life.

"Tell your Druid that there is no one in the dún," Gomrik finally managed to say. He looked at them savagely, the hatred plain to see in his eyes.

"You can tell him that the mountain is mine, that I claim it, and you can take your men back to the Druid's dún. When I have finished here, I will come and talk to the Druid, but for now you will leave this place at once, or I will order my men to kill you both."

Dubhghall hesitated, wondering whether he should call Gomrik's bluff, but the Formorians who guarded Gomrik had already drawn their weapons, and he knew it was pointless to resist, so he left, followed by a very shaken and terrified Díele.

There was a sullen silence in the dún, as the Formorians and Picts faced each other. In the tense atmosphere which at that moment existed between the two armies, the slightest provocation would have set off a full scale battle, but peace was maintained, and Dubhghall led his men from there, and back down to the plain to where the Druid was waiting for them.

The Druid's anger was greater than Gomrik's when Dubhghall and Díele told him what had happened, and what Gomrik had said.

"How can they have escaped!" he screamed, hardly able to contain his anger. Then it occurred to him.

"Last night's report of an attack on my camp was a feint to draw my scouts from the mountain. That is what must have happened. Ceolmhar led his people down during the night, while my scouts ran away. They must be hiding in the forest. It's the only place they could be."

He smiled.

"Ceolmhar is out in the open now," he said. The horror which had almost overcome him a few moments before was gone, and he began to feel that the victory which he had thought was lost would still be theirs after all.

"Look for Ceolmhar," he said to Dubhghall. "Out in the open with his women and children he will be slow and easy to find, and distracted by his need to protect them. You will have no trouble disposing of him."

"But what about Gomrik?"

"Do not worry about Gomrik," the Druid replied calmly. "His days are short, and he will soon join Vitrig. Let him shout for now and say that he is Master, because he will not frighten anyone for much longer."

The Druid's words and passive attitude calmed them also, especially Díele, who was still terrified. Things had not turned out as he had anticipated, and he regretted now that he had betrayed the high king, but it was too late for regrets and he knew it.

CHAPTER TWENTY TWO

"How do you feel now?" the queen asked Alfred. He was leaning against a tree, out of breath and exhausted.

"I shall be all right." With some effort he pushed himself away from the tree. "I'm sorry to be holding everyone else up," he said, but she dismissed his protests and ordered the rest of the group to go ahead without them. Two of Muireann's men helped Alfred to his feet, and they linked arms behind him, helping him to keep up with the rest.

"I shall be all right." He smiled at the obvious concern for his safety, but she could see clearly just how unwell he was, and hoped that their stay in the forest would not be for long.

It was a pleasant spring morning, and the forest was calm. The storm which the Druid had unleashed over the mountain had not touched the forest at all, and it as as if they had stepped into another, brighter world.

They knew nothing of what had happened only a short while before and they remained unaware that the Druid's magic had passed over Ceolmhar's dún but had done no harm except to the animals and livestock. Morna looked at the others who remained with her and Alfred, at Deirbhne who was at peace with herself at last, at Muireann and his four warriors who remained in close attendance and, as they rested in this peaceful and picturesque place, the queen thought to herself, that death should not come on such a day. It was not a day to die, yet she knew that many would die that day, and she felt sorrow for all of them, Formorian and Pict as well as her own people.

It was so peaceful in the forest, so calm, and the warm sunshine coming through the trees, as well as the noisy birds overhead, cheered her somewhat, and took away some of her gloom.

They were well into the forest, safe from the Formorians and Picts, and they rested without fear and at leisure until finally, Alfred decided he was able to continue. They moved slowly, out of consideration for Alfred and caught up with Aemrig and the others in a short while, because Aemrig had deliberately slowed his pace for that very reason.

Aemrig and Muireann and all the other warriors could not forget that Blamad and Ceolmhar and all their friends would soon be fighting the Formorians, and they could not help feeling that their place too was by Ceolmhar's side, but the queen had spoken and given them her command, and they obeyed her, no matter how they felt about it; yet they were restless for battle, and eager to be with their friends.

"I would rather die this day fighting the Formorians, than live a long life." Aemrig said to Muireann as they walked together.

"I too," Muireann replied.

The queen overheard their conversation. "I too would welcome death in battle. But there are other battles to be fought, and you have been chosen for these. If Ceolmhar and his warriors are killed today, it will be your task to teach the young men how to be warriors, you who will protect us and keep us safe until we can fight again. Is that not also an honourable thing to do? Remember, when you protect us, as you now do, you are serving our cause as much as if you were fighting by Ceolmhar's side. Some must live so that all will live again."

Aemrig bowed his head.

"You have spoken the truth," he said quietly. "And if we have forgotten our place, then we are both sorry."

Morna smiled. These were good men, she thought, and in Muireann she saw a future leader, a king perhaps, when he had gained more wisdom. He had already proved himself a capable and loyal follower, his skill as a warrior was acknowledged, and he had an easy, yet commanding way about him. A king for certain, she thought. If he survived.

A sound disturbed the calm of the forest, a strange sound, and Morna and the others were quickly alert, arms ready for battle, but it was Rory and three of his Danaans who rode into the clearing.

Each of the Danaans rode a white horse, each was dressed in white with a pure white cloak edged with gold, and they looked every inch the gods they were. Rory dismounted and went straight to Aemrig.

"Greetings, Aemrig," he said smiling. Aemrig, like the others, was astonished by the appearance of the Danaans, which was striking, but also by their knowledge of his name.

"Greetings also to you noble queen Morna," Rory said, turning to the queen and bowing very low, a bow which she returned with a smile.

"We have been watching your journey since you entered the forest. You have been under our protection for a while now."

"Who are you?" the queen asked, but already she knew who it was who stood before her. She was somewhat frightened, and suddenly remembered Blamad.

"Your thoughts are correct," Rory said smiling. "We are the Danaan whom Blamad told you about, your friends and, I hope very soon, your allies."

"I have heard much about your people these past few months," she said quietly, aware at once of the strange aura surrounding the young warrior and his companions.

"There is little time," he replied courteously. "The Formorians have taken Ceolmhar's dún, but they have already argued with the Druid's Picts, and it will take little to set them at each other's throats. Ceolmhar and the others are safe, but there will be a battle soon, so you must remain here. Soon, it will be possible for you to return to the mountain, but for now you will find all you need here, because we have provided food and shelter, which you will find a short distance from here."

He finished speaking, and turned and stood before Aemrig. There was a strangeness in his look which made the others uneasy, but not Aemrig, who felt no fear at all.

"You are to return with me," Rory said smiling. "It has been foretold that you shall fight your enemies today."

Aemrig looked at the queen, the pleasure of what he had heard clear in his eyes. She gave him her blessing at once.

"It seems that the gods have a greater hold on you than I do," she said. "Go with honour Aemrig, and farewell this day."

"What about me?" Muireann asked. "Am I not to go to battle also?"

"It is not yet your time," Rory replied quickly. "There are other, more important tasks ahead of you, tasks of which I cannot tell you, but about which you will soon find out."

Muireann nodded quietly, accepting Rory's words without protest or argument.

Aemrig and he embraced, long and hard they held onto each other, tears in both their eyes.

"Lead our people and protect the queen," Aemrig said, his voice filled with emotion. "I will be thinking about you, no matter where I am, and I shall be watching you."

"And I will be thinking of you, Aemrig," Muireann replied, equally choked with emotion.

"It is time to go." Rory remounted his horse and with the other Danaans, and waited for Aemrig to say his farewells.

"The gods be with you all," Aemrig said when he, too, had mounted. Rory led the way, and they quickly disappeared through the undergrowth, out of sight. No one spoke. A strange feeling hung over them as they realized that they would perhaps not see their friend again, and that thought saddened them all.

Ceolmhar led his men out of the forest, and back over the plain towards the Druid's camp by forced march, beginning even before the Druid's attack against the mountain had finished.

Blamad and Carriog led their men, who flanked the main force led by Ceolmhar himself, and when they came within sight of the Druid's encampment, they halted for a moment, before they commenced their final charge into the mass of tents and shelters.

The Druid was still recovering from the ordeal of unleashing the cloud, and his men had only just returned from the dún, tired and dejected after their encounter with Gomrik and his followers. Ceolmhar's sudden appearance caught them unawares, since they had not thought it necessary to protect their rear. The Druid realized his mistake when he heard the alarms sounding and saw the mass of men rushing towards his encampment, screaming with hate and vengeance, cursing him and the Picts, promising every kind of retribution for all the hurt and wrong he had caused.

They tried to organise themselves and prepare to meet the onslaught, but Ceolmhar had given them little time before his men entered the Druid's camp and began their slaughter.

"Stop them, stop them!" the Druid screamed in desperation, but there was already much confusion and panic as Ceolmhar's men ran among them, swords and axes raised, hacking at the Picts, or running them down with their horses.

Dubhghall tried to organise the archers. He ran to his horse and mounted up, but suddenly a voice filled with terror screamed close to him.

"It's Blamad!" Díele said pointing, his eyes wide with fear. "Blamad is leading them. We are destroyed. Ceolmhar's army is being led by a dead man!"

Díele ran in terror, hiding among a group of Picts, who looked with bitter contempt and hatred at the coward who hid among them.

"Stop snivelling and fight!" the Druid said screaming, his own panic and fear barely contained, because he had no time to make another storm to scatter Ceolmhar and his men.

Díele, stung by the Druid's words and by the sullen stares of the Picts around him, recovered his wits. He drew his sword and with a mighty scream of terror, went into battle.

The fighting became more intense, as more and more of Ceolmhar's men came into the Druid's camp, scattering and confusing the Picts, preventing any effort by them at regrouping or holding off the attack with any sort of cohesion or plan.

Some of the tents had been set alight and the smoke and fires added to the confusion of men screaming and cursing, animals bolting in terror from the fires. The smell of fear was heavy in the air as Ceolmhar's men relentlessly drove the Picts further and further back through their own encampment. Led by Blamad and Carriog, they could see the Druid's banner fluttering over his tent and drove themselves towards it, allowing nothing and no one to stand in their way.

Ceolmhar, meanwhile, had attacked the Picts from their left, and his men were fighting their way to where Blamad and Carriog were trying to reach the Druid.

Godrane and Branvig spotted Díele, still cowering among the Picts, still trying to hide himself, and they now tried to reach him. Díele, maddened by fear, and knowing what would happen if he was taken alive by Blamad's men, fought like a wounded wolf, screaming at those around him to kill their enemies. The Picts, catching his fear, also found renewed courage. They, too, fought desperately because, like Díele, they knew that their lives were forfeit once the battle was over and lost. The suddenness of Ceolmhar's attack, as well as the failure of the Druid's magic to destroy him, not to mention the appearance of Blamad whom they thought to be dead, instilled into their minds the thought that there was nothing now to save them, that they would be destroyed. In spite of this, they fought on. They did not believe in surrender, and they knew no other way to behave.

The battle at last began to go Ceolmhar's way, and his men now drove the Picts back, killing great numbers as they did so.

The Druid waited in his tent, seized with fear, for what he thought was the inevitable meeting between himself, Blamad and Carriog. He was unable to think, unable to shake off the feeling that, in spite of all his power, in spite of the magic he had used, he was beaten.

Outside, Godrane was killed by Díele, who roared with triumph as he hacked at his body, and the last thing Godrane saw was Díele's mocking eyes as he fell to the ground, dead. Branvig, maddened by Godrane's death, rushed at Díele, but the older man was more than a match for him, and held him off, filled as he was with renewed strength and courage.

It was at this moment the Formorians arrived.

Gomrik, intent on settling with the Druid once and for all, was surprised to find a battle raging, but did not hesitate to send his men to help the Druid. His men rushed in behind the retreating Picts, and held the line, until slowly they began to drive Ceolmhar's men back over the ground they had taken.

There was a terrible loss of life on both sides, but the Druid was safe. Gomrik's timely arrival prevented Blamad and Carriog from reaching him, and he left the battlefield with the other druids, going to higher ground to watch from a safe distance, the battle which had now begun to swing against Ceolmhar and his allies.

Blamad, Carriog and the rest fought desperately, but the combined strength of the Picts and Formorians was too much for them, and they were pushed further and further back. They left behind many dead and wounded who were killed where they lay by the Formorians and Picts, who were, after their earlier losses, thoroughly enraged and merciless.

Only with the coming of darkness was Ceolmhar able to disengage his men safely and withdraw in some order. He had lost many, and their strength was badly ebbed. He believed that the next day would see them destroyed, yet he drew some comfort from the fact that they had done great harm to the Picts and, but for a different touch of fortune, might have destroyed them, and the Druid too.

They moved away from the battlefield, and made camp close to the forest, where Ceolmhar held a council of war.

"We have lost nearly half our men," Carriog said gloomily. "Another day like today, and we shall all be dead."

"Godrane was killed today," Branvig said bitterly, deeply upset and distraught because he and Godrane had been great friends.

"He will play his harp in the Otherworld tonight," Blamad said quietly.

"He died a warrior's death," Ceolmhar added.

"Yes, and we shall all join him tomorrow," Carriog said bitterly. "We had them at our mercy until the Formorians came, Tigernmas take them all."

Mirrored on all their faces was the disappointment, coupled with the fear they felt, that they had come so close to victory, but now lay on the edge of destruction.

"The gods did not will it," Ceolmhar said, "and we must accept that. But for now my friends, we need rest. Tomorrow will be a hard day."

They took turns in keeping watch. They lit no fires, and sat or lay huddled close together, their cloaks wrapped round their shoulders. The cold night breeze blew across the plain, carrying with it the sounds and smells from the camp of their enemies, a short distance away.

They could see the lights from the Formorian and Pict camps, the fires, and this, coupled with what had happened that day, depressed Ceolmhar and his men, who sat for the most part huddled and silent, during a long night of waiting and anticipation.

In the Formorian and Druid's camp, it had been a stormy sometimes violent night, because Gomrik, enraged by the failure of the Druid's magic and the escape of his enemies forgot for once his fear of the Druid and spoke with unusual harshness and lack of respect.

"Your Power is useless," he shouted angrily, pointing his finger almost into the Druid's nose.

"You lost many men today because you did not guard the mountain properly. Your magic passed over the mountain with no effect. You were careless, and because you were so careless, I will take command tomorrow. I will lead our men into battle, and when we have disposed of Ceolmhar and the rabble he has left with him, we shall what is to be done here, between you and I..."

The Druid remained silent during Gomrik's tirade against him, but his eyes never left Gomrik's face and Dubhghall, who was watching the Druid carefully, realized that in spite of his passiveness, the Druid was not afraid of Gomrik, but was allowing him to say too much, to condemn himself by his own mouth. Dubhghall suddenly felt sorrow for Gomrik because he knew that the Druid would destroy him when he had the mind to. The Druid rose from his seat. He did not take his eyes off Gomrik for an instant, and Gomrik, himself, realized suddenly that he had said too much.

"You are swift with your words of anger. Perhaps you think that you are stronger because I have lost many men. But I warn you now, that I can destroy you and your men if I so wish, because I need no men to work my Power, only the skill and knowledge that is in my head. You are strong because I have permitted you to be strong. Without me, you would still be the barbarian pirates your people always were. Remember that if you wish to keep your leadership and your life, and remember also, never to speak to me in such a manner as you have done this night, or I will not be as merciful as I now choose to be. Tomorrow, you will do as I command, as all other men do. Before the noonday sun, Ceolmhar will be ours. Now, return to your men, and prepare..."

Gomrik seemed to shrink before their eyes. The Druid's words, carefully chosen and spoken in clear calm tones, had about them such an air of menace that Dubhghall and Garweng and the others present were also terrified.

Gomrik was horror stricken. He had seriously underestimated the Druid, and he now felt the full weight of the Druid's anger on his head, and he knew that the Druid would also find some way to punish him.

He left the tent, his forehead dripping with sweat, and staggered quickly to his own, hiding his face from his men in case they should see the fear written in his eyes.

Back in the Druid's tent, the Druid looked at Garweng and Dubhghall.

"Gomrik will not see tomorrow's sunset," he said harshly, his voice evil and cold, the bitterness of Gomrik's words still in his ears.

"We will destroy them all, and you will rule here for me, because the Formorians have shown that they cannot be trusted."

He spoke to Dubhghall, who bowed. Dubhghall promised that he would obey the Druid whatever he commanded, and the Druid smiled with something close to indulgence. He knew that he could trust Dubhghall. The Pict served him because he was powerful and because he knew that there was no one who could stand against his Power.

Garweng had remained silent, and the Druid had ignored him completely until the very end, when he said almost as an afterthought;

"You shall rule Brian's dún for me. You have served me as well as you could. But remember this, and be sure that it never slips your mind. You rule for me, not for yourself. If you forget that, you will die. As surely as Ceolmhar will die tomorrow."

Garweng smiled and bowed nervously.

"Thank you, Master," he said silkily. "You do me a great honour, and I will not forget, ever, that I serve you."

At dawn they lined their men, Gomrik on the left flank, Dubhghall on the right, while Díele took the centre, directly facing Ceolmhar's force, a short distance away. Díele was in a more confident mood, having come so close to disaster the day before and survived. Like every man in the Druid's force, he knew about Gomrik's humiliation at the Druid's hands, and he was confident that the Druid's power had not deserted him, so he faced Ceolmhar on this bright clear morning, actually eager to fight.

Ceolmhar and his men, having prayed to the gods, stood ready and waiting for the Druid's men to charge. Ceolmhar stood before his men, axe in hand, his cloak discarded, helmet also, believing that he stood on solid ground for the last time. Feeling the bright morning sun on his face, he was convinced that he stood no chance against the combined Formorian Pictish force, yet determined to fight bravely and to die like the warrior he had grown up to be. He was not afraid to die. He was always ready to die in battle, knowing as he did that if he died a warrior's death, then he would see the Otherworld as a warrior who would never know old age, or fear.

His one fear now was for the queen and the rest of his people, and he prayed they were all in a safe and sheltered place. The thought that they might fall into the hands of the Formorians filled him with dread, but he put this quickly from his mind, and braced himself for the final assault, which he knew would come soon.

CHAPTER TWENTY THREE

The Formorians and Picts began to move towards Ceolmhar's lines, and out from behind the lines of footsoldiers Formorian and Pictish charioteers steered their vehicles towards Ceolmhar's lines which stood ready to meet them. Ceolmhar mounted his horse. Suddenly from over the plain between Ceolmhar's army and the Formorians, a large group of horsemen appeared. Blamad leaned closer to Ceolmhar.

"More Formorians?" he asked, straining to see. He moved his horse towards the horsemen.

"I can't tell who they are," Ceolmhar said.

The Formorians, too, were watching the new arrivals, and their chariots had stopped their charge while they tried to find out who it was had come to join the battle at such a time.

The horsemen began to move towards Ceolmhar's lines and it was Carriog who first recognised them.

"It's Eornan and the Nemedians!" he said grinning. "I knew they wouldn't let us down. My people have come to help us!"

When they heard this, Ceolmhar's men began to cheer. This was the signal for the Formorians' attack to resume, and the chariots once more began to move.

Eornan and his men reached Ceolmhar who greeted him warmly, but who nevertheless had grim news for him.

"You are welcome here, but you have wasted your journey, my friend, because we are at the mercy of our enemies now, with little hope of seeing the sun set this day."

Eornan smiled, not in the least disconcerted by Ceolmhar's gloomy news.

"It is a long time since we behaved as warriors should," he replied. "Today we will make amends for that, and die as warriors, and hope that the gods will remember this when the fighting is over, and we are in the Otherworld."

"They will remember you," Ceolmhar said, delighted by Eornan's reply. He put his hand on the Nemedian king's arm.

"You will fight by my side today, and together we shall die like brothers."

The chariots were almost upon them, the screams of the Formorians in them and following behind, filling the air. The same screams and war cries which had terrified countless people over many years.

Ceolmhar raised his hand. From behind the first line of his men, his archers let loose a hail of arrows which fell into the advancing chariots, felling men and horses alike, but failing to stop the impact as the chariots reached his lines and scattered his men, wheeling and turning to charge at their rear, in a move designed to frighten and confuse them.

Ceolmhar and Eornan and their men at the centre took the full impact of the first Formorian charge, but they quickly routed the charioteers, killing all of them, ignoring for the moment the danger from behind as the Formorian footsoldiers reached them. Blamad and Carriog, who saw what was happening, wheeled their men in behind the Formorians, and the battle now began in earnest.

It was a vicious battle, bitterly fought, with no quarter asked or given. Sometimes Ceolmhar and Eornan pushed the Formorians back, sometimes they were pushed back, and for many hours this became the pattern as neither side gained full supremacy over the other. The Nemedians fought furiously, and by now they had lost nearly three quarters of their men, but there was no thought of running or leaving the battle, no thought of giving up. It was difficult to see during those hours who was winning, but by early afternoon, it was clear that the Picts and Formorians had begun to push Ceolmhar's men and the Nemedians, back.

Desperation bred resolve, and Ceolmhar and his men fought for every inch of ground they gave way. Blamad and Carriog stood by Ceolmhar and Eornan, each man protecting his own king. Branvig could not be seen, but was still fighting, somewhere to their right. He had several sword cuts, mostly arm wounds, but he also had a large gash on his face, from which the blood ran freely, but he ignored this as best he could as he fought to hold his ground.

Like Blamad and the others, however, he too was forced to give way, but he fought like a madman and made his enemies fight for every step they took. The battlefield was already littered with bodies, and more and more of Ceolmhar's men were falling to the increasing Formorian push, when from the forest a strange noise was heard. Then from the mountain behind came a thunderlike sound. A pure white cloud formed over the mountain, hovered, then began to drift down towards the plain and the battlefield, resting before the trees a short distance away.

The battle stopped as the warriors from each army paused to look at it, and listen to the noises emanating from it.

Another thunderclap filled the air, while again from the forest and the cloud, more strange noises were heard. Quite suddenly the white cloud disappeared completely and the Danaan king and his people were there before them, each of them mounted on a pure white horse, Oengus at their head, his gold helmet glistening in the sun, the spears and javelins and swords of his men, also glistening gold.

From his vantage point to where he had fled when the battle had turned against Ceolmhar the day before, and from which he again observed the battle, the Druid watched the formation of the strange cloud, and heard the noises with growing apprehension and fear. He knew at once what had happened, who it was who now approached the battle, ready to join in on Ceolmhar's side. He knew with deepening terror that he had lost, that the Danaans would win the battle because they had magic more powerful than anything he could ever conjure up.

There was real fear in his eyes, which Garweng and the other druids also saw, and they too were afraid.

The prophecy had been right after all, the Druid thought fearfully. The Danaans had returned to claim back their Power which he had stolen and corrupted.

"Get our horses," he said quickly, the fear obvious in his voice. "We will return to the dún. The battle is lost to us, but we may yet save ourselves. Hurry."

The battle suddenly began again as if by some unseen signal, though the sight of the Danaans had given Ceolmhar's men fresh hope, and had instilled into the Formorians and Picts a terrible sense of foreboding.

Oengus led his Danaans towards the battle, and Blamad saw with some surprise that Aemrig, his friend, rode beside the Danaan king. He smiled, and realized that for Aemrig, like himself, this was to be the last battle.

Gomrik saw that everything was going against him now. The Danaans seemed to be everywhere, yet they were nowhere. No one fought them, they killed no one, but the white cloud came and left, and came again, covering the fighting men, spreading confusion and fear in the Formorian ranks, at the same time guiding and protecting Ceolmhar's men.

Blamad and Carriog were joined by Aemrig. The three of them fought side by side, laughing as they killed Formorians and Picts as though it was the easiest thing to do. Their earlier doubts and fears gone, and since the arrival of the Danaans a new confidence had infused itself into their hearts. They fought fiercely, but their sense of victory and triumph was short lived, when Aemrig was suddenly killed by a Formorian sword, and fell dead at Blamad's feet.

The desperate Formorians were pressing in on them, and Gomrik fought like a mad man, but even he had to give way and fall back over the very ground he had fought all day to gain.

The Danaans swirled in and around him, confusing him, driving him wild with anger, and they melted before his eyes every time he lifted his axe to strike back. He could do them no harm, and they laughed and taunted him all the more for it as he cursed and swore impotently.

Dubhghall too was fighting desperately, but the Picts were by now almost annihilated. The losses they had suffered the day before and their losses now had almost wiped them out. The Danaans tormented the Picts also, but Dubhghall, who was not the man Gomrik was, broke under their magic and ran, trying to get away from the battle and the laughing taunting warriors who seemed to pass right through him. He ran straight into Ceolmhar who buried his sword deep into Dubhghall's body, then, with another mighty sweep of his arm, decapitated him, lifting his bloody head high for all to see, a grin of utter triumph on his face.

Díele was a desperate man. He knew that Blamad would torture him mercilessly if he took him alive, and the fear he had felt the day before returned to him a hundred fold, as he fought and hacked his way through the mass of bodies, hoping to escape by some means from the battlefield. He was hoarse from shouting, but some of his men were already running from the battle. It started slowly at first, but gradually more and more of his men began to throw away their weapons and scatter in all directions. Still the Danaans swirled in and out through the mass of fighting men, their phantom presence terrifying the Formorians as more and more of them began to turn and run. Ceolmhar's men however, were not in a merciful mood, and they cut and chopped and thrust at any of their enemies who came within reach of their weapons.

Díele saw that the battle was lost, and began to ease his way through the fighting men hoping to slip away unseen, and escape somehow to his own dún. He discarded his bright cloak and moved through the twisting and writhing bodies until, with a shock so sudden and complete that it almost killed him with fright, he came face to face with the man he feared above all others, Blamad.

"Here is your reward for treachery," Blamad said coldly. Without another word, he swung his axe, and swept Díele's head from his body.

Suddenly it was all over. Here and there among the fallen there was movement, but the battlefield was strangely quiet after the noise and clash of metal against metal.

Blamad's men went among the bodies looking for their own dead and wounded, killing those Formorians or Picts who were still alive. Blamad lifted Díele's head from the ground, and carried it to where Ceolmhar was standing. He laid it at his feet beside Dubhghall's head, the sightless, shocked eyes, seeming to look heavenwards.

Ceolmhar looked at the head for a moment, then with massive force, kicked it into the heap of corpses lying close by, then repeated the same thing with Dubhghall's. Eornan stood beside Ceolmhar. Both men were weary but happy, especially Eornan, who felt quite rightly that his honour had been vindicated, now that he had joined the battle as Carriog had urged him to do all those months ago.

"We have done it friend," Ceolmhar said happily. He looked at the scattered bodies of the Formorians and Picts, lying where they had fallen to be left there for the carrion creatures which would come in due time to feast on them.

"Thanks to you, and the Danaans, we have done it. Where is the Danaan king so that I can thank him?"

They looked around, but there was no trace of the Danaans or their king.

Carriog approached, carrying the body of Aemrig. He laid it down gently before Ceolmhar, who bent down and touched the ravaged face, already cold.

"Goodbye old friend," he said sadly, and with genuine grief. "You will be in the hall of warriors tonight."

Blamad and Branvig had already prepared a grave for Aemrig, and Carriog now lifted his body and brought it to the place prepared, and placed it in the ground. He laid Aemrig's sword and axe beside the body and, when they had filled the grave, they placed large stones over it, to prevent anything from disturbing it. It was almost dark when they had finished, and already overhead, birds circled and waited for the living to depart, greedily watching the feast waiting below, while from the undergrowth, many dozens of pairs of eyes also watched and waited.

"Gomrik is not among the dead," Blamad said. "We've searched again and again, but he's not there."

"We'll have to find him, and the Druid," Ceolmhar said urgently. "They must not escape. But first we must burn our dead before the vermin get at them."

The bodies of Ceolmhar's men and the Nemedians who had died with them were placed on a huge pyre which had been hastily constructed. The wood was lit and soon the evening sky was filled with the glow from the fire, which quickly devoured the wood and then the bodies on top. The bodies of the Picts and Formorians were left where they were for the rats, which were already coming out of their hiding places to gorge themselves.

Ceolmhar and his men went to the forest to find the queen and the rest of his people. He was still mystified by the disappearance of the Danaans. Sorry too, because he had wanted to thank them for what they had done but their disappearance had been as mysterious as their appearance.

It was dawn before they found the queen and the others. There was almost hysterical relief among his people when they saw that it was Ceolmhar who was returning from the battle and not the Formorians.

Those of Ceolmhar's men who had been wounded were taken by the women to be looked after. Ceolmhar and the other warriors went to talk with the queen who was resting. Deirbhne was by her side, keeping watch.

"We have beaten them," he said triumphantly when he stood before her. "The Druid and Gomrik have escaped, but their armies are destroyed, their Power is broken. We have won a great battle and brought peace to our people."

Morna rose slowly. She was feeling the fatigue of her time in the forest, but her spirit was high.

"You have done well old friend, my father," she said embracing him softly. "The high king will be well pleased."

"The news will race through the Otherworld about this victory," Ceolmhar agreed. He turned to Eornan, the Nemedian king, who was standing by his side, and put his hand on his shoulder.

"This is Eornan, king of the Nemedians without whose help we would all be dead." The queen smiled at Eornan, a soft grateful smile which he acknowledged.

"I can see that Carriog was a worthy ambassador for his people," she said. "We are all grateful for what you have done."

Eornan smiled.

"I thank you for your praise," he said quietly. "But it is not by my hands that Ceolmhar and I are still alive today."

She looked at him, a frown forming, but she smiled when he explained further.

"The Danaans came to join the battle, the Danaans who scattered and destroyed the Formorians, and made this meeting between us possible."

Morna looked at Ceolmhar. He sat down, weary and spent after the past two days of fighting and tension, and he told her the whole story, of how the Danaans had suddenly appeared, of the white cloud which came among them, helping them yet confusing and disturbing the Formorians. Finally, he told her about how Aemrig had ridden into battle with the Danaan king, and how he met his death, about which all of them still grieved.

Muireann, who was standing close by, looked shocked and dazed when he heard Ceolmhar speak about Aemrig.

"He is dead, you say?" he asked with a quiet, calm dignity, which impressed Ceolmhar even as he spoke to him. The young man would surely be a king one day, he thought. "Aemrig died a warrior's death, but now that the battle is won, it is to the living we should look, and I tell you Muireann, here before all our people, that you are now king of your people. It was Aemrig's wish that this should be so."

Muireann did not reply. He did not know what to say. He merely bowed slightly and walked away to be alone for a while, to think about Aemrig, his friend and king.

The queen watched him go, her eyes moist.

"They were like brothers, he and Aemrig," she said quietly.

Ceolmhar smiled.

"He is young and lacks experience, but that will come with time, and he will understand that what has happened was meant to be."

Morna embraced Ceolmhar once again.

"You are a wise man," she said affectionately. He smiled.

"You are thinking that there should be a new high king," she said suddenly. Ceolmhar looked at her and grinned.

"It is the law," he said lightly, amused that she had somehow read his thoughts. "We need a new high king, now that we have destroyed our enemies."

"I have one in mind," she said. "One who is fitted for the task. Your own son, Branvig. He has proved himself to be more than worthy, and when the council meets to decide, I will speak for him."

Ceolmhar was too stunned to speak.

"I cannot nominate my own son," he said quietly. "It would be wrong for me to do so."

"It will be done," she said smiling. Muireann rejoined them at that moment, and he stood before the queen.

"I am sorry, but Aemrig was my friend, and I will always remember him, and regret his death," he said quietly, obviously trying to control himself.

"There is no shame in grief, Muireann," she replied gently. "Even for a warrior. You have given proof of your loyalty and friendship for Aemrig with your tears, but now you must look after your own people. They will look to you for guidance and protection. You must be strong and show them that you are a worthy successor to a good king, as I believe you are."

Muireann bowed, and went to tell his people the news of Aemrig's death. Carriog and Blamad now approached Ceolmhar and the queen. There was a strangeness in Blamad's eyes, a look of detachment as he stood before them.

"We are going after the Druid. While he is alive and free he has the power to make more evil, so we are going to find him and destroy him."

"It must be done as you say, but I will give you more men," Ceolmhar replied. Blamad shook his head.

"We will do this alone." He looked into Ceolmhar's eyes, and the old chief nodded.

"You have served us well Blamad, the high king too, and he will know this when you meet him again."

He looked at the queen, who was staring at Blamad, as if she was seeing him for the first time. Without warning, she embraced him, and whispered into his ear.

"I was wrong to doubt you, I know that now. Will you forgive me?" He looked into her eyes, tears in his own.

"You understand?" he asked quietly, and she nodded.

"I understand at last," she answered, her voice choking. "May the gods go with you, and keep you safe."

She released her hold on him. The others had been watching, but only Deirbhne had heard what the queen had said to Blamad.

"We will never meet again," Blamad said to Ceolmhar. He gripped the old chief's arms.

"The gods keep you happy Blamad, you too Carriog," he said. He took Carriog's hands and held them tight for a moment.

"I will not forget you, either of you." They took their horses, and left the camp. Ceolmhar knew as he watched them leave, that they were obeying a higher authority than his, and this he understood, and he knew now for certain, that he would not see either of them again in this life. He turned around to find Rory standing where Blamad had been a few minutes before, smiling as usual. He greeted Ceolmhar warmly.

"You have done well, Lord," he said cheerfully.

The others gathered round the Danaan prince, this slight blonde haired man, who looked so delicate, yet who had such a feeling of power about him, that they were all in awe of him.

"Where is your king?" Ceolmhar asked. "I wanted to thank him for what he did to help us."

Rory smiled.

"It was intended that we should help you, as it was intended that when we did, that our time in this world would be finished, that we would be free of this life at last and cross over to the Otherworld. The others have already gone, even the great Dagda. I am the last of my people that you will see, and I too have only a short time left, enough, my friends, to talk with you for a while and bid you a fond farewell."

"Oengus bids me to tell you in his name that the sons of Dana will always watch over you and guide you, even from afar. He bids me also to tell you, that this world now truly belongs to you and your people, and to those of Nemed's race who remain. We are no longer of this world, and we have no more say or influence in its affairs. So my time too has come, and I must join my people who are waiting for me. Goodbye, my friends. Farewell all of you."

They did not actually see him leave, but he was gone before they could say anything, or ask him any questions.

"We have been through a strange and wonderful time," Ceolmhar said, his voice awestruck, his whole being alive with the feeling that they were close to the gods, all of them at that moment.

"Many strange things have happened since we started out to fight the Druid, things which we shall remember always, Storyteller."

Creidne, who had been watching and listening, approached. Ceolmhar, put his hand on his shoulder, while with his other he made a sweep of the forest.

"Remember everything that has happened," he said earnestly. "Those who died deserve to be remembered by their deeds."

"They will not be forgotten, Lord," Creidne said truthfully. "I have remembered everything that has happened since the day we first left the high king's dún. Not one Lord, will be forgotten. You have my word on that."

Ceolmhar smiled, satisfied.

"Now my friends," he said genially, "it is time at last for us to return home."

CHAPTER TWENTY FOUR

The countryside across which Blamad and Carriog now rode was free of the scars and tension of war. Already word of Ceolmhar's victory over the Druid and Gomrik had gone ahead, and there were people on the roads once more and peasants in the fields, as life quickly returned to normal and the evil times were forgotten.

A great flock of birds passed overhead, but this time Blamad and Carriog did not feel any fear or apprehension as they had done only a short time before when they had seen other flocks of birds.

The sun was hot, all traces of winter gone, all signs that there had been a war, and that evil had been master for a time. They savoured the sights and scents of the wild flowers which seemed now to grow in abundance, the lush green grass and the light, warm breeze which fanned their faces as they rode at a leisurely pace towards the coast.

They stopped at an inn when darkness began to fall. Inside, a group of men were arguing and talking, but when Blamad and Carriog entered, they stopped and looked at the two friends suspiciously.

They sat in a corner, away from the others, and the innkeeper came over to their table, a wary man, who forced a smile and tried without success to hide his nervousness. He was small and fat, grease- stained from constant proximity to his spit, and years of hand- wiping on his tunic. He smelled like a pig, but he didn't notice or care.

"What can I do for you?" he asked. He looked nervously at Carriog, noting the strange clothing and features, his gaze bordering on insolence.

"What's the matter?" Carriog asked impatiently, his voice sharp. The other men fell silent. "Haven't you ever seen a Nemedian before?" The man stuttered — tried to speak but could not.

"We'd like some meat and wine," Blamad said, breaking the tension, "and some bread if you have any. My friend and I are tired and hungry... and a little impatient, as you can see."

He smiled as he spoke, but the innkeeper, grateful though he was for Blamad's interruption, nevertheless wished that both of them would leave his inn, and him in peace. Despite this, and obeying the hospitality of his calling he bowed to Blamad. "My wife baked bread today sir," he said smoothly. "There is still some left. I'll bring it to you at once with the wine and meat."

When he had gone, Carriog and Blamad laughed quietly. The other men, the ones who had been arguing, had also gone back to their own conversation unable to meet the stern gaze which Carriog directed at them after he had shouted.

The innkeeper returned in a little while with the wine and food and two cups.

"Will you be staying the night?" he asked nervously, as he put the food on the table. Blamad nodded and the man clearly looked disappointed and more frightened than before. Carriog gripped his arm tightly — the man almost fainted with fear. "Have you seen any Formorians lately?" he asked, his voice soft yet filled with authority. The innkeeper was perspiring heavily.

"Well?" Carriog demanded, squeezing the man's arm even tighter so that his face twisted with pain.

"Yesterday about ten of them passed this way, but they did not stop. I'd barred the doors anyway because I had heard what they had done to other innkeepers, and I can't afford to lose this place. Anyway as I said, there were about ten of them, led by a man with really black hair, the blackest I've seen, an evil looking man if ever I saw one, and in this trade you see all sorts. He was screaming and shouting at the others as they passed. I was very frightened, because I thought they might want to come into my inn but they kept going."

"Gomrik?" Carriog asked. Blamad nodded.

"Sounds like him."

Carriog looked at the innkeeper once more, his grip still firm on the man's arm.

"Now tell me, have you seen any druids pass?" he asked.

"No druids," the innkeeper replied quickly. "I saw no druids."

He was telling the truth, but the very mention of the druids terrified him, because the Grey Druid had terrorised them for so long. He feared the Druid's Power, as did the others in the inn, and their friends in the villages. They did not believe the rumours circulating that the Druid had been defeated, because they believed he was too tough, too wily and dangerous to have been beaten in battle, or in any other way. He was just too powerful.

"The Druid's Power is broken," Carriog said reading the man's thoughts. For once the innkeeper found the courage to speak his mind.

"I do not wish to offend you sirs, but we have lived under the Druid's rule for long enough, to know that we are not safe from him, nor will we be safe until he is dead. As long as he lives, the Druid is to be feared."

"He will trouble no one again," Carriog said impatiently, and he let the man go.

"The man is right, you know", Blamad said. "Fear is the Druid's power, and as long as he lives, these people will fear him, and there will be no peace in this land."

Carriog did not reply. His eyes were distant — filled with hatred for the Grey Druid. For the rest of the evening they were left alone, and the innkeeper disturbed their solitude only to bring them a fresh jug of wine. The inn itself was old and very much run down, and a stale smell of decay pervaded the place. It was dimly lit, though warm, because a well stocked fire burned near where the other men sat talking, quietly now after their earlier arguments. They spoke in low tones, conscious of the presence of the two warriors. Sometimes a newcomer would enter and stare at them, but they were not disturbed or spoken to. Blamad understood. He and Carriog were uncomfortable reminders of the war, and though he resented the fact that they were treated with suspicion, he nevertheless understood it.

"We remind them too much of what has happened," Carriog said, again reading Blamad's thoughts. "We belong to the past, to what has happened. This is not our time."

"As long as they see men like us, they will not believe that the war is over, that the danger has passed, that there is no more danger. It's strange, is it not, that we who have been fighting for them now make them shake with fear?" Blamed did not answer. His thoughts were far away, on a distant lakeshore — a beautiful woman...

They went to bed late, losing in sleep all the fatigue of battle, but one of them always awake in case of ambush. They were not disturbed, and the innkeeper came to them at dawn with bowls of hot broth and newly baked bread.

After they had eaten, and feeling thoroughly refreshed and replete, they set off once more to find the Druid. The innkeeper and his wife watched them go.

"The gods be praised they've gone," she said, making a sign to ward off evil spirits.

"The gods be praised," he echoed vacantly.

The Druid had returned to the high king's dún, to the place where he had begun his quest for power. With Garweng and the other druids, he entered the almost deserted dún. Only a few old people remained. All the others had gone, those who had not accompanied him to battle, and they had taken everything with them, everything they could carry, stripping every house, every store, the stables of anything that could be carried. Not an animal remained, no trace of the horses which the Druid had captured, nor the slaves or the gold which he had taken from the high king.

He went to the high king's house, to the great hall. The other druids remained outside looking at each other nervously. They knew in their hearts that they were beaten, yet such was the Power of the Grey Druid and such was their fear of him that they stayed, unable to believe that he had lost the power to strike back at his enemies. Morc and Dichiu stood apart from Garweng, and they eyed him with growing and open hostility, feeling that he had no protector now to help him. Garweng felt fear. He knew that the other two would kill him at the first chance they got, but he was too cunning to be surprised, and besides, he did not share their belief that the Druid was finished.

In the hall, the Druid took the manuscript from its hiding place and put it on the table before him. From his pocket he took the pouch which contained the powder he had used on the fires to raise the cloud against Ceolmhar's dún.

He hesitated for a few moments, considering what he was about to do, remembering vaguely as he did so the warning he had received not to use the magic too often. Then he threw the powder onto the grate, bent down, lit the dry tinder with his flint, and waited a few minutes as the flames took hold and the smoke began to rise.

"YOU GODS OF THE ELEMENTS HELP ME NOW IN MY HOUR OF TRIAL. SCATTER MY ENEMIES AND BRING THEM DOWN INTO DISTRUCTION. STRIKE THEM FROM THE FACE OF THE EARTH. BRING TERROR AND DESTRUCTION TO THEIR HEARTS AND VICTORY TO ME ONCE MORE..."

His speech was followed by a terrible silence, during which time the blue smoke formed itself into a column, slowly swelled and began to fill the hall. A rumble filled the air, followed by a sudden flash of lightning, then the room was filled with demons, horrible screaming creatures that clawed and dragged at the Druid as the smoke spread itself over him.

He screamed in terror as they dragged him to the ground, tearing at him, passing over him, through him, under him, howling and wailing, filling his head with the most terrifying sounds of despair he had ever heard. He could not escape, he could not rise from the floor, as the demons came in ever-increasing numbers from the flames of the fire and the smoke which continued to fill the room. He was paralysed with terror.

The other druids heard his screams, and they too were filled with the most terrible dread. But they did not dare to open the door to see if they could help the Druid in any way, they still did not dare to disturb him because they feared him so much.

He lay on the floor as the room swirled in a fantasy of evil, but finally, with much effort and strength of will, he managed to drag himself to his feet, break free from his tormenters, and run to the door moaning and frothing at the mouth like a terror-stricken animal. He saw the three druids standing a little way before him, watching him, menacing him. He drew his dagger and with a horrible scream, rushed at the confused druids, who did not know what to do until they realized that the Grey Druid in his maddened state of fear, meant to kill them.

Acting from instinct they drew their knives and struck out at him, again and again. He hardly felt the pain because of the madness in his heart. For a terrible minute he pressed his attack. Just as they thought he would never stop, he fell dead at their feet.

"We've killed him," Garweng said, realising the full horror of what they had done. "We've killed the Grey Druid."

The other two druids looked at him coldly, their intentions suddenly clear.

"You have no one to protect you now," Dichiu said viciously. They moved towards Garweng, their knives raised. Terror filled his eyes as they struck him again and again until he, too, was lying lifeless on the ground.

"What are we going to do now?" Morc asked, suddenly terrified by what they had done. He was unable fully to comprehend the fact that he had helped to kill the Grey Druid, the most feared man in the land.

For Dichiu, however, there were no such problems. He kicked Garweng's body in revenge for all the indignities he had suffered at his hands. Then he looked at Morc, assuming leadership which the other man accepted passively.

"Take whatever valuables you can find," he said harshly. "We'll have to get away from here before Ceolmhar comes looking for us."

He looked towards the hall from which the Druid had run.

"Don't go in there," he said to Morc, who was already moving towards the door. "There is danger inside." Morc understood at once.

He looked down at the Druid's body and laughed. It had been so easy in the end that he wondered why he had feared him for so long. Now that the Druid was dead he, Dichiu, would become the most powerful magician, but he would not fail where the Druid had failed. It might take a long time, years even, but he would do it. He would return.

They searched everywhere, but they found little of value, as the Picts had removed everything worth taking. Because Dichiu was afraid to enter the hall where the Druid had conjured up the magic for the last time, he missed the precious manuscripts which would have given him the Power he so desperately wanted. He took the Druid's horse and Garweng's and they rode away from the silent dún before the avenging Ceolmhar arrived.

Blamad and Carriog reached the high king's dún a few hours after leaving the inn. They approached warily, but there was no sign of life. Carriog had to restrain Blamad from rushing in.

"Be careful my friend, it may be a trap," he said cautiously. The Druid was a cunning and treacherous man, and with each step they took Blamad and Carriog expected to hear the yells of ambush, but there was only an eerie deathly silence, as they rode through the gates their battle axes ready, into the open space behind the high king's house.

"There is no one here," Blamad said. He dismounted, and Carriog did likewise, and they tied their horses outside the king's house. An old man shuffled into view. Both men turned, axes ready, but they lowered them when they saw there was no danger.

"Who are you?" Blamad asked softly but the old man, a Pict, did not understand him. Carriog spoke a few words to him, and the old man replied.

"He says that there are about fifteen of them here, left behind because they were too old to follow the others. He says also that the Druid was here a short time ago."

He let the old man go, and they went into the high king's house, where it did not take them long to find the Druid's body, with that of Garweng lying beside it. Carriog lifted the Druid's body with his foot and rolled it over. He looked down at the fear-ravaged features, then suddenly kicked the corpse savagely, but Blamad stopped him from doing it again.

"Let him lie in peace," he said quietly. "He will do no more wrong. His punishment lies in other hands."

Carriog nodded quietly and went to look around. He entered the hall where the Druid had lit the fire, but by now the cloud had dispersed and there was no residue of evil left in the room, only the same terrible and deathly silence they had felt outside.

He looked around for a few minutes. Then he saw the manuscripts lying on the table where the Druid had left them and, with great care, he lifted them and read them with growing interest.

They were written in his own tongue, but he frowned when he read what was on the pages. Blamad joined him, and Carriog handed the manuscripts to him.

"This belonged to our people in ancient times," he said shortly. He had bent down to the fire and lit the remaining tinder as he spoke.

"It contains many great spells of magic, which the Danaans took from us when they defeated us in battle. Somehow the Druid managed to get his hands on it, though I do not know how. This was the source of all his Power, of all the evil he unleashed, these words and markings which look so formless to your eyes."

Blamad examined the pages. He could not understand what was written there, but he admired the script, and the artistry of the maker. Carriog rose from the fire, took the manuscripts from Blamad and threw them onto the flames without a word. Blamad looked at him with horror.

"What are you doing?" he demanded, but Carriog carefully stoked the fire so that the flames took hold very quickly. Without turning to face Blamad, he explained.

"As I have said, it was from these books that the Druid took his magic. I have burned them because it is the safest thing to do. Even if we guarded them and hid them away, there might come a time when someone else would try to use the Power they contain. It is better my friend, to burn them now."

They watched the flames consume the ancient vellum, which cracked and curled and turned black in front of their eyes, before finally disappearing forever into ash and dust. When he was satisfied that nothing remained of the manuscripts, Carriog rose.

"What about Gomrik?" Blamad asked.

"He will have taken ship by now," Carriog replied calmly. "There is nothing we can do about him. Perhaps in time, Muireann will take a fleet of ships to their island and destroy them once and for all."

"It will not happen," Blamad said. "That is not the way of our people. Ceolmhar will leave them in peace, Muireann too. They will say that they are damaged enough, that too much blood has been spilt already, and that will be the end of it."

Carriog looked sharply at him.

"If they do not follow the Formorians and destroy them, they will return one day. Many years ago, my people defeated them, yet spared them. They will come back again and destroy your people. Believe me, they will."

Blamad smiled, his thoughts in another world.

"If Muireann and Ceolmhar say they will not follow the Formorians, there is nothing I can do," he said. Carriog shook his head sadly. He could not understand it. The Formorians had returned when his people had spared them and had almost wiped out his entire race. Carriog knew in his heart that one day Gomrik or some other chief would return to the island, but he could not convince Blamad.

"You must tell Muireann and the others that they should follow them," he said, but Blamad merely smiled at him.

"I shall never see Ceolmhar or the others again," he said gently. Carriog looked at him. His face was calm and serene and there was a distance in his eyes, a softness; and suddenly Carriog understood. Blamad's time was almost up, he would soon return to the Otherworld. There would be no more playing dice, no more hunting, no more drinking the night away.

"I had forgotten," he said quietly, feeling an unusual emotion.

They went outside and remounted their horses. They did not look around the dún, or feel any further curiosity about the place, their business was finished .

"Which way do we go?" Carriog asked. Blamad pointed towards the setting sun.

"We will make certain that the Formorians have really gone," he said. They rode out of the high king's dún in silence, passed the lake and turned west in the direction Blamad had indicated.

Over the flat grassy countryside they rode, their horses responding to the lack of restraint from their riders, and they covered many miles before dark.

They camped in the open, sleeping peacefully and without disturbance, and resumed their journey at first light, refreshed and alert.

They had been riding for a couple of hours, when they came to hilly country. There were few settlements or villages in this wild, desolate territory, few men in a place where wolves and bandits roamed unhindered, a place the hand of man had hardly touched. They moved more slowly now, because the ground was hard with many loose rocks and stones.

"Look! over there," Carriog said suddenly. Blamad followed his arm.

A column of smoke was rising, standing like a pillar in the sky, from behind one of the hills which surrounded them.

"What do you think?" Blamad asked. There was a peculiarity about his manner which Carriog sensed at once.

"I think we should investigate," he replied. He looked at Blamad, examining him closely with his eyes.

"Are you alright?" Blamad smiled.

"I am fine, Carriog, really I am," he said lightly.

They rode towards the smoke. Coming nearer to the hill, they dismounted, and drew their weapons.

The smoke rose into the sky in a harmless spiral, but naturally it reminded the two men of the Grey Druid's smoke cloud. Voices spoke ahead, but they could not make out what was being said, nor in what language. Very slowly and cautiously, they moved up the hill to see who and what was on the other side.

They had barely reached the summit when the Picts, who had been watching them from their cover, rushed out screaming at them, taking them by surprise. There were about a dozen of them, stragglers from the surviving members of Dubhghall's army who had escaped from the battle, men who were trying to follow the rest of their people to the coast. They had seen Blamad and Carriog ride towards them, and had lured them closer to the fire, because they wanted their horses.

Blamad and Carriog fought like demons against the Picts, who found them no easy target, but it was still an uneven match. In a short while, both Blamad and Carriog lay dead, their bodies receiving even in death many more blows and cuts, as the Picts hacked at them, their bitterness and thirst for vengeance intense. With the two extra horses they now had nine, which meant three of their men having to double up. Having taken everything of value, they mounted up and in a final act of vengeance trampled over the two warriors bodies as they rode away towards the coast.

The birds circling overhead had been the only witnesses to the short but vicious battle, and when darkness began to fall, out from their many hiding places, the creatures of the night emerged, scenting their prey.

Gomrik stood on the deck of the ship, staring at the receding coastline, his eyes full of bitterness and anger as he thought of the men he had lost, and with their loss his own chance of power.

He looked at the others around him. There were so few of them, hardly an army any longer, just a ragged group, a rabble almost, lucky to be alive and to have escaped from the vengenance of Ceolmhar's people. One ship full of men out of a mighty army which Vitrig had brought with him to the island.

There would be many songs of mourning when they reached their own island, many tears and angry words. The women of the dead ones would weep long and hard, the old ones would nod their heads and say that the gods had been against them yet again.

Gomrik looked out over the sea once more. Perhaps they had offended the gods in some way, he did not know. He knew only that it would be a long time if ever, before he sailed to the island again. He cursed Vitrig for his foolishness over the woman, he cursed the Picts for their stupidity, he cursed the Druid one final time, and turned his back on the island forever.

The ship lay at anchor. The water was calm. Even the waves breaking on the shore were lapping the sand quietly and rhythmically. The woman stood on deck watching the waiting men on the shore.

Blamad stood with Aemrig, Carriog, Godrane and the other warriors who had fallen with them in battle. They were silent and fearful, some not yet fully realising what had happened to them or where they were. Only Blamad understood, only he was not afraid, and he tried to reassure his friends and companions.

"I have been here before," he said smiling. "No harm will come to any of us here."

The woman looked down at him, and smiled very gently, her lips hardly moving. By some means Blamad knew that she was thanking him for helping the others.

The sails on the ship which had already been unfurled, flapped in the breeze, but the ship, although it was not tied or held by any human agency, did not move from its stationary position.

"It is time for you all to come aboard," the woman said. Quietly and without murmur, led by Blamad, they obeyed her command. She watched them impassively as they came aboard. She smiled at Blamad as an old friend, and when they had all embarked the ship, again driven by the unseen force, began to move away from the shore.

It was a large ship whose great sails quickly took the wind and moved her over the water, passing between the two peaks before which Blamad had been stopped on his previous journey.

They sailed out into the open sea. The spray touched the faces of the warriors, who stood watching on deck, afraid to rest or close their eyes in case they missed anything on this incredible journey which, despite the apparent danger, filled each of them with excitement.

The sea became rough. The wind rose. The waves rolled higher and higher threatening sometimes to swamp the ship, but each time falling harmlessly away. The wind rose to a howling gale, and the terrified warriors held on to whatever they could, as the vessel was tossed about like a leaf on the wind. Some of the warriors, unable to contain their fear, screamed and looked to the woman for comfort, but she stood against the wind rigid and unmoving, as the storm raged around her.

"How can she do that?" Aemrig asked, his voice filled with terror. Blamad, who was holding onto the rail of the ship, answered over the noise.

"She has a guide to help her," he said, smiling, "someone else who commands this ship and protects it. We will not be harmed by this storm, just wait and see."

Aemrig was not comforted by Blamad's words, and lay against the side of the ship, feeling each roll and swell of the sea in the pit of his stomach, unable and unwilling to move from his prone position.

Quite suddenly the storm was over and they saw in the distance the outline of a mountain, coming closer all the time. In a few minutes they reached land, travelling at what seemed normal speed, yet at the same time covering a great distance over the water in less time than human effort could devise.

The ship sailed into a quiet cove. There was a smooth beach, and gentle green-covered hills sloping down to the strand. The ship beached on the sand, but strangely, it did not list or turn over, remaining upright as if it was still in the water and sailing.

"You may leave the ship now," the woman said softly, yet her words conveying a sense of command. The warriors jumped onto the sand and when the last of them had gone ashore, the ship, by the same supernatural agency which guided her, moved into the water once more, turned and went back to sea.

When it was out of sight, the warriors looked at each other. They were all unsure of what they were to do, or what was to happen next. There were no sounds at all, no birds in the air. Nothing. Even the water hitting the sand lapped at their feet in silence.

"Are we really dead?" Godrane asked, and suddenly the others laughed. The tension which had grown in the past while was broken.

There was a movement up on the hill behind the beach. A figure was clambering over the rocks and moving through the bracken towards them. Blamad and the others watched his progress, and it seemed to them that the man was familiar, though it was not until he was almost beside them, that they recognised the high king.

More men began to appear over the hill and approach the beach, which the high king had by now reached. He walked directly to Blamad, and embraced him warmly.

"My friend," he said, his voice filled with emotion, tears in his eyes. "You are welcome to this place. I have waited so long for you."

He looked at the others, smiling and crying at the same time.

"All of you are welcome. We are together at last. Brian is here and we have waited for a long time for this moment, but Brian will tell you this himself. Here he comes now..."

Brian came onto the beach. His arm was raised in welcome, and when he drew near the first thing which Blamad and the others noticed was that the terrible marks had gone from his face, and that he was no longer blind. He looked and was his old self again. The high king, who noticed their confusion with some amusement, explained;

"In this place, all traces of our past lives are removed, all wounds and scars. We remember who we were and what we were, but here such things are not important, and we begin a new life without the fear of war or treachery, without enemies. The gods are near to protect us and keep us safe from ourselves."

Brian greeted Blamad and the others warmly, and they spent a long time talking to each other, unable to say enough of how they felt of how much they had missed each other.

"You have earned the right to be here, all of you," he said to them, Nemedians as well as the high king's men. He even addressed some Picts and Formorians, who stood apart from the rest, still unsure of themselves and what their place would be in this new world they had entered. All of the men who had come on the ship were not as yet true parts of the Otherworld and their thoughts were still on those they had left behind, but the high king, who had gone before them, knew that they would forget their old lives in a short while.

"Here, you will find a new life, a life which will never end, one in which you will never grow old, or suffer any pain. Here all men are brothers. There are no Formorians or Picts. All men are the same, each respects the other. You will forget what you have been, and remember only what you are, what you have become. You will understand all these things I have told you, in a little while..."

He paused for a moment and from their faces he could tell that many of them had doubts, that this life was not what they had expected. He spoke again.

"This life will be as your old life was, but with those differences I have told you about. There is hunting here, an abundance of game, the wine is good and plentiful, and you will have merry nights and be completely happy forever. Now, forget your old lives, and come with me to this new home of yours."

He led them from the beach up over the hill and out of sight, and the gentle breeze blowing over the sand covered their footprints so that not a trace was left.

Away inland a fire burned in a warm, well appointed hall, and here the Danaans were waiting with food and wine for them, with many other of their friends who had reached the Otherworld before them...

EPILOGUE

It is winter again. The snow is heavy on the ground once more, and the wind whistles through the great hall. The blazing fire crackles and lights the room, and the assembled chiefs and kings listen quietly as the storyteller tells his tale.

Creidne speaks eloquently, slowly building his story, keeping them in suspense before telling them what they want to know, what they have come to hear, what they know already. He speaks with authority, of battles lately fought, of men whose names have not been forgotten, of the things they did and the manner of their dying, an eloquent and important part of their lives, more important perhaps than the life itself.

They listen attentively to his words. The high king's eyes moisten at the mention of a name, or a place, as he remembers what has happened and the friends he has lost. He remembers too, that it was their sacrifice which made him king, their example which gave him the wisdom to be a king. He is young but already he is wise beyond his years.

Aobhne sits beside Creidne as he speaks. She never leaves his side now, and their son sleeps close by in the king's house, a fine healthy boy who seems to have inherited some of his grandfather's strong temper.

Muireann, who sits close to the king will marry soon, and Deirbhne who was a king's wife, will be a king's wife again. She has learned to smile once more.

Alfred and Maron are now both dead. They did not survive the winter, and they too have joined Blamad and the others in the Otherworld. Only the queen and Ceolmhar are alone, and they sit close to each other, remembering. The winter is not a good time for the queen, and she has not yet learned to forget, while Ceolmhar is too old to forget. His only consolation is his son, now high king, a great comfort to the old warrior who has seen too many of his friends and comrades die, to be ever totally happy again.

Morna thinks of her son, who will one day be high king, if the gods spare him and war does not return, and that is a small comfort to her still aching heart.

The night is cold and well advanced when Creidne finishes. There is silence in the hall. Each person holds his words in their hearts, making in their minds a picture of what he has told them, each holding onto some memory of the friends they all miss. Through Creidne, they have remembered those friends, and relived the time spent with them. Through his words, their friends have come alive again for a moment, so that in spite the sadness they feel as they live again the past, they are glad he has made them all remember...